WESTERN

Rugged men looking for love...

Fortune In Name Only
Tara Taylor Quinn

Reunited With The Rancher
Anna Grace

MILLS & BOON

Tara Taylor Quinn is acknowledged as the author of this work
FORTUNE IN NAME ONLY
© 2024 by Harlequin Enterprises ULC   First Published 2024
Philippine Copyright 2024   First Australian Paperback Edition 2024
Australian Copyright 2024   ISBN 978 1 038 90272 6
New Zealand Copyright 2024

REUNITED WITH THE RANCHER
© 2024 by Anna Grace   First Published 2024
Philippine Copyright 2024   First Australian Paperback Edition 2024
Australian Copyright 2024   ISBN 978 1 038 90272 6
New Zealand Copyright 2024

MIX
Paper | Supporting
responsible forestry
FSC® C001695

Published by
Harlequin Mills & Boon
An imprint of Harlequin Enterprises (Australia) Pty Limited
(ABN 47 001 180 918), a subsidiary of HarperCollins
Publishers Australia Pty Limited
(ABN 36 009 913 517)
Level 19, 201 Elizabeth Street
SYDNEY NSW 2000 AUSTRALIA

Cover art used by arrangement with Harlequin Books S.A.. All rights reserved.

Printed and bound in Australia by McPherson's Printing Group

Fortune In Name Only

Tara Taylor Quinn

MILLS & BOON

A *USA TODAY* bestselling author of over 110 novels in twenty languages, **Tara Taylor Quinn** has sold more than seven million copies. Known for her intense emotional fiction, Ms. Quinn's novels have received critical acclaim in the UK and most recently from Harvard. She is the recipient of the Readers' Choice Award and has appeared often on local and national TV, including *CBS Sunday Morning*.

For TTQ offers, news and contests, visit www.tarataylorquinn.com!

Visit the Author Profile page at millsandboon.com.au for more titles.

Dear Reader,

I'm so excited to be an official part of the Fortune family! If you're new here, you're in for the best of the best. The best stories that grab you up and take you to a place you want to be. Stories that engage all the emotions and leave you feeling not just satisfied, but smiling. And the best news there is...there are always more Fortune stories to devour! You don't ever have to leave this newsworthy family!

If you've been with the Fortunes for a while, you already know all of that. And welcome home.

And this particular Fortune story...I got all the feels writing it that I always get when I'm lost in reading romance novels. Lily is a true heroine. Someone I admire. Someone I want to be. She didn't have a perfect, or even pretty, life. And yet, every day, she looks for the good. And Asa—well, he's a work in progress. Aren't we all? Mostly what I love about this story is the possibility that awaits when you have the courage to take a risk. To go off course for a chance to find happiness. I learn from all of my books. My characters teach me as they evolve inside me. And this one...I've taken a big risk this week, one I haven't taken before, but wanted to, because Lily showed me the way.

I hope her special approach to life blesses you, too.

Tara Taylor Quinn

DEDICATION

For Luke Sorrell, my three-year-old farmer who,
I feel sure, will one day own his own ranch.

CHAPTER ONE

"MA'AM, YOU CAN'T mean that." Turning his charm on full power, Asa Fortune also injected huge amounts of sincere emotion into his gaze as he looked the widow in the eye. "I've just offered you a generous amount, more than you're asking for the place."

The woman liked him. Asa knew she did. He rented a cabin on the ranch, boarded his horse there. Helped her out around the place.

When she started to shake her head, he burst into words. "Mrs. Hensen, you've put fifty years of your life into the Chatelaine Dude Ranch. You and your husband raised your kids here. And you also, in a way, raised me," he admitted without a bit of shame. "I was here with my family when I was little, and it was one of the best times of my life. Because of those days, I became a rancher. I bought Majority right out of high school," he told her, naming the horse that he was currently boarding at the Chatelaine. "Together, we've traveled all over the state of Texas, working ranches, learning, preparing for this chance. I can promise you, there's no one you can trust more to carry on your legacy than Major and I."

All true, although he'd never believed his young boyhood dream of owning the Chatelaine Dude Ranch would ever come true. As an adult, he'd just been hoping to have his own ranch someday. And for the past twelve years, he'd worked tirelessly toward that goal.

Asa saw the flash of hope cross her face. He didn't imagine it. So it made no sense when she shook her head again.

Maybe he was the one missing something?

At an uncharacteristic loss for words, he watched the widow's mouth move and could barely comprehend what he was hearing.

"I've realized that I can't bear to sell the place to anyone who isn't married."

What? His brain started to sputter a flurry of responses, but she continued before he could articulate even one of them.

"This is a family ranch," she told him. "My heart breaks at the thought of it not going to a couple who will love it, invest their hearts in it together, like my husband and I did. There are tough days running a dude ranch," she continued. "Times when something goes wrong, and families need reassurance at the same time. And times when you're so busy, you're too exhausted, and you might want to quit, but then your spouse reminds you of the great days and suddenly you have energy again. And holidays...they're celebrated like family here, with owners who *are* a family and who understand the importance of family..."

"I understand the importance of family!" Asa burst out, interrupting her. Could he really be so close to sweet success and still fail? Lose a lifelong dream when he'd already mentally moved in? There were other bidders for the popular ranch, though he'd heard none were full price. Still, chances were good some were married. "Family is why I moved to Chatelaine last summer, right before you put up your For Sale sign! My relatives have been in Chatelaine for as long as you have! Many were born here. It's family inheritance money, from my great-uncle, that brought me here..."

She already knew most of what he was rambling on about. The whole town had heard about the letters the Fortune grandchildren had received from Freya Fortune, the previous summer, summoning them to Chatelaine to receive an inheritance they hadn't known existed.

Just as they hadn't been privy to the whereabouts of their disgraced uncle for years, or been aware that he'd married Freya.

Asa just couldn't be holding his dream in his arms and let it slip away. Not when he knew he could not only honor the Chatelaine legacy exactly as Val Hensen wanted but help the business grow and prosper for generations to come. "I not only see your and Mr. Hensen's vision for this place, I share it," he told her in an impassioned plea that was totally unlike himself.

When he saw a second shake of her head, his system went into total freeze mode. Unable to process what he was dealing with, or come up with a way to smile his way to victory, he blurted, "You can't just turn down the highest offer because of my marriage status."

And knew he'd made a grave mistake, turning the conversation adversarial, before he even registered the tightening of her expression.

"You come back here with that offer and a marriage license and we'll talk," the widow said in a less friendly tone. "For now, I'm taking the place off the market."

That first Monday in March was supposed to have been the day his life's dream came true. Instead, it was turning into a nightmare.

With those parting words, the widow shut the door in his face.

LILY PERRY MIGHT have slowed her step as she saw Asa Fortune's truck turn onto Main Street right as she was deciding what to do on her break from work. The choice between heading to the bank and paying her electric bill, or stopping at the coffee shop was made for her when she saw him slow down. He might or might not head in for coffee himself, but if he was going to do so, she wanted to be there to hear his good news.

She'd been leaning toward the latter choice in any event. The bill wouldn't be late for another two days, which gave her a couple of more shifts at the café to earn tips. And maybe a chance to pay the bill without drawing on her somewhat limited savings account.

Not that anyone else in the world knew that piece of the puzzle. Both of her sisters, newly reunited with her, had the means, and, she was sure, the willingness to front her a loan if she ever needed it. But she'd die before asking.

Having provided fully for herself since she was seventeen years old, she knew how to make extra cash if she needed it. Had even driven a couple of towns over to clean house a time or two when she'd been strapped for cash.

Seeing Asa's truck slow just before the coffeehouse, all thoughts of personal cash flow flew the coop. The man had taken control of her senses since he'd moved to town the summer before. And while he'd dated seemingly every available female in Chatelaine except her, her heart still jumped at the chance to be the recipient of that magnetic smile.

And, maybe, secretly, it was also a bit thrilling to know that while Asa flitted from woman to woman, she was his one constant. The only female, according to him, who'd become a real friend to him.

Besides, he'd been going to make his dream come true that morning, and she couldn't wait to share his joy. He knew she'd understand. She'd told him about her personal connection to the dude ranch when he'd run into her and

his sister Esme having coffee at the café at the GreatStore.
She'd told him then how as a baby, she and her fellow-
triplet sisters had spent the day at the dude ranch with
their parents.

A few days after the coffee with Esme, she and Haley
had run into him downtown, and when Lily told Haley
then that Asa was buying the Chatelaine Dude Ranch, her
sister had told him why that day at the ranch had meant
so much to them. Those hours at the ranch had been the
last ones they'd ever spent with their parents. Haley had
told him what she knew about the one-car crash that had
ripped their parents away from them that night, saying
that she kept trying to find out more, but couldn't seem to.

Her sister had blurted out the story of old wounds that
Lily didn't want to reopen. Ever.

But when Asa had looked at Lily, she'd teared up.

She would never forget the compassion that had filled
his compelling brown eyes as he'd asked her how old she'd
been.

Nor could she escape the memory of how she'd felt…
comforted by his continued interest when she'd told him
she'd only been ten months old. She'd quickly turned the
subject back to him, in upbeat tones, telling him how she'd
keep her fingers crossed for him to get the ranch that had
always held such a special place in her heart.

Which was why it hadn't been a surprise to her when,
a couple of days before, he'd stopped by the café at the
GreatStore, to tell her he was making the new bid.

Wishing she was in something a little more sexy than
her waitressing uniform, she opened the coffeehouse door
and waved at the people who glanced up, all of whom she
knew. She had her usual smile on her freckled face as she
ordered her usual—a hot chocolate—and took a seat at

the only two-seater table left available. Her back deliberately to the door.

Which went against the grain for Lily in general. A girl who'd grown up with no real family, moving from one foster home to another, learned at a young age how to keep her own back covered. Even in a small town where everyone looked out for her.

The door opened. Was she the only one in the room not checking to see who'd come in?

If it was Asa, either he'd join her or he wouldn't.

She'd be fine either way.

Grabbing her phone out of her pocket, Lily hoped it looked as though she'd just had a text buzz for her attention. Or some such thing.

And then, just as quickly, pocketed the device. *What was wrong with her?* She was a fully grown, twenty-nine-year-old, completely self-sufficient woman. Not a starry-eyed schoolgirl.

Not that she'd know it by the silly flutter her heart gave when she saw a cowboy boot fall into her line of vision. "Mind if I join you?"

The voice…it was his, but something about it wasn't right.

Forgetting herself, Lily's gaze shot immediately to Asa's face. Noted the downturned lips, the flattened cheeks and more than that, the lack of a glint in his so sexy gaze.

"What's wrong?"

He looked like someone had died.

"Major's okay, right?" His horse was more family to him than any of the relatives he'd found when he'd arrived in town the year before.

Another thing they had in common—finding family in adulthood, rather than growing up with them. Though she'd known about her triplet sisters growing up, she'd had no idea where they were, and no money or way to find them. Turned out, Tabitha and Haley, who'd both had families, hadn't even known about her...

"He's fine." Setting his coffee on the table with a thump, Asa dropped to the chair across from her. Leaving her with no choice but to stare at his massive shoulders in the button-down shirt beneath his pouty face. Make that *gorgeous* pouty face.

"Your financing didn't work the way you wanted," she guessed then. While she didn't know the intimate details of his money, nor all that much about managing an inheritance of any size, let alone one as exorbitant as his, she'd known that he'd been overhauling his original purchase and investment budget. The Chatelaine ranch not only needed some updating, but he'd planned some additions, too.

A local horse training program for local children, being one of them.

When he shook his handsome, dark head, she frowned. Then leaned in toward him, her worried gaze meeting his. "What then?"

"She turned me down."

"She *what*?!" Realizing she'd raised her voice with the force of her shock, she bent further in to practically whisper, "Why? How can she even do that? You were offering over asking price."

With a look of total disillusionment, he shrugged. "Says she'll only sell to a married buyer. Something about having had this epiphany about it being a family place, and she'll only feel good about it continuing that way if it's run by a married couple. She had her list of reasons."

"She can't do that, can she? Pick and choose a buyer based on someone's marital status?"

"I have no idea. And it doesn't matter. She's taking

the place off the market rather than be forced to accept my bid."

Completely nonplussed, hurting for him, and quite a bit disappointed for herself, too, she stared at him in dismay. Ever since he'd told her he was upping his bid on the property, she'd been toying with the idea of offering to help him out as he took over at the dude ranch, just to give herself a valid excuse to spend time on the land she'd been on the last time she'd been with her parents.

Back when her life, her future, had seemed safe and secure.

When she'd had as many opportunities as her triplet sisters to make a great life for herself.

Not that her life wasn't great, it was. Just…

Asa's sad chuckle brought her mind straight back to him. "So, you want to marry me?" His eye roll told her how completely not serious the comment was.

She opened her mouth to offer a chuckle right back to him. A friend commiserating with a friend. And instead, what came out, with a burst of unfamiliar giddiness, was, "Okay."

"What?" Still wearing the smile that had accompanied his pathetic attempt at a laugh, Asa stared at Lily. As always, those hazel eyes captivated him. He'd never met a woman whose gaze always seemed to be telling him that she had something to say that he needed to hear.

But he had to have heard her wrong. Or her earnest expression was a cover for the laughter that would erupt as soon as he started to take her seriously.

Not that he felt much like being the butt of a joke at the moment. Even hers…

"Okay, I'll marry you."

Asa sat straight up. Fast. Cramming his shoulder blades into the back of the chair. Had the world gone mad?

Or the day just hadn't started yet, and he was caught in some kind of weird nightmare where he meets with a seller and isn't at all himself. And then gets proposed to by a woman who was probably his best friend in the world. If you could forge such a connection in the short time that he'd known her…

Taking a deep breath, he refrained from pinching himself to verify that, yes, he was really awake. Watching Lily, seeing her fidget, and noting how her freckles were growing more pronounced with the color forming on her cheeks, he took a sip of his coffee that turned out to be a gulp. Of steaming hot liquid.

Which burned the hell out of his tongue.

Yep, he was definitely conscious.

"You can't be serious," he said then. Enough time had passed to ensure that she wasn't about to burst into laughter.

"Why not?" She shrugged. The color on her cheeks intensified even more. Those freckles had become frequent visitors in his dreams. He loved how they gave him clues into Lily's thoughts. Or emotions.

How they set her apart. Like there was more to hanging out with her than with any other woman.

When he was done with his freckle obsession, he started to silently compile the dozens of reasons "why not."

"How about if, while you figure out all the why-nots, I tell you why?" Her voice hit him softly…but with the power of a ton of bricks. So much so that he nodded.

But didn't look away. Because for the first time since Mrs. Hensen had shut that door in his face, Asa was feeling something besides despair.

Of course, he knew there was no way he could ever

marry Lily Perry. First, because he wasn't marrying *any-one*. But definitely not the one person in the world he wanted to have in his life forever. In his experience, based not only on his parents, but his aunt and uncle, too, marriage and real life didn't exist well together. Instead, the recipe created rancor, resentment, tension, eventual affairs...

She'd given him a second to stop her.

He waited instead. Expecting her to retreat. If there was one thing he'd learned about Lily that he wished was different, it was the way she always settled for what she had, rather than reaching for more.

He understood. Her life hadn't been easy. He admired the hell out of the way she always found the good in things. And was secretly addicted to her perennial sunny mood. But she could do both. Find good and reach for more...

"For starters, I'm in kind of a slump." If he hadn't been seated, her words would have floored him. Had the woman read his mind? Using what he'd just thought about her against him?

Or was it for him? The morning was just getting too bizarre.

If he didn't know better, he'd think he'd been drinking.

"Ever since I reconnected with my sisters... I look at them, my triplets, who started out in the same womb with me, and now one is a mother of twin babies, the other a successful magazine writer, and me? I'm refilling cups and ketchup dispensers..." Seeing the shrug of her slim shoulders, with that long dark hair gracing them, hit him hard.

For no reason he could understand.

Then her mouth quirked, and she gave a little head tilt, admitting softly, "Truth is, I already had a plan to ask you, once the place was officially yours, if I could come help out, work for you, as you took over the business."

He had a feeling he knew where she was going with this but didn't want to make any assumptions, so he gestured for her to go on.

"I know it might sound a bit over the top, but I want to be able to have a good reason to spend time out there. I told you before I've always had a fondness for the ranch. It's the last place I was before I became an orphan in the foster system. You know? The last time I was a member of my own family." She shrugged again. Looked away.

"It's not out there. I get it." Asa forced himself to ignore the temptation to reach for her hand. Lily was off-limits. Sacred. She was a…friend. "But—"

"It wouldn't have to be for long," she said then, glancing back over at him.

She wasn't letting it go.

Not allowing *him* to let it go.

"Once the place is in your name…it would probably behoove us to, you know, stay together for a while."

"A while, huh?" he couldn't keep himself from asking. "Exactly how long are you thinking?"

"Just long enough to make it look like we tried…but think about it, Asa. Who on earth would ever believe that a woman like me—the perennial friend—would ever be able to keep a hunk like you satisfied?"

He saw no pain or mockery in her grin. Just the wide-open honesty that had drawn him to her from the first time they'd met.

But his own anger made up for her lack thereof. Leaning forward, he gave himself time for a deep breath and then gritted out, "Don't you ever, *ever* say anything like that again," he said softly. "You are worthy of the best man on earth, Lily Perry. It's the men who aren't worthy of you."

Her lips trembled. And she glanced away. He wasn't sure she believed him.

He meant the words with every fiber of his being.

Himself included.

If only there was a way he could make certain that he and Lily would never fight for real, never fester any resentment...

But, wait.

"You really planned to ask me to come work at the ranch?"

"It would be lot more challenging than delivering plated burgers."

"If we did this, and it's a big *if,* I'd be the one at fault when we separate. In some big obvious way..." What was he saying? *Thinking?*

Was he really considering this outrageous scheme?

Her nod seemed a bit...jerky. Had he scared her?

Talking like he was really going to consider the ludicrous idea?

"Rest assured," he quickly added, "there'd be separate bedrooms."

He saw her flinch that time, then noted her chin lift as she said, "I didn't see it happening any other way."

He almost grinned at her tone of voice. The woman might not ask much for herself, but she could most definitely hold her own.

Against anyone.

Him included.

Sitting back in his chair, he exhaled slowly, then locked eyes with her once again. "I need to think about it," he told her.

Her nod was circumspect.

But the smile that lit her face was something Asa knew he was never going to forget.

For better or worse.

CHAPTER TWO

HAD SHE LOST total sight of reality? Taking Asa's facetiousness seriously? She'd known he was kidding. Lily would be the last woman he'd ask to marry him.

If he even *had* marriage on the radar. As his best friend—she knew he didn't. His comments on the subject had been few, but he'd made it clear that he thought marriage was a risk not worth taking anytime in the semi-near future. That the institution put people into a position of being forced to deal with hard stuff together, which ultimately ended up turning love into...well...disdain. At the very least.

But...he was *thinking* about getting hitched?

Lily knew the thought of marrying Asa should scare her a little. Especially considering his comment about separate bedrooms. She was in love with the man. How could she live with him platonically even for one night—let alone however long their marriage lasted—without giving herself away? Or dying of want?

But if he was seriously considering the idea... Sighing, she watched him sip his coffee. Lily had no idea if he was thinking about the proposal right then, weighing pros and cons while he sat with her, or just waiting for her to finish her hot chocolate and get back to work—leaving him in peace.

For all she knew he was at the coffee shop to meet someone else.

A woman, perhaps, who could be walking in at any moment.

Still, just in case he *was* actually contemplating a marriage between the two of them, she did the same. Her whole life, she'd felt as though the only family she had was the town. The people, collectively. Her dream had always been to get married, have a home and family of her very own.

So yeah, maybe, as her sisters both claimed, she settled for less than she deserved. But a marriage of convenience, the chance to call the Chatelaine Dude Ranch home, to actually *live* there, in the same house as the man she loved, while being instrumental in making his own dream come true... No way she'd give up that chance. Even if it wasn't a real marriage.

At least she'd be taking the first step toward her own wished-for destiny. She'd have the marriage and the home for a while. And when the marriage ended, she'd still have the memory. She'd know what it felt like to be happy. And she'd be closer to having it for real one day because she'd finally have reached out for something she wanted. And had gotten it...albeit temporarily.

The clock ticked. Asa sipped his coffee. Watching her. Opening his mouth, then closing it again.

She had to get back to work.

As if reading her mind, Asa stood. Nodded at her. "You need to think about it, too," he told her, as if they hadn't just sat there with a good two minutes of silence between them.

"I don't need to think about it," she responded without hesitation, standing as well. Heading out the door with him and then into the bright sun, she turned to face him on the sidewalk. "I'm in for the reasons I've already told you."

And for the one she hadn't. The one he'd never know. That she was in love with him.

Because she didn't kid herself for a second that her living with Asa, then appearing as a real husband and wife to the town, would suddenly make him fall for her. If she had that hope, she'd run for the hills. She might not reach for things out of her grasp, but she most definitely watched out for herself and avoided known danger at all cost.

And thinking that Asa Fortune would fall for a simple, plain woman like her would be dangerous. She wasn't sexy, or glam, and her hair would always hang around her shoulders in a way that could never be considered amazing…

Yet at this moment, he was staring at her as if she *was* someone special, and her entire being warmed from the inside out.

"I can't believe you'd do this for me."

"I'm doing it for me, too," she reminded him softly. "Have you seen my place?" She nodded toward the part of town where she rented a tiny apartment. "Trading that for even one room at the Chatelaine Dude Ranch…" She shook her head. "No comparison."

She was making light of the changes her life would take. And the fact that they were only temporary. She knew and could tell he did, too.

Still…she thrummed with an energy, an excitement she'd never known.

Pulling her over toward the brick wall of the building, away from the middle of the sidewalk, he murmured, "We'd probably only have to stay married for like six months." He said it as though offering good news.

She nodded.

"You're seriously okay with this?" His gaze bore into hers.

She withstood the look without a blink. "I am."

His hand shot out toward her, and when she didn't react, he reached for hers. "It's a deal," he said, grasping her hand in the bigger, warm palm of his. And then he pulled her toward him, drawing her right up against the hardness of his body, and gave her a hug.

A bear hug. A *friendly* hug.

Yet it was the first time her body had ever touched his, full-on. And desire made Lily so weak, she had to hold on.

Tight.

ASA WAS NOT a man who fooled around. Or wasted time. He never had been. He was a man driven to reach his goals... who strove to make his life the best it could be. A man who was dedicated to working hard every single day and who wasn't afraid to dream big.

Knowing that he was maybe a bit over-the-top on all of that, some might call him pushy, didn't stop him from barreling ahead when he saw the path in front of him.

From his rented cabin on the Chatelaine Dude Ranch—his home since he'd arrived in Chatelaine in response to the inheritance letter he'd received the summer before—Asa called Lily that night. A quick reach out, begun and done in a matter of seconds, just to make certain she was fully on board with their plan. And to offer her more time, if she needed it.

With her go-ahead clear, he was up early the next morning. His first order of business was to drive directly to the jewelers as soon as they opened. He had to tend to every aspect of the plan, make it appear real, so Widow Hensen would be convinced. And legally, the marriage would be real.

His next stop was his lawyer's office. To have a prenuptial agreement drawn up, giving Lily a sizable amount of his net worth once the marriage was dissolved.

No way he was reaching for his own dream, changing his life forever, without equally changing hers. For the good.

She'd have no need to ever go back to the café or her rented apartment. She'd have the chance to do what she wanted to do for a living.

The marriage wouldn't last, but as far as he was concerned, the bond between them and the benefits the marriage brought most definitely would.

He knew she was working that day, and that shifts ended at four. A busy time at the GreatStore in which the café was located.

Dressed in new black jeans, shined black cowboy boots, a white button-down shirt, and leaving his Stetson on the seat of his truck, he entered the building at fifteen minutes before the hour.

He'd thought he'd mosey some, be casual, but as it occurred to him that she could have plans and run out as soon as she was off, he made a beeline straight for the café. And stood there, all dressed up, getting a few interested looks and a smile from a woman he'd dated a time or two the previous fall. A guy he knew from the ranch was heading down the main aisle of the store, right for him. While he was glad to have the chance at a firsthand witness to what was about to happen, most likely on its way straight to Val Hensen, no way he wanted to be stuck in conversation with another cowboy when Lily appeared.

Nothing left to do but head into the café and seek her out, even while she was still on the clock. He'd planned on waiting till her shift ended to do this, but now those plans had changed. Besides, it wasn't like she needed the job anymore. If he had any sway with her, she'd be quitting that day. She'd told him more than once that while she loved seeing the people who came in, loved being around town folk every day, she hated the work. It bored her.

If they were entering into a real marriage, he'd know he'd have some sway.

With that thought at the top of his mind, Asa saw Lily exit the café's kitchen, a filled salad bowl in hand, and head to a table.

He headed toward her.

Seconds later, he was a couple of feet up the aisle, blocking her way when she turned back toward the kitchen. Everyone seemed to be staring at him. He *hoped* they were at least, as he bent down on one knee, pulled the newly purchased ring box out of his pocket and opened it to show the glistening two-carat diamond he'd picked out that morning.

He heard gasps.

Only then did he look up at the woman he'd virtually trapped between tables and any exit. "Lily Perry, would you do me the honor of marrying me?"

His gaze was only for her. Steady. Letting her know, that she had every right to turn him down and he wouldn't hold it against her if she did, while at the same time, trying to look the besotted lover to all of his inadvertent witnesses.

The way Lily's mouth fell open helped his plan.

The doubt he thought he saw flash in her eyes, not so much.

She recovered quickly. Pasted a smile on her face. Followed by the light a normal fiancée would expect to see in his betrothed eyes. He'd known Lily was a great friend. An incredible person. However, he'd never known she was such a good actress.

"Yes." Her voice trembled, caught, so much in fact that he wasn't sure he'd heard the right answer.

Until clapping and whoops broke out around them. Thanking fates for the startling cacophony that was his clue to actually pull the ring out of the box, he grabbed Lily's left hand, and glided the ring on her second to last finger.

Shocked again, as a curious thrill spread through him as the ring slid home.

He knew why...because he was getting the ranch.

Asa just hadn't expected such an emotional reaction from himself. Wasn't sure what to do next. How far did he take a fake proposal?

They hadn't exactly discussed how it would all unfold.

Letting go of Lily's hand as he panicked for a second, disgusted by his lack of preparedness, he felt Lily's fingers close around his. Holding on to him as she pulled him up to his feet.

And into her body.

Sliding her arms around him, she held on tight.

Lifted her face to smile at him.

And he did the stupidest thing he'd done in...maybe ever.

He lowered his head and kissed her.

LILY HAD ALMOST backed out.

She should have said no.

And despite everything, she couldn't help the surge of sadness inside her as Asa's lips touched hers to the sounds of whoops and hollers and whistles. In front of friends and coworkers, whom she considered to be her family, she was living her greatest dream come true. Except that where it counted, in the heart of hearts, it was all fake.

The feel of those lips, though, the warmth, wiped out everything but Asa. Her mouth opened to him, and for a second, she forgot their audience. And their pretense. She kissed him back with passion, and when he pulled back, and she saw the thankfulness in his gaze as he looked only at her, she knew that she'd walk to the end of the earth for the man.

What was six months of her life to make his future right? Six months where she got to live a portion of her own greatest desires? Part was better than *nothing*, after all.

With that thought solidifying her choice, knowing that there was no backing out for her, she kissed him once more, just for the heck of it. And then, stepping back, she took a moment to smile at everyone coming forward to express their shock and delight, before she left Asa to deal with the scene he'd made and went to clock out.

ASA WAITED FOR LILY. A guy didn't just propose and then leave. Not him, at any rate. Accepting the well-wishes of a few people he knew, and more who'd known Lily her entire life whom he'd never met, he kept watch for his brand-new fiancée.

Only then fully grasping what he'd just done. What he'd gotten them both into.

If he hadn't been so worried that Widow Hensen would put the ranch back on the market and find a married buyer willing to offer more than asking price, selling it right out from under him, he might have had the sense to slow down.

To talk over parameters with Lily, at the very least.

He knew they weren't just entering into a platonic, limited time marriage for Val Hensen's sake. They were embarking on a union that everyone would think was real.

Chatelaine was an old-fashioned small town that wasn't progressive like other communities in Texas. The people there wanted things left just like they were.

And they were *not* the type of folks who'd likely look kindly on a man using one of their own to his own gain.

Feeling like a lout, he kept a smile on his face and

grabbed Lily's hand as soon as, purse in hand, she reappeared from the back room.

"We need to talk," he whispered directly into her ear.

Even if she had other pressing plans, she'd have to change them.

His fault.

He'd make it up to her.

But if he'd just sent a boulder down a hill to crash her world into pieces, he had to find a way to stop the descent.

She was busy accepting well-wishes and being stopped for hugs as they made their way out of the café. But she seemed as eager as he was to be alone.

To sort out the mess he'd made.

And, if they were going forward, to get plans in place for future public appearances.

He wanted his future.

But *not* at the cost of hers.

As he pushed through the door of the GreatStore, holding it for her, he could feel the sweat trickling down his back and promised himself he'd just made his last mistake where Lily Perry was concerned.

CHAPTER THREE

WE NEED TO TALK.

That kind of lead-in usually meant the conversation would not be good.

They'd reached the GreatStore parking lot.

Asa started talking. "We can take my truck, maybe head out to my cabin at the ranch. Word getting to Val Hensen that we're alone there together would be good, but we'd also have plenty of privacy."

And they'd be at the ranch. Their whole reason for getting married.

"I can't, Asa. Not right this second. I'm meeting my sisters for an early dinner." True. Though she didn't have to show up at the restaurant for another hour. She just wasn't ready for "the talk." Not ten minutes after he'd shocked her with the impromptu and incredibly romantic proposal in front of a crowd of people who'd known her all her life.

She'd needed it to be real in the worst way.

But it wasn't. And she had to get a grip on that before things went any further. So right now, with the way her body was humming and her heart was crying, being alone with him at his cabin was a *very* bad idea.

"Call them," he said, pulling her down out of the way of the store's entrance. "Make it an hour later, and I'll take us all out to the LC Club."

He said it as though visiting the ritzy oasis set twenty miles out of town with multiple balcony dining spaces overlooking Lake Chatelaine, wasn't a once-in-a-lifetime experience. For Tabitha, it wouldn't be. Probably not for Haley, either. But for Lily?

She'd never been.

And didn't want her first time to be a fake celebration. Most particularly not when she'd be there with the three people she loved most in the world.

Shaking her head, Lily pulled away from Asa. Secretly hating the way his brows drew together, like he was pained, but held her ground, just the same.

"My time with my sisters…it's still kind of sacrosanct to me. You know, having grown up without knowing them… I can meet you after," she said to him. "We can drive out to the lake, if you'd like."

We need to talk purported a need for privacy, and it wasn't like they could find that at the LC Club.

As soon as she saw his nod, she turned toward the employee parking area and was further put out when Asa kept in step beside her, until he murmured, "Just to keep up appearances."

At which point she nodded, grinned at him, and walked fast.

She still felt like she was racing as she sat, in newly donned jeans and a short-sleeved shirt, fork suspended over her chef salad, facing her triplet sisters an hour later.

It was like she couldn't catch her breath. Had been that way since she'd seen Asa down on his knee in front of her, holding out that ridiculously fancy diamond ring.

She'd taken it off the second she'd shut herself in her old beater of a car.

"Tell us already," Haley said, sounding more caring than exasperated. Lily saw the glance she shared with Tabitha, the beautiful blonde sister, as Lily thought of her. One more suited to Asa Fortune, for sure, if not for the fact that Tabitha had already loved, and lost, a Fortune. Weston Fortune's death had left her a single mother, raising their year-old twins alone.

"Tell you what?" Lily knew pretending was only going to stall the inevitable. When pretense had gotten her into this whole mess to begin with. And besides, she'd needed to talk to her sisters.

But just putting it out there…facing reality. Was she really ready for that? A part of her wanted to cling to fantasy for a second or two longer.

"We both got calls," Tabitha said softly, her blond hair falling perfectly against the sides of her face, her green eyes filled with questions.

"Within a minute of him asking," Haley confirmed.

"You knew we would." Tabitha again.

And Lily put her fork down.

"Trouble is, you aren't wearing the ring." Haley just kept coming at her. "And you sure don't look like an ecstatic, newly engaged woman."

"Which, considering how besotted you are with the guy, is a bit of a concern," Tabitha added.

They weren't going to let this go. And truthfully, she didn't want them to. She just wished, for once, she wasn't the poor fledging among them. The one who didn't have a life mapped out in front of her.

Because who else would enter into a fake marriage just to help out a friend?

"It's a favor," she leaned in to say. There. She'd put it out there. Quietly. Just between the three of them. And effectively ended the weird flight into make believe she'd been teetering around in. "But before I tell you any more, I need you both to swear that this goes no further," she said, looking between the two of them with a solid gaze.

Both women nodded immediately.

"I mean it," she reiterated. "No one." If word got out, the adventure was over. And Asa lost everything he most desired.

"Of course," Tabitha agreed.

"Goes without saying," Haley said. "We're our safe place, right?" Her glance encompassed Lily and Tabitha equally.

"Right," they both answered solemnly. In tandem.

As though they'd grown up together rather than just being part of the same birthing event, and sharing a home for the first ten months of their lives.

"So yeah, I'm a fool," Lily said with a beleaguered sigh, suddenly feeling a lot younger than her sisters despite the fact that they were all the same age. But looking over at Tabitha, the doting mother, and Haley, the incredibly talented magazine writer, she suddenly just knew. She wasn't going to change her mind.

No matter the eventual cost to her heart.

"What have you two been telling me for the past year?"

"That you need to expect more out of life," Haley answered first.

"That you deserve more than you allow yourself to expect," Tabitha chimed in with her version of the same.

"Right. Well, um, as it turns out, Asa can't buy the ranch unless he's married. So…"

"He asked you to marry him, to give up your life, so he can buy a *ranch*?"

Not a ranch. *The ranch.* "No. He made a joke. I'm the one who talked him into it."

"Still…he's letting you give up your life for…"

She shook her head before Haley could finish the sentence. "No," she stated emphatically. "First, I'm not giving up my life. The marriage is only temporary. Second, it's in name only, though as far as the town is concerned, it will be real. Basically, I'm moving from my apartment to the main house on the ranch for the next six months or so…" Assuming Asa's *talk* didn't change that.

"Ah, Lil…" Tabitha's look was full of…worry. "You love him. You think you'll share his daily life for six months and then just be able to walk away?"

Shoulders straight, she shot back, "What I think is that I'm reaching for what I want," she told them pointedly. "I want a home. Marriage. I want to be surrounded by family. And while this isn't at all what I'd envisioned, it's a hell of a lot better than waitressing at the café."

Both women kept their mouths shut, but their facial features expressed their doubts loud and clear.

"Sharing his life for six months is better than not ever having known what living with him is like," she continued, articulating thoughts she hadn't fully landed on yet. "Who knows, maybe Asa will turn out to be no fun at all in everyday life."

"And if he's everything you ever hoped for?" Haley asked again.

"Then I know what to reach for. Don't you see? You both grew up in a regular homes. You've had stability your entire lives. I never have. Besides, love isn't about what you get, it's what you give. I'm helping Asa's dream come true…"

"And when the marriage is over…you move back to your apartment, or one like it, and go back to work at the café?" Tabitha asked the question, but it blared from Haley's expression as well.

"No." She was never going back. To either. "I expect that Asa will keep me employed at the ranch for as long as I want to be…" Assuming she made it there at all.

As minutes passed, Lily grew more and more anxious

about that talk Asa had said they had to have. Surely, he wouldn't make a big public proposal and two minutes later cut her off.

He wanted the ranch too badly to do that, the more practical side of her reminded herself.

"I told him, when I was giving him my reasons for wanting to help him, that I'd already been planning to ask him for a job as soon as he got the ranch…"

Ignoring the salad in front of her…her stomach was too knotted to eat much… Lily nibbled on a dinner roll as she gave her sisters a rundown of the reasons she'd used to convince Asa to marry her. Ending with… "And the bottom line is… I want to do this," she told them both. "It might be dumb, I might get hurt, but at least I'm daring to live bigger…"

When Haley and Tabitha both nodded, Lily's stomach settled some. She might be walking into heartache, but she was doing so consciously, by her own choice.

"And who knows," Tabitha said, sharing a glance, and a small smile, with her triplets. "Maybe he'll fall in love, too, and the marriage will become real."

Haley's brows raised, her eyes wide, and, glancing at Lily, she added, "I can't imagine any straight man living with Lily for six weeks, let alone six months, without falling for her…"

Lily got that her sisters were trying to make her feel better. But she'd been residing in a town that was full of eligible men her entire life and not one of them had ever tried to snatch her up.

And it didn't matter, because the last thing she needed was false hope.

What she *did* need, however, was to get out of there, call Asa, and get every second of living she could out of the next six months.

Asa almost didn't pick up when Lily's call came through. From practically the minute he'd left her at her car in the GreatStore parking lot, he'd been getting calls from his siblings and cousins, congratulating him. He'd wanted word to travel fast. He'd just never expected the deluge that rained down upon him.

But then, he was still reeling somewhat from the huge changes life had brought him. A decades old mining tragedy that had driven his grandfather and great uncle out of town, after they'd pinned the blame on someone else, had turned into a windfall for their heirs Asa had been shocked when he'd received the letter telling him that he was the beneficiary of a fairly large sum of money. Even then, he'd never, in a million years, expected that the family members he'd never met would welcome him home as if he'd lived there all his life.

Turned out his Fortune cousins were so much in his life that they'd been noticing how much Asa and Lily hung out together and had been hoping that he'd be bringing another one of the Perry triplets into the family.

While Tabitha wasn't officially a Fortune, with West, a former federal prosecutor, having been killed before they'd been married—before he'd even known he was going to be a father—her twins were most definitely carrying Fortune blood, and the entire clan had welcomed Tabitha in as one of them.

And his own sisters...well, they'd been giddy over the idea of him actually getting over their rancorous upbringing and settling down.

Which, of course, wasn't happening at all.

Still feeling the sting of guilt over keeping the truth to himself about his impending nuptials to Lily, he'd glanced at his ringing phone on the fourth ring and saw that it was his bride-to-be.

"Hey!" he answered, anticipation replacing all of the other emotions that had been rolling around inside him. "I thought you'd be another hour or so..."

"I can meet up with you later, if you're busy."

"Now's just fine," he told her, arranging to pick her up at her place in five minutes. And as he hung up, he couldn't help feeling relieved that she was back to her easygoing, accommodating self.

Not that he wanted her to always let him have his way. On the contrary, he'd like to show her, during their time together, that she didn't always have to fit into everyone else's plans. Just like earlier, outside the store, when she'd turned down his dinner invitation.

She could say no, and it wouldn't change anything between them.

In fact, he wanted her to feel comfortable asking for what she wanted from *him*, and he'd do his best to give it to her.

That thought in mind, as soon as she climbed into his truck, he said, "I want this marriage to be a two-way street." No hello. Just him, pushing forward into his future.

Which was now hers, as well, at least for a time.

"You're the one friend in the world I think I've ever wholly trusted, Lily, and I don't want anything to ever jeopardize that."

What the hell was he doing?

"What's going to jeopardize it?" she asked, looking cute and comfortable in her jeans and shirt. No makeup, hair just flowing naturally. That was Lily.

And he wouldn't have her any other way.

"You not benefiting in a big way from it as well."

He'd intended to wait until they were parked at the lake to get into it with her. Had planned to take Major out for half an hour before he met up with her again, too.

To have some soul-calming family time.

He told her about his conversations with his lawyer. The prenuptial agreement he'd already had drawn up.

"That's ridiculous, Asa, you don't have to do that."

Glancing over at her, he pulled off onto a dirt road, parked by some trees, and turned to her. "This marriage is changing my life forever, Lily, giving me my future. It needs to do the same for you. No way you just go back to working at the café, not unless you loved the work, and remember, this is me? I already know you don't. You love seeing the people, being a part of their lives, every day, being able to keep up on everyone's news. But the work…"

Her smile was more self-deprecatory than filled with humor as she conceded the point with a nod. They'd had a long talk over beers one night about their jobs. Him needing to move on from ranch hand to ranch owner. And her not knowing what she'd move on to.

"I don't want to be bought." Her words were barely above a whisper. He felt them to his core.

"Are you marrying me for money?" He met her gaze in the early evening, shaded sun glow.

"Of course not! How could you even ask that?" Her hazel eyes glared at him, like pinpricks of gold and steel.

"Then you aren't being bought." He waited a second for his words to settle over her before continuing. "You're working toward your future," he told her. "You want a home of your own. You said so. That's one of your dreams to the point that you're willing to settle for six months of having one, rather than never having the chance." He huffed out a breath. "But I can't do that to you. Just let you taste your dream and then snatch it away. You're doing this to make me happy, well, I need to make you happy, too. When we get married, you'll be getting a home for life. For the first six months, or so, you'll be sharing mine. After that, you'll have the resources to choose one you want."

Saying the words aloud, knowing she was hearing them, settled some of the qualms inside him. "It's the only way I can do this," he told her, holding her gaze tightly. "This arrangement can't be a one-way thing."

She didn't look away. Lily wasn't a wallflower. She didn't hide. She just...*expected less than she deserved*. Words she'd told him months ago, again over beers, repeating what her sister, the mother of his second cousins, had said to her.

When she nodded, she didn't look happy, but she didn't seem upset, either. She seemed to have lost, or at least fully contained, all of the agitation his impromptu proposal had raised in her.

"About this afternoon," he began, glancing at the diamond he'd placed on her finger, liking the way it glistened there, "I'm sorry for the way that went down. I was..."

"Being you," she said, with a real grin. "Getting the job done."

"Yeah." He grinned back. "But I could have let you in on the plan ahead of time," he allowed.

"Might have been a good idea."

"So...we're good?" he asked.

"Yep."

He gazed at her fondly. "You know I love ya, right?"

"I figured, maybe."

"You want to get a beer?"

When her usual positive response didn't immediately follow, Asa's gut tightened again.

"I just...if Widow Hensen suspects that this marriage isn't real...you still won't get the ranch," Lily reminded him.

"I know." He figured that went without saying, literally. "The whole point of the proposal was..."

He stopped when he saw her frown. "What?" he asked.

"In public, Asa...we're going to have to act like it's real. Holding hands. Sitting next to each other at the table, having conversations with our heads close together sometimes..."

He'd had the same thoughts but was trying not to dwell on them too much.

"You have a problem with that?" he asked her.

"No."

"So...you want to get that beer?"

Her smile was still lighting him up inside as he parked outside the Corral, the popular rancher bar just outside of town, where they'd met the previous summer. Aafter exiting the truck, he reached for her hand.

He felt her softer palm and fingers intermingle with his calloused ones. Didn't hate it.

Two friends, lifting each other to their futures.

Life had never been better.

CHAPTER FOUR

LILY PUT HER notice in the next day at work, but agreed to work a few more days, just until management could fill her schedule. She could pretend that life was going on as normal—other than the huge rock surrounded by a setting of smaller ones she was carrying around on her left ring finger—except that nothing about the following couple of days felt at all normal.

Everyone who saw her in the café either congratulated her or asked about a wedding date. Her sisters were both calling daily to check up on her—and wanting to know the same.

Plus every single one of the Fortune cousins currently in town, and Asa's two sisters, had called, or stopped by to welcome her to the family—all of them offering to help with wedding plans. And it got to the point that on Friday, after work, she had to take matters into her own hands. Her last day at the café had culminated with a surprise shower for her, gifts consisting of things she'd need for a wedding, like certificates for a manicure and pedicure, a waxing— like she'd have any reason to need that—a hair appointment, and a pile of gift certificates for the GreatStore.

She and Asa had been meeting in town for dinner each night, usually at the Chatelaine Bar & Grill, the nicest place in town, to be seen as much as to eat, and she started in on him as soon as she joined him in the red-leather booth.

Rather than asking if he'd been waiting long—she'd been late due to more well-wishers stopping her as she tried to get out of the café—she slid onto the chair directly across from him and started right in. "I think we need to get this over and done with," she told him. "Let's just go to Town Hall and get married." She could use the gift certificates making her purse bulge as Christmas gifts or something.

Asa quirked a brow. "Right now?"

"Probably best to wait for them to open, but Monday morning, for sure. People can throw whatever parties they want to for us afterward. Or we can have a big housewarming at the ranch once the closing happens."

His glance at her seemed a little worried. And she sighed. "I've just spent twenty minutes trying to get a word in edgewise with my sisters, regarding me having a dress suitable for marrying a Fortune. Tabitha wants me to wear the wedding dress she had made to marry West, but never got to wear. If we don't get this done, we're going to have one-year-old twin ring bearers and a magazine spread of the big day, too."

Her sisters, bless their hearts, were trying to make everything so real and perfect in the hope that Asa was going to fall in love with her—not just love her as a friend. In the hopes that the marriage would turn out to be real. And by then the wedding would already have happened, robbing Lily, in their opinion, of the chance to have her big day. And pictures and memories to cherish forever. They wanted to make sure she had that.

Didn't matter how many times she told them that she didn't care about that kind of stuff.

Asa suddenly pulling out his phone, as though her conversation wasn't worthy of his attention, didn't sit well, either. Not right then, after a busy day at work, and too much pressure coming at her.

For a second there, she wished herself back to the non-entity life she felt like she'd lived since she was ten months old. Invisible, or slightly visible, under the radar at least, wasn't all bad.

Not wanting to chance anyone witnessing a cross word from her to him, she picked up the menu as though she'd hadn't just read it the night before. And wished they were over at the Corral, having wings and chips. At least there the conversation was louder and the mood lighter.

"There's a seventy-two-hour waiting period after you apply for the license until you can get married."

She glanced across the booth at her pseudo fiancé. He'd been reading about getting married? Not finding something more important than her wedding woes on his phone?

And of less importance, but easier to deal with in the moment, "We have to wait until next Thursday to do this? That's like…almost another whole week from now!"

Another week in which Val Hensen could find some married person to buy the Chatelaine Dude Ranch. Asa would lose his chance. And she…really and truly wanted her chance, too. She wanted to marry the man, to make the deal, to change her life, build her future into something more than her past had been. If they had to wait, they had to wait, but it was going to be a very nerve-wracking week on so many levels.

He leaned in toward her. "Let's go to Vegas."

Heart jumping, she stared at him. Saw the seriousness in his gaze. And a new light there, too.

"Vegas?" She didn't squeak, but almost. "I've never been outside of Texas." In fact, she'd never been more than a hundred miles from Chatelaine. Excitement pumped through her. "Is it like you see on those old CSI, Las Vegas reruns?"

"Pretty much," he told her. "Though we can stay off the strip if you'd like. They have marriage chapels around the town."

"No!" She blurted so loud, one of the managers from The GreatStore, who was seated with his wife at the table next to them, glanced over. "I want to go!" she finished, not much quieter. "I want to see it all."

And a fake wedding where she had her groom all to herself…the groom she loved for real…sounded better than anything she'd ever dared dream up for herself. There'd be no worrying about what other people saw, or thought. No pretending. Just a woman eloping with her best friend, knowing that he wasn't going to have sex with her.

Just her and Asa on the most incredible road trip…

He talked to her about wedding venue options, looked up flights, and booked them two seats for Sunday morning, then moved on to hotels. Eventually choosing what he said was one of the most opulent, in the best part of the strip, he got them the honeymoon suite plus. The plus part was that in addition to the lavish master suite, the accommodations included a second, smaller bedroom. For her, she assumed. Which was what she preferred anyway. No way she wanted to sleep alone in a big romantic wedding room bed.

Of course, for show, they'd be able to bring back photos of the amenities, including a heart-shaped bed, chocolate-covered strawberries, and exclusive champagne.

It was working out perfectly. In a way, she was getting the wedding of her dreams. Just her and Asa, all alone, on a magical trip, in Sin City, staying in a room that would surely feel like paradise to her. For those two days and one night, she'd be a princess. And he'd be her prince.

Grown-up version, of course.

And not having to go through a wedding in Chatelaine, where everyone would be watching, where her sisters would be looking on, knowingly, where she'd worry every second that someone would call them on the pretense...that relief was palpable.

Lily was still flying high as she and Asa left the restaurant, their plans all firmly settled. So much so that she slid her hand behind his elbow and down, linking her arm with his. He stiffened, but then immediately relaxed, hugging her arm close to him, and she couldn't help thinking what a perfect moment it was.

Right up until they started down the sidewalk to their vehicles and Baylor Minser turned a corner and started toward them. The tall, thin, glamorous blonde with her perfect make up and long, flowing, flawlessly styled hair was one of the women Asa took out on occasion.

Had he called her? Let her know the marriage was a fake?

Even as Lily had the thought, she was admonishing herself. Asa wouldn't do that to Lily. Or risk sabotaging his chances of getting the ranch, either.

Smile, just keep walking, get past her, Lily was saying to herself.

"Asa! Hello!" Baylor called out, as though just then noticing them. The woman's gaze was firmly on Asa, her smile inviting more than just words, even as she said, "I hear congratulations are in order..."

At which point Baylor gave a quick up-and-down glance over Lily. With a smirk filled with disdain before turning her gaze, accompanied by a bright smile, right back on Asa. "I wish I'd known you were in the market for more than a good time," she said, with a little pout. "I'm sure we could have worked something out..."

She let her words trail off as she passed them—on Asa's side—making sure that the side of her hand grazed his thigh as she did so.

Lily couldn't say how Asa reacted. She was too busy trying to keep her own despair firmly under wraps. Clearly, whether her marriage to the handsome cowboy was real or not, there were some women who were still going to be available to him.

And...

"I need you to promise me something," she blurted, all sense of euphoria giving way to panic. But at least she had her feet firmly back in her own world where they belonged.

"What?" Asa didn't seem the least bit different. As though seeing Baylor had had no effect on him at all. Good or bad.

Because he knew he'd be calling her for a little *on the side* action the woman had made clear she'd still be willing to offer?

"I know our marriage is pretense, and this is asking a lot of a guy like you, but I can't do this if I'm going to be humiliated."

"A guy like me?" He was still walking...still holding her arm. But more loosely. And his tone had a more distant edge to it, too.

"You're sexy, Asa. Virile. You have healthy desires and places to assuage them..." What the hell. She was going to start spouting like some kind of virginal heroine of a melodrama now? "I just...you need to promise me it won't be in this town. Or with anyone who lives here. Not as long as we're married."

"What won't be in this town?"

He was going to make her spell it out? Maybe even was teasing her some? Getting a little fun out of it? Fine. "Your sex life. Or partners."

He stopped. Right there in the middle of the sidewalk. Then took hold of both of her arms and held her in front of him. So close, if she leaned at all, their thighs would be touching. Glancing up at him, she saw his gaze boring into hers. "There will be no sex life, period," he told her gruffly. "At least not on my part. You think I'd do that to you?"

At that moment she didn't have a thought. Not a single one of them. She had tears welling inside her, though.

And, almost as if he knew the things she couldn't show, knew the battle inside her, Asa leaned in and kissed her.

It was all for appearances, she knew. For the benefit of the folks out and about who'd probably witnessed at least parts of their interaction.

Which was definitely why Lily kissed him back.

She flooded with warmth, too.

Asa was her closest friend. He was going to have her back. Not only during the marriage, but afterward, too.

And that was a win for her future.

HE HADN'T THOUGHT about sex.

Or rather, entering into six months of total celibacy.

It wasn't a deal breaker. Not even close.

But he should have given the matter thought. Enough to assure Lily that he was not going to be unfaithful to her before she'd had to ask. He would not have her known as a woman whose husband cheated on her during the first year of their marriage. In a town the size of theirs, she'd carry that with her for the rest of her life.

He'd die first.

For that matter, he had no desire whatsoever to be labeled as that guy, either. He planned to be in Chatelaine, owning and running his dude ranch, until he was old and gray. No way he was going to smirch any of it with rumors of infidelity.

Having grown up with all four of the major adults in his life—parents and his aunt and uncle—cheating on their spouses, he'd promised himself he would never put himself in such a situation. One reason he didn't ever intend to marry for real. Or at least not for a very long time.

All of which he'd still been thinking about on Saturday when Lily called him, just after noon, saying she was ready for his truck. With firm wedding plans in place, she'd given notice on her apartment and had been told that, instead of having to pay the full month's utilities, if she was out by the end of the weekend, she'd get her full deposit back. The owner knew of someone else needing a place as soon as possible.

She'd known of someone, too, she'd told him. A cook at work whose twentysomething son was moving back to town to help his father out with their horse breeding business, and she'd hoped the new renter was one and the same.

Asa had wanted to provide boxes and help her pack, but she'd staunchly refused his offer, to the point of refusing to accept his help moving her things from the apartment in town out to the spare bedroom in his cabin, if he didn't stop.

He'd stopped. Asa had figured her sisters would be there, helping her, but was surprised to find her alone. With a tattered blue suitcase, two large moving boxes, and a small closet's worth of hanging clothes wrapped in a blanket and lying over the couch.

"This is it?" He regretted the question as soon as he'd asked it. Making it sound as though her belongings weren't enough.

But in a perfectly satisfied-sounding tone, she told him that the furniture wasn't hers. Her apartment had come furnished.

Standing there, looking at her small, incredibly neat

haul, he had to hold back a surge of emotion. H
moving around his entire adult life and he had t
much stuff to lug around with him everywhere he

"It's not like I have family photos or childhoc
mentos," she added. He took the reminder as a cue
his butt moving.

Carrying her boxes down one at a time, Asa found
self seeing Lily in a new way. It was like he was some
entering more of her world, even as he moved her it
his. He'd known she'd grown up in various foster home.
Nickolas, head bartender at the Corral, and also, as it had
turned out, one of Lily's foster brothers, had told him she'd
never been in one home long enough to feel a part of a
family. Nickolas had only lived with her for part of a year
before he'd aged out of the system. But the married man
and father of two clearly looked after Lily.

Nickolas was why Lily frequented the Corral, she'd once
told Asa. She could have a beer, alone, yet not feel lonely.
Plus, she'd help him out in the kitchen, making wings if
he got overly busy, and she'd get comped beer.

Asa had known her childhood had been vastly different
from his. He'd just never put himself in her position until
that Saturday afternoon. Or truly understood how much
their marriage was going to impact her life.

And he told himself once again, as they headed out to
the Chatelaine Dude Ranch, that he'd make certain his
friend never went back to a life of two boxes, an old suitcase, and some hanging clothes.

Unless she wanted to do so.

Wanting to give her plenty of time to unpack, he left
her to it and drove to the freeway, following it to the first
exit that promised plenty of shopping choices. He wasn't
after much. Just a new set of luggage for his bride-to-be,
and, as an afterthought, a box of expensive chocolates, too.

She'd raved about a box a customer had left her at the café over the Christmas holiday. He'd thought maybe the drive would open his mind to seeing how out of hand his scheme to get the ranch was getting. Instead, he took the Chatelaine exit feeling pretty damned good about the future.

For him and for Lily.

She deserved so much more than he was giving her, but at least she'd be getting a home, the new way of life she wanted, as she searched for the rest of her future.

The thought was still on top of his mind a couple of hours later, as he and Lily—who'd seemed more embarrassed by, than happy with, his gifts—made their way to the front door of the main house.

Both of them in jeans and short-sleeved shirts, they stood together, their sides touching as they waited for their summons to be answered.

Val looked shocked to see him, but smiled almost immediately as she invited them in.

"That's okay," he said quickly. "We don't want to take up your time, and actually have a lot to do before our flight in the morning. But I just wanted to let you know that I'm getting married."

They hadn't told anyone else of their plans to elope. And weren't planning to tell Val—only that he was going to be out of town and had arranged for Jack to take care of Major for him.

"I heard!" the older woman exclaimed. "But I thought…" She clamped her mouth shut on whatever she'd thought, and Asa had a feeling he didn't want to know.

He just needed to know that she wasn't going to sell the ranch out from under him while he was gone.

"I've been in love with Asa since last summer," Lily piped in, sounding not at all like the woman he knew. "He'd wanted to make our relationship public, but I…well, I just work at the café and I was afraid people would think I was a Fortune hunter…" Lily looked embarrassed for a second, and then said, "literally," with a chuckle. "But when I heard that you weren't going to sell him the ranch because I was afraid of what people would think of me… I couldn't let that happen. I told him if he wanted to make our relationship known, I was okay with that." She blushed. "Of course, I had no idea he'd do it in such a big way, proposing to me at work like he did, but it's a memory I'm going to cherish forever."

The words rolled so naturally from her lips, Lily had Asa believing them in their entirety. Until he made himself remember what they were doing and why. Maybe Lily had a future onstage…

The absurd thought flew off as Val said, "I heard about that! And the ring. Let me see the ring."

Holding her hand out, and as Val oohed and aahed, Lily talked kind of shyly about being half afraid to wear it, and Asa was fairly certain that she hadn't been faking that one at all. Again, he'd bumbled, doing his thing, solo, as he did. Buying a ring expensive enough for a Fortune, instead of thinking about his bride-to-be and what might have been more suited to her.

He had a lot to learn about being a true friend, apparently. And made it a silent wedding vow to work every day of the next six months to rectify that situation.

He had a ton to do, just getting the ranch ready for the summer season, and was chomping at the bit to get at it…

"I remember your parents," Val said to Lily, stopping Asa's thoughts in their tracks. How did a woman recall one couple from nearly twenty-nine years ago…

"You girls were such a treat that day you were here… in your triplet stroller. They took you to the petting zoo, and I was working there that day, and your parents got you out and you were all just starting to walk. It was absolutely adorable watching you girls toddling around..." The widow hitched in a breath. "And when I heard about the accident the next day I just..." Val teared up.

Lily might have, too. But Asa couldn't see the face she'd turned toward the setting sun.

"We've moved Lily's things into my cabin," he said then, feeling like he needed to rescue his friend. "I'm hoping that's okay with you. I realize I should have cleared it through you first. I just... Lily, as you'd obviously assume knowing the circumstances, couldn't wait to actually live here..."

All true. And would remain true if that was what she wanted. Maybe he'd sell her a cabin on the ranch. Give her lifetime occupancy or something.

Maybe he was getting in over his head.

And couldn't stop the avalanche from rolling forward. Lily had quit her job. Given up her apartment. It was too late to back out now...

"It's fine," Val said, her smile a bit wobbly as moisture still filled her eyes. "Of course she can stay here. I'm honored to have one of the triplets back on the ranch."

Lily still appeared to be admiring the landscape. He heard a sniffle. "What makes more sense than to marry my best friend, who I truly love?" Asa spit out into the moment. All true. Lily *was* his best friend. And he truly loved her. As a friend.

"I married my best friend, too," Val surprised him by saying, drawing Lily's gaze sharply back to the older woman as well. "I wish everyone could. I think it's what made our marriage so strong and healthy for so many decades."

He didn't know about that. Figured, on the inside, behind the family dude ranch scenes, there were some things not as pretty as Val would have them believe. There had to have been some tense times. Fights. That led to…

"And Asa," Val interrupted another pointless train of thought. "You two go get married, and when you return with your marriage certificate and your wedding rings on, I'll have the sales contract ready for you."

Asa found his usual charm long enough to say, "My latest offer still stands." And then, slipping his hand into Lily's, pulled gently, meaning to lead her away. But when she turned instead, looking up into his eyes, he didn't go anywhere. He planted his lips on hers. Right there in front of the widow.

He hadn't meant to kiss Lily. But the way she'd been looking at him, as though he was everything in her world, the light of her life, he'd just bent his head to her lips.

She'd been playacting—for Val's sake. He knew that. But the desire she stirred in him? That couldn't be faked. So much so that Asa pulled back as soon as he felt himself starting to grow hard. There'd be none of that.

Still, as they'd walked back to his place, to share a box of macaroni and cheese and then retreat to their own rooms for a few hours' sleep before needing to get up for the couple of hours' drive to the airport to make their 6:00 a.m. flight, Asa couldn't quite lose the memory of that look in Lily's eyes.

Or the soft touch of her lips beneath his.

CHAPTER FIVE

SHE HADN'T EVER flown before. However, not wanting to come across as a bumpkin in front of her husband on her wedding day, Lily kept the news to herself. They made it through airport security, followed the signs to their gate, and then before she knew it, they were on the plane. As she buckled herself up, it almost felt as though she'd been doing so all her life.

Finally experiencing something she'd only heard about occupied every single one of her thoughts—and most of her emotions, too—right up until she was sitting there, waiting to take off, anticipating the speed she'd be moving at with a mixture of excitement and trepidation. To distract herself, she thought of her destination.

Vegas.

The strip she'd only seen in movies. The noise and lights. Millions of people. Maybe, if she'd been heading there alone, she'd have been afraid. As it was, knowing that she'd be experiencing it all with Asa, she couldn't wait.

Wanted to savor every moment.

Didn't want the next two days to ever end.

But at the same time, she didn't want to think about her upcoming wedding. It wasn't that she was getting cold feet. She wanted to marry Asa and had no thoughts of backing out. She just wanted it to be honest and real.

And even though they were marrying under false pretenses, deep down in her heart, her vows would be truthful.

He didn't know that.

His wouldn't be.

She *did* know that.

"Maybe we should write our own vows," she said as the plane taxied down the runway for takeoff. Lily would not reach for him. She couldn't need him *that* much. Instead, she kept her hands in her lap, firmly clutching each other. "That way we can control the lies," she added as they lifted off. "Maybe work our way around them so there aren't so many of them."

Asa's easy agreement was a gift. A distraction.

And got her through takeoff.

They'd said they'd sleep on the flight, since they'd had to get up in the middle of the night to make it to the airport, and Asa drifted off almost immediately. Lily, in her newest pair of jeans and a long-sleeved button-down shirt, closed her eyes, dozed, but couldn't quite get herself to let go and really sleep. Instead, she thought about the one girlie dress she owned, which was probably getting wrinkled in her suitcase, and the shoes she'd worn only once, She'd purchased both for a function she'd gone to with Tabitha's wealthy adopted family shortly after the triplets had reunited.

She'd wanted to get her hair done, but the certificates she'd received were only good at the local shop in the next town over from Chatelaine, and she doubted she had enough money in her checking account to pay for a Vegas hairdo. Like she was some kind of celebrity.

She thought about dipping into her modest savings account for the first time ever, to do just that—get her hair done. And her nails and fingers as well.

If she and Asa ever did get together romantically, as her sisters kept insisting they might, and the day ahead was going to turn out, someday, to be real, she wanted pictorial memories of herself looking...prettier than normal... standing next to her gorgeous cowboy husband.

Plus, people in town, her sisters at the very least, and maybe Asa's too, would want to see photographs from their wedding.

Giving up on sleep, she signed her phone up to the plane's free Wi-Fi and started surfing for hairdos with long straight hair. But eventually settled on beachy waves, not even sure they were still in style, but she figured they'd go best with the kind of longer, rather than round, shape of her face.

She'd need flowers, too. Maybe one in her hair?

The plans seemed to take on a life of their own, and by the time they landed, Lily was too focused on her wedding to pay all that much attention to the crowds, the noise, the sheer cacophony that was the Las Vegas airport and then strip. Slot machines seemed to be everywhere—even along airport walls—as they'd exited the plane with their carry-on suitcases and made their way down the longest escalator she'd ever seen on their search for ground transportation.

Glittering lights and advertisements were everywhere. From the walls of the airport, hanging from the ceiling on the sides of cabs and buses, on billboards...and all of it was like background to her as she thought about standing with Asa and saying, "I do."

But by the time she was in the elevator up to their suite—a feat in itself to reach from the hotel desk—she was overstimulated and ready to escape the crowds.

Yet excited to get back to it, too.

Asa, on the other hand, seemed to take it all in stride. She didn't ask, but figured by the way he knew his way around, that he'd been to Vegas before. He seemed fully focused on getting them where they needed to be, checking them in, arranging the chapel time, and choosing the two dinners, from four choices, that would be brought to their room later as part of their wedding package.

He was kind to her, polite, consulting her on every decision, and all business. She didn't want to dwell on that.

As soon as she entered their suite, she made a beeline for the smaller bedroom. Didn't even look at the larger one. Or the view.

Instead, she locked herself in her bathroom, the farthest place from the rest of the suite, and started a three-way video call with her sisters. She couldn't get married, even if it was fake, without letting them know.

After their exclamations of shock over her flying off to Vegas to elope without letting them know, Lily looked from one to the other on the small screen and asked her sisters the question she'd been refusing to ask herself. "You think I'm making a mistake?"

Because even if she was, she wanted to marry Asa. To live with him, regardless of the fact that it was only for six months. To live on the ranch.

And, though it wasn't her reason for marrying Asa, she wanted to be able to at least buy her own home when the six months was through.

"I think you're following your heart," Tabitha said softly, easing some of Lily's stress.

"And who knows," Haley added, "Maybe the marriage will turn real…"

She knew better, and still, that tiny bit of possibility made her tear up—and smile—as she told her sisters she loved them and hung up to their chorus of the same.

She'd told Asa she needed a couple of hours before they got married, but in the end, it didn't take that long at all. He'd told her to charge anything she needed to the room, and, as it turned out, there was a salon right on the premises that offered all of the services she needed, as well as some she didn't recognize.

He might just be closing a deal, making his dream come true, but she was still in the process of reaching for her own dream. And, just in case her marriage to Asa could, by some miracle, turn out to be it, she needed the day to mean more than Asa buying a ranch. Even when it was the Chatelaine Dude Ranch.

He'd suggested that they meet at the suite and ride down to the hotel's on-site chapel together, but she'd demurred, saying she'd meet him at the chapel.

As she'd have done on a real wedding day.

She'd taken her dress and shoes with her down to the salon, not wanting to run into Asa upstairs, and her hour there turned into an impromptu little bridal party with aestheticians gathering around her to take over getting her ready.

It wasn't as good as having her sisters there with her would have been, but Lily actually had a great time, letting herself be pampered for the first time in her life. She exited the place feeling, not exactly like a princess, but more beautiful than she'd have thought she could feel.

The woman who'd done her nails had offered to show her how to get to the chapel, and Lily figured it was kind of like having a bridesmaid there beside her as she arrived outside the room where she'd be making vows that were going to alter the rest of her life.

Then she just plain stopped thinking. She'd waved goodbye to the nail technician, had opened the door to the chapel, and there stood Asa.

Not in the jeans and cowboy boots she'd expected to see on him, but in a full tuxedo. The jacket was black, with silver undertones, and then her eyes drank in the rest of his ensemble. A light gray shirt, tie, shiny black shoes…

If she hadn't already been over-the-top in love with the man, she'd have fallen hard, just at that first sight of him.

He was drop-dead gorgeous.

And in that instant, the small grain of potential possibility lingering inside Lily's chest exploded into full-blown hope.

She let it loose, took ownership.

Telling herself it was just for that one magical day.

WHAT IN THE hell had she done? Catching his first glimpse of Lily as she walked through the door of the chapel, Asa couldn't breathe.

He'd known she'd brought a dress—they had to in order to keep up appearances. Same reason he'd rented the tuxedo. They'd be getting photos as part of the wedding package.

And people in Chatelaine—Val Hensen, yes, but also his family members for sure—were going to be asking to see them, to share the day.

But… *"Wow,"* he said as Lily walked up to him. He smiled. It was the thing a guy did when a woman got dressed up and walked toward him.

"Too much?" She grimaced, giving him a glimpse of the friend he was going to be spending the next six months of his life with, the friend he loved and trusted, but when she quickly looked away—something she didn't often do with him—he was like a fish out of water again.

"Not at all," he said thickly. "You look…beautiful."

More than he'd ever needed to see. Far more.

The hair, the makeup…she'd been transformed into a bewitching stranger. One his body was responding to in a way that he didn't want to respond to Lily.

The same way it had when he'd kissed her at the Great-

Store after their engagement. And at Widow Hensen's front door.

He was not going to go all guy on himself and let sex get in the way. No amount of physical pleasure was worth losing his best friend over.

She still wasn't looking at him. "You want to forget it?" he asked, softly. They still had time to back out. Could walk out that door and call the whole thing off.

Yeah, it would go down as the shortest engagement in Chatelaine history, but that was better than losing Lily, too...

Her face had swung toward him, and her lovely hazel eyes, they seemed to peer so deeply into his that it felt as if she was seeing his innermost thoughts.

"Are you getting cold feet?" Her question had been the last thing on his mind.

"No."

"Neither am I. I want to do this, Asa." Linking her arm through his as their names were called and the inner door to the chapel opened, she confessed, "There's no other man on earth I'd rather marry today..."

Today. He got the disclaimer. Added it to the fact that she didn't even have a boyfriend at the moment, and did that math.

Relieved on so many levels, he was wearing a genuine smile as they approached the pulpit, behind which a character resembling Elvis in a white suit and glasses stood.

Music started. Ended.

The Elvis look-alike, pseudo preacher man—a pretense for their pretense—read a line or two about matrimony, then invited the two of them to face each other, hold hands and say their vows, looking at Asa first.

"Lily Perry, as your husband, I promise you my complete fidelity," he said, the first of the five things he'd come up with on the plane, while trying to fall asleep. "I promise to always have your back. I promise to listen. I promise to keep your needs a priority. I promise to love you for the rest of my life." That last part of the vow was the one he most wanted her to believe. She was his wife for six months, but his friend *forever*. He wasn't in love with her, but what he felt for her was even better. He loved her as a friend. Someone he could argue with, maintain separate though attached lives with, and because he was free to do those things, his love would have no reason to turn into resentment. Or worse.

She hadn't blinked. Or taken her gaze from his. He figured maybe she'd glassed over, was just gliding through the moment that wasn't meant to be real in any way.

"Asa Fortune, I promise to love you for the rest of my life…"

Asa nodded as she repeated his words right back at him. He didn't blame her for not being more prepared with her own set of truth. Hell, he owed her a lifetime of not blaming her in return for the gift she was giving him today.

"I promise to be your wife for as long as you need me in your life." He frowned, looking at her. Not sure where that one had come from. "I promise that you are and will be the only man in my life."

While they were married, he finished the sentence for her. The words she couldn't very well say aloud.

"And I promise to work beside you to make dreams come true."

He smiled at that one. Figuring it to be the best one of all—from either of them.

"Do you, Asa Fortune, take this woman…" Asa held Lily's gaze, trying to let her know that she had nothing to fear and only good to gain as the white-suited man finished his question.

"I do," Asa said.

"And do you, Lily Perry, take this man, Asa Fortune, to be your lawfully wedded husband?"

"I do."

A weight lifted off his chest. He had no idea of its source. Hadn't even realized it had been there.

"Then in the powers vested in me… I now pronounce you husband, and wife. You may kiss the bride."

The smile on Asa's face slipped away. He hadn't anticipated that last line. Hadn't actually given the formal little questions they'd have to answer any thought…

However, the worry in Lily's gaze had him taking a step forward. As a camera flashed, he lowered his head to hers. And understood. She'd been concerned about the photographs. Their proof to the world…

Letting go of some of his tension, he let his mouth open over hers, kissing her as he would any other beautiful woman who was willingly in his arms. Saw flashes behind his closed lids and lengthened the kiss. Because Lily was playing right along with him.

Her arms around his neck pulled his head closer, and he pressed his body against hers…

The next thing he knew, Pretend Elvis was clearing his throat.

Embarrassed, Asa pulled away. He'd gotten a little too caught up in the part they were playing for the camera. And took note.

No enjoying certain aspects of the role he might be called upon to play from time to time.

But figured, as he and Lily went out to the lobby of the chapel and finished up the business of being married, including providing an email to which their wedding photos could be mailed, that there was no reason two friends couldn't celebrate the different, but very coveted futures they'd just locked in for the both of them.

"You want to get a beer?" he asked Lily, dropping her hand as the chapel door closed firmly behind them.

When she said, "Sure," in a perfectly normal Lily tone of voice, he filled up with celebration energy. And it hit him.

Lily had never been to Vegas.

To thank her for being such a sport that day, dressing to the nines to make their marriage appear real, he was going to show his friend the time of her life.

And since they were married, in a deal they both wanted and understood, he didn't have to worry about it seeming like they were on a date.

Watch out Vegas, best friends from Chatelaine Texas, on the loose...

CHAPTER SIX

LILY LET HERSELF float on cloud nine during what she considered her wedding reception. She knew it was all make believe, but then everything about Las Vegas perpetuated the sense of an adult fairy-tale land. The lavish resorts that went on for blocks, the opulence, the five-star dining, the oodles of money...

Asa insisted that she try out some slot machines, just for fun. And to her delight, she won, in one push of a button, ten times what he'd given her to spend.

They made their way down the strip, Asa showing her the special features of every resort, like the garden in the five-star hotel where they were staying that was always a different theme, different scene, depending on time of year, but everything was made out of real flowers. The working, full-sized carousel at another place where the entire visible surface was always living plants.

There was the canal through a version of Venice, complete with gondola rides, which they took. Then the fountain that danced to music and an accompanying light display. Another resort was a replica of a New York City street, and the next one—her personal favorite—had a mock Eiffel Tower that they rode up in. Everywhere they went, he had her drop a little into slots.

And every casino they stopped in offered free beer to slot players, too. She could take a bottle with her and walk down the street with it to the next place.

It wasn't a place Lily would ever want to live in, or even visit often, but for that one afternoon and evening, in this stolen moment in time with Asa, her new, *very legal* husband, she was on top of the world. Even after they descended from the tallest tower in the city.

They didn't talk about their pasts, or home. Didn't mention memories or anyone they knew in real life. Didn't talk about families or ranches, dude or otherwise. For those hours, it was just the two of them celebrating in a world of strangers.

Until it was time to head back to their suite for dinner. Asa had called the hotel—twice—to put off heading back, but the ten o'clock final serving time was approaching. They'd snacked on appetizers at one indoor establishment that replicated Greece, complete with full-sized statues, an ornate Parthenon ceiling and painted blue sky overhead.

Still, she was ready to head back. To settle down and eat a full meal. To switch to one glass of champagne along with iced water instead of beer and start to get her feet back under her. To begin to prepare for the vastly changed real life that would be waiting for them when they flew home the following afternoon.

Dinner was served in front of a full wall of windows that overlooked the strip that was as busy at night as it was during the day—with such a glorious array of lights she figured she could just sit and watch all night. And when they were done, and neither of them were quite ready to put an end to the day, Asa suggested they watch the Marvel movie that was being advertised on the nearly theater-sized screen that had been on in their living room when they'd come in.

She'd kicked off her dress shoes the second they'd walked in the door. Had been sad to see Asa shrug out of his tuxedo jacket and vest. And when he asked if she wanted to share the last of the champagne, she nodded, not quite ready to return to real life.

Curling up with her filled glass on the couch, she understood why Asa sat down closer to her than the living room ensemble required. Their seats were directly in front of the screen. And also had access to the table where they could set down their glasses and still reach them.

The movie was good—oddly, the first they'd seen together. He wasn't a talker, for which she was glad. She liked to escape into the films she watched, even when, as was the case that night, she'd seen it several times before.

It was a slow wind down. A bittersweet ending to a fantastical day.

Except that, when the credits were rolling at the end of the movie, she still had a little champagne in her glass and, as tired as she was—having been up since before dawn—she wasn't ready to have the day end. Asa wasn't jumping up, either. Leaning her head back against the couch, she smiled dreamily. "I can't believe we're married."

His lips pursed, then he smiled, too. "I know. Can you believe how much that preacher guy looked like pictures of Elvis?"

"Preacher guy" was the last thing on her mind.

"Your vows were…really nice," she told him, then, turning her head to look at him. "They sounded like wonderful, real wedding vows, and yet, at the same time, fit our situation, too. You didn't lie."

"Nope." He grinned back at her. "You know, even though we aren't lovers and aren't planning to stay married for long, that doesn't mean we don't have a special relationship. Or that we don't care about each other. Personally, I think what we have is a hundred times better."

His words hit her right at her core. Down below and in her heart, too.

She'd have thought going through the fake marriage with Asa would make the love she felt for him seem tarnished. Distant. But as she sat there with him, she realized she was more in love with him than ever. They'd had so much fun together that day, laughing, goofing around, teasing, and yet he'd been completely attentive, too. Had made her feel as special as any real bride would have felt.

His eyes seemed to be speaking to her, holding her gaze for a long time. Until he bent to help himself to one of the chocolate-covered strawberries left over from dinner. She watched unabashedly. Saw the strawberry juice drip out of the corner of his mouth.

And the small piece of chocolate that clung to his upper lip.

Earlier in the day, she'd have teased him about that chocolate. However, this late at night, she was all teased out. "You have chocolate on your lip," she whispered, and reached over to get it for him. Without thinking.

Just doing what she'd do for anyone she loved.

He didn't pull away. Or grin. Instead, his gaze on hers, he leaned forward. Placed a light kiss on her lips. A friend thanking a friend.

Except that she was a wife on her wedding night. One who was so in love with her new husband, she found herself opening her lips, winding her arms around his neck and beckoning him closer... Right or wrong, for this one singular night, in a city where things happened that wouldn't happen anywhere else, he was hers.

And as he deepened the kiss, and his tongue started exploring her mouth, she quit thinking altogether. With inhibitions tempered by the champagne, control lessened by lack of sleep, and a longing desperately eager to be assuaged, instincts she hadn't known she possessed took over.

So when he groaned and pushed gently against her, laying her on her back on the roomy couch, she went willingly. Accommodating his body as he lay halfway on top of her, his thigh between her legs.

She felt air hit her back as the zipper on her dress slid down, and then her breasts were more free to strain against Asa's dress shirt as the back fastener on her bra came loose.

She wanted it all off. Her dress, her bra, his shirt, and when she realized that was his goal, too, she helped him make it happen.

His broad, muscular chest, full of dark hair, was glorious. Her fingers explored every inch of it, before she plastered her palms against him and lowered her head to run her tongue over his nipples.

She didn't know herself. Didn't care.

She'd changed that day. Was never going back to being the Lily Perry she'd been. She had a new legal name. *Lily Fortune.*

And Lily Fortune wanted Asa's pants undone. Her dress came up as his zipper went down, and she opened to him as though there was no other choice. Because for her, there simply wasn't.

He scrambled for his wallet, retrieving a condom. She took the time to stroke him with her hand. And then to help him apply the protection, before she took a deep breath and finally found out what paradise was like.

She'd had sex a time or two. But had never felt such an instant burst of pleasure. Or actually reached completion simply from a lover moving in and over her.

When it was over, and she was basking in sweet coital bliss, she dreaded going back to reality. So instead, as Asa collapsed against her on the couch, she simply closed her eyes and drifted off.

She was happy. Really happy. For the first time in memory.

COOLNESS AGAINST HIS backside woke Asa. Or the warmth on his front did. Reaching for covers, he found a naked thigh instead. Not his own. And slowly regained consciousness. Realizing, not only that he was with a woman, but which woman.

Lily?

He'd had sex with *her*?

He had to take it back.

Moving slowly, he extricated himself, but thankfully she didn't wake up as he settled her against the couch. Then, still naked, he went into his room, pulled the sheet and blanket off the bed, and used them to cover his...what?

His best friend. Lily was his best friend.

Wife in name only.

Oh God, what in the hell had he done?

Had he blown everything on the first day? Ruined the one marriage he'd felt good about having before it had even been twenty-four hours old?

Wearing only the jeans he'd worn for travel the day before, he paced his room, figuring he needed to jump in the shower. He glanced out to the living room. Saw the form on the couch.

Pictured, though with the covers, couldn't see, her lovely dress balled up around her waist. He'd taken it off her shoulders, and pushed it up over her hips, but hadn't even taken the time to fully undress her. Of course, neither had she, but...

He'd treated her like some kind of animal.

Acted like one.

And didn't want to risk waking her yet.

Not until he had something to say to her that could somehow save the future.

Lily already thought he was a player. He dated a lot of women. But not because he needed the variety for pleasure. He'd needed it to keep women from wanting more from him than he was willing to give. Things like commitment, exclusivity...

He paced. Ignoring the heart-shaped bed. And couldn't believe he'd been so incredibly thoughtless the night before.

Sex, in an exclusive situation, brought in the strong chance for other kinds of emotions to emerge. Which muddied his and Lily's crystal clear waters. And brought with it the high probability of expectation. Disappointment. Rancor.

He'd lose Lily's friendship. The thought brought on a new surge of anxiety.

He wasn't going to lose her.

But...what if the condom failed and she got pregnant?

Sweating, he thought back several hours to the moment he'd taken the thing off. Reassuring himself there'd been no failure in the process.

He had to figure out a way to turn back the clock.

To return them to who they'd been the day before, prowling down the Strip, drinking beers, having a great time together. Probably one of the best days off he'd ever had.

This wasn't about saving the ranch—his marriage certificate was signed, sealed, and ready to present to Widow Hensen. It was about safeguarding his friendship with Lily.

She'd follow through on the deal, either way. He was certain of that. But their six months together could get ugly if their hearts became entangled in one another as life mates not just friends.

A future together wouldn't work. Not well. And as soon as they divorced and he started playing the field again... the last thing he wanted was for her to get hurt. And she would if they continued down this path.

"Asa?"

Hearing Lily's voice call sleepily out to him, he didn't answer. Wasn't ready...

"What's going on?" she asked, wiping her eyes as she came to the doorway of the room he'd been frantically walking, as though, if he did his penance, he could be shown the way out the situation he'd created.

He never should have kissed her. Not at the GreatStore, not for Widow Hensen's benefit, and very most definitely not the night before.

He'd been stupid. Surely that didn't have to ruin his entire life.

And Lily's...

Looking over at her, it hit him. "I'm trying to figure out a way to apologize to you," he told her. "I'm beating myself up over breaking my word to you, coming on to you, taking advantage of the moment. I swear to you I've never done anything like that before in my life. And I just need you to know that it won't happen again. Ever."

Her frown didn't bode well.

"But..."

He had to cut her off before she told him she was having second thoughts. "Our arrangement, our marriage, but more importantly, our friendship—which is the one thing that we promised would last forever—is at stake here, Lily, and I can't lose you." If he sounded as though he was begging, maybe that was because he was.

Begging her to let them both forget.

To let go of what they'd done the night before. And to never ever let it happen again.

Because if it did...they were doomed.

Her nod, a knowing look in her eye, told him she got the message.

He stood frozen, awaiting her response.

Was it over before it had fully begun?

"I can't bear the thought of losing you, either, Asa," she said, and turned away from the door.

He wanted to go after her.

Wanted to know if she'd enjoyed their sex as much as he had.

But stopped himself and mustered the control to gather his things and get into the shower instead.

AFTER THE INITIAL drop of her heart, leaving a heavy weight in her stomach, Lily walked away from Asa's door just as she'd walked away from every foster home she'd had. Losing one home after the other over the eighteen years of her growing up, never being in one more than a year or two, she knew how to get the job done.

And how to survive.

Asa was just…being Asa. He'd been honest from the beginning about what he did and did not need from her. Or *want* from her.

Just as every foster home had been temporary—by sheer definition of foster as opposed to adopt. And, like Asa, none of the families she'd been with had wanted to hurt her. To the contrary, they'd all been good to her. She liked to think that a couple of them had even loved her.

They'd just had circumstances change, had no longer been able to foster for one reason or another. A husband leaving, a woman being transferred and not allowed to take Lily out of state, an unexpected pregnancy, an illness— the list went on and they'd pretty well all been completely understandable. Even to a young girl craving a family of her own.

It was her silly heart that continued to breed the hope that got her into trouble.

And this time, she wasn't losing her home. To the contrary, she was moving into the place she'd always wanted to live. Temporarily.

But the next time she moved, it would be to her very first home of her own. One she could keep forever if she chose. One no one could ever tell her she had to leave.

And most importantly, this time she wasn't losing family. Because Asa would always be that to her. She'd married him legally. Had taken his name. And they were best friends.

He'd promised to be in her life forever.

A promise no one had ever made to her before.

And...that pesky pinprick of hope that just wouldn't leave her in peace, reminded her, as she packed her bag, that a lot could happen in six months' time.

Men had fallen in love, as opposed to just loving like a friend, in less time than that.

She'd dared to reach out for what she'd wanted, accepting Asa's joking proposal, and look how far she'd come in just a week.

The thought kept her buoyed as she left the suite with Asa.

And on the flight home, too.

Her spirits faltered a little as she rode beside him in the truck back to Chatelaine, to the world where everyone knew her as Lily Perry, the freckled foster kid who was a boy's best friend, not his girlfriend. Who'd grown into a woman who, until the night before, had only ever had sex with a couple of men who'd moved to Chatelaine and then, for various reasons, had left again.

"You've gotten quiet."

It wasn't something he'd have called her on in the past. Friends had their boundaries.

"It was a really busy twenty-four hours. I'm having an

energy letdown." She gave him the truth she'd have delivered sitting at The Cellar over a beer. Surface version.

"It seems like there should be some fanfare, you riding back into town as Lily Fortune, married woman." He was grinning.

Looking sexy as hell.

His ring glistened as the sun shone through the windshield, and she looked at the matching white gold band on her own hand.

And it hit her. In that moment, she *was* a married woman.

In every sense of the word.

The realization put a smile on her face, too.

CHAPTER SEVEN

THE SECOND HE pulled onto the long drive leading onto the Chatelaine Dude Ranch, Asa was hit with a need to get busy. First and foremost, visit Major, let the boy know he was back and still the same old Asa.

And to check on the rest of the horses, too, most of which were used by patrons of the ranch. They'd been his responsibility since moving to town. Something he'd offered to do for Val Hensen when she'd agreed to take him on as a permanent border in one of the family cabins that had always only been used as vacation rentals.

Dropping Lily off at the cabin, he purposely left her alone, giving her time to move about the space alone, to get her bearings and handle any phone calls she might want to make in private.

He knew she'd been living alone a long time, and he wanted her to have the time and space to do whatever it was she did at home.

And maybe he was running away for a few hours. Just to find his own bearings. Getting back into his routine would help him put everything—the old and the new—into healthy perspective. Then all he had to do was keep it there.

A quiet ride on Major helped solidify the calm his mind had finally found.

And just as quickly, any sense of peace he'd found flew

the coop as he rounded the lane toward his cabin and saw Val Hensen's golf cart at the front door.

He'd been planning to visit the widow in the morning, with a check in hand.

Pulling the truck into his usual spot beneath the trees at the side of the cabin, he jumped down and tried to look as casual as he could as he hurried inside.

Lily was sitting on the couch with Val, and Asa stopped just inside the door of what had been his bachelor pad until a day ago.

He'd had a lot of different living quarters over the years, but hadn't shared them with anyone since he'd left home at eighteen.

Even before then, he'd had his own room. A place where, when the door was shut, no one was permitted entrance without him there.

Lily glanced at him. "I've just been showing Mrs. Hensen…"

"Val, please," the widow interrupted. "I told you, please call me Val, Lily. We're going to be family now with you and Asa adopting my husband and mine's firstborn, the ranch…"

"I've just been showing Val our wedding photos," Lily said then, turning her phone so he could see the current shot. Of him in his tux, standing in the gondola, holding a hand up to help her down.

Val reached for her purse and pulled out a thick envelope. "I brought the contract for you to sign," she said, her tone changing to all business. "Lily's already shown me the wedding license…"

She unfolded several long pages, joined at the top, and moved to the wooden table that served as both eating spot and desk to him. He joined her there.

Skimming the contract he'd already seen when he'd first

submitted an offer to buy the ranch months before, he took the pen she offered and signed his name.

It took all he had not to let out a huge whoop and holler as he handed the pen back to her. The moment was solemn for the widow. No matter how badly she was in over her head and wanted to be able to travel to stay with her kids for longer periods of time, signing away a lifetime had to be incredibly difficult.

"And now you." He heard Val's words. Saw her hold out the pen in Lily's direction.

What was going on?

Had the two of them...

"Me?" Lily asked, and Asa grew warm with shame. Thinking for one second that Lily would have gone behind his back, made some deal with the widow...but...

"I'm selling to a *family*," Val explained. "Asa knows that. Come on, sweetie, it's your new life, too..." When Lily looked at Asa, not standing to join them, Val said, "Unless you don't really want the ranch. If this is just Asa's choice and you..."

"No!" Lily jumped up. "You of all people know what the Chatelaine Dude Ranch means to me," she said, moving slowly toward the table. She didn't even look at Asa as she took the pen and signed her name, just beneath his. On a line that read *spouse*.

That's when reality hit Asa. The whole of what he'd done. Letting Lily do him a favor. Knowing he'd return the gift in kind. It wasn't anything as simple as that. They'd gotten the law involved when they'd run off to Vegas.

And while he didn't doubt for one second that Lily would sign the ranch over to him when it came time to dissolve the marriage, he no longer felt like whooping and hollering.

At all.

Instead, invisible bands of truth and desperation, of subterfuge and shame, wrapped around him. Trapping him right where he'd sworn he'd never be.

In a relationship from which he couldn't just walk away when unhappiness took root.

SHE COULDN'T STOP SHAKING. Inside, and a little bit outwardly, too. Hugging her arms, Lily sat and listened as Val explained the workings of the ranch, much of which Asa already knew so she didn't go into all that much detail. She turned over a key to the office, talked about bookings that were going to be arriving over the next few weeks— even in February—and said that she'd been packing for weeks and had arranged over the weekend to have movers there the next day.

Lily heard her, took it all in on some level. Mostly she just heard her head repeating the same words over and over. *I'm part owner of the Chatelaine Dude Ranch!*

It meant nothing. She knew that. No way she'd hold that signature over Asa's head when it came time for them to divorce. She valued their relationship, and her own integrity, far more than any piece of land. No matter how precious to her. Or how lucrative.

And, still…

I'm part owner of the Chatelaine Dude Ranch?

For twenty-nine years, her life had been predictably unremarkable. The biggest event had been moving from one home, one bedroom, to another. Having to learn a new address and foster parent phone number.

But in the course of a week, she'd gotten married to the man she'd been besotted with for months, had had hot, passionate sex with him, had quit her job, moved to the land she held most dear… And now owned half of it.

She could be forgiven for having a case of the jitters. And a moment or two of surreal mental aberrations.

Val was thanking them, holding out a hand, which Lily took, and then walking out the door. When that wooden structure closed behind the widow, Lily would be alone with Asa, in the two-bedroom cabin meant to be a vacation rental for families.

A cabin that they both now owned.

There was so much to think about, to learn, reins they would need to take up immediately. The ranch had a handful of employees, people who'd be doing their jobs during the transition, keeping things running smoothly, all folks who'd been working with Asa over the past months.

While Lily, the new owner for a few months, blathered silently about none of it.

"Feel like getting a beer?" Asa's question, the normalcy of it, reached out to her like a lifeline.

The Corral. *Their* place.

"Sure." She grabbed her keys and then dropped them in her purse. She wouldn't need to drive separately.

They'd be leaving from and returning to the same place.

Not at all normal.

Downright weird, really.

Especially when one considered the twelve-pack of his favorite brew she'd seen in the cabin's refrigerator.

HE SEEMED TO be losing Lily. Couldn't figure her out.

The Corral had seemed a logical solution. Not only because they'd met there, but because the majority of their friendship hours had been spent there.

Just running into each other and hanging out.

But as soon as they walked in together Monday, wedding rings on their fingers, the place erupted into clapping, and then, as they sat, they were besieged by a series of visits to their table from well-wishers.

It took an hour for them to finally get some peace.

At which time he said, "You okay?"

"Yeah."

"It doesn't seem that way." *Don't talk about sex. Please don't talk about sex.* He didn't want to hurt her. Or to want her again, either.

Head lowered, she looked up at him. "It's all so strange. I can't find anything that feels like me." She looked around them. "Even this place, tonight."

"Yeah, but look, it's already settling down in here. The rest will, too."

She nodded and sipped the one beer she'd been nursing since they came in. "The signature means nothing," she said then. "I have no intention of taking half of your dream. Or forcing you to change the plan."

"I know." But it felt good to hear her say it. Did that make him scum of the earth? "All that stuff Val was saying tonight, about duties she's expecting you to take over…you don't have to do any of it." She'd said when she'd first accepted his facetious proposal that she'd been planning to ask him if she could help out at the ranch once he owned it. But that was just so she could spend time on the property.

She was frowning. "What else would I do?"

"Take the time to figure out what you want to do for the rest of your life. Take some classes if you want." Granted, opportunities were limited in a town the size of Chatelaine. And she'd told him many times that she had no desire to leave the town, ever.

It had come up when she'd mentioned some guy she'd dated briefly. He'd moved to town as part of a team doing road improvements for the state and had asked her to leave with him, to see if they could make a relationship work.

"I want to work at the ranch." She'd raised her head, signaled for another beer, and was looking him straight in the eye. "Everything Val said…the list of events coming up, bookings, the growing wedding venue side of things, the little café that's open during the summer months—that's a given for me—I want to do it, Asa."

Her eyes had the old light in them. Pre-engagement. Something he most certainly hadn't seen since she'd appeared in his doorway in Vegas that morning.

"Then you shall," he told her, finding himself more relaxed, and strangely more excited, too.

"Okay." She grabbed a small notepad out of her purse, pulled the little attached pen out of the elastic at the side, and started writing as she spoke. "I handle guest relations, planning and arranging events, administrative and staff management duties where it pertains to any of that, and you handle everything ranch related. The petting zoo, farm animals, obviously the horse and horseback riding as you're already doing, tours of the property and wooded trails, maintenance staff, and whatever else you envision. How does that sound?"

Better than he'd thought it might. Good, actually. "Fine," he told her, nodding.

"Then sign here." She passed the small notepad over to him.

He read the brief agreement she'd drawn up, then looked over the list. Added, *and anything else that comes up*, to his part of it, and signed, passing it back to her for countersignature.

There was no touching. Not even a finger brush. Nothing at all that could be considered "more than friends."

Merely two people getting on with the rest of their lives. Just as they'd planned.

THAT NIGHT AFTER they got home, Lily called the bathroom first, and then retreated to her room, closing the door firmly behind her. And on Tuesday, they both hit the ground running so fast there wasn't time to think about marriage and sex—or even to dwell on basic matters of the heart like being head over heels in love with a man who only saw you as a friend.

She and Asa kept in contact over radios, both listening to the channel active for the small staff, and then talking to each other on a private channel Asa had set up for them.

All business.

She was the new face of the Chatelaine Dude Ranch to the public, and to the staff. The learning curve was huge. But she found herself catching on, knowing what to do, without a whole lot of guidance. Val was there on Tuesday, showing her everything. The widow, who'd bought a small place in town, had said she'd be available by phone whenever Lily needed her and offered to come out to the ranch to help out in the office if she was needed.

Lily hoped not to have to make that call.

Gaining confidence by the second—she'd always been an excellent student—she'd mastered the online booking system, the basic filing system, and the banking all before noon.

With a full afternoon ahead of her.

The one personal conversation she had with Asa that day was borne from her new confidence. Bolstered by the fact that she'd dared to reach for more, for her heart's desire, and had found a life she hadn't even imagined for herself.

A temporary one, for sure, but once she'd gotten the

hang of going after what she wanted, rather than settling and finding her happiness with what she had, who knew what lay ahead.

She called Asa on his phone, midafternoon, from the bare kitchen in the main house, not on the radio.

"Lily? Is everything okay?"

"Great," she told him. "Though we're going to need to make a run to Corpus Christi to buy kitchen supplies. And furniture. My pot and pan, and your little toaster oven aren't going to fill even one cupboard of this place. And all the empty rooms..."

"Fine. You can start by ordering whatever you want that'll ship, and we'll set up a time for furniture shopping. I'll open an account for you at the bank as soon as I've finished out here with the cows. I'm hoping to start some basic rodeo activities to offer guests by summer..."

She listened as he talked about adding calf roping and a controlled cattle drive, then went on to talk about skeet shooting, but didn't let herself get distracted from her purpose.

"Asa? I have a request. Not quite a condition, as it's a bit too late for that, but it's important."

"What?"

"Dinner. I want us to eat dinner together at night."

Silence met her on the other end of the line.

She'd been prepared for it.

"First off, it's what families do, what I've missed my whole life. And since this is supposed to be the start of my dream come true, as well, and my request doesn't change the boundaries we set forth, I feel that it's a fair ask. Second, it'll be a set time each day we can discuss ranch business. After just one full morning at it, I can see where we're going to be too busy to see each other much, and we'll need some quiet time to discuss things."

"Request granted." His response didn't lag even a second. And she smiled.

Pictured him smiling too on his end.

She and Asa really were best friends. They knew each other, understood each other.

And if that was the most she ever got from the man, she'd be happier than she'd been before she'd known him.

More content than she'd ever been.

And there came a point when allowing yourself to be happy with what you had was just plain smart.

CHAPTER EIGHT

Asa DIDN'T CARE a whole lot about the furniture he used. He needed it to be there when he needed it. And to comfort tired muscles as necessary.

Realizing that if they didn't get to Corpus Christi—the nearest town with enough shopping choices—and get some furniture in the house, they'd have to spend another night cooped up in what had turned out to be a far too small cabin, he'd taken off at midafternoon on Tuesday, emptied out the back of his truck, and picked up Lily.

He'd even managed to have the forethought to call her first and obtain her consent to the plan.

The hour-long drive to Corpus Christi had been consumed with ranch talk. And they hadn't even covered a quarter of what he wanted to discuss with her. So far, they'd just been getting started with current and pending business. He had ideas he wanted to run by her. A slew of them.

But first, "Seriously Lily, pick what you want. What you think the house needs." They'd found a huge furniture store, divided by types of rooms and were still just in the living room portion. They had both a living and a family room in the house. One had a wall of windows with screens that looked out over the ranch. The other had a fireplace.

"It's your house, Asa. Tell me what you like. Or, if its easier, what you *don't* like."

He didn't like having to choose. And told her so. "I trust

your judgment. Everything you've had me sit on was fine, other than that gray sofa set we both disliked. Besides, it's your house, too, at the moment. And when you move to a place of your own, you're going to need furniture there. It's only fair that you get half of whatever we have together."

The thought had only occurred to him as he said the words, but when he saw the surprise, and then warmth spread over Lily's expression, he knew he'd come through. Not just for her, but for himself, too.

She was helping him build his dream future, and he would do the same for her. Not when their marriage was through, but from day one, just like she was doing for him.

That's what you did when you loved someone.

Even as a friend.

FURNITURE PURCHASED, AT least the start of it—with the two bed frames, headboards, footboards, and mattresses loaded in his truck, and the rest, including a third bedroom set for the guest room, living room set and kitchen table, on schedule for delivery to the ranch on Wednesday—Asa suggested dinner out.

It wasn't a date. Not even close. Just the dinner they'd agree to have together each night to discuss business.

He just hadn't been prepared for the first order of business that came up. She'd taken charge of the meeting from the time they'd been shown their booth in the Mexican restaurant they'd both wanted to try.

"I need to know something," she said, holding his gaze when he'd been about to peruse the menu. He was hungry. She had to be, too.

"What?" he asked, hoping it was about the different types of jalapeños the waitress had described as she'd seated them.

"Would you be willing, assuming that I do a good job,

to keep me on in my duties at the ranch once our marriage agreement ends?"

Not a food question. Or one that he'd been at all prepared to be hit with.

"It's not a deal-breaker, Asa," she said, her tone carrying no disappointment with him. "It's a practical consideration, really," she continued, putting her napkin in her lap. "There are a couple of weddings on the calendar, including your sister's, by the way, but I'm guessing you knew that. In any case, one is for fall. And then there are the bookings, and café menus, which I'd like to change according to season. But if I'm going to jump in and start all of this, but not be there to finish—most particularly with the weddings—I feel as though I should alert customers to that fact. We can just say I'm only working temporarily until we can find someone to handle the management duties..."

One of the things that had first drawn him to Lily was her ability to see through minutia and focus on matters at hand. The first night he'd met her, there'd been a run on wings at the bar and she'd slid off her stool, washed her hands, put on gloves, and cooked up more wings.

All that *after* she'd already put in a twelve-hour day at work and would need to be back for the early shift in the morning.

Then there'd been that night where there was talk in the bar of family trouble with someone everyone knew, serious trouble, and Lily had sat there on her stool, chatting with him, sorting out emotion from fact as though the problem were her own. She'd homed in on what she'd figured was the real problem—jealousy—and she'd turned out to be right, too.

"My personnel problems aren't yours to worry about," he started in, seeing her leap into action to problem solve for him because that was just Lily's way. He was absolutely not going to take advantage of her.

However, he knew the second the words left his mouth, they'd been the wrong ones. "That didn't come out right," he said then.

"No." She didn't let him get anything else out. Opened her menu. "You're absolutely right," she told him in that tone that had always seemed normal to him, but suddenly sounded distant. "I don't think I'm going to try the jalapeño tasting plate…"

With one finger, he pushed her menu down so that he could see her face.

And she could see his.

"Lily… I feel like a real jerk here, getting everything I want while you… I just don't want to take advantage."

There. He'd said it. And then more came. "What I need to know is if you want to work for the ranch…past our agreement. But how could you possibly know that if you haven't done the work yet? What if you hate the job?"

"I guess then it would be like any other. I'd put in my notice. Whether we were still married or not."

She wouldn't. Not while they were married, at least. He knew her well enough to put his life on that one. But six months wasn't all that long to do something you hated.

If it turned out she hated it.

"I wasn't kidding when I said I'd already been planning to ask you if I could work at the ranch before the whole marriage thing came up," she said then. "I was just thinking about maybe helping out at the little café or something…"

"Just because you wanted to be on the property regularly." He reiterated what she'd told him. He'd paid attention.

"Right, but also because I didn't even think about being

able to actually quit my job and do a lot more. I loved every minute of what I was doing today," she told him then, her eyes glowing as they had a time or two in Las Vegas. "My head is spinning with plans, changes I can make to have things run more efficiently, like the seasonal menus at the café, and maybe a cotton candy machine in the summer, and caramel apples in the fall…"

She took a breath and then said, "I'm applying for the job, Asa. Right here. Right now. I'd like to know if it's available and if I'm a likely candidate. Before I invest too much of myself into it."

Wow. He smiled. He couldn't help it. He'd wanted her to bloom, rather than just accept what was in front of her, and she was sprouting petals all over the place.

With flecks of gold, he thought, taking in the freckles that set her apart from any other women he'd ever dated.

"The job is available. And you're hired," he told her. And he could not, absolutely would not, touch her again. He'd rather die than be the cause of her wilting. "With the caveat that if you find that you don't like it, or want to do something else, you let me know. Whether we're still married at the time or not."

She smiled. "Deal," she told him, and gave her attention back to her menu.

Leaving Asa to wonder how on earth he'd turned out to be such a lucky guy.

LILY HADN'T KNOWN it was possible for her to be so happy. Other people were the blessed ones. Not her.

She'd have figured they'd be tired, arriving back at the ranch after nine o'clock Tuesday night. Had expected they'd spend one more night in the cabin, and unload their beds in the morning. But Asa cracked open a couple of bottles of beer, handed one to her, and told her to pick her bedroom.

She chose the one at the back of the upstairs hallway, right next to the bathroom, and with a view of the ranch. Leaving the master, with it's bath included, for him.

It made the most sense, since he was the one who'd be living there long-term.

It didn't take him long to get her bed set up. When she'd said she was going to take the four-wheeler back to the cabin to gather sheets and a bag of things for the night— towels, toiletries, clothes for the morning, pajamas—he'd opted to go with her, to get his own.

The entire way there, and part of the way back, he'd talked to her about plans for the ranch. Wondering what she thought of adding rodeo-like activities for guests, and maybe allow local kids who had an interest in rodeo to come out to work in the same corral, for real, when guests weren't using it.

She'd told him she'd call their insurance company in the morning, to see what kind of coverage the activities would need, and work up a cost estimate for him.

It was all businesslike.

And yet…invigorating, too. Two weeks ago, she'd never in a million years have pictured her and Asa riding in a four-wheeler across the Chatelaine Dude Ranch together, ever. Let alone at night.

"You want to take a detour and drive by the rest of the guest cabins?" he asked her. The housing units were all in the same general area on the ranch, six arranged in a semi-circle around an outdoor swimming pool and playground equipment and four others, Asa's being one of them, set off alone for more privacy.

"Of course." She sipped from the beer he'd opened for her, not caring that it was getting a little warm, and felt the cool, sixtyish degrees night air against cheeks suddenly warmer as his arm brushed hers.

Who cared about making beds or getting some sleep? She felt alive, really alive, and didn't want to miss a second of the joy by sleeping it away.

The thought was fanciful, she knew it even as it came to her.

And she thought of her sisters, figuring they'd be proud of her, as she sat there thinking about putting her hand on Asa's thigh.

He'd said no more sex.

But he'd wanted her. She might not have had a bevy of lovers as he had, or had much experience at all, but she'd felt his urgency even before he'd entered her.

And had taken that ride right along with him, too, ecstasy and all.

She'd talked to both Haley and Tabitha when she'd returned from Vegas the day before, and again that morning, too. Keeping them updated on what was going on. She hadn't told them she'd slept with Asa, though.

That was private.

During the course of their conversation, she'd invited them to come out and take a walk around the ranch with her. To come out anytime they liked, in fact.

While the ranch was her home, she wanted them to consider it theirs, too. To share the place with them, as the three of them had shared it with their parents on their last day on earth.

She'd like to think her parents were happy for her.

"Esme called today," she said then, naming his younger sister, who was also her friend. "Since she wants to have her wedding here, at the ranch, I told her to come over tomorrow and we'd get started on the planning..." She was rambling. Filled with so many emotions that had no business spilling all over him. "But...before I actually speak to her, I need to know a couple of things."

"Name them." If only she could be a little more like him, taking everything on the chin instead of in the heart.

"First, I need to know what you told your sisters. About us."

"Same thing everyone else knows. We're married."

"And they believed that? Knowing you? And me? They really think we're in love and married for real?"

His shrug didn't give her much. Except more desire to be as calm as he was.

He glanced at her as he said, "You're the only woman I hang out with on a regular basis, and have ever since moving to town. It made perfect sense to them."

Which meant she was going to have to play the loving new wife to her new husband's sister—her friend. And... it was what she'd signed on for. But it didn't mean it would be easy.

"You said a couple of things." Asa nudged her with his elbow. "What's the second?"

"Everyone's asking me...are we going to have some kind of reception? People want to party with us. Personally, I'd much rather not, but I know Esme's going to press me about it tomorrow and..." She glanced at him. "I think if we want everyone to buy into us together—and most particularly Val Hensen—then we need to do something..."

"So let's have a party. And if you're willing to take them on, I'll leave the details up to you."

As if life was just that simple. But she agreed. Because to not do so would bring on a conversation she wasn't prepared to have.

Asa had slowed their pace as they approached occupied cabins and he talked about updates he'd like to make to them. Painting. Some new cabinets and fixtures. He mentioned that he'd been hoping to put an indoor pool in, as well, but with the higher price he'd paid for the ranch, figured that might have to wait a year or two.

And she smiled, then, thinking that, as of that night, she could count on still being on the ranch then.

As long as she didn't put her hand on Asa's thigh.

He was accommodating all of her needs and wants, and she had to give him the same. He'd made it clear that he didn't want a real marriage.

She couldn't push that.

Another sobering thought struck her then. What if his excitement on their wedding night, his desire, had been a product of Vegas, of alcohol, of him imagining he was making love with any of the sexy women they'd seen on the strip that day. What if...

She stopped the thought.

Wouldn't disgrace herself, or the memory of those moments with Asa in their honeymoon suite by entertaining what-ifs.

And yet, a small voice reminded her, she wasn't Asa's type. He'd been honest with her about not wanting sex with her.

"What's wrong?" He'd stopped the four-wheeler in front of a currently vacant cabin with occupied ones on either side of it.

"Nothing, why?"

"You just tensed up," he said.

"It was just a chill."

His brown gaze was compelling as it focused on her beneath the security lights shining around the pool in the distance. "You sure?"

She met his gaze. Held it. Valuing his friendship and all that they were doing together far more than mere sex. "Yep," she told him and took another sip of beer.

The look in his eye, the raised brow, the shake of his head, all left her knowing that he wasn't convinced. But he didn't call her on her lapse, either.

When you were just friends, there were some things you didn't share. Besides sex.

"Just friends" had boundaries that didn't allow some of the heart-wrenching honesties shared by husbands and wives.

And, finishing her brew, she said, "You ready to head back? We need to get those beds made and get some rest. We both have long days of work ahead of us tomorrow."

He gave her one last long look, and she hoped, for a second there, that he'd refuse to head back just yet. That he'd push her for more.

Instead, he nodded, put the four-wheeler into gear, and shot them at top speed back into the life they'd agreed to share.

CHAPTER NINE

FOR A SECOND, Lily thought about doing her hair, dabbing on a little bit of the makeup the salon had sold her in Las Vegas, for Esme's visit the next morning.

She was supposed to look different, right? The glowing bride?

In the end, she pulled on jeans and a long-sleeved button-down white shirt, slipped into her only pair of cowboy boots—purchased for a country dance at some point—and ran a brush through her hair. Leaving it hanging long.

Because, yay, she no longer had to pull it back, or pin it in a bun, for work at the café.

And made a mental note to do some online shopping for a few more shirts. Her entire adult life, she'd spent more hours in her uniform than anything else, and her closet contents didn't support even a week's worth of different outfits for ranch work.

Esme had been new to town just before the holidays, showing up nine months pregnant with her baby boy to be with family after a hard marriage that ended when her husband died. Poor woman had then found out that her three-month-old baby had been switched at birth and wasn't hers after all. Good news was, she'd ended up with two baby boys, instead of one, and a loving man as a bonus. Lily had heard the saga every step of the way as it was happening, in stereo. Asa's version as he retold parts of it to her at the Corral. And Esme's version, too, as the younger woman and Lily had hit it off the first time Esme had stopped at the café, a bit harried, as her newborn had decided to wake and let her know he was unhappy right when she'd been in the middle of shopping. Lily had let her use the break room to feed her little guy in peace.

The fact that Asa and Esme had turned out to be brother and sister had been like an omen to Lily. What it had been predicting, she didn't know, but she'd been glad to be friends with both of them. They were orphaned, too, though as adults, and in Lily's world, that had kind of given them a special bond.

One that mattered to her a great deal.

Which made her nervous when she heard the ranch's reception door open a little before ten on Wednesday. Her office, in the back across the hall from the coin-operated laundry room available to guests, was blocked from view of reception and the check-in counter, but she could see via security camera who'd come in.

And went out to greet her friend.

She was surprised by the big hug Esme gave her, but returned it in kind.

And then realized that the affection was based on them being new sisters. Only, she knew they'd only be such for a few short months.

The pang that accompanied her as she led Esme back to her office seemed to be growing inside her, in spite of the joys that were also abundant in her new life.

She didn't lie to her friends.

And, other than her sisters, she was duping the entire town that had been her only family since she was ten months old.

"Where are the boys?" she immediately asked, as she noticed her friend without either of the four-month-olds she was raising.

"Ryder has them. Just until I get back," Esme said, her creamy skin creased into a smile that lit the room. The lovely brunette had most definitely lost the shadows that had clouded her green eyes the first few months Lily had known her.

But as she smiled at her friend, she felt a prick of envy, too.

Which was absolutely *not* her. Jealousy served no good purpose and opened the door for bitterness to grow.

Something a foster mother had told her along the way. She couldn't remember which one. She'd been pretty young. The words had been offered lovingly, not in a mean way. And they'd stuck.

Esme deserved every single good thing that had come to her.

And maybe Lily reaching for more wasn't such a good thing after all. There she was, with more than she'd ever dreamed of having in her lifetime, and she wanted more? Wanted Asa to love her like Ryder loved Esme?

Wanted to have babies with him?

Shaking the thoughts right out of her head, she sat down with Esme, conscious of her VP fiancée's family merger and acquisition business responsibilities, and her friend's need to get back to her babies.

She pulled out a snapshot book of previous weddings held at the ranch, intending to show them to Esme, but her friend shook her head. "Uh-uh. Not yet. First, tell me when and where you and Asa are having your wedding reception? Because you have to have one, Lily. If anyone deserves to have the whole town showering her with gifts, it's you."

Asa had left it all up to her. Kind of a deflating thought. Who wanted a party for two that only one cared about?

"Well…"

"Good," Esme said, with a nod. "Bea was going to call you, but I told her I'd talk to you about the party when I saw you today. I already called Haley and Tabitha, and they are on board with the idea...so if it's okay with you, we'd love to throw you and Asa a wedding reception. We were thinking at the LC Club."

The same place Asa had wanted to take her and her sisters the night they'd gotten engaged.

And she still didn't want her first visit to the place to be a fake celebration. He'd left all the details of a celebration up to her. Clearly hadn't had interest enough even to make suggestions.

"I really appreciate this...but would it bother you all too much if it was held at the Corral?"

She saw the surprise cross Esme's face. And continued, pushing forward when, in any days past, she would have simply nodded and gone along with what was being offered. "It's where Asa and I met. Where...we...fell in love. And maybe more people could come, you know..."

Because not everyone had a lot of money. Some of her friends from the café, for instance. And Nickolas, with his wife and family...they did fine, but no way she'd want them to fork out money for a babysitter, plus gas out to the LC Club, and then...even the drinks there were twice the cost of the Corral. She'd looked online once.

"No, that's great!" Esme said, all grins as she sat forward. "I love it! And my brother will probably thank the heck out of you..."

They talked about dates. Esme wanted to wait a couple of weeks, because if they did it too soon, more people would be booked up, and then, when Lily started to make a suggestion or two, perhaps catering in some food from the café being one of them, Esme shook her head. "No way, girl. This one's being done *for* you. Not *by* you."

Not used to being the center of attention, Lily nodded.

She wanted to tell Esme to let everyone know not to bring gifts. But had a feeling that even if she did so, she'd be ignored on that one.

And if her marriage to Asa was real? Would she still say no gifts?

She wouldn't.

But who wanted a bunch of reminders of a broken heart? Which was what she was likely going to be left with when the union ended.

Turning the wedding book around and shoving it across the desk right in front of Esme, she turned the talk to a real wedding. One conceived in love.

Asa, ON THE FOUR-WHEELER, was heading back from the horse barn, when he saw his sister's vehicle parked outside the reception area. He was about to head up and say hello to her when he heard voices hollering.

"Jimmy! Jimmy!!" The first voice was male. The second female, and ending on a scream.

Making a sharp turn, he headed down the road toward the cabins and met up with the distraught couple on the way. Stopping, he got the gist in a couple of seconds.

Their four-year-old son was missing. They'd been walking the family path in the woods with him and their three-year-old. The little one had fallen and both parents had turned to him. When they turned back, Jimmy was gone.

The younger boy, Willie, was riding on his father's hip, and still sniffling.

On his radio immediately, Asa alerted all staff that a four-year-old blond boy named Jimmy was missing and for everyone who could to report to the family trail immediately.

He heard from Lily before he'd even signed off. On

his cell. She was on her way down. Esme was helping to search up nearer the office in case he'd headed up for some candy or something.

Telling Lily to arrange the search party of the woods, Asa left the parents and took off on the four-wheeler. He'd seen the little guy the day before, by the fishing pond not far from the cabin area. If he'd wondered off...

The pond wasn't all that big. An acre, maybe. Man-made and fed, too. But for a young child...

If the boy had only been missing a few minutes, even if he'd fallen in, there was still time to save him if he didn't waste a second. None of the three families on-site that week had signed up to fish that day. Chances of anyone being at the pond to help the kid were nil.

He took the four-wheeler as far as he could. About thirty seconds up the road, and then took off on foot. The boy, even running, wouldn't have been at the pond long. He would only have had five minutes on Asa at most.

Ripping through trees, his boots clomping through brush, Asa broke into the clearing near the pond and nearly wept.

Jimmy was sitting on the ground, a kitten in his lap.

Out of air, Asa slowed his step, calmed his breath, so as not to scare the boy, and walked slowly toward him.

"What have you got there, buddy?" he asked, while he was still far enough away for Jimmy not to feel immediately cornered. The boy was right on the edge of the water. Asa didn't want to scare him into falling in.

"A baby cat," the boy said, looking over at him, his voice still more baby-like than Asa would have expected. "You're the man with the horses." The r's were rounded.

Asa smiled. "That's right." He pulled out his radio. Quietly announced his location and that he had Jimmy in sight as he approached the boy.

Jimmy seemed more interested in the kitten shoving its head into the boy's palm than the man coming toward him. "There's a cat at the horse barn," the boy said, rubbing a hand on the kitten's head.

Kneeling down close to the boy, Asa murmured, "There's more than one of them." Wild cats that hung around. The Hensen's had allowed them to breed to help keep mice and other rodents under control.

Asa and Lily hadn't yet gotten anywhere near as far as discussing the presence of the cats. Or what to do with them.

"Maybe this is one of her babies. I had to rescue him so he didn't get too lost…"

"Maybe it is. If you come with me, to my cart, we can get you back to your Mom and Dad, and then I'll take the kitten to the barn," Asa offered.

"Okay, but only if you promise to take care of him," the boy said. Standing, and with the kitten hanging over his arm, he lifted his other hand toward Asa, as though expecting them to hold hands for the way back.

Taking that little hand in his own, Asa felt a clutch at his heart. Picturing his four-month-old nephews…thinking of them at Jimmy's age. Or Willy's. Running all over the ranch…

And for the first time, thought about, maybe someday, having a son of his own. He didn't see how that would happen, didn't want to muck up another life as his parents had mucked up him and his sisters.

But in a perfect world…it might be cool to have a little guy around all the time. To help him grow into a man.

The thought wasn't even complete before Lily showed up on the four-wheeler he'd given her to use as her own, Jimmy's parents and little brother aboard.

And where Jimmy might have received a scolding—

after the frantic hugs from both of his parents—Lily intervened. Jimmy had told his parents why he'd run off, and both of them had started in on him about how dangerous that had been and not minding his rules. Lily interrupted, suggesting that they all drive the kitten to the horse barn together, returning it to his parents, just like Asa had returned Jimmy to his. Pointing out that as scared as Jimmy was for that little kitten, wanting to get it home, his own parents had been even more scared about him.

Speechless, Asa sat there, staring at her.

Had the woman just taught the boy a lesson he wasn't likely to forget? Without a single harsh word?

Asa had no way of knowing, of course, as they all drove off to the horse barn, leaving him alone at the pond. He even told himself he was overreaching.

That the whole marriage thing, finally owning his ranch, was kicking him a bit off-kilter. He'd be more himself in another day or two. Once he settled into the routine that had driven his entire adult life.

Then, returning to the matter at hand, he got on the radio to thank everyone for their quick responses and rode off to the cow pasture.

Where the manure he got himself into washed right off.

SINCE WORD OF Jimmy's having been found had been sent over the radio to those searching up by the store, Lily had expected Esme to be gone by the time she was heading back to her office. They'd already outlined the basics of the wedding before the 911 radio alert had come through. She should have known Asa's sister—the new mother of two baby boys—wouldn't leave until she heard all the details.

She picked up Esme in the four-wheeler when she spotted her friend walking along the road she'd sped down half and hour before. Immediately, Lily relayed the news of Jimmy not having so much as a scratch on him.

"What a relief!" Esme exclaimed. "I stayed on the road the whole time. I figured, if anyone came this way with him, I'd see them," the young mother told her as she climbed in.

Lily shuddered at the chilling possibility that had been clearly weighing on Esme's mind. That Jimmy had been kidnapped by someone who'd looked decent enough to get onto the property, but who was rotten on the inside.

Reminding Lily of the other woman's not so distant rough past. With a man who'd promised to love and cherish her, but who'd broken her heart instead.

Lily wanted to hug Esme. And had an aha moment, too. An hour ago, she'd been envious of her friend. But when she looked at her own life…she'd only ever been treated with decency.

And that was something for which to be deeply thankful.

For which to feel lucky, even.

She filled Esme in on the kitten details. And then said, "Another good ending, just like with your boys. Them being switched at birth was just accidental, not some sinister plot."

"Absolutely," Esme said, then added, "I still wonder about that mysterious volunteer who was there that night, but knowing that the nursing assistant realized she put the wrong bracelets on the babies…it's always good to have faith in humanity reaffirmed."

"Always," Lily concurred with a nod. "Asa's the one who found Jimmy, by the way."

"I'm not surprised," his sister said, smiling.

Pushing the gas pedal, Lily turned and headed back toward the office as Esme confided, "You have no idea how thankful I am that you hung in there with him."

Hung in there? Frowning, Lily shook her head. "I don't get it."

"Asa's a master at blowing off the women in his life. He does it kindly, of course. From the very beginning. Letting them know that he's not boyfriend material, or open to any kind of ties or exclusivity, as I'm sure you know. He'd have done it with you, too. But you didn't let him push you away."

They'd reached the office. Lily needed to escape inside. To put her mind to the hundreds of tasks awaiting her. The myriad of things to learn.

Not sit and be reminded of unrequited love.

Or dwell on having to lie to the woman with whom she'd developed a real bond within a short period of time. A woman she'd love to call sister for real.

Another random foster mother quote came to mind. Something about tangled webs you weave when you deceive.

"He...didn't push me away," she said slowly. Thankful that she could speak the truth, in this matter at least. "But I never acted like I expected anything from him, either," she added. "Because I didn't." All factual.

Which felt better than any alternatives she'd come up with. Like saying out loud that what made her different from all the rest was that Asa had fallen in love with her. She just couldn't give voice to the lie.

"Maybe that's what did it," Esme said then, her tone growing even softer. "Women have always been all over him."

"I noticed." Lily's dry comment just slipped out. Accompanied by an eye roll.

Esme patted her hand, still on the steering wheel—as

though she could drive away from the entire conversation. "Like you have anything to worry about," she said then. "You're the only one who's ever snagged him."

She found that a little hard to believe. In his adult life, yeah, but when he was younger... "Even in high school?" she asked, and then felt like she'd been unfaithful to Asa by doing so. Going behind his back for information on his life was so not her way of doing things.

"Especially in high school," Esme said. "He had his eye firmly on the door, not on finding any reason to hang around." Esme's sigh carried a lot of lived-life in it for one so young. "I don't know how much he's told you about our growing up, but it wasn't pretty. Or kind. Our parents fought. A lot. They had affairs on each other. I found books. Fairy tales, and later love stories. Feel-goods. When there was fighting in the house, I'd take my books and escape into the woods with them."

"That must have been very difficult for you as a child," Lily said quietly.

"Yeah, it was, but the upside is that even though I grew up with unloving parents, I still believed in love. Couldn't wait to grow up and fall in love and have a family. Which—" she shrugged "—maybe made me a little too eager to find it the first time." Esme shook her head and then continued. "Asa, on the other hand, stayed there, like he had to make sure no one got hurt or something. To make it worse, our aunt and uncle were the same way, unfaithful to each other. Always fighting. And it left him, I feared, unable to believe that romantic love even exists. Until you."

Tearing up, the younger woman touched Lily's hand again, squeezing it. "I'm just so thankful he has you." She sniffed. And then straightened. "And now, before I make a total fool of myself… I'm off to rescue my fiancée from our sons…"

With a smile, she was gone.

And Lily, who had so very many things to do, sat in the drivers' seat, going nowhere at all.

CHAPTER TEN

ASA WORKED LIKE a madman the rest of that week. Taking care of the horses, as he'd already been doing, getting a corral ready, with bleachers just outside it to accommodate the new family rodeo activities he wanted up and running by summer. He worked with the two young men Val had hired full-time to help with the running of the ranch, promoting them both, which basically meant giving them more responsibilities, putting one in charge of updating the petting zoo, new paint, fixing boards in stalls and fences, and the other in charge of the new corral. Even though Val had already hired a local man to come in and mow once a week, Asa knew they needed more regular help, so he went ahead and hired a recent high school graduate, a young man who'd grown up in foster care, to work at the ranch full-time as their landscaper.

He also called a pool guy to refinish the pool and to fix the heating system.

In the meantime, Asa put himself in charge of setting up horse riding lessons for the local kids who didn't live on ranches, and put both of his cowboys on schedule to teach them.

And he spent time on Major, re-riding every inch of the ranch, taking notes and pictures. And just taking time to let it all in. To believe he'd actually made it.

What he didn't do was leave time to run into Lily. They were in touch on their private radio channel all day long.

And he kept his word to her—met her at the house for dinner every night. Sometimes fixed by him, if she was still in the office, other times, prepared by her and he'd come in when it was ready. They discussed ranch business while they ate. And then he made it a point to keep himself busy outside the home until he saw her bedroom light come on upstairs.

It wasn't right. Wouldn't last long-term. He knew that. But for that first week, it got him through.

He missed breakfast with his sisters on Saturday. They tried to get together every week, but he couldn't get himself to make it happen, using his newly acquired ranch as an excuse. There was just no way he was ready to sit alone with them, or with Lily, and have them picking at his marriage.

They'd do it lovingly of course. But he wasn't ready to have them looking too closely.

Not after he'd gone and had sex with his best friend.

He'd been finding himself noticing her at odd times throughout the week. Seeing her on the four-wheeler, leading a new family to the cabins on Friday, for instance.

Not one damned thing sexy about that.

But his mind had gone straight to Lily's gorgeous body moving temptingly beneath his on that couch in Las Vegas.

He just needed time. Distance from the wedding day.

So much was happening so fast. Monumental life changes. As it turned out, realizing his dream after twelve years of backbreaking work was a lot to process.

So it made total sense that he'd feel some backlash.

Lily had detailed some of his sister's wedding plans for him over their nightly dinners. Discussing the somewhat luxurious lodge that the Hensen's had used for all kinds of events, from barn dances to wakes to weddings. Lily wanted to repurpose a barn that had once housed the Hensen's small, personal beef cattle operation into the event center, take out a part of the back wall of the lodge, making it floor-to-ceiling windows overlooking the woods filled with hiking trails, and adding an outdoor gazebo with cleared ground for seating for the actual weddings to take place when weather permitted. She was hoping to have some of the work completed in time for Esme's wedding the following month.

He'd seen his sister's vehicle on the property a couple of times. Had smiled each time. Couldn't be happier for her.

And felt a major prick in his sense of well-being when she texted him on Saturday, asking him to meet her and Lily at the lodge—a rustic, though quite nice place, complete with ballroom area for holding events.

The fact that she'd sent the request, not Lily, made him uneasy.

His business partner had conceded the task for a reason. He didn't like not knowing what it was.

As if Lily and Esme were in cahoots. Concocting something he might not otherwise go for.

And, perhaps, he was letting his conscience get the better of him—pretending to be in love, and married for life—and needed to just suck it up and quit overreacting to everyday things.

It was just… Esme, with her soft heart and quiet intelligence, tended to see through him more than most. Which could prove to be a major problem for obvious reasons.

"If the gazebo isn't ready, we could do the ceremony here," Lily was saying as he walked in through a back, service door. "With the right lighting, maybe strings of little white lights, it'll make the place look more magical. I can set this area off with white lattice room dividers, white wooden chairs for the guests, and the aisle would come from there." She pointed to a hallway leading to the restrooms and a back area currently being used for storage. "I'll have that room cleared out, carpeted, with changing areas, couches, mirrors…make it into a bridal suite…and then the reception can be in the ballroom area."

Her words broke off as she and Esme noticed him.

He was smiling. Couldn't help it. Lily was the best.

Whether she was serving coffee or planning dream weddings, she gave everything to the moment.

"Don't let me interrupt," he told them.

Esme grabbed his arm, pulling him toward the potential wedding area. "You aren't interrupting," she responded, dropping his arm. "Ryder and I want a simple, traditional wedding," she said then. "We're each picking out a couple of our favorite passages from books to read as part of the ceremony. Lily and Bea are my bridesmaids…"

He looked at his friend at that one. She hadn't mentioned that she'd been asked to be in his sister's wedding. She'd need money for the dress and…

They hadn't had a single personal conversation in days. He hadn't even asked how she was doing.

"…and Ryder's brother Brandon and Linc Mahoney are the groomsmen."

He'd been left out. Disappointing, but best that he not be paired with Lily, walking her down the aisle.

"The two couples will each be walking a stroller down the aisle with the boys in them," Esme was continuing. Painting a picture for him. One that made him happy for her. "That part was Lily's idea, because I wanted them included somehow…"

Asa looked over at the woman he'd married the week before. Wondering if it was hard for her, planning a real wedding when hers had been…not that. Knowing she'd never let it show.

He wanted to tell her that she'd get her chance. As soon

as they were divorced and she embarked on her new life, in a real home of her own, she'd meet someone, fall in love…

The idea didn't make him feel all that much better. More conscience backwash, he was sure.

Her attention all on Esme, Lily didn't even glance his way.

"And then the next part is where you come in," Esme was saying, yanking Asa's gaze straight to her. His sister grabbed his hand and pulled him a step closer. "I'm hoping you'll walk me down the aisle, Asa. That you'll give me away."

Him? In a tux again so soon? Walking down a wedding aisle? Esme deserved someone who believed in that stuff.

But… "Of course I will," he told her. And as she teared up, he didn't nudge her as he would have done any other time. Or lighten the moment with teasing. Instead, his chest tightened and he pulled his little sister into his arms. Silently promising her that he'd give her away, but not completely. Not ever completely. He'd be having her back until the day he died.

It wasn't until he'd pulled back that he realized Lily had walked away.

She was inspecting the back storage area. Giving him and Esme their private family moment. As a friend would do.

Funny, how it bothered him so much, her always ending up alone like that.

If anyone deserved to be included in close family moments, it was Lily.

Not him.

ESME HAD BEEN gone about an hour on Saturday, when Asa stopped by the office.

"This place looks great," he said, looking around from

just inside the door. It was the first time he'd been to her new space since their first day of ownership.

Lily had rearranged furniture so she had a picturesque view of the property from her desk. She had also thrown out two grocery bags of things that were of no use to her and Asa, and had been through the entire filing system. Fortunately, Val Hensen had kept great records, and had them in easy to follow order.

"It's getting there," she told him with a happy sigh. "Now that I know I'm going to be working here long term, I'm thinking I'd like to paint the walls—they're so smudged and dirty—but that can wait a good while." Business. It was all they talked anymore.

"You want to go get some beers?"

He wanted to go to the Corral? Had he read her mind? Did he know how badly she missed his friendship? "Now?"

His shrug was off, not easy and casual like before. "Maybe after dinner."

"Okay." She glanced over at him, still bothered by the somber look on his face. "Or we could go now and have wings for dinner."

It was the Corral. It *wouldn't* be a date.

And dinnertime was for business talk, so if that was what he needed, if he had something to discuss with her that he wasn't sure she'd like, best do it at the Corral.

Where her feelings would be under wraps, as though held by the people in town who, collectively, were her family. In the house she was currently sharing with Asa, she felt too raw.

Made no sense, but there it was.

He offered to drive. She accepted. No way she could see him riding around in her little beater. And it would be too weird for them to drive separately. In the past it had made sense. They'd been coming from and returning to two separate places.

So much change, so many nuances, she hadn't considered.

She led the way into the bar, waving at people as she went, heading for the only open table, in a back corner of the front room. She and Asa usually sat at the bar. But for some reason, she didn't want to eat up there that night.

He didn't say anything about her change in seating location. Just dropped into the chair across from her and pulled the wing menu out of the metal holder at the end of the table. He suggested a combo platter. She agreed, and, rather than waiting for table service, he went up to the bar to place their order. Came back carrying two beers.

She took hers. Sipped. Telling herself to relax, as she faced another first.

The first time she was nervous sitting at the Corral with Asa. They'd promised to be friends forever, but it was beginning to seem like, after only one week of marriage, they were hardly friends at all.

His gaze almost accusing he asked, "Why didn't you tell me that Esme asked you to be in her wedding?"

Whatever she'd expected to come her way, that was *not* it. She frowned, not at all sure where he was going with the question. "Because she didn't want anyone to know she'd chosen her bridal party until she asked you to walk her down the aisle."

"Why not?"

"I have no idea." She told him the truth. "I didn't ask." Then added, "But I can take a guess if you want me to."

A muscle ticked in his jaw. "Please."

"She didn't want to make the announcement without you in it."

His features relaxed for a second. But not long. And she

waited. They might not be acting as friends, or in any way normal around each other, but she'd known him, adored him, for a lot of months, and could still at least read his expressions with some accuracy.

"You haven't spent any of the money I deposited into an account for you."

Again, not anything she'd expected him to be bothering about. Him going crazy having her living in the same house as him...*that* wouldn't surprise her. But this threw her for a loop.

"I haven't needed to," she told him. "I've been working full-time since I graduated high school, and it's just me. I've got a little bit of money put away."

"And?" he asked when she stopped talking, keeping the rest to herself. Maybe she wasn't the only one who could read faces.

"And I don't like it that you can see the account, see what money goes out and where." There. She'd said it. "If we were really married and had a joint account, then I'd be fine with it, but it makes me feel like I'm your charity case, or kept woman or something, you having ownership on my bank account. Or even depositing into it like that. I'd rather just get paid from the ranch like everyone else."

He watched her. She could see his features softening, almost like he was morphing back into the man she knew right before her eyes. "Or, for the time we're married, we could have a joint account, with all profits from the ranch that aren't going back into the business, deposited into it, and we both spend from it personally as needed."

Her heart leaped. He wanted a joint bank account? You didn't do that if you were only into something for a few months.

"And when we split, we'll divide whatever money is in the account equally. Then the ranch can start to pay you."

Or maybe you *did* do it even if you were only in it for a few months.

Remembering her sister telling her to hold on to hope that the marriage could become real, Lily nodded. And felt like she'd been thrust over rapids and come out intact on the other side. She nodded as Asa told her he'd take care of it on Monday, as though they'd been discussing... fat veins in beef. Something he'd have talked to her about in the olden days.

So hard to believe that had only been a week and a half ago.

Putting his beer down after a long sip, he said, "This is all really strange, huh?"

"Yeah. Kinda." Completely, one hundred percent.

He signaled for another beer. Took a long sip after it arrived, and said thickly, "I feel like I'm losing you."

Her heart leaped up and started to thud. Hard. "You aren't going to lose me," she assured him, able to pour herself fully into that response. "If you haven't figured it out by now, I value your friendship more than just about any other."

Or, maybe more than any other, period. Her gaze dropped to her beer. From the night she'd met Asa, something in her had settled. As though she'd met her soulmate.

Which was why she was in the predicament she was in—tangled up in truth and pretense. Because Asa had needed her, so she'd needed to be there for him.

His finger touched the back of her hand, briefly. Enough to get her to look up at him.

"You know that I consider you my best friend, right?" he asked.

She'd thought so. *Hoped* so. Then nodded, more tentatively than she'd have liked.

"The sex is the problem," he blurted then. Softly. But

it hit her like a megaphone to her ear. "It's like there…between us…holding us apart."

Was he saying he wanted more of it? That wanting it was what was in between them?

"We can't go back and undo it," he continued.

"Do you want to?"

"Hell, yes." His head dip emphasized the words even more critically. To the point that her mouth dropped open in horror.

Apparently her expression was so filled with shock, she didn't even notice until Asa said, "Oh, hell, Lil, that didn't come out right." Reaching over, he took her hand. "I'm not saying it wasn't great. Because it was. But that's the crux of the problem, right? If it hadn't been good, we'd both have shrugged it off, and it wouldn't still be here mucking things up between us."

She'd never, in a million years, have considered their lovemaking to be something negative, but with what Esme had told her the other day about Asa, about them growing up, and him living his whole life ensuring that he was never ensnared as his parents had been, she understood what he was saying.

Enough to lose some of the anguish his *Oh hell* had immediately stirred within her.

"It's not mucking things up for me," she told him then. Thinking of him. And of herself, too. "We're healthy adults, Asa. We'd had a bit to drink. Things happen sometimes. Like…sometimes, when there's white cake around with buttercream frosting…sometimes I just eat too much of it. It's there, tempting, and I'm free to help myself to it, right? So sometimes I do. That's all."

Not quite. By a long shot. But, sort of.

"White cake, huh?" he asked, a slow grin spreading across his face.

She shrugged. "Only with buttercream icing. None of that whipped crap for me." She grinned back. Just as she'd have done any other time they'd been sharing beers together.

He nodded. "White cake," he said again.

"This is what I missed this week," she told him then. Something inside of her pushing to be heard. "This right here. You and me."

His face sobering, he nodded again. Looking her in the eye. "Me, too."

And she wasn't quite done. She could roll with most punches. Could take all the change happening overnight. She just didn't want lose him. She'd bear it if she did. She'd find her happiness wherever she ended up. A lifetime of doing so told her that.

But she couldn't just sit back and take it this time. She had to fight for him. "It seems to me that people quit being friends when they quit sharing...whatever it is they share," she told him. "This..." She pointed between the two of them, their beers, their conversation. "This is what we share."

"And right there is why you're my best friend," he told her, grabbing her hand again, giving it a squeeze. Sending her insides into a major quiver.

Giving her hope.

And then letting go.

CHAPTER ELEVEN

SATURDAY'S CONVERSATION WITH Lily at the Corral stayed with Asa as he dived into ranch business the following day. They'd stayed for hours, drinking and then sobering before he drove home. Discussing ranch business a lot of the time, but only because they were both so invigorated by the task they'd taken on together.

Their chitchat the night before was what prompted him to stop by the office for her when a call came in about a water leak in the cabin they'd just rented the day before. A young professional couple looking for a few days away from work was staying here. "Since you're the one who checked them in, I thought maybe you'd want to do your thing with them, make sure there's nothing else that's not to their liking, while I fix the sink."

"You thought maybe I'd entertain them while you fix the sink," Lily said, grinning as she followed him out to his four-wheeler. "You're definitely a guy who likes to be left alone when he's on a project." She stuck out her tongue as she finished.

And his groin grew instantly.

At the sight of that teasing, moist, tongue.

What the hell...

However, his immediate problem disappeared as quickly as it had arisen when he pulled up to the cabin to the sound of tense voices coming from an opened window.

Lily glanced at him. "Maybe there's more than just a water leak? You sure that's all they said was wrong?"

The couple had called the ranch's maintenance number, which rang to a cell phone Asa was carrying until he could hire a full-time maintenance man. Mr. Hensen had handled a good bit of the ranch's fix-it problems himself during his lifetime, but after he died Val had called a guy in town anytime she'd had a problem.

"That's all they said," he told her, grabbing the plumbing bag he'd put together when he'd sorted through tools earlier in the week.

Tense sounds came again, male that time. He couldn't make out the words.

"Maybe we should come back," Lily said, but he shook his head.

"I told them I was on my way."

She didn't have to accompany him. He was still glad she did, though, as he climbed the couple of steps to the cabin's front door.

He'd barely ducked under the kitchen sink before he quickly diagnosed the problem—a crack in the trap—and went to shut off the water, pulling a new trap piece out of his bag as he returned to the kitchen. Grabbed his little can of purple PVC pipe glue, too. And the pliers he'd need to unscrew the old trap and apply the new.

Then heard Angela Larson, one of the cabin's two guests, say, "I think maybe we're going to check out early." Clearly addressing Lily.

He stopped forward motion just as he was about to slide back under the sink. Stood up. And saw Brad Larson, standing in the middle of the living area, hands in his pants, looking at his wife as though she'd sprouted some kind of body part he didn't recognize.

Looking as bewildered as Asa had felt the night before.

"Because of the leak?" he asked inanely, when he had no business doing anything but fixing a leak and letting Lily refund part of the couple's payment to the Chatelaine Dude Ranch.

"No," Angela said, looking at her husband, before turning her gaze to the two of them. "Because once we got here, we figured out that there was nothing we wanted to do."

"I want to fish," Brad said, as though needing to point out the lie in his wife's statement.

"I want to horseback ride," Angela shot back.

Lily shook her head, frowning. "We offer both of those activities here."

"Yeah, but the whole point of this trip was to do things *together*." Angela again. She looked from Lily, to Asa, who'd started to sweat a bit, then toward her husband, and finally back to Lily. All the while Asa's head was ordering him to vacate, telling him he should have listened to Lily and retreated, rather than putting himself in the vicinity of a marital battle.

He'd had enough of that growing up. Always thinking he needed to stick around so none of the people he loved— including the parents who didn't seem to love each other— got hurt. Or did something irreparably stupid.

"We've…kind of…grown apart," Angela admitted then, addressing Lily specifically. "I'm a lawyer, he's in finance. We both love our jobs. And…"

"You hardly talk to each other anymore?" Lily asked, glancing at Asa, who stood there, watching her.

And then heard himself say, "My wife can tell you, I learned, not too long ago, that the way to find your way back to each other after a…separation…is to talk to each other. Not as husbands and wives, but as the friends you were before you got married."

He was speaking to Angela. Sort of. Mostly, his gaze kept straying back to Lily.

Realizing in that moment that their conversation the night before had been far more momentous than he'd realized. He and Lily would make it through their temporary marriage, intact, as long as they continued to be friends throughout the process.

He could do that.

And, of course, he'd have to stay off the white cake for the duration. No matter how tempting the buttercream icing might be in the moment.

"Do you like to hike?" Lily asked then.

"Yeah." Both of their guests said at once.

"So maybe you quit trying so hard and head out to one of the trails. We've got all skill levels. Getting back to nature, away from the world, exercising, working off tension, doing something you both love…might be good for you," she said.

That was his Lily. Always able to get to the meat of the point and toss out the minutia that smothered so many chances of reaching an understanding.

"And talk," Asa blurted, feeling like, as the host, he should be a part of the solution, too. "Just talk like you used to. Even if it's about work."

He'd had a great time the night before, better than he had all week, discussing business with Lily. Once they'd figured out how to be "them" again.

"I'm guessing there's still good feeling between you both, or you wouldn't be here," Lily's soft words hit Asa strongly.

Good feeling.

Yeah. That's what he felt when he hung out with Lily.

Angela glanced at Brad, who was looking right back at her. "There's definitely still some of that," he said tenderly.

At which point Asa dived for the sink. Sliding himself into the cupboard and attacking the plastic. He didn't need to witness any of the mushy husband-and-wife-making-up stuff.

He and Lily definitely wouldn't be needing that.

LILY SPENT THE rest of the day Sunday buzzing inside with replays of her and Asa that morning with the Larsons. She and Asa…marriage counseling? It was ludicrous. And it fit, too. Asa wouldn't live in a rancorous marriage. He'd fix it, or kindly end it, taking the brunt of all burden in doing so upon himself. He wasn't a guy who hung around in unhealthy situations.

Asa just didn't seem to see that about himself.

The Larsons had walked up to reception together, later, to thank Lily, asking her to pass their thanks onto Asa, too, for caring enough to share a little bit of marriage advice with the two of them.

Apparently it was all they'd needed, a middleman to help them see through the job tensions and distractions to find their way back to each other.

They'd scheduled horseback riding for the following day. And had rented fishing poles, too. Two of them.

Asa came in to make dinner with her that night—a first, them in the kitchen together—and she told him about the visit from Angela and Brad.

"I guess we got it right, because being best friends kind of is at the core of having a successful marriage," she said, brushing against him as she reached for the colander hanging from a decorative holder she'd put on the wall—her breast touching his chin for a second—while she was talking. He stopped peeling the cucumber he'd had in hand. Just stood there at the sink, saying nothing.

Minutes later, as she'd poured hot pasta into the colander resting in the opposite side of the sink, she caught him looking at her breasts.

And tingled all over.

He looked away.

She did as well.

And they both tried to pretend it hadn't happened.

Over dinner, they talked ranch business, as always, and the moment with the colander seemed as though it hadn't been.

Which put Lily into another quandary. Had his reaction just been an involuntary male reaction to his skin against a breast? Because a ladies' man had locked himself into six months of celibacy? Or...just because he was a guy who couldn't help it that he liked breasts?

Or had it been an *Asa* to *Lily* thing?

She liked broad shoulders. But Asa's shoulders were the only ones she'd ever been so wildly turned on by in the throes of passion, as they were moving above her, that they drove her over the edge. And, even now, drinking in his big, strong presence made her ache to go to bed with him all over again...

She swallowed hard. But she doubted he felt the same way about her. She was very much aware that, with her freckles, her stick-straight hair, and her lack of sex appeal...she'd never been anywhere near the smoking hot category that Asa fell into.

Still, when he asked her if she wanted to sit out on the porch and have a beer before turning in, she couldn't help remembering that electric moment between them at the sink.

Wondering if...just maybe...it had had something to do with his invitation.

She sat on the porch swing. Asa took a big wooden chair

bowed at the back as if made to fit a human spine. They talked about Esme's wedding some.

Asa mentioned that Jimmy and his parents and little brother had stopped by the barn that day, before they left, to visit with the kitten. He'd ended up giving it to them.

"You what?" she asked, stopping the swing to stare at him. "That's really cool, Asa! And you're only just now telling me?"

He shrugged. "It's just a kitten."

"Maybe. Or perhaps, to that family, it'll be just a kitten like Major is just a horse."

His glance up at her was probing. Like he was looking for more than was there. Reminding her of their wedding night.

And she got hot. Inside. And so very wet.

Couldn't stop staring at his mouth. Remembering...

Until she almost fell off the swing. And stood instead. Her nearly empty beer bottle in hand, she made to move past him. "I...um...think I'll turn in," she stammered. "We've got two check-ins in the morning, and I want to double-check the cabins to make sure they're ready, plus I've got another three weddings on the books—all from out of towners—and have to get working on the lodge if I hope to have a decent bridal suite in time..."

She was rambling.

Trying not to look at his mouth again.

And ended up with her gaze on his crotch instead. Outlined in those sexy, tight jeans.

Completely visible by the light through the living room window in front of which he sat.

Of course, she tripped. Because of the bulge. The sight of it had taken every ounce of her focus. Then, to her dismay, the toe of her slipper, caught the inside of his boot,

right at the arch, and she would have fallen, if he hadn't
caught her.

In one arm, due to the beer bottle in his other hand.

Laughing, embarrassed and jittery, she quickly righted
herself.

Or tried to.

Asa's hand that had steadied her, caught hers. Yanking
her down to his lap, and before she could figure it all out,
his lips were on hers.

Devouring her.

Then his hands found her breasts and she arched against
him.

Opening her legs, she straddled him in the big chair.
Riding his very obvious desire through their two pairs of
jeans, and still getting herself off.

Right before she exploded, Asa stood, holding her in
place against him with one arm, as her legs wrapped tightly
around him.

He made it inside the front door. To the couch. Kissed
her again as his fingers worked her fly. He stripped down
her jeans, undid his own fly, and was inside her, riding
her as she bucked, until they both came to full pleasure
at the same time.

Euphoria had never been so all-encompassing. So intense.

Or so fleeting.

Lily knew, the second she came down, that while Asa
had most definitely found physical pleasure, he was not
sharing her joy.

He'd stiffened almost immediately. Pulled slowly out
of her. And then had jumped up off the couch as though
he'd been burned.

Closing his fly and fastening his belt, leaving his shirt

hanging over it, he was still breathing a little heavy as he said, "I'm sorry."

She'd been a little slower at gathering herself. Was only just getting her jeans up over her hips when she heard the words.

And had no idea what to do with them. Was he apologizing to her? Or just sorry in general that he'd done what he'd done. Did it matter?

"Me, too," she told him. Because at that moment, after what they'd shared, to hear him say he was sorry about it...she wished it hadn't happened, either.

How did a woman feel good about her future, her chances at happiness, when the man she loved with her whole heart regretted making love to her?

"Look, I don't know why this is happening, but it can't mean anything, Lil. And we can't keep doing it."

The distress in his tone was so clear, so painful, she knew that for both their sakes, she just had to accept the truth.

Not fight it.

"I know," she said, heading across the room toward the stairs. She stopped with one foot on the bottom step. "But just so *you* know, Asa, I enjoyed it."

CHAPTER TWELVE

I ENJOYED IT.

What in the hell was the woman trying to do to him? With one hand she'd fully accepted that sex would not be a part of their lives. Had never once tried to convince him otherwise. Yet with the other hand, she tempts him?

To be fair, she hadn't done a thing to bring on sex that night. She'd tripped over his big, booted foot.

He'd done the rest.

With her cooperation, yes, but no surprise there. He knew how to please women. He'd had a lot of experience.

And she hadn't.

No way the woman was teasing him.

To the contrary, she'd been nothing but the friend she'd been since the first night they'd met. Sincere. Loyal. Accommodating. Asking for...so little.

Too little.

Which was why it had felt great to give her so much. A way out of the dead-end life she'd been living. Fulfilling her heart's desire with a home of her own. A permanent job at the ranch for as long as she wanted it.

He was the one who was blowing it.

She hadn't changed. Not even in the clothes she wore. With decent money at her disposal she hadn't splurged on designer clothes. Wasn't wearing makeup or having her hair and nails done.

So why was he suddenly so attracted to her?

Because the question just brought sexy visions of Lily to mind—visions he absolutely could not entertain—Asa pushed the wondering away and did what he always did when faced with a problem. He moved through it, over it, or around it.

Except…without knowing why…how did he define the problem? Sex was the result. But what was the problem?

And then it hit him.

On their wedding night, when they'd had sex, the look on Lily's face, the abundance of happiness in her gaze… he'd felt like a million bucks, being the guy that gave that to her.

So…maybe it wasn't about the sex. It was about making Lily happy. Maybe it was *that* look he was craving.

Satisfied that his deductions had a great chance of being accurate, Asa hooked his horse trailer up to his truck, left the ranch before dawn Monday morning, and headed out of town to a ranch he'd once worked for. They were nationally renowned for breeding some of the best quarter horses in the States. A family business, they'd been breeding horses known for their temperament and longevity for more than twenty years.

He'd thought about calling first, to make certain that he'd find what he was after, but decided just to show up. And pour on the charm and even resort to past relations, if he had to, to make sure that he left with a gorgeous young mare.

One that had been earmarked to keep for breeding.

"I'm not going to breed her," he told Mark, one of the brother owners, and the man who'd offered Asa the top management position to get him to stay on. "I'll sign paperwork saying so. I'm not trying to compete with you. I just want the best of the best for…my wife."

Why the words came out Asa had no idea. He hadn't

been planning to spread word of his marriage any further than Chatelaine. Partially because then he'd pretty quickly have to spread news of the divorce, too.

But Mark had to know how vitally important this gift was to him. Why the quality mattered.

"No way, man! You're *married*?" Mark glanced at Asa's left hand. Saw the ring there, grabbed his hand and shook it. And then kept shaking his head all the way to the barn. "I can't believe it! Asa Fortune has gotten himself hitched! There must be broken hearts all the way across Texas..."

Asa took the ribbing in stride. He'd earned it.

And would be back to earning it again at some point.

He also paid for, loaded up, and took home his first-choice pick. A two-year-old dam—old for breeder weaning, but the average age at which the bond between foal and mother naturally ended.

A gorgeous, shiny brownish red, the girl was a beauty. He couldn't wait to get her back to the ranch. Played with various scenarios as the miles passed behind him. He'd pull up to the office, have Lily come out to the trailer. Let her lead her girl down into her new life.

Or...maybe he'd get the dam set in her stall in the barn—the one right next to Major—and decorate a little. Make it more like a wrapped present. And let her and the girl bond there in privacy.

He thought about saddling her up, asking Lily to go riding with him, and when he and Major and Lily and the girl were out on the ranch, telling her that the dam was hers.

He'd texted to let her know he'd be gone for the morning, had even told her he was visiting the ranch he'd worked on prior to moving to Chatelaine. To see the owner.

Because they were business partners and he'd be leaving her alone on the ranch.

Because he hadn't wanted her to need him and not be able to find him.

Because he wouldn't be on the ranch radio if any problems arose.

Like a missing kid.

The thought reminded Asa of the little guy reaching for his hand that day at the pond. And him having an out-of-body moment where he'd thought he might want a kid of his own someday.

What had *that* been about?

His mental question went unanswered as another flash occurred to him. The previous night. On the couch.

He hadn't used a condom.

He'd hit the call button on his steering wheel before the period planted on the end of that sentence. Told the automated system who to call.

"Asa? Are you back?" Lily sounded as though she'd been involved in something when she picked up the phone. Like she wasn't giving him her full attention.

"No, not yet."

"Is everything okay?" she asked worriedly. "You sound—"

"We didn't use a condom," he blurted. There were things she could do. Take a morning-after pill. He'd had a woman tell him about it once when she'd asked him not to use a rubber because she didn't think it felt as good.

He'd opted out of sex that night, instead.

"I'm protected, Asa. I take contraception for…female regulation."

Something he most definitely should have known about his wife. Even in name only. He tried to hold himself in check, to remain completely calm and serious as the relief flooding through him made him slightly giddy.

"Was there anything else?" Lily's voice came over the phone.

And a vision of her—pregnant—came to mind. Not a horrible sight.

She'd be radiant.

Wearing a Mona Lisa smile.

She'd be the best mother ever, too.

He just wasn't going to be the father.

"No," he told her.

And hung up.

LILY WASN'T AT the ranch when Asa returned. His phone call, the obvious horror that had prompted the call, had driven her to the phone. Asking her sisters to meet her at Harv's BBQ for lunch. They'd ordered and eaten—Lily picking at her food more than eating it—before Haley asked, "Are you going to tell us about it or not?"

At which point Lily shrugged. The whole triplet thing, knowing each other so well—she'd have thought there'd be none of that with the three of them. Other than their womb time, and the first ten months of their lives, they hadn't known each other until adulthood. She'd lived almost twice the number of years without them as she had with them.

And still, as Haley and Tabitha remained silent, just sitting there watching her, she admitted, "Asa and I slept together."

Both woman hissed in excited breaths.

"No, no," Lily told them. "He says it can't happen again. That it'll ruin our friendship."

She didn't tell them what Esme had told her about their growing up. About her fear that her brother would never let himself fall into romantic love or marry for real. But it had been on her mind a good part of the night as she'd lain awake in bed.

"The thing is," she said slowly, "I don't know how I'm going to survive when the marriage ends. I'm afraid my heart is going to be too crushed…"

"That's the most drama I've ever heard out of you," Haley said. The words might have been off, in the moment, if they hadn't been offered softly. With obvious compassion.

"You'll survive as you always have, Lil," Tabitha said then, with equal caring evident in her tone. "You're the strongest one of us. You're like a rock compared to me…"

"You survived the loss of the love of your life, while pregnant, giving birth to twins, and now are raising them all alone," she told her sister. "I'd hardly think living alone in an apartment and working at a café as giving me any real strength."

"How many foster homes were you in?"

"Eight." What did that have to do with anything?

"Eight times you entered a residence, looking for home. For family. Eight times you were forced out again. And here you are, loving with your whole heart. That's strength." Tabitha's eyes were steady and unwavering as she said the words.

"He clearly cares a great deal about you, Lil," Haley said then. "Maybe it won't progress any further than friendship for him. But maybe it will. Do you want to cut off the possibility before you have the chance to find out?"

She didn't. Of course she didn't. And she thought of something else, too. Haley finding her and Tabitha. She'd had no idea what she'd find. What kind of reception she might receive. Her sister had been facing possible rejection, anger, indifference. And still, when she'd turned eighteen and had found out that she had triplet sisters, she'd gone full force to find Lily and Tabitha. And then to write to them, asking them to meet.

Because that's what love did. It put itself out there, made itself available.

It didn't run and hide for fear of being hurt.

And neither did she. Just as Tabitha had said. She stayed in a home for as long as it would have her, hoping that she was becoming family.

The thought was firmly on Lily's mind as she pulled onto the ranch half an hour later on that Monday. She'd thought about refusing to have sex with Asa if the chance ever came up again. About stopping it if it started.

And knew she wasn't going to do that, either.

If love was going to have any chance to grow, she had to let it live freely.

And if it ended up killing parts of her spirit, irreparably damaging her heart, she'd find a way to live with that, too.

All of which didn't stop fear from striking her as she parked in the house's garage, climbed into her four-wheeler and headed toward the office. What if Asa really did start to resent her? Like he feared would happen. To the point that he didn't want her to work on the ranch?

And what if a tornado hit them and wiped them all out? The thought sprang to mind.

Along with a well of sadness for what wasn't.

For her of all people, who'd never had a home like her sisters both had, to be the first of them to get married—and have it be fake...sometimes fate was a little cruel.

She texted Asa to let him know she was back and was just heading inside, when she got a text back asking her to come down to the petting zoo.

They'd talked about getting in a couple more animals. A llama, for one. With all of the families already booked for the summer, they were going to be bringing in enough money to hire a full-time caretaker for the zoo animals as well.

And once word got around about the rodeo activities, the dedicated wedding lodge, and other improvements and updates, they'd likely end up booking out completely months in advance. Asa knew his stuff. He had already put out feelers with his contacts who would send people his way.

And that was without the Fortune family in town spreading the word. Which was already happening.

They would need more staff. But for now, he must have had some day visitors descend on the petting zoo, for him to need her help.

Expecting to see several cars in the visitors' lot as she passed, Lily was surprised to see only two, belonging to the guys who'd come in early to go fishing. Kids were in school. Maybe a school bus had descended that she hadn't known about?

Things were relatively quiet, as a Monday in March would be.

Peaceful. Though she was looking forward to the craziness of summer in a way she never had before. To spend all day, every day with families vacationing on the ranch... she couldn't wait.

Pulling up to the petting zoo, Lily frowned. No one was there. The animals weren't even out. Just one of the horses.

Why did Asa need her help? Was one of the animals sick? Or more than one? They were all stalled separately, lambs with lambs, ponies with ponies, rabbits and ducks and...

She jumped off the four-wheeler and went inside the barn that housed the animals. And stopped when she saw Asa standing at the gate leading into the outdoor "zoo" area. Facing the barn door. As though he'd been waiting for her. Major stood beside him.

Oh, God. Please don't let anything be wrong with his

horse. Major was Asa's immediate family. The one creature who had his whole heart.

"What's up?" she asked him, approaching slowly.

He didn't say anything for a long minute. "Asa?" She was almost up to him.

"Come on," he told her, grabbing her hand and pulling her toward the opened gate. Major walked just behind them, right on his owner's heels.

The horse was more doglike in the way it served Asa. Followed him. Stuck by him.

Asa let her go as they stepped outside. The area had fresh straw on the ground, looking newly cleaned and ready for visitors. Only the one horse was there.

"What do you think?"

"About what?"

"Her." He nodded toward the horse.

That was it? He'd bought a new horse? She walked over to the obviously young mare. "I don't know all the much about horses, Asa," she told him. Lily knew how to ride—she'd been fostered on a small ranch when she was thirteen—but that was about the extent of her knowledge. "She looks gorgeous."

Going up to the horse, wanting to be of use to Asa if he was asking her opinion on something, she ran her palm along the mare's neck, not even sure of the breed.

She loved the softness. The warmth. And when the horse turned, putting her nose to Lily's neck, she held the mare's head to her. "She's lovely," she said then. "How old?"

"Two."

They'd have at least twenty years with her then...

"What's her name?"

Asa came up to stand beside her. "She doesn't have one yet."

So he was thinking about buying...

"She's yours, Lil. She's purebred quarter, from the best lineage in the state. I bought her this morning..."

Lily heard him. Noticed Major nosing the freshly laid straw a few feet away from them. As though he was keeping watch from afar.

She shook her head. "I don't get it."

"Family, Lil." Asa's soft words dropped into her world like little stars. "I've got Major. You've got her. She's all yours. For as long as she lives..."

Tears sprang to her eyes. She couldn't help it. Fighting hard to blink them away before he saw them, she pressed her cheek to the side of the young horse's head.

That he'd get the horse for her...and give it to her where she'd last been with her parents...

It meant the world to her.

"I love her," she said, hiding her face against the horse's shoulder, petting her. Not wanting to let her go. "Thank you." So much more wanted to tumble out. She gave it all to the horse instead. In long steady, warm caresses.

Asa was there, in the background, watching. "You want to take her out? She's saddle broken. Major can show her around the property..."

Hell yes, she wanted to.

She wanted to throw her arms around her husband, too. To hold on tight and tell him how very much she loved him.

Instead, she hugged the horse and said, "I'm going to name her Laura. After my mom." And didn't even care that her throat caught with emotion as she said the words.

Asa, in his own way, had just given her another part of her heart's desire.

Immediate family to call her own.

Family that wouldn't stay behind if she had to move on, but that would go with her, as Major always went with Asa.

Family that would be there when she needed her. That would need her, too.

Family that would be with her for however long their forevers lasted.

Asa knew.

He understood.

And he'd given her Laura.

Because the horse could give Lily what Asa could not.

He might not be able to be the husband she wanted, but he was the best friend a woman could ever hope to have.

CHAPTER THIRTEEN

ASA WAS STILL giving himself a thumbs-up for buying Lily the horse later that week, still feeling the high that had come over him as he saw how much the gift had meant to her.

Other than sex, he'd never seen her let go of the band of steel she kept around her emotions—until Laura.

It was a high he figured he didn't have to lose. Even after the divorce, he could still find little ways to give to her, to keep that smile on her face. Lord knew it wasn't a hard thing to do.

She'd had so little given to her growing up, the woman was grateful for a new toothbrush.

He'd found that out when he'd run into town for some things, had picked up a new toothbrush for himself, and had given her the second one that had come in the pack.

You'd have thought, by the smile on her face, the way she'd looked at him, that he'd bought her another diamond.

Maybe, if they were still married by her birthday, he'd buy her a pair of those, too. Diamond earrings to match her ring.

They'd added another meetup to their daily routine. Before dinner each night, they took Major and Laura out. Sometimes the ride was only fifteen minutes or so, but they did it together, looking out for their property he'd told her the first night he'd suggested it. And giving the horses some exercise.

Not that Major needed any extra. Asa was on the horse as much during the day as he could be. Riding Major in lieu of taking the four-wheeler, more and more often.

They'd taken to dropping Lily off at the house, to fix dinner, while he and Major led Laura back to the barn. By the time Asa had cooled and bedded down the horses, dinner was ready.

As he stood on the porch Thursday night before bed, sipping the rest of the beer he'd had as he'd gone over the books Lily had brought home for him to inspect, enjoying the stars in the vast night sky, Asa could hardly believe he'd reached such a perfect place in his life.

And when he heard the door open, and the small thump of Lily's boots stepping outside, he figured he'd finally found his own true Narnia.

A ranch of his own. A best friend who shared his business acumen and a love for the place. And a town with both of his sisters living in it. He and Major had finally hit gold.

"I'm firming up the guest list for Esme and Ryder's wedding next month," Lily said, "and I haven't heard back from your cousin, Bear. I sent his invitation to the address Esme gave me, somewhere across state from here. I'm figuring, maybe he doesn't know who I am. Have you heard anything from him?"

Asa shook his head. "I knew Bear as a kid, of course, but I haven't seen much of him since we grew up. I'm not even sure what he really does for a living."

"Esme didn't know, either. She just told me to check with you, in case you knew more."

He shrugged, thinking back to some of the few fun days he and his cousins had spent together as kids. Times when their parents hadn't been fighting with their spouses. Or off having affairs. "It's possible he wouldn't RSVP and still show up," Asa said then. "Keep a place for him, just in case. It'd be cool if he was there..."

More family back together.

Without the fighting.

Asa had never thought, before the previous year, that they'd all be living in the same town and growing closer by the week.

Bear would probably be as shocked, and maybe as pleased, as Asa was.

Finally finding a place where he wanted to stay.

A place to call home.

Lily leaned against the porch railing next to him. Reached for his beer bottle and took a sip.

Something she'd done before, at the bar, when she didn't want another one, but wasn't quite done partaking.

It had been his suggestion that she share his, the first time she'd expressed the predicament, a month or so after they'd met.

Tonight, seeing her full lips covering the nose of his bottle, he was instantly hard.

Something that had never happened in the bar. Not even close.

"What?" With her lips hanging open for the edge of the bottle, Lily stopped midsip to look at him.

Asa stiffened. He must have been staring at her. "Nothing," he told her.

Taking another sip and then handing him back the bottle, she said, "Tell me you'd rather not talk about it, or to mind my own business, but don't lie to me, Asa. Please."

She didn't look away.

On the contrary, she was standing right up to him. Not letting him off the hook.

Something else new.

And because he respected her—because he wanted to

keep her friendship and receive the same courtesy in re-turn—he said, "It really was nothing. Just when your lips touched the bottle…it reminded me…"

He let his words end there. No point in filling the moment with any more erotic imagery.

She licked her lips.

A natural response to having them talked about.

And it took every bit of strength in the whole of Asa's body not to lean over and kiss them. Instinctively, he knew she wouldn't stop him. It was in her body language. The way she was still there in the moment with him, holding her ground…

"I'm going into town," he said, overwhelmed by the tension, the wrongness of wanting something that would ultimately hurt them both.

And leaving his beer bottle sitting on the rail, he turned and strode through the house, out the side door, and didn't slow down until he was strapped into the driver's seat of his truck.

He didn't look back. Just drove. Needing lights. Even if it was just streetlights and those emanating from the Corral's front window.

He needed distraction.

Time to cool down. To breathe.

He could do this. Would be fine. They were just learning how to do it all—run the ranch while living together as friends who were pretending to be married. There were bound to be some stumbles along the way. They'd figure it all out.

He'd intended to just drive it off, but by the time he reached town, a full-blown fog had fallen. Asa pulled into the park.

What in the hell was the matter with him? He'd been hanging out with Lily for eight months or more, with no problem. Why was he suddenly having a problem keeping his hands, his lips, the rest of him to himself?

Was it the proximity?

Because, he had to face it, at the Corral, there hadn't been a chance in hell of kissing Lily without an audience, so it had never been an issue.

Was that really it? That he was really such a player that he had to have any woman he was alone with? Ones that he liked, of course, and who liked him back.

Ones who wanted it.

Yeah that must be it, he reassured himself. It was just a sexual thing...

His thoughts suddenly broke off as he was distracted by someone in a hoodie. From the slight build and average height...he couldn't tell if it was a man or a woman... or someone he knew...but he watched as the person went up to the community bulletin board. Attached a note to it.

He got out. Figured shooting the breeze with someone else, even a total stranger, would be better than sitting alone in his truck making an inconvenience into a way bigger problem than it needed to be. But before he'd taken his first step, the person had hurried away. Asa couldn't even tell in which direction because of the fog.

Still thankful for the distraction, and curious, he went over to the bulletin board anyway. The whole situation struck him as a bit weird. After all, who came out late on a foggy night to leave a note on a community bulletin board?

He didn't get his answer. But when he saw the note, he needed to know who'd left it more than ever.

The note wasn't signed.

And it wasn't just any note.

51 died in the mine. Where are the records? What became of Gwenyth Wells?

What the hell?

He didn't know the gritty details, but he knew enough. His grandfather had been involved in that mining disaster that had happened long before Asa was born. And not in a good way. From what he'd heard, his grandfather, Edgar, had been at least partially to blame. And had run off...

Which was why Asa had only just been introduced to Chatelaine, where his Fortune ancestors had lived.

Grabbing his phone, he took a photo of the note and sent it in a group text to his great-uncle Wendell, his grandfather's older brother, and to Freya Fortune, the widow of his great-uncle Elias, asking if either of them knew who Gwenyth Wells was.

Freya had been the one who'd written letters, bringing Edgar and Elias's grandchildren, Asa and his cousins, to town the previous summer to receive their portion of the inheritance their great-uncle had left them.

It was late. Wendell and Freya were probably long in bed.

But they'd see the text first thing in the morning and be aware of what he'd found before anyone in town started talking...

As he was putting his phone away, Asa saw the open text message as he'd left it, except that there were little dots scrolling, as though someone was typing. Figuring it was Freya, who he knew sometimes had trouble sleeping, he stood there waiting for her response. Would she want him to remove the note?

Would that be ethical?

The dots were gone. And a new text binged.

Not from Freya.

It was from Wendell.

Yes, Gwenyth Wells was the widow of the foreman who died in the '65 mine disaster and got the blame for the collapse from Elias and Edgar. Her family was ruined. I don't know much beyond that.

Asa was heading back to his truck when his text binged again.

Freya had finally sent a response.

Oh, how awful, no wonder her name was familiar. Elias must have mentioned it over the years in sorrow.

Shaking his head at his family history, Asa climbed back in his truck and headed home.

Elias and Edgar Fortune had left a dead man's widow thinking her husband had caused the collapse, when they'd known full well it had been their own fault.

Somehow, feeling desire for a woman he couldn't have didn't seem like such a horrible cross to bear.

And unlike his uncles, he'd do the right thing.

One way or another, he'd figure out a way to quit wanting to have sex with his temporary wife.

Because, also unlike his uncles, he had no intention of losing friendships or leaving town.

LILY WAS DEVASTATED. Full-out falling apart inside. Pacing the dark, from kitchen to front porch, she wore an imaginary path in the wood floors Val Hensen had had redone before she'd put the place up for sale.

Asa had gone to town. Why? To be with another woman?

No, he wouldn't do that to her.

Or to himself. He wouldn't be *that* guy.

But he'd do just about anything to not have sex with Lily. And they almost had...again. After only making love with Asa a couple of times, she already recognized that look in his eye when he was losing himself to desire for her.

It was a heady look.

One she'd never seen before on a man's face. At least not directed at her.

If she'd turned away, Asa would still be there with her.

She should have turned away.

Easy to see from the outside looking in, but when they'd been standing out there...she'd been captivated by the powerful want between them, too.

No way she could have walked away.

So he had.

He'd told her where he was going.

To town.

Close to midnight on a Thursday night. She knew full well what there was and wasn't to do in town.

Meet up with someone.

Or go to the Corral.

There were no other choices.

Except, maybe, going to another town. Where he could take care of his needs without anyone in Chatelaine, anyone who knew Lily, finding out about it.

Stop it.

At the door out to the front porch, Lily paused. Staring out.

Could see writing on the wall almost as though it had been printed in big letters across the night sky. Her nights with Asa, being married to him, would be repeats of the current one. Him leaving at night, even to go into the Corral just to drink.

Something he used to do with her. Their precious time together.

Now his time to get away from her.

Turning, she started her trail back across the room

again. She had to buck up. To lift her chin and look for the good. In just a couple of weeks' time, her entire life had changed. Giving her more than she'd ever thought she'd have. Making dreams come true that, in her previous twenty-nine years, she hadn't even come close to achieving.

At the kitchen sink, she glanced out, could see lights in the distance. She knew one of them was the security light at the barn where Laura was probably sound asleep.

Stomping her foot, as though she could crush that night's pain beneath it, Lily headed toward the stairs. When had she ever wasted time walking around feeling sorry for herself?

She needed to go to bed. Get some rest. She had a busy weekend, and an equally hectic week ahead. More check-ins, and a lot of renovating to oversee to get the ranch as ready as it could be for a full summer. And the following Saturday, just eight days away, was her and Asa's wedding party. In the back room at the Corral.

They'd agreed one night over dinner, the day that they'd both had texts from their sisters telling them to save the date, that they had a ton worth celebrating. The ranch. A home—albeit hers would be changing, it was still out there someplace, waiting for her to find it. But no matter where she ended up living, the two of them would be working here together long into the future. A forever friendship. Even Laura's advent into their lives was a true blessing. So, while others celebrated the legalities of a marriage certificate and rings on Lily's and Asa's fingers, the two of them would be toasting to having found the futures they'd dreamed of having.

In her bathroom, Lily scrubbed her face. Hard.

Getting rid of the grit that had tried to take over her mind downstairs.

Just standing in that bathroom, in a real home, she had so much more than she'd ever had. And she wanted Asa in her life, as best friends—forever.

It was all well and good to reach for dreams.

But not to the point of killing a different version of a dream that had actually become reality.

CHAPTER FOURTEEN

ASA AWOKE ON Friday feeling as though he'd managed to walk across fire and not get burned. He'd faced temptation with Lily and had gotten them both out of the situation before flames had consumed them.

And he knew that having done so once, he could do it again. As many times as necessary. He'd found the wherewithal to beat the demon that had been threatening their lifelong friendship. For however long desire continued to tempt him, he'd just get in his truck and drive. He had his escape hatch.

With the success giving buoyancy to his step and lifting his mood, he sought Lily out in the office midmorning. There were no more check-ins due until late that afternoon. And no checkouts. Everything else could wait.

"You feel like getting lunch in town?" he asked her. And then, so as to ward off any hint of a return of the demon, quickly added, "I have to make a stop and would like you to go with me. We could order takeout, make the stop, pick up lunch, and eat it on the way home."

Home. His and, for the next several months, hers.

The thought brought no threat. No feelings of danger. Just...satisfaction.

"Of course," Lily said, standing. "Where's the stop?"

"My great-uncle Wendell's." It felt right, taking her with him. Not for show—though formally introducing Lily to the Fortune patriarch would further solidify their marriage in the eyes of anyone who could possibly have doubts—but because something truly weird was going on. Something worthy of mention to someone he trusted most.

And Lily was his someone.

His best friend.

She'd stopped at the edge of her desk and was looking at him. Frowning. "Why would we be stopping there?"

Only then did it occur to him that Lily wasn't just his best friend. She was also the woman who'd grown up in foster care and, until recently, had lived in a tiny old apartment, and had worked serving food to others in a café.

"You're going to love Fortune's Castle," he told her then, grabbing her purse, handing it to her and heading toward the door. She wasn't a foster that no one kept for long anymore.

Hadn't been for a long time.

She'd become a woman who would do anything for anyone. Who put others first and always found the good in any situation. Who brought a smile with her into pretty much every moment of her life.

And for the time being, she was his wife. As far as he was concerned, that meant she would always be a Fortune.

And before they divorced, he would see to it that she never, ever felt like she had to hesitate again before walking in anywhere.

LILY LISTENED AS Asa told her what he'd seen in the park the night before. She picked up on his escalated energy, his need to find out why on earth someone would have left a note about a decades-old mine collapse.

More, she felt almost light-headed with relief to know that he hadn't gone to the Corral to drink without her.

Or to seek comfort in a woman.

He'd driven to the park.

And parked.

The thought brought the threat of tears, and to avoid them, she tuned in to what he was saying about Freya Fortune. She already knew about the letters his great-aunt had sent to him and his siblings and cousins. Everyone in town did. But the fact that Freya had said that her late husband had probably mentioned knowing the mining foreman's widow after Asa texted her about the mysterious note he'd found tacked to the community bulletin board the previous night, *was* intriguing.

And... Asa was taking her to his family's famed castle. She could hardly believe that she was actually going to see inside the place known all over the state for its elaborate feat of architecture, hidden rooms, and supposedly secret messages buried in the cement. She'd heard that Wendell Fortune's art collection was impressive as well.

She'd driven by the place more times than she could count.

And now Asa wanted *her* to be a part of that piece of his family legacy.

Like he was giving her an official admittance into the Fortune family.

Shaking off the lofty thought, Lily spent the rest of the drive reminding herself that she was and always would be...herself.

And that self took things as they came. She didn't get dramatic and fanciful.

Those were the types of emotional forages that could take the cheer right out of a woman. Or a little girl being shuffled from home to home.

Still, she couldn't help the sharp intake of her breath at her first step into the renowned masterpiece. The place was huge, with high colorful ceilings. She could only imagine all of the hidden messages in the barrage of art, and as they walked through to the room where Wendell sat, waiting, she really found the place kind of bizarre.

Fascinating, ornate, and glamorous, but an odd thing for a man to build as his family home.

She'd seen Wendell before, of course, as Martin Smith, the man he'd been posing as all of her life. He'd been at town functions. A ribbon cutting in the park.

She'd glimpsed him often enough to know that the man in the big ornate chair, who welcomed them in with kindness, but not a tone of warmth, had truly grown frail.

"Thank you for seeing me," Asa said to the patriarch, his formality reminding her that he'd only met his great-grandfather's older brother the previous summer. "First, I wanted to introduce you to my wife, Lily."

The old man nodded. "I've seen her. One of the Perry triplets. Terrible tragedy there…" Wendell shook his head, and Lily warmed up to him in a way she'd never ever have expected to.

One of the town's founding fathers, or a relative of such, knew about her parents. Knew that she'd been born a triplet to loving people.

She and her sisters and parents had been *memorable*.

It didn't change anything about her, or her life.

And yet…in a strange way…it did.

If nothing else, it changed how she viewed herself.

"Secondly, I just keep thinking about last night's note," Asa told his great-uncle. "Do you have any idea what became of Gwenyth Wells?"

Wendell's chin quivered a bit as he said, "I don't, but I remember that she was ruined. I heard that she knew that my younger brothers were responsible for the mine collapse." He lifted a shaking hand about an inch out of his blanketed lap, then let it drop. And continued, "She knew that they were the ones who'd placed the blame on her husband, the mine's foreman, who died in the collapse." He paused again, the wrinkles at his neck moving with the breaths he took.

Because Asa sat silently, so did Lily.

"It was rumored that she'd vowed to seek vengeance on Elias and Edgar, but they'd already fled town," Wendell continued after the brief pause.

Sitting on the big leather couch with Asa, Lily wanted to place a hand on his thigh as his grandfather was mentioned. She settled for leaning enough that her shoulder touched his.

"And she was never heard from again?" Asa prompted the older man. "Did she have any relatives in the area? Any other family?"

"She had a daughter, Renee, I think her name was." Wendell frowned. "She was a handsome young woman, as I recall. Seventeen or eighteen. Sure gave her father a sleepless night or two." Wendell's tone lightened, though the man's expression didn't change much.

"So is she still around? Married? Going by a different name?"

Wendell's headshake was minimal, but there. "She left town with her mother soon after the disaster, and I never heard of either one of them again until last night."

"So what do you think of the note?"

The old man shrugged and readjusted the blanket across his knees. "My guess...someone's playing a prank. Or is out to cause a stink. These young kids today...just don't have enough hard work to keep their minds out of trouble."

While Lily didn't agree with that statement—she figured today's kids had way more to deal with than even she had growing up, with all of the information coming at them instantly all day long—but she understood Wendell's views came from an era when even kids worked on

the ranch from sunup to sundown. With education coming in as a luxury. Or at the very least, coming in second.

And she told Asa as much a short time later as they
stopped in town to pick up their lunch and head back to
the ranch.

There followed a conversation about the internet and
social media, and the pressures they brought—as well as
the plethora of mind opening information—all the way
back to the ranch. They didn't judge the past against the
present. Didn't even compare. They just talked.

Sharing thoughts. Impressions. Memories.

Just like any of dozens of evenings they'd spent together at the Corral.

They didn't talk about his family's history. Or the fact
that Wendell Fortune knew who she was and remembered
her parents.

But there was comfort in knowing that she and Asa
knew those things about each other.

Knew that they came with emotional investment.

And held the information safely.

Because that was what best friends did.

Asa woke every morning with a sense of anticipation.
Finding the life he'd dreamed of even better than he'd
imagined. Far better.

It wasn't just hard work so that he could be the boss of
his world. It was taking on all kind of tasks, challenges,
being creative, and getting to meet interesting people
among the vacationing strangers who were happy to share
his property.

It was about knowing that Lily was sharing the days
with him. That had been his missing piece. Not doing it
alone.

Plus the fact that she was loving the work as much as

he was—the challenge, the opportunities to grow something bigger and better—was a satisfaction he hadn't even known how to conjure up. And the knowledge that she wanted to continue to be his partner on the ranch even after their marriage ended? Well, that was more than he'd ever have envisioned for himself.

The days all rolled by one after another, each one different in the tasks that cropped up, and each one the same, too. There were no days off. Not until they'd gotten a firm grip on every aspect of the business, made some initial changes, and hired a few more staff.

But he and Lily had started taking a little more time, when they could, for their afternoon ride. It had become kind of like the Corral to him, those hours with Lily, he on Major and her on Laura, instead of on their barstools.

Up on separate horses, there was no danger of anything physical cropping up between them, just as there hadn't been sitting at the bar at the Corral.

And they could talk about whatever came up between them.

Like the upcoming wedding party being thrown for them. He was uneasy every time he thought about it. Such a public display of pretense. Everyone there together all at once. The ones who knew them best. He figured he and Lily needed a strategy—some kind of plan they could work out together—but wasn't sure what it would be. Or, even how she felt about the gathering.

Not that she'd share her feelings about it with him.

The one thing he and Lily rarely talked about—the one thing he couldn't ever remember hearing her talk about—was her personal emotions.

Not that he was any scholar on that front himself, it was just…with all of the women he'd ever dated—and there'd been enough to have a pretty good cross section—

he hadn't had to wonder about what they were thinking or feeling. They'd all made it pretty clear.

Good and bad.

Like when he and Lily had run into Baylor Minser on Main Street. The woman had left no doubt of her disdain for Lily.

Or her willingness to take Asa on whatever grounds he offered. Married or not.

Lily hadn't shown any obvious reaction then, either.

On Thursday afternoon of the following week—with the party only two days away—he rode silently, trying to work out a way to approach the topic. They were out on a longer ride, checking all of the ranch's wooded hiking trails. Their current one was an easy, flat family trail that wove by a natural little rock waterfall into the small creek that ran through part of the property.

"Sometimes, when we're out here, I can't help wondering if it looked the same when my parents took our stroller on these paths," Lily said, throwing all party strategy conversation starters out of his mind. "It's almost like I can see us here with our whole lives stretched before us…"

The words stunned him. Or maybe it was her tone. Whenever she'd mentioned her parents in the past, it had always been with cheer. But her voice had changed before it had drifted off completely.

Filled with a longing so acute, he felt inept to deal with it.

Slowing Major to a stop, Asa glanced over to see the unusually melancholy look on her face. And pictured a ten-month-old baby version of her. He felt his heart swelling with sorrow for her. Regret. That little triplet girl had had parents, a father who'd have given her away at her wedding, a mother who'd have intervened with common sense when Lily announced she was marrying her best friend so he could get his ranch.

Or so he thought. Because in his gut, he knew it was wrong for her to go to a party filled with everyone she knew and cared about, pretending to be something she was not. The lie would be with her forever.

As would the divorce.

Even if the failed marriage was all his fault, she'd still be the woman who'd only been married six months. The one who'd made the poor choice to wed him.

Even if it was for the best reasons. To help a friend. And reach for her own hearts' desire in the process.

"They'd be proud of you, Lily," he said, feeling inane, and yet, confident, too, as the words came with a power that forced him to deliver them.

She shrugged, looked at him, and started to speak, but a call came over the radio with a crackle, followed by the voice of Jack, one of Asa's two full-time ranch hands. "A stray dog's been running through the cabin area," he said. "He's got no collar, looks like he's been on his own for a while, kind of mangy, too skinny. Mixed breed. About thirty pounds. Brown and white. I tried to catch him but he ran off. We're taking care of the barns and corrals now, making sure the entrances are closed and he doesn't get in and spook the animals…"

"We'll keep an eye out," Asa replied when Jack had finished detailing the steps being taken, wishing the interruption had come at any other time. Lily hardly ever spoke of her parents. She'd been opening up to him—needing him?—and when she heard the message, set off immediately in search of the dog.

That was his wife, always putting others before herself, but at what cost?

Would there come a time when the pain the woman bore silently and alone rose up and damaged her happy spirit?

Was being married to him contributing to that cost?

Asa didn't like the questions.

Or their probable answers.

CHAPTER FIFTEEN

THEY'D BE PROUD of you, Lily. As Lily listened to Asa talking to his ranch hand, warning him about the stray dog and making certain that the barns and petting zoo were being checked, the entrances closed off, she kept hearing Asa's earlier words ringing simultaneously in her head.

She sighed. More than anything, she hoped they were true. Glancing around a 360-degree perimeter of land in sight, she saw trees, with spring leaves just starting to show up in force. And acres of ground with the residue of crushed fall leaves, twigs, and branches broken by storms. All was still. Quiet.

Peaceful.

No evidence of a dog running wildly through the woods.

The horses would surely notice, as well, if another animal was in their vicinity. Both of them were standing calmly, Laura's head just a foot from Major's thigh. Major, probably bored by their slow pace—and the fact they'd now stopped altogether—looked about ready to take a nap.

And...the path ahead of them on the trail...it jogged off to the left. Then immediately right. Then left again. Like an S. And in the middle of the jog, a red oak tree.

A curve around a tree...

Heart pounding, she slid down from Laura, keeping the horse's reins loosely in hand, to lead her ahead of Major and Asa. Toward the small double curve.

It couldn't be, could it?

Her hands were shaking so hard as she pulled out her phone that she had to push twice to access the picture gallery. The photo she wanted was the first one in the gallery.

The last one taken.

It was a photo of a photo.

One Val Hensen had found in some old ranch boxes she'd been going through and dropped off to Lily earlier in the day. Lily had snapped the phone photo and put the original in the office safe. Needing time to process it on her own before doing anything else with it. Or telling anyone else about it.

Including telling her sisters.

Glancing from her phone, to the S the trail made in the ground, and the placement of the tree in that formation, she knew she had to be seeing things.

It couldn't be the same.

She was just emotionally in over her head. How could she not be? With her fake Vegas wedding, then the work at the ranch and planning Esme's legitimate marriage, and her and Asa's wedding party looming on Saturday...it was a lot to take in.

Lily wanted to believe that was all that was happening. Her mind playing tricks on her. And yet...

"What's up?" Asa had come up behind her.

She turned without thinking, paying no attention to the tears on her cheeks. She was that far gone.

He didn't ask again. Just took Laura's reins out of her limp hand, tied the mare and his gelding to a couple of trees and walked back over to her.

"It's too much, I know," he said, his tone softer than normal. Compassionate. A sound she'd heard directed toward his beloved Major before. "I've been trying to figure out a way to bring up the party on Saturday, and just..."

Shaking her head, she cut him off. He'd thought she was

crying in front of him because of a party she'd get through, just as she'd come through every other difficult moment in her life? She'd planned to enjoy herself Saturday night.

Making the most of a gathering that starred her and Asa together.

Wiping her eyes, swallowing the emotion, she bucked up and handed him her phone.

"What the..." The way he glanced sharply from her phone to the trail had her heart thumping all over again.

Could she possibly be right?

She saw him look at the phone again. Enlarge the clearly old photo. Look at her.

And then... "Look at the tree root." Followed immediately by, "Is that... Oh my God, Lil. It's you and your sisters, in your stroller, with your mom, isn't it? Right here."

It couldn't be. It was just too...

She glanced at her phone again. But hadn't needed to. She'd stared at the photo so long that morning that it was forever ingrained in her memory. She was the middle one. Tabitha's hair was lighter. Haley's face more beautifully round than Lily's oblong features.

When the tears started down her face again, there was no way Lily could contain them.

She was standing on the very ground her mother had stood on, pushing her and Haley and Tabitha, and looking like the happiest, proudest, woman on earth.

HE REACHED FOR her without thinking. Seeing Lily cry... tore him up. She wasn't a crier. *Ever.* And now...he had no idea what to do. How to console her.

There was nothing he could fix about the current situation. No way to make the past better for her.

Or less painful.

But when her arms slid around him, holding him, he

could let her do that. Could embrace her, just as tightly, be there for her, a friend at her back—or wrapped around her—so that she knew she didn't have to be alone anymore.

He didn't try to find words. There were none.

Holding her firmly around the waist, pressing her body against his so that his presence, his warmth was solidly there—ready to support her completely if she started to fall—he stroked his other hand through her hair. Slowly. Again and again.

Not patting her head, either. Truly caressing her hair, across her head, over her shoulders, down her back. Even losing his fingers in its silky lengths, hoping that it felt good to her, could reach her, in the midst of whatever agony she was allowing herself to release.

Good with the bad, that's what she'd always told him. The way she'd always gotten through any hardship was to focus on the good.

He had to give her good to focus on.

When he felt the bone-deep shudder against him, he slid his hand under her hair, going straight for her back. With both hands. Running his fingers slowly down each side of her, still pressing her to him.

She'd never really been sobbing, just, in pure Lily fashion, quietly crying, but then her breathing changed, giving him the impression that her tears were abating.

Until it changed again.

To a rhythm his senses recognized.

And responded to. With his groin.

Her arms around his neck tightened, and she lifted her head from his chest, looking up at him.

She didn't say a word, just looked.

And he knew she'd felt the hardness that had sprung up against her.

But he wasn't pulling away. No way he could tear those soft, feminine arms from the warmth they were clinging to.

No way he'd add his rejection to her grief from a lifetime of loss.

She needed him. He was not going to let her down.

He'd be strong.

For both of them.

And he was.

Right until her lips lifted and planted against his. Her eyes had been wide-open as she'd done so.

Her gaze connected to his.

She'd moved slowly. Watching him.

And he'd watched her, too.

Knew the second she closed her eyes.

Just before he felt those soft, smaller lips touch his bigger ones.

There was nothing tentative about Lily's kiss. Nothing at all weak.

But the caress was most definitely filled with need—of a different kind.

Surging with sudden flame, he kissed her back, let her lead him down to the ground by the old oak tree, and then led her toward the dance that was coming.

It wasn't slow or sweet, but frantic and hungry.

She kicked off one boot while he pulled down her jeans and got both of her legs free. She went for his belt buckle. The fly was so tight he had to help with the button and the zipper, and the second he sprang free, he slid into her.

The ride was his shortest ever. A few strokes. She came. He came.

And there they were, half-naked on one of their family hiking trails, with their horses tethered just feet away.

He'd tried to give her a feel-good rub on her back. But

the intensity pouring through her had obviously needed much, much more than that to counteract it.

She'd reached for the good.

And he was glad he'd been there.

Had been about to tell her so when Major snorted, Laura stepped back, and a flurry of fur came charging through the woods in the distance, aiming straight for the half-naked people lying on the ground.

ASA HAD HIS pants up and was sitting down, in front of Lily, before the dog almost reached them and then veered away. Still watching them.

"You can go after him," she hissed, as she scrambled to get back into her jeans, pull them up and then, sitting down, pull on her boot. She didn't kid herself that what they'd just done designated any change in their relationship or future plans.

Worst case, he'd had pity sex with her. But she didn't really think that, either. Asa was virile, and she was the only woman in his life for the next several months.

"Stay down," he said, not moving. "He ran from those running after him. Let him come to us."

Still reeling from everything that had happened, half-numb, all emotion spent, she did as he asked. Boot on, she remained completely still, expecting the dog to get so close and then, change directions and head off.

Instead, as it approached again, it slowed, tail wagging, and came closer.

Head down, it stopped a few yards away.

Reaching into his pocket, Asa pulled out one of Major's sugar cubes and held it out to the dog. "It's okay, boy," he called softly.

Lily, who'd had a couple of dogs in her growing-up

years, pets that had been with the families she'd entered and stayed with them after she was gone, held her breath.

Somehow, awash in so many different emotions as she was, it seemed as though, if the dog would come to them, that somehow meant that she and Asa were okay.

Dogs could sense trustworthiness.

He didn't run right up to them. Didn't approach at all at first. But his nose started moving the second Asa reached his hand further out. And with each sniff, he came closer. One step at a time.

Asa took out a second cube. Held it in his other hand, closer in, and slowly, with those cubes, eased the dog in until he stood there of his own accord.

She expected Asa to grab him then. Gently, of course, but to make sure the dog didn't run off again.

Instead, he petted the dog's head.

His back.

Reminding Lily of the way he'd first comforted her such a short time before.

She smiled. "You're a good boy, aren't you?" she asked the dog, in a tone of voice she'd use for a child.

She didn't reach out for him. She had no sugar. And didn't want to scare him off.

The dog looked from Asa to her, and then, to her complete shock, he came right up to her, sat on her lap, and gave her a lick on the chin.

Burying her face in his fur, choking back a new wave of tears she'd thought completely spent, she hugged him, kissing his mangy fur. And finally, when she was emotionally able, stood, still holding on to him.

She couldn't ride back with him. She wasn't that strong.

But she could carry him to the horses. Still holding him in her arms as she approached Laura, she turned to trade the dog for Laura's reins as Asa untied the horses. Laura didn't wait for Lily to get the reins. The young mare moved with Asa, straight toward Lily, nudging the side of Lily's head softly with her own.

Much like the dog had sat in her lap.

A complete stranger.

They knew.

It was like, on some level, Laura and the dog were telling her she wasn't alone.

Almost as though, for those moments, the animals had claimed her as theirs.

She'd never ever felt so loved. She really did have her own family. A growing one. Laura, for sure, who was all hers. And Asa, her forever friend. Maybe her family wasn't a conventional one. It wasn't mom, dad, and the kids. But her dream was coming true.

She'd come full circle. Right there, on the same exact earth where she'd been Lily Perry, precious triplet baby whose mother glowed with happiness just because she and her sisters existed.

As she handed over the dog to Asa and climbed up on Laura for the trip back, Lily truly felt like her parents were there in her midst, smiling.

In her mind, they were happy to see her so loved.

And, in that moment, she was truly happy, too.

CHAPTER SIXTEEN

Asa needed space. Time to breathe in air that didn't contain an excess of...everything. The confusion of feelings that had bombarded his life would not get the best of him.

He just had to have a chance to rope them one by one and get them back where they belonged. Most of them in the ether, where they would evaporate and mess with him no more.

He'd called the animal shelter as soon as he and Lily had returned to the house with the dog. No one had called looking for their pet. While he'd given the dog a bath, figuring him for part cocker spaniel and maybe some small shepherd breed, Lily had made up fliers to post around town, inserting, as the last piece, the newly cleaned dog photo Asa took for her.

She'd insisted, without any fight from him, that they'd make certain that the dog ended up in a good home.

While she made up a chicken and rice concoction to feed him, Asa gladly escaped to head into town to put up the fliers, and to stop at the GreatStore for dog food, treats, and maybe a toy or two.

Before he pulled out of his drive, he texted the picture he'd taken of the dog to Devin Street. Asa had only met the man a couple of times, at the Corral, but he'd liked him. Respected him. Owner of the *Chatelaine Daily News*, Devin not only got wind of everything going on in town, he was also known to foster dogs.

He was barely on the road before his phone rang.

"You got a new dog, man?" Devin asked as he picked up the phone.

"He was running loose on my land. You recognize him?"

"No. He's a cutie, though."

"You want to take him?"

"I would, but I'm fostering a huge Great Dane at the moment, and believe me, you wouldn't want a little one around here right now. Chumley's all I can manage…"

Sharing an understanding chuckle with the man, Asa told him about the flyers he'd be putting up and Devin said he'd keep his ear to the ground.

Asa's first stop was at the community bulletin board. The note he'd seen put up the other night was still there. Seeming to glare at him with unanswered questions.

He tacked his dog flyer on the opposite end of the board.

And spent the next forty-five minutes on Main Street, going from place to place to ask permission to hang his lost dog missives.

The task itself wasn't such a time suck—it was all the chatting, backslaps, and well-wishes he got every place along the way—congratulating him on his wedding.

Asking him how married life was treating him.

All reminders of the very things he'd needed to escape.

He'd left his sister's place on Main Street for last—wanting to get a look at the progress she was making. And also to see if there were problems, if she needed help, if anyone was giving her a hard time in the final stages of creating her down-home Western-style restaurant.

In other words, his usual MO.

Cowgirl Café was slated to open the following month and if there were any snags, he'd be there to help her through them. Bea had always loved to cook. But that didn't mean she was on top of every aspect of opening her own business.

"Wow, this is impressive," he heard himself saying once inside, giving her a hug as he looked around. The post and beam interior and Western flavor looked far better than he'd envisioned them when she'd first told him about the place.

"You want to see the menu?" she asked, pushing one beneath his nose. "They just came today."

Taking it, he read the list of solid cowboy/cowgirl favorites, from five kinds of chili and corn breads and po-boys to mac and cheese in crocks.

"Now you've made me hungry," he grumbled, handing it back to her. "I don't suppose you have any samples back there." He pointed to the opening that led to the kitchen.

"Go home to your wife, little brother. She just called to say she over made the rice and is doing up a chicken and rice casserole for dinner. She wanted my mushroom sauce recipe…"

There'd been a bounce in Bea's step from the second he'd walked in the door and caught sight of her. The smile that was on her face as she sassed him went far beyond her mouth, too. Her eyes seemed to glow in a way he hadn't seen in a long time.

"Yes, ma'am," he retorted, as she took one of his fliers from him before he'd even offered it to her.

"She told me about the dog, too, now git. Knowing you, you still have to stop at the store and the casserole will be coming out of the oven in less than an hour…"

"You know, bossy bosses aren't all that popular…" he told Bea with a grin as he grabbed her for a quick kiss to her head, and left.

Feeling better than he had since he'd pulled his pants back on after being with Lily in the woods.

His sister hadn't looked so excited about anything since her divorce, and her happiness made him happy.

Turned out, buying dog stuff wasn't such a bad gig, either.

Figuring it was best to overbuy rather than end up not having something Lily wanted, Asa bought up two grocery bags worth of food, treats, and toys, and grabbed a dog bed, too, on his way out of the aisle. The stuff could all go with the dog when he went home.

Or be donated to the shelter if the dog's owner didn't want them.

He had a feeling the supplies would make Lily happy.

And that lifted his mood, too.

THE DOG—MAX, she was thinking of him in her mind—occupied Lily before dinner, through it, and afterward, too.

Turned out, he was a chewer.

And a clinger. He didn't like to be alone in a room for long.

He was also house-trained, she discovered just as the buzzer was going off, indicating it was time for her to get Bea's casserole recipe out of the oven, and Max went to the door and whined.

She didn't have a leash or collar yet, so she grabbed the rope Asa had fashioned to serve as both holster and lead when they'd first found him. Slipping it on Max, she took him out. He did his business so fast it was like he'd held it to the last minute.

And she made a note to self to offer him outdoor opportunities more often.

She wasn't calling him by any name. Wasn't letting herself start to think of him as her own. But having been a foster, she wanted to be a good foster parent, even if only for the night.

The dog's presence made Asa's return much easier to take in stride. Not only did the little guy wiggle and wag and demand attention, but he was like a third in the room. Allowing them to avoid talk of what had happened between them in the woods.

"I think he's still young," Asa said as they finished up dishes together, and he asked her if she wanted to have a beer on the porch. "The chewing, and the overexuberance seem to point that way."

He had a lot more experience with dogs. Was probably right.

"I choose to think that he's just thrilled to not be running scared in the woods." After all, fosters had to stick together.

"That, too." Asa chuckled, tipping his bottle to her as they each took one of the two big white wooden chairs, with a holstered dog lying down between them.

As though he'd accepted that he had a place for the night and exhaustion had finally hit him.

"This is nice," Asa said after a few minutes of relaxing night air filled only with the sounds of an occasional breeze. The birds that chirped and called their various melodies during the day had settled in for the night as well.

And all Lily could think about was the sex she and Asa had had earlier.

It had been different. Not just sex between a hungry man and woman, but between her and Asa. Best friends with an understanding of the other's needs, insecurities, and motivations.

Where she got that notion, she didn't know. She acknowledged to herself that he might not have experienced anything of the sort. But the way he'd reacted to that photo of her mom and sisters and her...it was as though he'd been right inside her heart. He'd felt her.

She'd felt him in there. Sharing her anguish.

Right before they'd ripped one another's clothes off.

"This is paradise," Asa murmured. "This right here... it's what I longed for as a kid but never had."

"You don't remember a time at all when your parents got along?"

He sipped from his beer, staring out into the night, and shook his head. "Nope. I think my dad's affairs started early in the marriage. Mom's came later."

"And you guys knew about them?"

"It was kind of hard not to. They threw them in each other's faces. And then threw my aunt's and uncle's liasons in each other's faces, too, as though that justified their behaviors." He shook his head.

And she hurt for him.

She thought of what Esme had told her about Asa's lack of belief in a true love that lasted. His sister thought Lily had cured him.

If only that were possible...

"I love that you called Bea for recipe suggestions tonight," he said then, sliding a glance her way.

Lily smiled. "It's nice, having a group of people with various skills who are happy to hear from you and help out."

"It's called *family*, Lil," he said, laconically, but kindly, too. As though he was pleased.

The word got her. *Family.*

His sisters would only be her family for a short time and then...

She'd stood on the exact spot where her mother had stood with a heart full of love for her.

She still couldn't wrap her mind around that one. To the point that, other than Asa, no one else knew. She'd thought she'd call her sisters, but with the dog, and well…everything, she hadn't done so.

Silence fell between them, and he sat forward. Turned to her. "You and I, we're family now," he told her. "You married me. Took my name. And even after the divorce, we'll be family. We promised each other forever."

Her throat clogged to the point that she couldn't speak. She wouldn't let tears fall. Not in front of him again. Not in the same day.

So she nodded. Sipped from her beer.

He knew that having grown up without a family to call her own, family meant everything to her. Being a part of one was her heart's biggest desire. The only dream she cared to reach for.

She thought about the two of them. Her past…and his. How it affected them both. Envisoned the future, what it would probably look like. What it could look like.

What she most *needed* it to look like.

And when she could speak calmly, normally, she found herself saying, "The Hensens were married almost fifty years, worked together every day, and the way Val talks about her husband, their love holds true ever after death," she said. And then she talked about one of her high school teachers who'd opened her home to Lily for a graduation celebration because Lily had been living alone in her one room apartment by the time that June had come around. The woman Had been near retirement. Had been married for over forty years. Had grown children of their own. And they'd worked together to give Lily a special day of her own.

"I didn't know they'd done that," Asa remarked, glancing her way. "That's such a cool thing. Why didn't you ever mention it before?"

For the same reason she hadn't told anyone except him

about the picture she'd received that morning. The things that meant the most to her were cherished inside where they couldn't get crushed.

Just as the things that hurt the most weren't talked about, either. She wouldn't shine a light on them. It would only give them the power to hurt more.

"It just never came up," she answered. "The point is, Asa, there are happy marriages. A lot of them. You must at least hope that Esme and Ryder will be happy together for the rest of their lives…"

She wasn't sure if he shook his head, or just gestured with it. He'd stopped midmovement to take a long swig of beer. "Of course, I hope it," he told her. "But I don't feel certain that will be the case. When you watch relationships erode, one day at a time, you see what happens… I don't know how some do it. I just know that I can't take that chance."

He glanced at her, and though they were sitting with only the light from the front window, she could see the steely resolve in his gaze. "How could I gamble like that? On the possibility that we might come out okay? Because if we're wrong, I lose you."

She smiled as best she could. Nodded. Then looked out into the night.

"I can't lose you, Lil."

At the sincere emotion in his tone, she glanced over at him. Smiled for real, and said, "I can't lose you, either, Asa."

And told herself, as they took the dog and went upstairs that night—and Asa veered off to his own room without any hesitation at all, asking her if she wanted to keep the dog, or have Asa take him—that she had to give up on the idea that she and Asa would ever have a real marriage.

Or children to share it with them.

He cared about her deeply.

Loved her even. As a best friend.

And that was far better than anything she'd ever had.

It was just that she'd just begun believing in the possibility that she could have whatever her heart desired. Or that she could at least keep trying for it, keep reaching, until the day she died.

As long as she kept believing.

With that picture of her own mother looking so gloriously happy with her babies firmly in mind, alongside Asa's support and lovemaking that afternoon, she felt like she was at a crossroads.

And wasn't sure which path to take.

CHAPTER SEVENTEEN

LILY WAS ALREADY down in the kitchen, feeding the dog, when Asa came downstairs after his shower the next morning. They'd agreed not to call their new companion by a name since they didn't know what his actual name was.

They'd both already figured the dog had had an owner, even as young as he was, because he'd been neutered.

Listening to Lily talk to the four-legged bit of happy energy as he headed toward the kitchen, he hated to think about her giving the dog away again.

But when it happened, he knew she'd take it all in stride. With a smile on her face.

Lily was used to losing what she cared about.

Which was why he had to get his ass in better gear for her. Keep his hands off her. Get divorced, and settle in for the forever part of their vows.

He couldn't let himself think about happy marriages.

He would *not* be one of her losses.

"I had an idea for the ranch last night," she told him as he came into the kitchen to prepare his usual bowl of cereal and toast, while she munched on her granola bar and a banana.

The words, the easy tone in her voice, settled some of the tension inside him. He knew he hadn't given her the answer she'd wanted the night before. And had been half prepared to deal with a new distance between them.

Instead, so Lily-like, she was forging into her future at the ranch.

Breathing a silent sigh of relief, he said, "What's that?"

"I'm thinking maybe we look into a horse therapy program…"

She paused just as his toast popped. Reaching around her to grab it from the toaster, he met her gaze.

And smiled. "I think it's a great idea," he informed her, moving quickly away. "The ranch I was on before I moved here had a program, and while I was skeptical at first, it was really kind of cool. They worked mostly with displaced teenagers. Horses have a natural ability to sense human emotions and even just the nonverbal support was a thing to see…"

"I read about a place once, when I was having to leave another home. It was a boarding school that offered equine therapy outside of Corpus Christi, and I wanted to go, but…" She tilted her head back and forth. "Clearly I didn't have the money."

"Did you ever mention the idea to anyone? Or try to find out more?"

He wasn't surprised when she shook head. "What was the point? My monthly foster care amount wasn't nearly enough. It wasn't like I knew anyone with money, and I saw no point in getting my hopes up, or wasting anyone else's time, when I knew it wasn't going to happen."

Because she didn't reach for what she wanted.

Or she hadn't. Until she married him.

And now she was thinking about other teens like herself, wanting to provide for them.

If it was possible, Asa's pool of love for his best friend grew even deeper.

LEAVING THE DOG, with his new holster collar and lead, at the barn with Asa later that morning, Lily went into town to meet her sisters for lunch.

She'd thought she'd tell them about the picture Val Hensen had given her, but wasn't quite ready to share yet. For so long, her sisters had had family, while she hadn't.

For a minute or two, she wanted to savor seeing who she'd been, all on her own.

Tabitha had the adoptive mother she'd grown up with. Haley, the mother who'd fostered her, and was her mother still.

Their mother was all Lily had. She wasn't ready to share. Her sisters would get their copies of the photo. It was theirs as much as hers.

She wasn't trying to be selfish, or in any way slight them. But the photo was just such a huge thing for Lily, representing so many things. She needed some private time to process.

They'd have questions…suppositions…especially Haley, whose journalist brain couldn't stop digging. And Lily wasn't ready to start wondering yet.

She'd grown up knowing her parents had been killed in a car accident. But had never wanted to know more. Because doing so would make it bigger, more painful, within her.

Yet seeing her mother's smiling face…she kind of did want to know…as though, her mother deserved for Lily and the others to find out, to have her daughters know her as completely as they possibly could.

But not that day. Lily was already riding on crests too high to sustain her, over undertows strong enough to take her down.

Which was why, as soon as Asa had left the house that morning, she'd called Tabitha and Haley to request a get-together. They were the only ones who knew the truth about her marriage.

She'd told them both she'd needed to speak with them before her wedding celebration the next night.

Who she was, what her marriage was, where she was going...she couldn't seem to get straight in her own mind and heart about it. She'd spent much of the night lying in bed with her heart and head fighting each other. Another first for her.

In the past her heart had just shut up.

She'd eventually invited the dog up on the mattress with her, and, with his warmth pressing her through the covers, had finally fallen asleep.

Only to wake with the same battle raging inside of her.

There was no rush to figure it all out. She was under no time constraint except her own emotional one. She needed to have something right within her before she went to that party with Asa.

As soon as she'd opened her eyes that morning, she'd known she had to talk to her sisters. Haley was practical—she'd take the mind part of the war. And Tabitha...was a mother. She'd be the heart.

Maybe, listening to the two of them go back and forth with their opinions, she'd see where she needed to be. Who she sided with most.

By previous agreement, the three of them connected in the diner's parking lot, but before Lily could even get more than a thank-you out, a woman she'd never seen before came up to the three of them.

"Do you know if there's a hotel in town?" she asked, leaving Lily to wonder how the young woman could have missed it. It wasn't like Chatelaine was all that big.

"There's just one motel," she answered, figuring the unknown woman, with her wavy short brown hair and green eyes, had just broken up with someone, or found out some other bad news. She seemed distracted—and not in a happy way. "It's called the Chatelaine Motel," she continued. "You can't miss it, it's right at the tail end of Main Street here. It's an old two-story motor lodge with rooms that open onto the parking lot, has a second level walkway and is desperately in need of some updating. But it's clean."

She was babbling, wanting to help, needing desperately to unload on her sisters, and getting odd vibes from the stranger in their midst.

"I'm Lily... Fortune," she said then, stumbling over the last name in her attempt at friendliness, at which time Tabitha rescued her with, "I'm Tabitha Buckingham and this is our sister, Haley Perry."

"We're known around here as the Perry triplets," Haley told the younger-looking woman.

So weird, as soon as they tried to be welcoming, the woman kind of turned away from them, hunching her shoulders, as she half mumbled, "My name's Morgana," and hurried off down the street.

Haley, always the journalist, watched her go. "Interesting," she said, with that needing to know more tone in her voice. "She definitely didn't want to give her last name. I'll bet there's a story there."

"Yeah, she did react kind of odd..." Tabitha was saying, as Lily moved them toward their destination.

Lily had no focus for Haley's penchant to make a story out of everything. She'd only squeezed out enough time for a quick sandwich before she had to get back to the ranch. With it being Friday, they had two check-ins that afternoon. And then it would be tomorrow and her and Asa's celebration would loom...

If nothing else, she needed to let her sisters know she might need a little help keeping up appearances at their soiree. They deserved to understand why, after all the trouble they and Esme and Bea had gone to throw the party.

As it turned out, she only ordered coffee—because it's all her sisters wanted and she was glad for the faster service. And to not have to choke down food.

"I need to talk to you both about Asa," she said as soon as they had their cups in front of them, Lily on one side of the table, Tabitha and Haley on the other.

It just felt better to her that way.

"What's up?" Tabitha asked the question, but both sets of eyes were trained on her, sending compassion in waves.

Which was exactly why she'd called them. She wasn't all that good yet at sharing private details of her life with her siblings, but for some reason, it suddenly all came tumbling out of her. Probably more than should have. *Way* more than Asa would have wanted to share. She told them more about making love on the couch in Vegas on their wedding night. About the night on the couch at the ranch. And then, leaving out the part about the photo and the S in the trail, about having had sex with her husband in name only out in the woods the day before.

She didn't mention the dog, either.

"He loves you," Tabitha said softly, a smile on her face.

And Lily shook her head, saying, "He loves me like a friend. He's not *in* love with me. Every time, as soon as it's done, he reverts back to just friends. We've had sex, but we've never slept together. Or even been in bed together. And when I tried to talk to him about giving the marriage a real chance, he adamantly refused."

Haley swore mostly beneath her breath.

"Did he say why?" Tabitha asked.

Lily gave her sisters the abridged version of the things Esme had told her, and then added, "In his mind, to try is to risk failure, and he'd rather have me as a forever friend than take a chance at losing me."

Tabitha's eyes grew a little moist. Haley raised her brows and shrugged.

"So you just have to show him differently," she said, shocking Lily. Haley was supposed to have been on her *give-up-on-him* side of the battle. The side who knew she wanted children, and if he wouldn't give them to her, she couldn't settle for less.

"I agree," Tabitha told her. "You're head over heels in love with this man. How can you even consider giving up on a chance that he'll change his mind?"

Lily's heart clunked at that. She'd been so deafened by her own inner war, she'd failed to think about Tabitha's having lost the love of her life to death.

Failed to even think about the fact that her sister knew exactly when it was that you had no chances left.

"People change all the time." Haley's tone was unusually soft. She started pointing then, as she threw out a list of to-dos. "Play the femme fatale," she suggested. "Make him see you as more than just his buddy. Be the woman in his life. Do your nails. Put on makeup. Buy a sexy teddy. Hit him where it hurts."

Lily glanced at Tabitha, who was nodding. Could something that...doable...really work? It wasn't her, but neither was dressing up as she had for her wedding. She'd done it once, so she supposed she could pull it off again. All except Haley's last suggestion. She had no desire to ever hurt Asa. Period.

"And I'd talk to him some more about it, too," Tabitha said. "Let him know that as long as the two of you keep open communication, and work at it, you can get through the tough times."

Something Tabitha hadn't had a chance to do with her baby's daddy.

But it made sense.

Reaching over, Haley slid her opened hand beneath Lily's on the table and then clasped her fingers. "Bottom line, though, sweetie? You have to trust your heart. It will tell you when to go, if it comes time to do so. Until then, you keep trying."

That. Right there. Truth rang loudly within her. Settling both her heart and her head.

Giving Haley's hand a squeeze back, she reached for Tabitha's, too. "I love you both. You know that, right?"

It wasn't something she generally said aloud.

And she held her sisters answering avowals of love close to her heart as she insisted on being the one to pay for their coffee and headed for the door.

On the way to the rest of her life.

One way or another.

LILY WAS IN the four-wheeler, escorting a family back to their cabin, when Asa got the call about the dog. The exuberant guy had been with Lily since she'd returned from town, and Asa headed up to the office, letting himself in with his key, helping himself to a soda from the cooler in the little store that took up one side of the reception area, and then heading behind the desk to drop money in the drawer.

He was killing time.

Waiting for Lily to return.

Needing to prove to her that they could make their future work. There at the ranch together. With their horses and other animals. Maybe even with them both living on the premises.

They'd have the best part of a lifetime partnership without the traps that eventually got to one or both parties and turned love into hate.

The dog came bounding in before her, dragging his leash, and he could hear Lily laughing at the boy's antics. The little guy ran in and jumped up on Asa, as though it was his job to welcome Asa to his own property.

Lily didn't look as happy to see him. "What's up?"

From her reaction, Asa could tell she knew he wouldn't be at the office at four in the afternoon if there wasn't a situation.

"I got a call about the dog." He started in and stopped when she interrupted him.

"I figured," she told him, sounding calm, businesslike. "As soon as I saw your four-wheeler outside. How soon is he leaving?"

"That's what I needed to talk to you about," he said then, moving closer to her. "It turns out that someone recognized him from the photo. There was a rancher renting a place just this side of town who moved on without warning, leaving in the middle of the night. The dog was his. And, it appears, was left behind on purpose."

Lily was staring at him. And he could read in her expression the things she wasn't saying.

"So...you want him?"

Eyes narrowed, she studied him. "Do you?"

"Yeah."

"Me, too." There was nothing businesslike or sedate about her as she ran around the desk she'd put between them and went straight for the dog, bending down to put her arms around him. "Oh, and, if it's okay with you, his name's Max," she informed him, before letting loose with a slew of baby talk that cut him out completely as she let Max know that he was home, and would be loved and have a happy life.

Max, Juniper, Sunshine…any name was fine with him.

As long as it brought that radiant smile to his wife's face.

"I think he approves." Lily looked over at him and giggled as the dog gave a lick across her chin.

Asa joined the two of them on the floor then, needing to be a part of the moment. To play with the dog—Max—and let him know that he was a part of them now.

He watched in amusement as Lily grabbed a toy and started playing tug-of-war with their new pup.

Max grabbed hold, pulled, and was growling playfully. Chuckling, Lily looked over at Asa, handing him her end of the rope.

Inviting him into their game.

Taking the rope, he pulled, but not too hard. He didn't want to break the young dog's teeth. Or get too rough with him, either.

When Max tired, helping himself to a drink from the dish Lily must have put down earlier, and then lay down, watching them, Lily sat there on the floor and smiled at Asa.

"Thank you," she told him.

"Right back at you," he murmured back.

And just like that, they'd become parents.

CHAPTER EIGHTEEN

IF LILY HAD had any doubts about the seduction she'd planned for Friday night—having stopped at the Great-Store on the way home to pick up everything she'd need—Asa's involvement with Max had silenced them.

As good as he was with a stray dog...she knew he'd be a hundred times better with a little human. The man was father material all the way. She'd had enough of them in and out of her life to be able to tell the greats from the maybe nots.

He'd grown up with a definite no for a father.

But that didn't mean that all men were that way. Asa being a case in point.

He'd done so much for her, and now she was the one who was going to have to fight for their future.

To that end, she had the night all planned out.

She took Max out and then, taking him with her, excused herself to bed while Asa was still going over bids and figures for some of the remodeling projects they'd talked about doing before summer. She needed their newest family member shut in her room, hopefully asleep on her bed, when she made her move.

She'd washed her hair that morning and covered it so it didn't get wet during her quick shower. The lingerie thing...she'd never in her life thought of herself wearing one.

It was one piece, red with black trim and lace, and

mostly see-through. The silk garment came with spaghetti straps up top and snaps for an easy open crotch.

She felt naughty just putting it on.

Her first glimpse of herself in her bathroom mirror almost had her calling off the whole thing. And then she heard her husband's boots on the stairs and knew that she couldn't give up. She couldn't let fear—hers or his—win.

Shivering, noticing how clearly her tightened nipples showed through the fabric, she grabbed the makeup she'd purchased for her wedding day. Applied it as best she could as the artist had done it for her in Vegas. And then took her new, wide barrel curling iron and did her best to reproduce the waves the hotel's expensive stylist had created out of her usually boring, straight dark strands.

She'd looked at shoes, too, but the GreatStore's selection was most definitely not femme fatale, so she had decided to paint her toes and just go barefoot. She'd done that, giving them time to dry, before pulling her socks and boots back on in time for check-in.

The one thing she hadn't done, in Vegas, or that afternoon, was go the artificial nail route. Her fingers lived on working hands, and that was just fine with her. She could dress up to please her husband at night after work, but she couldn't be dealing with pieces of plastic sticking out on the ends her fingers, worrying about breakage, all day while she worked. She'd smoothed and buffed her short nails, though. Lily wanted to tempt Asa, to show him a different side of her, not pretend to be someone she was not.

She was attempting to give him a lifetime.

Not a moment in time.

Asa had been upstairs fifteen minutes, long enough for his nightly rinse off—something she knew about because, for the past weeks, she'd heard his shower running as she lay in bed, picturing him naked in there.

Her time had come.

Unless she was going to put it off...give herself more time to think about it...give him more time to come around on his own.

Standing at her bedroom door, with Max snoozing on her bed, just as she'd hoped, she stared at the doorknob.

Was she chickening out?

Or being wise?

Hanging from the doorknob was the new shirt she'd purchased to wear to their wedding party the next night. Feminine. Silky. White. Would look great with the new black jeans she'd bought.

And...if there was any chance that a celebration of her and Asa's love could be for real...it was now or never.

She opened the door. Shivered as the cool night air hit her skin. Then turned the knob, held it, and let it slowly release as she closed Max in behind her.

Lily stepped lightly down the hall. Not to be sexy, but because she didn't want Asa to hear her until she was right there. In his face.

A seduction in the hall didn't have any ring to it.

Pulse racing, she faced his closed bedroom door.

There she was. Doing it. Just as her heart had directed.

A light shone beneath the door.

Was he reading?

Still in his attached bathroom?

If she just walked in with no warning, would she be interrupting something that was none of her business?

Maybe she should wait until the light went out.

Or...knock first.

With a shaking hand, she rapped lightly, once, and then reached for his door handle and turned it. Stiffened her shoulders. Feeling more like she was going into battle, not moving toward sex.

He'd been in bed—slept in the raw, she saw—but was halfway out of it by the time she stood in the doorway. His pillow was propped up, his tablet on the bed.

And...

"Lily? What in the hell are you doing?"

Not at all the response she'd expected. Perhaps she should have waited until his light was out...

"I'm hoping I'm about to have sex." The words tumbled out, sounding less awkward than she felt. "You're good at it, Asa. And while you aren't doing it with anyone else, and since we've done it before..."

In some part of her mind she knew that rambling wasn't sexy.

Nor were the words spitting out of her.

But the way he was looking at her...with some kind of fascinated horror...

She should have opted for the putting-it-off choice minutes before in her room. Given herself more time to think it all through.

Because he wasn't moving, or speaking, she took a couple of steps toward him, worried that she wasn't pulling off the teddy look after all.

Then stopped herself, just barely, from wrapping her arms around her chest.

When he didn't stop her advance, she continued forward, stopping only when she reached him, standing there nude beside his bed.

That's when she looked down.

And saw his body's response to her presence.

She was most definitely, gloriously wanted.

The sight, the knowledge it brought, emboldened her, and she reached for his chest with both hands, sliding her fingers through the springy hair there. Purposely gliding over his nipples.

Asa groaned. He reached for her.

And...

Gently pushed her away.

"We can't, Lil." His voice sounded strained. But then he moved briskly toward the pair of pants thrown over the chair in the corner of his room.

He had them on, up, and fastened before he turned, grabbed a robe off the back of his bathroom door, and tossed it to her.

"Here, put this on."

She did so at once. Not for his sake, but for her own. Never in her life had she ever wanted to cover up so badly.

But she wasn't running.

She'd been right to know she was walking into battle.

And, humiliation aside, her reason for being there was stronger than ever.

"We can't do this," he said, standing there in the middle of the room, his arms crossed.

"Yeah, we can. We've already proven that." Her words weren't planned. They were coming from a desperate place, a hurting place, that had been given free rein.

He shook his head, seemingly not the least bit affected by her continued presence in his room. "And as great as those moments were, Lil, we have to live platonically so that nothing gets in the way of our partnership, running the ranch, and most importantly...us. Our friendship."

"I know that's your take on it," she said then. "But there are two of us here, Asa, and a true partnership has to consider both sides." She'd come up with that on the drive home that afternoon.

"Yes, when the agreement is being made," he countered, without even a pause to think about her side. "But our marriage, our relationship...that's a done deal. Based on a mutual agreement. One party can't just suddenly decide to change everything up after the deal has been signed."

The deal under which they'd signed their wedding license.

He wasn't budging. Clearly he had no intention on hearing her out.

Dashing her hopes.

Except…he wasn't throwing her out. Even as he rejected her, kindness emanated from him.

Because he cared that much.

It was that—the love he'd professed, the love she felt—that kept her from apologizing, excusing herself, and slinking quietly away.

Because their lifetime of living and loving together, of having a family, was at stake.

She might not get what she wanted.

But she could no longer live with herself if she didn't reach for her stars.

SHE WASN'T LEAVING.

He had logic, fairness, decency, even rationality on his side. Everything that ruled successful interpersonal relationships.

And was in the right on a critical point that would protect them for the rest of their lives.

If it had been anyone else but Lily standing there, he'd have extricated himself from the situation.

However, he couldn't do that with her. Not just because they were legally married…but because he truly loved the person she was. He wanted her in his life. Valued her friendship more than any other single thing. All of which he'd already told her.

She moved and relief flooded him, until he saw that she was heading for his bathroom door, not the one leading her back to the hallway, to her own room, outside of his suite, which he could lock as soon as she exited.

His robe fell off her shoulders as she moved, and by the time he realized what she was doing, returning his robe to the hook on the back of the door, he was already hard again.

Staring at that incredibly beautiful body in the tantalizing piece of man-killing lingerie.

He wanted her so badly it scared him. Truly sent shivers of fear through him. How was he going to control his desire for her if she was throwing herself at him like that?

Knowing she wanted him made it a hundred times harder.

"You do realize that if we continue to have sex, I'm going to start wanting you like all the rest of the casual women in my life, right?" The words spewed forth out of desperation.

She stood her ground silently.

"Sex always brings issues—heightened emotions...expectations...and when one can't meet them, there are over-the-top disappointments, too..."

"We've already had sex, Asa. You can't undo that."

He didn't know how to get through to her. Almost panic driven, he gritted out, "You're asking for something I can't give you, Lil. Believe me, I want to give you everything your heart desires, but I can't do this." He knew his words were hurtful and regretted having to say them.

However, the stricken look he'd expected to see on her face wasn't there.

Instead, her gaze seemed to be filled with compassion.

"You're free to choose to give us a try, Asa, in a legitimate marriage. It's not that you can't. Esme was talking to me about the way you guys grew up. She told me about reaching too soon for love with her first husband, because she was so desperate to find what she knew was out there…" She paused. "It's clear that the acrimonious home your parents raised you three in affected you all deeply. And *differently*. I'm not saying there aren't valid reasons for your concerns. I understand where you're coming from. But it seems criminal to allow your parents' and aunt's and uncle's mistakes, and your fear of repeating them, to deny you your greatest happiness."

"I already have my greatest happiness. Right here." He raised his arm, encircling the air around him. "This ranch. And your friendship. The rest, the sex…that's transitory. It makes people do things, promise things, that aren't right for them, because in the moment, they're so consumed by physical need they can't think straight."

"Have you ever, once, promised anyone anything during sex?"

His tension grew. "No." Because he'd specifically made it a point to say what had to be said before he ever got to that point with a woman. Including her.

And yet…somehow, there he was.

"You have no guarantee that it will turn bad between us, Asa. We can talk things out…just like we are doing right now. We care about the same things—the ranch, the people in our lives. We honor family. I'm so in love with you that I can't fathom life without you. And you've shown me over and over that you care enough about me to keep my feelings in the mix, too. We wouldn't be having this conversation otherwise."

He heard all her words. But the *I'm so in love with you* part was what kept reverberating through him.

She couldn't be. And if she was, then it was up to him to save them.

"There've been a lot of couples who've made it work for a lifetime, Asa. We might very well be one of them.

All I'm asking is that you give us the chance to have it all. A real family. Maybe even kids someday."

Kids. Like Esme's little guys. A flash of himself at the fishing pond, with little four-year-old Jimmy putting his hand trustingly in Asa's hit him. Along with his thought of having a son of his own someday.

But not at the risk of making an eventual enemy out of Lily.

"Kids are one of the top reasons married couples fight." Money and sex were the other two. He'd looked it up. "Because of the strong emotions they bring." Just like the other two. She was making his point for him and didn't even seem to grasp that.

"People fight, Asa. There's a difference between healthy disagreements, and the kind of acrimonious dissension you grew up with."

When he opened his mouth, she held up a hand and said, "Look, how about we just try it for the six months we agreed to stay married. I'll know, going in, that it's only a trial. If it doesn't work, we'll divorce as planned and be friends only…"

"But you knew going in that the marriage was going to be platonic and in name only." And there she was less than a month later, trying to change the whole agreement on him.

"But we both broke that original agreement, mutually, on our wedding night. And then again downstairs on the couch. And yesterday…out in the woods…"

His mind immediately shot to—and away from—that memory. It was one he knew he couldn't dwell on.

"I'm not trying to make you someone you aren't, Asa. If, after trying this, you still feel as strongly about not taking a chance on a real marriage, then I will respect that choice and still love you with all my heart. As forever friends. All

I'm asking is for you to open your mind to the possibility of something *more*, and give us a shot."

For a second there, he thought about it. Seriously wanted to consider the idea.

But, though she had good talking points, he told his truth. "It's not just about the sex, Lily. It's about being free to walk away." He didn't know how to articulate what raged inside him, but he did his best. "That's what always brings you back, knowing that when you need a breather, you have the ability to walk away. In a marriage, you can't do that. In a marriage, you're promising *not* to walk away. And that puts chains around you. Chains made of expectations. And when the chains get too tight, you go into fight mode. It's a natural reaction. Instinct." Which was something no amount of talking, or even wanting, could change.

He knew the second she gave up. Her face flattened. Became one he recognized from his first months of knowing her. The face she gave to the world.

Hiding herself behind it.

And a part of him was relieved to have that friend back. The rest of him just ached.

CHAPTER NINETEEN

LILY HADN'T PLANNED a worst-case scenario.

She'd expected stipulations and conditions. But not Asa's point blank refusal to even attempt to see if they could make a real marriage work.

And his response to her mention of having kids with him?

That children were one of the top three reasons couples fought?

His definition of fighting between married couples, and hers, were vastly different. She'd lived in enough homes to get the gist of the whole husband and wife dynamic. Yes, there were definitely arguments. Strong disagreements, even, like when Sandy and Tom, her twelfth-year parents, had had to give her up to move to Wisconsin where he'd had a tremendous job offer. One that would allow them to afford lessons and opportunities for their own kids, including sending them to college. She hadn't been meant to overhear that particular argument, but it was one she'd never forgotten.

And what she'd learned was that when people truly loved each other, were honestly and wholeheartedly committed to each other, that love showed them each other when push came to shove. And, seeing each other, instead of just themselves, helped them to find what was best for both. And for their family.

Lily stood there, in her ridiculously revealing piece of cheap lingerie, and felt the cold, hard truth settle over her.

The problem between her and Asa was that they were not both wholeheartedly devoted to each other. She was fully committed to loving him forever. Had accepted that he was a piece of her heart and soul.

But to him, no matter how good things might be between them in bed, she was and always would be his freckled friend in the GreatStore uniform.

In his own way, whether he realized it or not, that was the truth he'd been trying to tell her all along.

She didn't blame him. She couldn't. After all, he could no more help how he felt than she could.

And he'd tried so hard to spare her. Had given her every piece of her heart's desire that he had to give.

But it wasn't enough.

And *that* was her truth.

She'd seen that look on her mother's face. The pure joy involved in pushing her babies in a stroller. She might not ever have that, but she could no longer go through life without giving it her all. Her parents would expect that of her.

And she, an offspring of them, owed it to them, to honor the too shortness of their lives, by making the most of every moment of her own.

Lifting her chin, she looked the love of her life straight in the eye and said, "I can't do it, Asa. I can't stay in the house, sleeping down the hall from you, sharing groceries and furniture with you, knowing that there's no chance of us ever being a real family together." Instead of losing air due to a tight chest as she spoke, she found herself breathing more freely. Her voice growing stronger as self-honesty poured out of her. "I'll honor our agreement. I'll attend the party tomorrow night and pretend. I'll stay married to you for six months, and even live on the ranch, in the cabin you used to occupy. But that's it. I'm going to sign the ranch over to you this week. And when the six months is done, so am I. Here. And, maybe, with you."

She faltered there. Felt her throat thicken, but said, "If I can be happy meeting you at the Corral for drinks now and then, okay. But if not..." She shook her head and then settled her gaze straight on his again. "I want a real marriage, Asa. I want children. A home. I deserve a family of my own. And I don't think I'll ever find that as long as my heart is close to you."

Turning her nearly naked fanny on him, she held her head high, her shoulders straight, and walked out of his room.

In her heart, she'd just walked out of his life.

ASA HELD HIS ground as Lily walked out. Told himself that she'd calm down. Change her mind. He went to bed. Even slept some. On and off.

In between bouts of waking up, having reality and panic hit him simultaneously, it took a great deal of effort to fall back to sleep.

Fortunately, by the time he was out of the shower Saturday morning, he was feeling better. On top of the fear and confident that everything would work itself out.

It always did.

Then he saw Lily's note.

She'd be taking care of the office for him in the short go, but he needed to be looking for a full-time employee to assume the duties as soon as possible.

He told himself it was just the disappointment and hurt feelings talking, that when a little time passed, she'd still want to work at the farm—not because of him, but because of her own attachment to the place. Because it was as much her dream to own the dude ranch as it was his.

And then he saw the Horse For Sale sign tacked up to the community bulletin board outside the public restrooms and showers by the pool in the cabin neighborhood.

Laura?

She was selling Laura?

Staring at the picture of the horse he'd bought for Lily, the horse he knew for certain she loved, he could no longer talk sense into emotions that were roiling through him.

She was removing Asa, and things associated with him, from her life in an effort to take back ownership of her heart and move on to a future that held her dreams.

To find her heart's greatest desire.

A family of her own.

Tearing down the sign—he'd buy the horse if he had to—Asa raced his four-wheeler back up to the office area, looking for Lily. Her four-wheeler was parked in its usual spot. As was her car.

He breathed a sigh of relief until he strode into the office, intending to drop the wadded up For Sale sign on her desk, to meet her calm, clear gaze, and hear, "Sorry for the note."

Finally. She'd calmed down. Was coming around.

Shoving the wadded-up paper into his back pocket, uncaring that there was hardly space for it, he accepted her apology with an, "That's okay."

"I just wasn't sure I'd see you this morning, and I want to give you all the time you need to find a replacement for me."

What?

Getting up from her desk, she let him know that ranch business was all in line for the day. Their part-time desk help was already on-site. And finished with, "I'm going upstairs now to pack my things. I'll be moving into the cabin before we head to the party tonight. What time do you want to meet up to head in?"

"Head in?" His head was spinning.

"We'll need to drive together tonight," she said, sounding like a waitress serving a customer. "To keep up appearances."

Right. Their wedding celebration.

"Six," he told her robotically. Not even sure what time they were supposed to be there.

"Okay. I'll meet you right here," she said then, and moving by him, leaving a good two yards between them, she walked out on him.

Again.

Asa turned to go after her. Took a couple of fast steps... to do what? *Say* what?

Frustrated, unable to find anything that sounded good to him, he kept walking fast. Just not after Lily. He got into his truck and drove into town. Not bothering with things like speed limits and turn signals.

Partially because there was no one else around who could be hurt by his actions.

But as soon as he hit city limits, he wanted to turn around and go back.

To what?

Instead he went to the park. The place he'd gone the night after he'd walked out after sex. Not only was it too early in the day for beer but things like alcohol and mouthing off didn't work when it came to his feelings for Lily.

He'd never had a friend like her. One who'd be missed so much when he moved on that he'd think twice about going.

He walked around, mostly kicking rocks, feeling more pent up than ever, and headed back to his truck.

"Asa!" Spinning, he saw his great-aunt Freya heading toward him from across the street.

And thought about how lucky he was. Living his dream because of the older woman's generosity.

He greeted her with a smile. Asked how she was doing. Then walked with her toward his truck.

"You coming to the party tonight?" he murmured.

"I wouldn't miss it." Her words sounded strong. Certain. But she was frowning at him. "Except that, why do I get the feeling you're not looking forward to it as much as I am?"

It was almost as though she knew...

Guilt gnawed at him. Freya had opened her heart to him and his siblings and cousins, had moved to town to be near them, to watch them enjoy their inheritances, and he'd cheated to use her money to buy his ranch.

"I screwed up, that's why," he told her. Somehow thinking that if he owned up to the original wrongdoing, it would somehow be able to right the mess he'd made of his friendship with Lily.

Freya didn't seem fazed. "I've lived a long time and have seen a lot of wrong turns in my life. Usually turns out there are ways to right them." They'd slowed to a stop on the sidewalk in front of his truck.

"Not this one." He was working up the words to tell her the truth, and when he opened his mouth to say them what came out was, "I lost Lily."

"You *what*?" the woman's near screech didn't sound at all kind or supportive.

"The way I grew up... I can't do a repeat. I told her so, thinking she understood, but she didn't. I love her, Aunt Freya. I told her that, I just..." And there it came. The news about the fake marriage, fashioned to get Val Hensen to sell him the farm. He and Lily writing their own wedding vows, pledging to be friends forever. Her telling him she was in love with him.

And confessed his own response, too. Almost word for word.

What a pitiful picture he made. Big tough cowboy that he was, in his jeans and tough boots, big shoulders casting shadows on the older, more frail woman in front of him—whining to her like a little kid.

The silence between them, when he finally stopped was a relief. He waited for her castigation. And probably her demands that he tell Val Hensen what he did and give her the right to void the sale of the Chatelaine Dude Ranch. For the Fortune good name if nothing else.

He was almost ready to hear it, too, when she opened her mouth. "It's very clear to me that you love Lily."

Not at all what he'd been expecting, and so the truth popped out. "Of course, I do. She's my best friend."

Freya's headshake made him frown.

"No, not just as a friend. As a woman. A wife. As a life and love partner."

Those last four words…struck him. A punch to the gut.

"Go get your woman, Asa. Make it right. Before tonight so you all can enjoy your wedding celebration for real."

Life and love partner. Exactly. Life and love best friend. Life and love partner.

That's what Lily had been trying to tell him. They were already there. Living it. Except that he'd been too obstinate to see it.

Marriage. Husband. Wife. They were words. It was the people, their actions, and how they felt, that made them successful ventures, who gave their hearts and souls to the roles they'd vowed to honor for life.

And the chains…partners gave each other the freedom

to express their needs. They listened with a need to understand. Not to change the other.

Just as he and Lily had done from the beginning.

Life and Love Partner.

Oh, God. What had he done? He had to get to her...

Bending, he gave the older woman a hug, and then, with barely a thank-you, jumped in his truck, backed up and sped out of town.

BEFORE SHE COULD think about packing, Lily had to wash her sheets and pillowcases. She'd soaked the latter with tears during the night.

And again that morning.

She had to be done crying. And figured, the clean sheets would signify the tears' final demise.

Lily had no idea what she was going to do with herself once the marriage ended. But at least she'd have some financial resources. She was going to hold Asa to his monetary agreement with her, just as he was holding her to the friendship only part of their deal.

The thought of leaving town had occurred to her. She could go to college somewhere. Get far away from Asa, at least long enough to get him out of her system.

But Chatelaine was her home. The town was her family.

And no way could she lose her sisters again, after finally having them in her life. Tabitha was going to need help with her little guys as they started walking and getting into things. And Haley...she needed someone to remind her that life was more than unanswered questions. At least if she wanted to find love for herself.

Maybe Lily had been too hasty, quitting her job at the ranch. She loved the work.

And what better way to get over a man than to have

him for a boss? To work for him every day and, be around enough to see the women coming in and out of his life.

Maybe she'd even end up falling for whoever he hired as a new ranch hand.

When that thought brought more tears right as Lily was folding her newly cleaned sheets, she sniffled and kept folding.

Then, leaving packing for another time, she took Max with her down to the barn and went to find Laura.

· The dog needed something besides tears and a maudlin woman for company. She'd hugged him plenty, but had barely spoken to him since she'd returned to her room the night before. There was just no way she could find words for the chaos going on inside of her.

With Laura it was different. The mare was a female. And didn't need words.

She was also named after the woman Lily needed so desperately in the horrible aftermath of her botched bedroom encounter with Asa. Maybe if she'd had a woman who'd been through the ups and downs of adult romantic relationships, guiding her through every phase of her journey into womanhood, she'd have made different choices the night before.

Wouldn't have pushed Asa so far into a corner that he'd had to fight his way out.

Up on the horse, she rode for a while, feeling somewhat better as she breathed the fresh air, enjoyed the blue skies and sunshine. She didn't purposely head for the family trail with the notable jog around an old oak tree, but felt a little less alone when she saw it ahead of her.

And when she stopped at the curve, sitting atop her horse close enough to the tree to touch it, she knew it was right that she'd come to her mother as she, once again, saw her life heading into another rebirth.

She knew how to do it—how to re-create her home life. How to forge a place for herself wherever she ended up. And thankfully, she now had the money to choose that home for herself.

Of course, it would have to be a small place. She wasn't ever going to be rich. And maybe she'd have to take out a mortgage to finish it. If she built new.

But...

Laura's head lifted, turned back toward the trail they'd come down, snorted.

And then Lily heard it, too.

Horse hooves. Heading their way.

Putting a hostess smile on her face, expecting to see Jack, one of their ranch hands, with a guest rider, she felt her whole being slide into nothingness as Asa and Major appeared instead. Two strong male beauties. The one brought her a sense of comraderie. Acceptance. Understanding.

And the other...the muscled cowboy on top of the horse...looking so ruggedly handsome...ripped her heart a little more.

"Jack told me he saw you head this way," he said, as though he had every right to seek her out in her private time.

She nodded. Didn't want to fight with him.

Ever.

She loved him. Flaws and all.

Understood him.

She just couldn't be *in love* with him anymore.

When he rode Major right up to her, within a foot, she sat straight. Didn't flinch. Or give in to the temptation to give her mare's sides a slight nudge and gallop off with her into the sunshine.

He climbed down from the saddle. Then with a gentle tap of his hand to Major's front paw said, "Back."

Lily watched, starting to wonder if the man had been drinking.

She saw Major bow—one front leg bent under him as he went down—and hold the position. Lily was so busy watching the horse, it took her a second to realize that Asa had done the same. And was staring up at her.

"Lily Perry Fortune, will you please give me a chance to take that chance with you that you offered last night, minus the six-month getaway clause?"

Her heart pounding, she stared down at him.

"Asa? What are you doing?"

"I'm begging," he said, as though it was obvious. "I love you, Lily. Like a man loves a woman. You saw it. I think I did, too. I just couldn't get past my own deeply ingrained barriers to acknowledge what was right in front of me."

Tears sprang to her eyes again. She didn't bother to blink them away. After the night before, she hardly felt they mattered. "This is because I'm quitting, right?" she asked. "You want me to stay here on the ranch with you."

"I do want that, yes. But that's not why…"

Was he going to shatter her heart completely before he let her go? "Don't do this, Asa, please?"

"I have to, Lily. I love you."

He'd said the words to her before. They didn't change anything.

Major stood up. Asa did not.

"I want you in my home, in my bed, and to have my children."

She could hardly breathe through the tightness in her chest. Was shaking in her saddle. "Don't, Asa. It's not what you really want. Not what you believe in. Which means it will probably end up just like you fear it will."

He shook his head. "You're wrong."

She wanted so badly to believe him, she almost slid down off her horse to throw herself in his arms. But she couldn't fool herself anymore.

She'd never find her dreams that way.

"What changed between last night and today?" she asked him, finding the strength to resist him.

"Four words," he said, and for a second there, she went back to thinking he'd been drinking. Though, even that was so out of character it was hard to believe. Asa didn't drink during the day unless there was some kind of party, and he never drank to the point of talking out of his head.

"Four words?" she prompted when she could.

"Life. And. Love. Partner." He said each word like it was its own sentence. And then, "That's when I got it. Marriage, husband, wife...those words, what they stand for in my mind, scare the hell out of me. But I am so in love with you, Lily, that the thought of losing you is making me want to sell the farm. Will you please be my life and love partner until death do us part, and beyond that, too?"

"Life and love partner," she repeated, her heart tumbling over itself in fear. On a race to a joy she couldn't let herself grasp.

"Aunt Freya... I told her what I'd done, that I'd lost you and she said those words. They clicked, Lil. They honest to God clicked. Because they described us exactly. It's what you said. We're partners who always consider each other's needs as well as our own. A person is only trapped if he can't get out, and as along as he is out, being heard..." He stopped, shook his head, as though he was getting too much to fast. "Please, please, will you be my life and love partner?"

With tears streaming down her face, Lily slid down off her horse, and would have fallen if her husband hadn't stood and caught her up in his arms, lifting her feet up off the ground with the exuberance and strength of his hug.

"I love you, Asa Fortune, and I'll very happily and sincerely be your life and love partner until death do us part and beyond," she promised against his neck, right by his ear.

He kissed her then, slowly lowering her feet to the path.

And as she kissed him back, she knew her feet were never going to touch the earth in quite the same way ever again.

Her step would be lighter because she wasn't walking alone.

No matter what the future brought them, she and Asa would live it together, until death and beyond.

Just like her mother's love had continued to live in Lily, even when Lily had refused to think about her.

Because love carried that much power.

THE PARTY WAS in full swing. With Lily in a sexy white blouse and black jeans, and him in his own white shirt and black jeans, they had walked in holding hands, to a roar of cheers and flying confetti. They'd made their rounds, taken ribbing and heartfelt congratulations, had fed each other cake, danced their wedding dance alone in front of everyone, and toasted champagne.

The pile of gifts was overwhelming and wonderful—mostly because of the look of awe on Lily's face when she'd seen them—and were being sent to the ranch for opening later.

She'd asked him for a few minutes alone with her sisters, and while Asa visited with everyone around him, he missed her. Had hardly been able to leave her side all day—not because anyone or anything was holding him there. Except his own desire to be close to his beautiful bride.

The need would dissipate to a more normal level of togetherness. He knew that.

Or, as Lily put it, faith in their togetherness would make it less necessary for them to be with each other every minute of the day.

He wasn't really buying it, though. It made sense to him that some life and love partners were just made to do life together—work and play.

As Lily had pointed out, the Hensens had done so.

And now he and Lily were carrying on their legacy.

When Val Hensen came up to him, giving him a warm hug, he hugged her back and said, "Thank you." He'd been thinking the words yet hadn't meant to say them out loud.

"You bought the ranch fair and square," she told him.

He shook his head, "No, thank you for forcing me to propose to and marry the love of my life," he told her.

And glanced up to see Lily, just approaching from the side of him. She'd heard his words. He could tell by the glow in her eyes.

She licked her lips. Just as she'd done out on the trail that afternoon, asking for a repeat of two afternoons before. And then again, after they'd moved her things into his bedroom. She licked her lips and he was lost.

"You trying to kill me here?" He leaned over to whisper in her ear, and then kissed her.

Longer and deeper than he probably should have in front of an entire town's worth of their family and friends.

The catcalls that rang out that time were mostly calls for the two of them to get out of there, and when he looked at Lily, and she nodded, he scooped her up into his arms and headed for the door.

They were almost outside when Tabitha and Haley appeared in front of them.

"You're a very lucky man," Tabitha told him, her eyes brimming with tears as she looked from him to her triplet in his arms.

"And a smart one, too," Haley added.

That was it, along with a glance that passed between the three sisters, speaking without words, messages he didn't need to know.

Messages that comforted him just the same.

Lily might have grown up without family of her own, but she'd spend the rest of her life swimming in it.

His. Hers. And theirs.

And, if he had any say in it, they'd start adding to it, too, as soon as nature gave them the chance.

He'd found his life and love partner.

And the dream he hadn't known to dream had found him.

* * * * *

Don't miss the stories in this mini series!

THE FORTUNES OF TEXAS: DIGGING FOR SECRETS

Follow the lives and loves of a complex family with a rich history and deep ties in the Lone Star State.

MILLS & BOON

Reunited With The Rancher
Anna Grace

MILLS & BOON

Anna Grace justifies her espresso addiction by writing fun, modern romance novels in the early-morning hours. Once the sun comes up, you can find her teaching high school history or outside with her adventure-loving husband. Anna is a mediocre rock climber, award-winning author, mum of two fun kids and snack enthusiast. She lives rurally in Oregon and travels to big cities whenever she gets the chance. Anna loves connecting with readers, and you can find her on social media and at her website, anna-grace-author.com.

Twitter: @AnnaEmilyGrace
IG: @AnnaGraceAuthor
Facebook: Anna Grace Author

Visit the Author Profile page
at millsandboon.com.au for more titles.

Dear Reader,

I'm so glad you've returned to Outcrop, Oregon, for Piper's story! The matchmaking city girl of the Wallace clan comes home to help her community, and winds up head over heels in love!

It's been years since Whit and Piper were rivals on the college debate team, but they still find plenty to argue about as they team up to help Whit run for office. Neither is ready for the complications of a relationship, but ready or not, this unstoppable duo can't stop love.

If you want to make my daughter mad, mention a romance where a successful businesswoman gives up her career for a small-town love interest. This is *not* that book. But how can Piper stay true to herself, while embracing the possibility of love?

It's hard to believe this is the final book in the Love, Oregon series! I'm so grateful to Dana Grimaldi, Katie Gowrie, Kathleen Scheibling and the team at Harlequin for embracing my debut miniseries with Harlequin Heartwarming.

Happy Reading!

Anna

DEDICATION

**For my daughter, Margaret Grace.
For the love of city adventures, good espresso,
just the right outfit and short-legged dogs.**

CHAPTER ONE

SHE WORE DESIGNER SUNGLASSES, gazillion-dollar jeans, and she held a long-bodied, short-legged dog wearing a hand-crocheted bonnet to make it look like a frog.

Whit would have recognized Piper Wallace anywhere.

She clipped across the parking lot of Eighty Local with the same speed and sense of purpose she'd had moving across the central quad at Oregon State University.

It wasn't exactly a surprise to see her. Whit had been working with her brother Ash for over a year now as part of the Central Oregon Ranching Federation. The Wallaces were key supporters in Whit's bid for county commissioner. But Piper's name rarely came up, and only when Ash or another member of the family was relating a funny story about the city-girl sister. Piper's brothers had no idea how central she'd been to his college experience. Their relationship had balanced on a knife's edge between friends and enemies, with the handle of that knife firmly in Piper's grasp.

And now she was headed straight for him.

What do you say when your college nemesis is charging across a gravel parking lot, in all likelihood heading to the same place you are? Did she even remember him, or that they'd been rivals on the debate team? He'd have to say hello at some point. It would be weird not to.

Piper stopped abruptly.

"Whitman Benton."

Her tone hadn't changed since college, either. She still managed to say his name in a way that felt like a cross between an accusation and a greeting.

He pulled his Stetson off and nodded. "Piper Wallace."

She readjusted the dog in her arms and glanced over her shoulder toward Main Street. "Thoughts on the emu mural?"

"I'm sorry?"

"There's a twenty-foot mural of Larry the emu squawking 'Welcome to Outcrop!' on the old press building, right as you pull into town."

"Yeah, I saw that—"

"So. I'm asking for your thoughts. Emu greeting, yea or nay?"

Whit stared at Piper. She'd always been beautiful, but had somehow grown more fully into her beauty. Her clothing was classic with a stylish edge. She'd cut her hair, the shiny brown and blond strands now barely skimming her shoulders. With age, her confident stance looked less defensive, more natural.

He finally shook his head. "Piper, it's been seven years since we've seen each other. The first thing we're going to discuss is an emu mural?"

She had shades on, but he knew she was rolling her eyes. "I'm sorry. What did you want to talk about?"

Whit gave an incredulous laugh. "Uh...nothing in particular. Normally, when you see someone from the past you say, 'Hello, how's it been, what are you up to these days?'"

"Oh, I was supposed to acknowledge the passing of time?" Piper shifted the dog again and held out a hand. Whit shook it and was immediately transported back to facing off against her before a debate, the same grin suggesting he had no idea what he was in for.

"Hi, Whit. Seven years, huh? Wow, time flies." She

pushed her sunglasses up onto her head, exposing wick-edly sharp brown eyes. "Did you see that emu mural?"

He glanced up at the bright blue sky, then back at his college hate-crush. "You haven't changed a bit, have you?"

She blinked at him, shocked. "Why would I change?"

Whit laughed, holding up both hands. "Okay, Piper. You win. I like the emu."

"Me too!" she said. "I wasn't sure at first. I'm very particular about public art, but I kind of love it."

Whit took a deep breath. Conversation with Piper could feel a little like bull riding; you had to just hang on for as long as you could.

"Did the new mural bring you here?" he asked. "Or are you on other business?"

"My family has a thing." She gestured at the events center behind Eighty Local, confirming his fears. The meeting he was heading into was stressful enough already. His campaign manager, Dan, and a very few select supporters were assembled to work out the mess he'd gotten himself into.

Was Piper the last person on earth he would have invited to this meeting? Maybe. No, his sister Jana would be worse. Piper was only the second to last person on earth he wanted here. And she was still talking about the emu.

"—but no one told me about the mural. I was driving into town and nearly hit a mule deer, I was so shocked. Larry's my nephew."

She continued her march toward Eighty Local, and now Whit was scrambling to keep up with her physically *and* conversationally. The whole situation felt like a surreal flashback to college, where she'd always been two steps ahead of him and slightly out of reach.

"That emu is your nephew?"

"Right. You remember my sister, Clara?"

Clara was the sweeter, more empathetic of the twins, the one most of the guys fell for. "Of course."

"Well, she married Jet Broughman. And he has all these emus, so they're *like* my nieces and nephews. But I just count Larry because he's the only one whose name I know. Ergo, my emu nephew. Do you have nieces and nephews? Or emus?"

Whit's eyebrow twitched. He rubbed the tense muscle with two fingers. If your family's painful rift keeps you from ever meeting your niece and nephew, do you actually have them?

"I'm not related to anything with feathers." Before she could speak again, he pointed to the improbably shaped dog. "Is this your only child?"

She laughed, then raised her brows, as though impressed that he'd made a joke. "Sadly, I'm dogless." She leaned down and brushed the dog's nose with her own, then spoke in something between a baby and a Muppet voice. "I'm just babysitting the good pupper for the summer."

The *good pupper* soaked up her words, then glared at him over her arms.

"I hear you're in Portland now," Whit said, wrestling things back to something approximating normal. He was a champion debater in college; he knew how to take the reins in a conversation.

"Yes. Best city ever. I couldn't love it more."

"What do you do there?"

"I'm a matchmaker. Clara and I started Love, Oregon out of college."

"A matchmaker? That's—" *dangerous* "—unusual. How's business?"

"Brisk. We knew there was a need, in this busy age of cell phones and social anxiety. But we had *no idea* how it was going to take off. We run a boutique service. We don't just set people up, we get them ready for a relationship and provide the tools they'll need to succeed."

"That's cool—"

"Are you single?"

Whit sputtered as all of his organs seemed to flip inside out. "Uh... I..." He stumbled for words, then let out a breath.

This was just what Piper did. She had a way of drawing you in and making you feel comfortable. Then she spun the tables and turned the chairs into hot seats. Whit was twenty-nine and fully capable of not getting caught up in her verbal gymnastics, or in her. He had important business ahead of him, this morning and over the next three months. There was no time to get caught off balance.

He stopped walking and looked down at Piper. "I am single. I'm not interested in a long-term relationship right now. But if I ever am, I'll remember to contact Love, Oregon."

This race for county commissioner was the battle of his life. It was one he intended to win, no matter what the polls currently said. There might be time for a relationship down the road, but right now he barely had time for breakfast, much less anything as complicated as love. Casual dating was fine, but the complexity of a long-term commitment would pull his focus away from the task at hand. Having witnessed the meltdown within his own family, he didn't have much faith in his ability to commit to anyone. Logically, he understood it was messed up, *he* was messed up. But this was not the time to dwell on the past, or future. Once he resolved the issues facing his community, then he could think about addressing personal issues.

Unfortunately, his casual dating had become a target for his opponent. But Whit's campaign manager had a plan and seemed to think they could bounce back from this smear campaign stronger than ever. Whit had his fingers crossed that whomever Dan asked to help with this situation was easygoing and calm about the whole thing.

"Okay, that makes *no* sense, but we're talking about you, so, par for the course." She gazed critically at his outfit, then focused on the hat he held. "Did you take over your family's ranch?"

How would she know that? Had Ash said something about him to Piper? Had she asked?

As though reading his mind, Piper gestured to his clothing. "You're wearing the dressed-up rancher uniform."

Whit looked down at his khakis and chambray shirt. *Right.* "Uh, yeah. I took over the family place a few years back. We're outside of Tumalo."

She grinned at him. "Ah yes, it's nice to live *outside* the city limits of Tumalo. I'm sure the crush of the other 499 residents can get to be a lot."

Whit's heart rate picked up, as it always did when he sparred with Piper. He raised an eyebrow and shot back, "I do appreciate the quiet of my ranch. Tumalo can get intense, especially when cars get backed up at the Pony Espresso stand."

"Pony Espresso?" Piper wrinkled her nose. "Please tell me there's not seriously a coffee cart called the Pony Espresso."

"I can't take it back now."

"End times are coming," she said, lifting the dog and looking in its face as she spoke in her baby-Muppet voice. "I can feel it."

Whit took a step in front of Piper and opened the door into the events center for her. End times would be here if he failed to win this campaign.

"Wait. Are you here for this whole awful commissioner situation?" she asked.

Whit kept his hand on the door, gazing at her. Did she not know he was running for the position? Her right eye narrowed slightly, and he realized he was staring at her, not answering her question.

"Yes."

She rolled her shoulders back. "Ash called and needs my help or something. I'm not super political these days, but it sounds like the current county commissioner is terrible. I'll help out wherever I can."

"Me too." Whit drew in a deep breath.

He needed all his strength for this coming meeting. Unfortunately, Piper Wallace had a habit of illuminating his every weakness.

PIPER HAD TO pass awfully close to Whit Benton as he held the door for her. He smelled the same, like standing in a pine grove fifteen minutes after a troop of Old Spice employees had been testing product. It wasn't a bad smell, but it *was* distinctive.

Yeah, he smelled the same, but he looked even better than he had in college. Not that she noticed. Or that it mattered.

But he did legitimately look good. He'd been working out.

In a way, she was glad he was here, as glad as anyone can be to unexpectedly run into their old nemesis from the debate team. It helped her redirect her angst and give her a worthy adversary. The vague fog of dissatisfaction and self-doubt she'd been floundering in for the past year was hard to fight head on. Whit was more straightforward, and at least in college, he'd always been up for an argument.

Plus, if he was here to help deal with the whole county commissioner thing, the opposition better watch out. Whit was fiercely brilliant. Even if he did frequent a place called Pony Espresso.

Piper stepped from the bright sunlight into the events center at Eighty Local, scanning the room with a show of defiance to mask her apprehension.

Her brother, Hunter, and his fiancée, Ani, were bringing food in from the main restaurant, laughing together at some secret joke. Hunter's twin, Bowman, stood patiently while his gorgeous doctor-wife, Maisy, inspected a cut on his arm that he'd probably gotten fighting a fire somewhere and never bothered to tell anyone about. Ash was talking with some guy Piper didn't recognize, his fingers intertwined with Violet's as she spoke to Ash's son, Jackson. And Jackson apparently had no respect for Piper's wishes. Her nephew had gone ahead and grown a foot taller and was going into his junior year this fall, despite her direct request to stop growing up so fast.

Piper felt an uncomfortable pressure behind her eyes as her gaze landed on Clara. Her sister and best friend in the world seemed to shine with light from within as she smiled up at her husband and their newborn baby. She was *so* happy.

Piper swallowed hard. It got worse every time she returned to her family. She was acutely aware of all she was missing, aware of how much she missed *them*.

She was aware of being different.

Piper couldn't love her siblings more, and the noisy cocoon of being home. But she was a city girl. She couldn't remember not loving the shuffle and energy of busy streets. She loved her downtown loft, her morning cappuccino at the corner shop, all the well-behaved little puppies of her Pearl District neighborhood.

But while she was off enjoying the hum of the city, everyone was moving on back home. Their lives were interconnected: working together, running into each other everywhere, even living on the same property in the case of her brothers. She had to make do with instant messaging and trips home twice a month. If she ever asked her family members to come visit her, they would. But it always made more sense for her to come here, where one person was inconvenienced by the trip, rather than the whole family.

She was the odd duck who'd somehow flown off course and wound up living apart from the rest of the flock. When she was dating Liam, she assumed they'd get married. Then she and her siblings would at least be in the same stage of life together, even if those lives were dramatically different. But *that* wasn't happening. Liam had dumped her over an argument about breakfast foods. Is there anything worse than being dumped by someone you were only settling for in the first place?

The foggy sadness started to expand behind her rib cage. Piper focused on her sister's happiness, determined to stop the self-doubt before it could take root. Clara's smile shone as her son gripped her pinky finger, pulling it toward his mouth.

As though she could feel her watching, which she probably could, Clara turned suddenly. *"Piper!"*

Piper plastered on a bright smile and held out one arm as Clara rushed her, and then her sister was hugging her—and the dog—tight.

"Who's this friend?" Clara asked, bending down to speak to the dachshund. "Oh, she has a frog hat! She's a frog-dog! So cute!!"

"This is Bernice. I'm babysitting for two months." Piper glanced around. "Speaking of babies, I hope Jet's not planning on hogging Bobby all day."

"Oh, always."

Piper glanced over to see Jet with the tiny infant in his

arms. He was now deep in conversation with Whit. Super weird. How did Jet know Whit?

"Is everyone here because of the county commissioner thing?" Piper asked. The crowd included her siblings and a handful of others, fewer than twenty total. She couldn't exactly remember what Ash had said on the phone. Just that there was some disaster, and he needed her help. Piper would never admit to Ash, or anyone else, how good it felt to be needed.

Clara's face grew serious. "It's really bad. Thank you for coming."

"Of course."

Clara wound her fingers through Piper's and kissed her cheek. "You are literally the best."

"No, you're the best."

"Don't argue with me."

"I'm stating facts. Speaking of which, it is a fact that it's been a week and a half since I've held my nephew."

Clara grinned then waved her husband over.

"Okay, Jet! Hi," Piper called. She held out her free hand. "Baby, please."

Clara's husband gave her an indulgent smile. As always, he was happy to see her, reluctant to give up his son.

At this point, the rest of the family caught on to her presence, and the trepidation began to evaporate then vanished entirely. There were hugs, as brothers and their significant others came at her from all angles. Bowman pulled out one of the plush benches, and Piper settled Bernice next to her and patted the other side for her seventeen-year-old nephew, Jackson, to sit. She quizzed him about his friends and summer football practice as she opened her arms for the newest family member, Bobby. Clara's newborn gazed up at her then yawned.

He was an unbelievable miracle.

Jackson, a full head taller than he'd been six months ago, grinned at her. Also an unbelievable miracle, and one that seriously needed to stop growing.

"Literally the two best nephews in the world," Piper declared.

"What about Larry?" Whit asked from where he was setting up a computer and projector.

Piper considered this. "I like that emu, but to be considered a best he'd have to be more…"

"Human?" Ash guessed.

"Well-groomed, I was going to say."

Piper turned back to Jackson, who was holding out his finger for Bobby to grip. "He's gonna play receiver," Jackson predicted.

"What do the receivers do again?" Piper asked.

Jackson groaned. "Aunt Piper, we've been over this a million times."

Piper started to respond, but the guy Ash had been talking with was glaring at her. She narrowed her right eye and glared right back. "Is something wrong?"

"Are you settled?" he asked, with an awful lot of sarcasm for someone who wasn't a family member.

"Yeah." She gestured to Jackson and Bernice with the baby. "I am."

"Then maybe we should start the meeting?"

"Sure?" Piper instinctively glanced at Whit. He repressed a smile. "What? Meet away. I'm just trying to be a good aunt over here."

Jackson patted her shoulder. "You're always a good aunt."

The grumpy man stalked to the raised dais, where Whit remained with the computer.

"I don't need to thank you all for coming today. I know this is top priority for everyone. We're here because Marc

Holt as county commissioner threatens our way of life."
The man glanced at Whit, then moved to the computer and
projector setup. "Do you want to get people up to speed on
where we are, then I can go over the campaign strategies?"

"Sounds good, Dan." Whit widened his stance and
clasped his hands behind him, sending a flood of nostal-
gia through Piper. It was almost like she hadn't known
she'd missed those days of college debate until now. She
and Whit had been on the same team, but bitter rivals,
competing for spots in tournaments. More than once, their
coach had required them to work together, which generally resulted in a near-death experience for the two of
them, and a win.

"Marc Holt was elected as county commissioner four
years ago. He's from out of state but ran a good campaign
and promoted himself as being in favor of small businesses
and family farming operations. During his tenure in office,
he's been popular. He meets with constituents regularly
and has important friends. But his policies are decidedly
anti-family business. He's in favor of raising taxes on any
land holding under 10,000 acres. He's consistently moved
against protection of wildlife and recently proposed guide-
lines that would make it prohibitively expensive to practice
the modern, sustainable ranching techniques that Outcrop
has pioneered in the area. This alone would be enough for
us to run a candidate against him."

Piper ran her finger across her littlest nephew's cheek.
Bernice nestled closer, trying to help her care for the baby.

"But that was before we learned about Hummingbird
Ranch." Whit clicked a button on the computer, and an
aerial view of Deschutes County appeared, crisscrossed
with lines and numbers. "Backers from New Jersey have
proposed building a community of luxury estates—second and third homes for people who want to own multi-

ple vacation properties. It would divert water from local ranches, and all the infrastructure would be funded by property taxes levied on year-round residents. You'll see in this illustration that nearly all the farm and ranching land surrounding Outcrop is included in the project. If Hummingbird Ranch is approved, Holt will do whatever he can to force local owners to sell. That includes impeding business, higher taxes and the creation of new, restrictive building codes."

"I'm sorry." Piper raised her hand but kept talking without being acknowledged. "What does that mean exactly?"

"It means that Jet's organic ranching business will effectively become illegal," Clara said.

Hunter gazed back at her. "It means the taxes on Eighty Local will double within the year."

Bowman gripped his wife's hand, then gave Piper a sad smile. "It means I can't build a house for Maisy and me out by Fort Rock. There's a policy that prohibits building a second home on land with one established residence already."

"What? This is…no. This is a no. You can't even build a house on our property?"

"Not if Marc Holt has his way. The idea is to make it hard for families to hold on to their land, so that over time we all sell out to Hummingbird Ranch," Ash said.

Piper bristled. Bernice bristled beside her. "So, what are we doing about it?"

Ash answered, "Whit here is running against Marc."

"You are?" Whit flexed his brow, then nodded at Piper as though this weren't optimal. It was the *best* news. "Okay then, that's that. Whit will win. He's, like, a local rancher who's smart and good at arguing. What are we worried about?"

Whit let out a breath. Dan put a hand on his shoulder and said, "It's not your fault."

Whit shrugged in silent disagreement. "My fault or not, I have to fix it. Guess we should play the ad?"

Dan addressed the group again. "This advertisement will air Thursday. It was sent to us as a courtesy by the Holt campaign."

"More like a threat," Whit mumbled.

He pressed a key on the computer, and a commercial played on the screen.

"Who is Whit Benton?" the deep, suspicious voice one only hears in political ads boomed. It showed a picture of Whit at a backyard barbecue, holding a beer and smiling as though maybe it wasn't his first beer of the evening. "He wants you to think he's a local rancher."

"Isn't he a local rancher?" Piper asked Clara.

"Yep. And he has the audacity to want people to think that."

The commercial flipped to a picture showing Whit floating in an inner tube on the Deschutes River, laughing with a group of people. Okay, he'd *definitely* been working out. And sure, this might not be the top "Elect me!" photograph, but tubing on the Deschutes was legal. And fun.

Suspicious announcer man continued, "Who is he, really?"

Creepy music played as the commercial ran through a number of pictures of Whit, each with a different woman: out to dinner, playing golf, skiing, having coffee, sipping martinis, a sepia filter making something like an innocuous golf date look seedy.

"Someone's been busy," Piper muttered.

"You're one to talk," Hunter shot back.

Piper opened her mouth to argue, then shut it. Hunter was right. She'd been on a streak of revenge dating since Liam dumped her. She wasn't in a strong position to judge.

"Whit Benton is twenty-nine years old. He's never held political office. He doesn't even have a real job."

The room reacted strongly. Piper's anger built. When Ash asked for her help with the county commissioner election, she hadn't realized the situation was so dire.

The music changed, and a squeaky-clean couple in their midsixties appeared on the screen, walking through a field, surrounded by a passel of matching grandchildren. The announcer lost the suspicious tone as he went on to talk about Holt's experience and credibility.

"Okay, Marc Holt is gross." Piper scratched Bernice under the chin and spoke to the dog, "He's a gross, yucky man."

"Totally gross," Clara agreed.

"And his wife's hair?"

"Inexcusable."

"This guy cannot win," Piper said. "Not on my watch. What can I do?"

Dan cleared his throat and looked at Ash. Ash exhaled then nodded.

All in all, it seemed uncharacteristically ominous.

"What?" she asked.

The room stilled. Everyone seemed to know what was up. She glanced at Whit for answers, but that guy looked stunned.

"Wait." Whit's eyes were wide as he looked first at Dan, then at Ash and finally at Piper. *"Her?"*

OKAY, WHIT WAS man enough to admit he was still a little bit afraid of Piper Wallace. And that fear was completely justified.

"What do you mean, 'Wait, her'?" Piper asked. "'Wait, her' what?"

"Piper, I need you to listen to me," Ash spoke calmly.

Dan shook his head in frustration. "I don't think she's gonna work at all."

Piper turned on Dan, baby still in her arms, frog-dog giving a throaty growl next to her. "Not gonna work for what?"

Ash stepped in front of his sister like she was an unruly colt, then he knelt down to look in her eyes. Whit could see why the guy was so successful with horses. "We need someone to act as Whit's long-term girlfriend, just for the next few months until the election is over. We need to project a new image for Whit."

"Holt has him looking like a frat boy," Dan said.

"That couldn't be more wrong," Piper said. "Whit never stepped foot in a frat. He was too busy trying to steal my library cubicle."

"That cubicle didn't belong to you."

"But it was my favorite."

Dan shook his head. "Ash, this *isn't* going to work"

"This—" Piper gestured between herself and Whit "—doesn't *need* to work. He's obviously capable of getting a date on his own."

Whit stepped forward, desperate to get the situation back under control. "Piper, the problem isn't me getting a date. We're taking on a ruthless man who will do anything to win. There's a lot of money at stake for the backers of Hummingbird Ranch. I have to present an irreproachable image. I can't be criticized for anything."

"Then keep your shirt on the next time you go tubing."

Whit shook his head. "Wow, Piper." He sighed. She hadn't changed a bit. He turned to Dan. "You're right. She's not gonna work. Piper, if I'd had any idea Ash was thinking of you, I'd never have gone along with it."

Piper bristled. "What's wrong with me? I mean, I don't want to do this, but I'd make a fine fake girlfriend."

Whit put his hands in his pockets and studied his boots. Then he looked up at Piper and fired off the most obvious misgiving. "Well, to begin with, you're a matchmaker. I thought they were setting me up with a professional woman."

A groan escaped from the Wallace family, as though he'd simultaneously sucker punched the entire clan.

"I'm sorry." Whit raised a hand. "I didn't mean matchmaking isn't a profession. I just assumed he meant a lawyer or something."

Piper rolled her eyes. "My apologies for making an excellent living helping others."

Whit widened his stance. He might not be perfect, but he was a good man and was willing to sacrifice everything for his community. Piper didn't get to make him feel bad. And if he'd learned one thing in college, it was how to argue against her. "Then there's just you."

"Me?"

"You're not exactly a rancher's girlfriend. I mean…" He gestured vaguely. "You live in Portland. You're wearing what I assume are designer clothes. You're carrying a dachshund in a frog hat. No woman on a ranch would ever have such a ridiculous dog."

Piper's jaw dropped. She looked at Clara then Ash's fiancée, Violet, then the other women in the room.

"Oh my God, *you're* a ridiculous dog." She turned to Ash. "I can understand now why someone has to pretend to date him."

Whit shook his head, unable to keep himself from arguing. She'd always lit this spark in him that made him want to debate whatever she was saying. "Come on, Piper. What even is that thing? Its body is a foot long, it's got stubby little legs. You must be overfeeding it because its belly practically drags on the ground."

Piper's eyes flashed. "She's pregnant."

Whit eyed the grumpy, suspicious dog. "That *cannot* be comfortable."

"Are you body-shaming a dog?"

"I'm not body-shaming it. I'm saying it looks like someone took all the spare dog parts lying around and made an improbable creature just to laugh at it."

"Maybe she thinks your legs are too long. Maybe she looks at you and feels sorry that your momma put you in a silly hat."

"It looks like a *frog*."

"That's the whole point! It's cute." She eyed him. "And you're really not one to be criticizing anyone's outfit. Hello, non-ironic khaki pants?"

Whit massaged the twitch in his temple, muttering to himself, "It all sounded so simple when Dan suggested it."

This was bad. He needed to come back looking strong and responsible after the smear campaign. Now he felt like he might as well be wearing a hand-crocheted frog bonnet himself.

"Hey, Piper?" Bowman, the least voluble of the Wallace siblings, spoke quietly. "I know you hate anything that's inauthentic, and pretending to be in love with someone goes against everything you stand for." He looked up at the ceiling then back at Piper. "But Whit's a good guy. Holt's gonna be hard to beat. We wouldn't ask you to do this if we didn't think it was necessary." He smiled at her, and Whit noticed for the first time that he had a small, slightly off-center gap between his front teeth. "Plus, it might be kinda fun for you. Outsmarting Holt. If anyone can do it, it's you."

Piper shifted. Bobby stretched and fussed briefly in her arms. She stood and paced with the baby, easily settling him.

"How come it has to be a pretend girlfriend? Clara and I could match him up with someone he'd actually like." She glanced at Clara and raised her eyebrows.

Clara started to respond positively, but Whit interrupted her, "I can't. This campaign takes everything I have. I'm not great with relationships, as evidenced by the video." He met Piper's gaze. "When this campaign is over, I promise you, I'll figure out what my problem is. I might even hire Clara to help me figure it out. But right now, I need someone I'm not gonna offend when I don't call twice a day or when I beg off from commitments because I have too much work to do. I have to be selfish with my time right now to win this election."

Piper studied him for a long moment. Then she did the one thing he never had been able to resist. She smiled, a real smile, eyes lit up, dimples flexing in her cheeks. "You're too selfish for a real girlfriend?"

Whit nodded. "That's right."

Her smile only grew, like she knew what it was to be too self-involved to commit to anyone else. "*That* I can understand. I'm in." She turned to Dan. "When's our first date?"

CHAPTER TWO

PIPER PUT HER car in Park halfway up the private road to Whit's house. His cattle gazed at her from their pasture, slowly chewing their cud as they blinked their big eyes with moderate interest. Piper pulled out her phone and texted her sister.

Please remind me why I'm doing this.

Bubbles popped up immediately, as though Clara had been waiting at her phone to offer encouragement.

Because Whit needs help to win this campaign, and you are uniquely suited to the task.

That's too selfless and aspirational, Piper texted back. Give me a better reason.

It took a little longer for Clara's text to appear this time, but she finally came through.

Because if Marc Holt wins, Bowman won't be able to build a house on our property. He and Maisy will live in the bunkhouse forever, and we'll never get to redecorate it.

Yes! Piper texted back. That I can fight for.

Keep your eyes on the ultimate goal.

Piper stamped a heart on the text and continued up the drive. She crested the hill to find Whit pacing on the long veranda of a midcentury modern home. He offered a curt wave as she parked. He wasn't any more comfortable with this get-to-re-know-you session than she was.

Bernice perked up from her seat next to Piper and growled, signifying that none of them wanted to be here.

After the meeting the day before, Piper, her fake boyfriend and his campaign manager had hashed out a plan. The ad campaign aired on Thursday. They had to head it off by changing their social media status today, then they would go on a series of very public dates, starting with the Outcrop Rodeo on Friday night.

But before they could do any of that, they needed to learn a little about each other, take selfies to post and lay the ground rules for pretending to be in a loving, committed relationship.

Piper took a deep breath, opened the car door and hauled herself out. Bernice followed, sniffing carefully for any problems.

"Good morning." Whit nodded to Piper and bent down to greet Bernice. The dachshund eyed him, then sniffed her way around him.

Piper pulled off her sunglasses. "This is your home?"

"Yep."

"It's nice." She wasn't sure what she'd been expecting, but it wasn't this. The structure stretched out along the crest of a hill, a deep veranda offering spectacular views.

Okay, technically, the main view was of Tumalo, but still. From a distance, the little town was kind of cute.

"Yeah." He turned around and glanced at the house, as though reminding himself of what it looked like.

"You didn't grow up here, did you?"

"No, I was raised in Bend. This was my grandparents'

place. I spent my summers here and every holiday until…"
His words trailed off, then he shook his head. "Until a few
years back."

Piper looked around the wide porch, then at the grounds
stretching out from there. "Where are they?"

"My grandparents?"

"Yeah."

"Um…" He blew out a breath. This, Piper was learning, was Whit's signal to her that she'd asked the wrong
question.

Unfortunately for him, she interpreted it as a signal that
she'd asked the *right* question, and he just didn't want to
answer.

"They no longer live here." He gestured over his shoulder with his thumb. "Wanna come inside?"

"No. I want to stay on your porch forever."

Whit rolled his eyes and headed for the front door. Bernice loped up the steps ahead of him.

"You brought the dog?" he asked, pulling open one half
of the massive oak door.

"Obviously. I'm puppy-sitting."

Bernice trotted into the house, then scrambled to get
purchase on the tile floor.

Piper walked into the entryway and scooped up the pup,
but before she could soothe her, she caught a glimpse of
the home stretching out around her.

It was stunning, built and furnished with attention to
detail sometime in the 1960s and well cared for ever since.
Red tile floor ran through the entryway and into what she
assumed was the kitchen. A sunken living room unfolded
before her with views to the west, all the way to the Cas-
cade Mountains.

"*This* is completely fantastic." Piper jogged down into
the living room. From there, she could see the massive

kitchen and an open dining room that could seat her whole family, even with the recent additions. Piper shot across the living room, peeking into the kitchen, then sped down a hall with Bernice waddling at her heels.

"Piper?" Whit called.

What was it about exploring other people's homes that was so appealing? She loved her little Portland loft and didn't aspire to own a traditional home. But other people's homes? Those she couldn't get enough of.

Whit trotted after her, stammering out something about a tour later. But there was a breakfast room! There were pocket doors!

"Love this!" she commented, playing with a door. Something that must be Whit's office was on the other side, and he reached around her and slid it shut. Piper spun around and kept exploring.

"Did you keep all the original furnishings?" she asked, poking her head into a bedroom.

"Yeah. I—"

"Love your grandma's taste!"

"Piper," he said, loudly.

"What?" She looked back to see Whit looking panicked. She stilled. "Sorry. I like your house."

He stared at her, then shook his head and chuckled. "Thank you? Thank you. Can we—" He gestured back to the living room.

Piper craned her head, really wanting to explore the rest of the house.

"Okay." Piper stalked back toward the living room. "We'll be fake dating for months. I guess I can explore the rest of your house later."

Whit shook his head. Maybe it was time to lighten up on the guy.

"You're a lot," Liam used to say when he got frustrated

with her. There were so many ways in which she and Liam had been a solid match, but he didn't like it when she got too caught up in things, when she was *"too much."* But what was she supposed to do about it? Try to be less?

Piper's breathing slowed, then seemed to stop at the memory. The heavy, underwater feeling of confusion and self-doubt came sloshing back, pulling her down again.

He'd broken up with her during a fight about avocado toast. They were heading to the coast for the day, and she wanted avocado toast before they left because she was hungry and that sounded good. He'd gotten so frustrated, unable to understand why she couldn't just eat a protein bar. Piper had started to banter back her reasoning because it was fun to illuminate the benefits of avocado toast over a protein bar. He stopped the car a half a block from her apartment and broke off their relationship. "This isn't what I want" were Liam's last words to her.

After all the time, the plans, the conversations, the intimacy, those were the five words he left her with. *This isn't what I want.*

Bernice pushed at her ankle, soulful puppy eyes gazing at her. Piper reached down and scooped her up, cradling her close. The silky warm puppy settled her, the dog's heartbeat somehow kick-starting her own.

This heaviness weighing her down was so unexpected, so uncommon for Piper. She didn't have the patience for it. She didn't see herself as the type of person who got depressed. So not only was she sad and in a funk, she was mad at herself for feeling this way. She was trapped in a cycle of sadness and self-reproach that felt like trying to escape from an M.C. Escher print.

And the person she might have leaned on, her beautiful, wonderful sister Clara, was busy with her first baby. She wasn't going to ruin one minute of Clara's happiness because she was sent into an existential crisis by a man whom she'd only ever been settling for in the first place.

Piper ran her hand along Bernice's shiny fur, then kissed her head. This was the real reason she was puppy-sitting. She needed something, anything, to focus on other than her own stalled and sad life. She wasn't taking care of Bernice for the summer; Bernice was taking care of her.

"Piper?" Whit gestured to the living room, his eyes questioning her unexpected stillness.

"Right." Piper shook out of the memory. She clipped into the living room and sank into a surprisingly comfy Danish modern chair. She started to comment on it, then refocused on Whit. "Hi. Thank you for having me. Your home is lovely."

"Thank you for coming over, and for agreeing to this."

She shrugged. "We need to get you elected. If this helps, I'm in. Now, how long have we been dating? Or how long did Dan tell you we've been dating?"

"Two months. We became reacquainted through your brother."

"Which one?"

"Ash."

"Did he set us up?"

Whit's face constricted. "What? No."

"Um." Piper wrinkled her nose. "In my family, some-one always claims the match. So, like, Hunter thinks he set up Jet and Clara. Ash claims Bowman and Maisy. Jackson set up his dad and Violet. I take all the credit for Ani and Hunter."

"You have a weird family."

"Says the guy living in the massive family home alone." She scanned the space. Bernice slipped out of her lap and resumed her olfactory exploration of the room. "Seriously, if this were my family, there'd be like five other people here right now."

Whit stared out the window for a moment then sighed. He took measured steps and sat on the sofa facing her. "Let's go over some basic questions. What's your favorite food?"

"Espresso."

Whit laughed.

"No, I'm serious." Piper crossed her legs and leaned toward him. "What's yours?"

"I like Mexican food."

"All of it?"

"I think so." He furrowed his brow. "I like everything that's been presented to me as Mexican food. Cheap, expensive, chain, artisan, street, I like it all. I'd have to spend several months in Mexico to know for sure, but my guess is yes."

"Okay, that's our dream vacation then. We're saving up to go on a food tour of Mexico."

Whit straightened, nodding his head. "Okay. Thank you. That's nice of you to consider my desires for our fake relationship plans."

She grinned at him, feeling a little better. Generosity in a fake relationship was better than no generosity at all. "Any time. I really appreciate the bouquets of carnations you send me."

"I send carnations? Not roses?"

Yeah, this guy probably sent out a dozen long stems each time he had to break off anything in danger of becoming a real relationship.

"Carnations. I like the way they smell. It's like a spicy scent. They're way prettier than people give them credit for, and they last forever. Most guys go for the expensive bouquet, you go for the bouquet you know I love."

Whit studied his hands, smiling. "Is your favorite color still that golden yellow?"

Piper blinked. "Yes. I love a rich, sunflower yellow." She couldn't believe he remembered that. Then again, she'd worn a *lot* of yellow in college. "What about you?"

"Blue—"

"You can't say blue."

"Why not?"

"Men always say blue."

"Sorry. I like blue."

"What kind of blue? Cobalt? Slate? Indigo? Teal?"

He shook his head. "Just blue."

She narrowed her right eye.

"Fine. I like…" He gazed around the room, finally pointing out the window. "Sky blue, how's that?"

"In as much as the sky changes color all day, every day of the year, it's not super specific, but fine, we'll go with it."

Whit let out a breath and scrubbed his hands through his hair. "Do you challenge all your boyfriends on their favorite color?"

"Just the fake ones." Piper crossed her arms and walked to the window. Bernice waddled after her. "Just the ones I'm taking days out of a really busy schedule for to help win an election."

The sigh seeping out of Whit suggested she'd gone too far, again. Maybe Dan was right. Maybe she wouldn't work for this at all.

"You don't have to do this, Piper. We can find someone else."

Wait. Was he dumping her? Was she getting dumped from a fake relationship? It was almost funny: a matchmaker who can't even succeed in a pretend relationship.

"You want to swap me out for someone with a 'professional' job and a more suitable dog?"

"Someone who doesn't dislike me and doesn't want to fight on every issue."

Piper turned around to find Whit slumped in his sofa, hand resting across his face. "I don't dislike you. Didn't I just plan a fake food tour in Mexico?"

He let out a weak laugh. Encouraged, she continued, "And I *do* like arguing with you. I always have."

He folded his hands, then looked up at her. "We had some battles on the debate team, didn't we?"

She'd felt alive, so in the moment in debate. The flow of adrenaline, combined with the mental rush of keeping up with Whit in an argument came back to her. "We did."

"You were a worthy adversary, Piper Wallace."

"Maybe I still am?"

He caught her gaze and nodded in acknowledgment.

"Look, Whit, I want to help with this. Holt's a monster, and you'd be a great county commissioner. But I am who I am, an argumentative woman who loves clothes, espresso and short-legged dogs. I can pretend to be your girlfriend, but I can't pretend to be anyone other than myself."

"That's fair." He looked down at his hands. "My favorite color is still blue though."

"Fine. Point conceded. What else should we know about each other?"

He chuckled. "Tell me about your life. You graduated college and took off for the big city. How'd you become a matchmaker? I'm curious. I wouldn't have pegged you for a relationship expert when we were in college."

"What would you have pegged me for?"

Whit raised an eyebrow. "Leader of the free world?"

The laugh that bubbled up inside her caught Piper by surprise. Whit continued, "I never would have expected this." He gestured between them. "If one of us were to run for office, I'd have assumed it would be you."

Piper returned to her chair, crossing one leg over the other. "You never expected you and I would be sitting in your fabulous huge home planning our fake relationship because you date too many women for people to vote for you?"

"About that—"

"Has Dan considered just asking all your former girl-friends to vote for you? Because that's gotta be a power-ful block."

Whit reddened, holding out his hands like he needed her to stop. "I haven't dated *that* many women." His gaze connected with hers. "I just don't have time for a relation-ship. I don't have time to do it right, and I hate disappoint-ing good women because I'm too busy to commit."

Piper shifted, tucking her legs up under her. "I get it."

"You do?"

"Absolutely. I don't just get it, I've been there. I *am* there."

That had always been Liam's biggest complaint, that she was too involved in her own life, too inflexible in her habits. He said she was selfish. She could own that. She liked things the way she liked them. It was sad, so sad, to think she might never find the type of love she helped others find. But it was what it was.

Whit cleared his throat, and Piper realized she'd been staring morosely at the arm of the chair. She shook her head.

"I became a matchmaker because I believe in the power of love and relationships to transform the world. Love will solve all the problems, people connecting and bringing out the best in each other. It can happen through any number of relationships—friendship, family, community. But I deal in the one most people seem to have the greatest amount of angst creating."

"Hmm."

"What's 'hmm' mean?"

He leaned toward her, like he used to during their informal debates. "I think we should transform the world on a political level first, then happiness will follow."

"Forgive me, but politics aren't looking real great right now."

"They won't look good until good people step up and do their civic duty."

"Ugh. That sounds *so* unappealingly Greek to me."

"It might be unappealing, but I'm right."

"You can't just say you're right. That's not an argument."

"I wasn't arguing." Whit held her gaze, his smile slowly growing as he raised an eyebrow.

"Not the eyebrow," Piper commanded, but Whit just raised the brow even more dramatically.

"It's so unfair that you can raise one eyebrow and I can't!"

He laughed.

"I'm serious. I can kind of get one a touch higher than the other, but you have the full-on Bond-villain raise. Less than a quarter of the population can do that."

"I guess that means I win."

"I thought you weren't arguing."

"Touché."

She could understand his appeal to women. He really had grown to be quite handsome over the last few years.

Piper scanned the room because looking into Whit's eyes wasn't working for her. "This must be amazing for all your family get-togethers."

Whit's smile froze, then fell. "Yeah. My family doesn't really get together much anymore."

"Oh." Piper unfolded her legs. "I'm sorry."

He shook his head. "It's a pretty common story, right?"

"I don't know the story, so am unable to comment on how common it is."

He let out a short laugh. "Well, my grandparents divorced. People took sides. Those sides became political. Now we can't even be in the same room together."

"Not even this room? Because there's a ton of space."

"Not even this room." His gaze met hers. "I've never even met my niece and nephew."

Piper stood and walked toward him, then stopped. What was she going to do? Hug him? Pat him on the back and say she was sorry? If he were one of her brothers, she'd browbeat him into reaching out to his sister and repairing their relationship. But of course, if he were one of her brothers, they wouldn't be in this position to begin with.

She stood next to him as he looked up at her, a smile growing as he realized she didn't know what to do.

Then she spun around and sat back down across from him. Maybe a little honesty might help this fake relationship.

"I'M THE ODD duck out." Piper leaned forward, hands clasped.

"What?"

"In my family. Yours doesn't get along, and that's horrible. In mine, we're super tight, but everyone else is deeply connected to Outcrop, and to each other, while I'm off in Portland. I'm the odd duck."

Whit stilled. It was the first time Piper had shown any weakness or insecurity, ever. She wasn't exactly the sympathetic type. But rather than laugh at his family drama or dismiss it, or worse, try to comfort him, she'd sat down, looked him straight in the eye and admitted a family problem of her own.

"Are you? Because it seems like your siblings love you." On various occasions, he'd heard the Wallaces relating funny stories about her and boasting about her achievements.

"Oh, they do. We love each other. But they're all here and small-town and ranch-y. I'm all there." She gestured in the direction of Portland. "Big-city and busy."

"But does that make you the odd duck out?"

"Absolutely. Although I'm not one-hundred-percent sure *duck* is the right term. I've never actually seen an odd duck. Ducks are uniformly normal."

Whit thought about it. "Maybe you're the odd emu out?"

"Um?" She scrunched her face up. "No. All emus are odd. If you're an odd emu, you fit right in."

He grinned at her. "This is what I look like when I'm refraining from calling your family odd."

She grinned back, meeting his eyes for a brief moment. Something moved between them, like a new level of understanding. Whit felt stronger, happier, as though they were now on the same team.

Then, like the New York City-cab driver of conversation that she was, Piper abruptly changed lanes. "What are you wearing?" Whit glanced down at his completely normal outfit. Piper kept talking. "Remember when we were in college, and you always wore sweatshirts from other colleges?"

Whit chuckled. "Yeah. The college sweatshirt is always a safe bet when you're in college."

"But other colleges? It felt antagonistic. Like there we were at Oregon State University, and you come to class rocking a Montana Tech."

"The choice was in no way adversarial."

"Are you sure?"

"I'm sure."

"Well, we need to take some selfies, and what you're wearing is not going to work."

"Piper, this is for *my* campaign."

"But people have to believe that *I'd* actually go out with you. If my clients see me, with you, in that, they'll know something's up. Which way to your closet?" Piper started walking toward the main bedroom.

"That's not—" Whit scrambled after her. "That's not the way to my room."

But he was too late. Piper was already rifling through the closet in the primary bedroom. She pulled out a shearling-lined denim jacket and threw it on the bed, then sent a Pendleton wool shirt flying in the same direction.

"You've been holding out on me," she accused. "Look at this!" She held up a suede jacket from the 1970s. "You're a hipster!"

"I am *not* a hipster."

"You are, too. You just never wear your cool stuff." She gestured with two fistfuls of clothing. "You're a closet hipster."

"This isn't my closet."

She stopped abruptly. "Whose closet is it, then?"

"I guess that's my grandpa's old stuff."

She stared at him. "You didn't bother to clean out your grandpa's closet?"

"I don't ever come in this room, much less go through the closet."

Piper furrowed her brow in confusion. "Why not?"

Whit walked over and slid the closet door shut. "Piper, I'm estranged from my grandparents, who are estranged from each other. I bought this place from them because I still have wonderful childhood memories of my summers here, and I couldn't bear to see the land leave our family. I'm still hoping for a reconciliation."

Piper gazed at him, confusion and sympathy shifting through her eyes. "I'm sorry."

"I'm sorry, too. Not all families are like yours."

"I know," she said defensively. Knowing Piper, she *understood* that all families weren't like hers, but she wanted a full report on why they weren't and what they planned to do about it. She set the clothing down on the bed and smoothed out an old pearl-snap shirt. "I can't imagine what that's like for you, not even having met your niece and nephew. I regret bringing it up."

"It's okay. We just need to figure out where our boundaries are, you know?"

"You're right." She kept her eyes on the clothes she'd tossed on the bed, sifting through the shirts and jackets that Whit associated with his grandfather during much happier times. "We should definitely set our boundaries, and I'll do my best to remember them." She glanced up at him, her dimpled smile helping him to forget he'd ever been frustrated with her. "But can you do just one thing for me?"

"What?"

"Wear this?" She held up one of his grandpa's old woolen Pendleton shirts.

The woven pattern of yellows and blues had faded over time. This was one of Grandpa's standards. Whit remembered being little, the arms clad in this shirt helping him scramble up into the truck to go get donuts on a Sunday morning. The underlying connotation was that the two of them were in cahoots on a secret mission to secure a sugary treat before 9:00 a.m. Those had been good days.

"Okay."

"Okay?"

Whit took the shirt from Piper. "I'll wear the old-man hipster shirt for our photographs."

She clapped her hands, then turned back to the clothing strewn across the bed. "You cannot find vintage Wranglers like this in Portland. Not for less than three-hundred dollars."

"Three hundred bucks for someone else's old pants?"

"We could literally fund your entire campaign with the contents of this closet."

Whit looked down at the dog and quoted Piper's words from the day before. "The end times are coming."

Piper spent several more moments exclaiming over his grandpa's old clothes, then headed back to the living room to set up their photoshoot while he changed. Whit took a moment to look around the room. He rarely came in here as a child, and less frequently as an adult. He'd bought the house and property the day before his grandma planned to list it with a realtor and hadn't had time to update or make it his. Truth be told, he still didn't think of it as his; this was the family's home. He'd chosen one of the guest rooms as his bedroom and didn't spend much time anywhere but the kitchen and breakfast nook. He was just a placeholder, until his family came back together.

Whit sighed. That wasn't happening. But maybe one day, when this whole county commissioner situation was over, he'd have time to meet someone, form a real relationship and make this place a home. The cattle operation was thriving, despite his struggle to find good ranch hands. He'd made a name for himself in the local ranching community. He wanted to put down roots here, but he couldn't think about that now.

Grandpa/hipster clothes on, Whit headed back to the living room. Piper stood at the window, gazing out at the west view. It was as still as he'd ever seen her.

He hoped it wasn't the hipster shirt talking, but Piper's energy was different. In this moment, with nothing to do and no one to challenge, she seemed sad. Whit was fascinated but felt like he was intruding. He cleared his throat, and Piper spun from the window.

A mischievous grin spread across her face. "You look good."

"You look like Piper Wallace."

"So, completely fantastic?"

Whit chuckled as he jogged down the steps into the sunken living room. "That's the textbook definition, or so I'm told."

She pulled out her phone. "You ready for this?"

"It's as though I've been preparing my whole life to run in a tight race for county commissioner and pose for pictures with a fake girlfriend."

She gestured for him to join her at the window, then held out her phone for a selfie. Upon seeing the screen, she frowned, then set the phone down and turned to him. She reached up to adjust his hair, her fingertip brushing his forehead.

She stilled, her fingers against his forehead. A soft warmth moved through him at Piper's touch. Her gaze connected with his for half a second, and then she muttered something about him needing a haircut. Whit fought the urge to mess his hair back up so she'd have to fix it again.

Piper held out her phone and leaned into him. Whit felt wildly awkward and pretty sure any smile he managed was going to look as fake as Bunny Holt's eyelashes. Then Piper wrinkled her nose and said, "You smell like Grandpa."

Whit laughed out loud, gazing down at Piper just as she took the picture.

She flipped the camera around. "I think we've got our shot."

Whit stared at the photograph, confused. "That's actually a good picture. We look—" He flailed around for the right word.

"Happy." Piper knit her eyebrows, gazing up at him. Then she shook her head. "Okay. Let's post this bomb."

She stalked back to her chair. Bernice waddled over, and Piper scooped her up, texting at the same time. "Sent it to you."

Whit pulled his attention away from Piper to the picture on his phone.

It looked authentic. Piper was smiling, textbook definition of beautiful, as always. Whit was laughing at her joke, gazing at her. The vintage shirt made him look somehow relaxed, like a solid guy. Whit took a deep breath and uploaded it to social media, then changed his status to *in a relationship with Piper Wallace.*

Who'd have ever thought they'd see the day?

Seconds later, his college debate coach and favorite professor liked the post.

"Dr. Arturo just liked us!"

"She did?" Piper asked, looking up from her phone. "I loved her so much."

Bubbles popped up under the picture. "She's writing a comment." Whit adjusted his phone and read the comment out loud before it sunk in. *"Finally!"*

He set his phone down.

"Finally?" Piper questioned.

"That's what she wrote." She looked as baffled as he felt. He stared at the comment, saying, "That's…uh, not what I was expecting."

Then again, with Piper, he never knew what to expect.

CHAPTER THREE

"HOLD STILL," Piper commanded.

"I need to show this guy our tickets." Whit gestured to a heavily inked man in an orange vest scanning tickets for the Outcrop Rodeo.

"You have a string hanging off your sleeve," she fussed.

He sighed. "This T-shirt is fifty years old. It's advertising a feed company that went out of business in the last century. You're worried about a string?"

Whit had diligently put on the outfit Piper commanded him to: vintage feed company T-shirt, worn-in jeans, with a Pendleton wool shirt and shearling-lined jacket for when it got cold later. Mercifully, she'd allowed him to wear his own boots and Stetson.

Piper pulled a tiny pair of scissors out of her purse and clipped the loose thread as Whit held his phone out to the impatient man. "The shirt is cool," she explained. "The string is sloppy."

Whit rolled his eyes. "I'll take your word for it."

The man chuckled, then asked, "Aren't you that guy running for county commissioner?"

Whit nodded. If nothing else, Marc's smear campaign was getting him recognition. "I am. Can I count on your vote?"

The man shook his head. "No offense, but I'll probably vote for the other guy. He's got more experience—

and no strings hanging from his shirt," he added with a straight face.

"I respect that everyone will have their own reasons for voting as they do." Whit glanced over his shoulder then back at the man. "But I can tell you, even though I'm half Holt's age, I've lived in Oregon twice as long as he has."

The man pulled his head back in surprise. "I didn't know he's from out of state."

Whit shrugged. "My campaign never made a big deal out of it because we want to focus on the issues. But yeah. He was county commissioner in Colorado before he came here." He glanced at the shirt under the man's vest. It was advertising a bow hunting shop. "You a hunter?"

The man nodded. "Born and raised. That's how I provide meat for my family. I've been hunting in the Upper Deschutes my whole life."

Whit pulled his phone back once the tickets were scanned. "You know Marc Holt wants to open the Upper Deschutes area to development. It's one of several places that will be closed to hunting within the next five years if Holt's plan for Hummingbird Ranch comes through."

The man looked stunned. "Can he do that?"

"The county commissioner has a lot more responsibility and power than most people realize. Holt was county commissioner in a similar area in Colorado five years ago, where Hummingbird Ranch is now building a huge development."

"Okay." The man looked thoughtful, then nodded. "I might have been wrong about you. I'll check out your website."

"Thank you." Whit touched the tip of his Stetson. The man responded by touching the tip of his ball cap.

"I'm impressed," Piper muttered under her breath as they walked away.

"I've said from the beginning, we'll get the votes if people have the information."

"Well, you got his vote," Piper said.

"I think I did."

"Only a hundred and twenty-five thousand left to go." Piper slipped her hand into his and tugged him into the crowd. "Let's take a picture with the Rodeo sign."

The place was packed. People came from all over to the Outcrop Rodeo: old, young, urban, rural. The Outcrop Rodeo was a modern, humane affair, and while solidly the product of a cowboy town, it had the benefit of being close to both Bend and Eugene, bringing in curious city dwellers. But of all the people here, the only person Whit was concerned about was Marc Holt. He'd be campaigning tonight, too.

Music blasted over the speakers. Piper turned back and grinned at him, yelling, "I love this song!"

Okay, there were two people here tonight who made him nervous, and one of them was holding his hand, dragging him deeper into the crowds. If he was uncomfortable with his outfit, he was even less comfortable with Piper's. She wore fitted Wranglers, a tank top that showed off her toned arms and a straw cowboy hat that somehow made her eyes look even more mischievous.

"Let's get a picture of you with the rodeo queens!" Piper said, pointing to a group of young women posing with rodeo patrons.

Whit stopped in his tracks and raised one eyebrow. "You want to post more pictures of me with random women?"

Piper wrinkled her nose. "Right. Sorry. Let's go find a baby cow or some such."

"Much better idea." Whit placed his hands on her shoulders and guided her to the arena. He noticed several people staring at the two of them.

"My social media has been blowing up in the last forty-eight hours," Piper said. "How about yours?"

Whit nodded. It had been blowing up all right. He'd heard from old friends, old coworkers and all of his and Piper's shared college professors. Everyone had a politely shocked but happy reaction. One of his buddies posted that if it weren't for the picture, he'd never believe it, but the look in Piper's eye said it all. Whit spent a lot of time examining the picture for the "look in Piper's eye" after that one.

"I think we can do this," she said. "Like, it feels weird, but doable."

Whit gave her hand a squeeze. "We can."

"Hey! Michael, Joanna! You've got to meet Whit." Piper waved to a couple, and they were off.

Within a half an hour, they'd collected every kind of fried food known to humanity, and most of Piper's family members. Whit had enjoyed getting to know the Wallaces through his work with the ranching federation. But with Piper in their midst, the energy seemed to kick up a notch.

"Did you see that Nate Rayson is working as a rodeo clown?" Clara asked Piper.

"No way! Good for him."

"Unless he gets himself gored." Clara shuddered.

"Nate's not going to get gored. He'd have to stop making bad jokes if he did."

"Who's Nate?" Whit asked, a twinge of identifiable emotion sending his eyes roving for this Nate.

"Just a guy we knew from high school. He was a good bull rider." Piper glanced around, as though looking for him. "Probably makes a lot more money this way."

"Uh-oh," Hunter muttered.

"What?" Piper asked.

Hunter nodded toward the elephant ear stand, just as Marc and Bunny looked up and saw them.

There were a lot of things about Marc Holt that Whit didn't like, but his least favorite thing about his opponent was the look in his eyes. They were a watery gray that always seemed to be looking for the next thing to hate. His eyes held a mix of arrogance and fear that chilled Whit to the core. Whit was confident taking on any reasonable person in a debate on issues. Marc wasn't reasonable, and the way he dodged the issues in this campaign made it abundantly clear that he didn't want voters to know the real reason he was running for this position.

"Anyone else feel the sudden shift in temperature?" Clara asked.

"Good thing you brought that jacket," Piper quipped, waving at his opponent like there was no one she'd rather run into at the rodeo.

Bunny gave the slightest inclination of her head. Marc waved and started to walk toward them. Whit could feel his blood starting to roil.

Then Piper's hand came to rest on his cheek, and she turned his face toward hers. He found himself looking into her eyes, her lips much closer than he ever imagined they would be. Her lids lowered just a touch. Then she leaned toward his ear and whispered, "Can you at least *try* to look like you're in love with me?"

His eyes skipped from Piper's face for half a second, and he saw Marc drop his hand, annoyed that his jovial wave had been interrupted.

"This is what I look like when I'm trying," he whispered back.

Piper's breath brushed his neck. "Try harder."

Then she gave his cheek a pat and grabbed one of his fries and popped it in her mouth.

The whole move was brilliant. She'd been publicly polite to Marc and Bunny but stopped their advance while making Marc look foolish.

Back at the elephant ear stand, Bunny Holt let out an unconvincing peal of laughter and patted her husband on the shoulder as though he'd said something funny. Keeping his eyes on the Holts, Whit whispered, "You've got to admit I'm better at faking love for you than Bunny is with her husband."

Piper grinned at him. "Conceded. But she's a low bar. Like, limbo championship low."

Whit gazed down at her, then let his eyes flicker over to Marc again. Bowman might just be right about Piper being the perfect person to take on Holt.

He ran his hands down her arms, as though they were a couple, then wound his fingers through hers. "May I escort you to our seats?"

"Nope, I have to escort you. I changed our seats." Piper tugged him in the opposite direction.

Whit refrained from rolling his eyes in an effort to look besotted. "Why?"

"Um. Let me think about that." Piper mimed thoughtfulness, then said, "Because."

Whit shook his head, forcing his face into a smile, but Piper was already onto the next thing.

"Yo. Family! Let's go get our seats."

"WE'RE OVER THE CHUTES?" Whit asked, scanning the best seats at the rodeo as though they were covered in hot coals.

"Obviously." Piper gestured to his chair. "You're sitting behind your campaign sign, right over the central chute.

It's like you're advertising your advertising. People won't be able to look away. And even if they wanted to, this is where the stock comes out. If anyone wants to watch the rodeo, they have to look at you." She took her seat and grinned at him. "So look like you're having fun."

Whit faked a smile. "How's this?"

Clara leaned across Piper to address Whit, "Literally the worst." She looked down at Bobby in the front pack carrier. "He's the worst fake smiler," she said to her baby. "Nobody's worse at fake smiling than Uncle Whit."

"Uncle Whit?" he asked.

"For the next two months." Piper brushed a piece of lint off his shirt.

"And then what? Little Bobby just kicks me to the curb?"

"For someone with strained relationships with your siblings and no emus, you need to take your uncle-ing where you can get it."

Whit let out a dry laugh. Piper looked down at the baby, who had his mouth open like he wanted to smile but wasn't quite sure how it was done yet. She would really love to see that first smile. Piper slipped an arm around her sister and pulled her closer.

She'd stayed with Clara for three weeks when Bobby was born and hadn't missed a moment of his first days in this world. But now it felt like every time she made it home, he'd changed dramatically. And Clara was changing too. Of course she was. She was a mom now.

"How'd you get these seats?" Whit asked, startling Piper out of her thoughts.

These seats were a good reminder: her job right now was to keep Marc Holt from getting elected. In three months, she could worry about time passing, the world changing and her profound loneliness.

Piper nodded to her sister. "This is all Clara."

Clara pointed into the announcer's box. "I set the master of ceremonies up with his wife. They are *very* happy together."

Piper raised her chin and gave Whit a smug smile. "Like I said yesterday, all the world's problems can be solved by love."

He flexed his brow, then nodded to where Marc and Bunny were sitting. "Even that one?"

Marc Holt was watching her with that creepy smile-glare. She wanted to shudder but was not going to give him the satisfaction. Instead, she fixed her eyes on Whit. "They're watching us."

"You think they buy it?"

"You think I care? We just need to make them look petty and like their smear campaign was not only wrong, but mean-spirited. It shouldn't be too hard."

His gaze connected with hers, and he shook his head, then settled an arm around her shoulder. So they'd look like a real couple. His arm around her had *nothing* to do with anything other than this election.

But it sure felt good all the same.

"You're getting awful cozy with my sister," Bowman grumbled from the seat behind them.

Piper twisted around and batted his leg. "You can't get all protective of me. This is a fake relationship," she whispered. "You were literally the person who convinced me to do this."

"I can get all protective if I want. Maybe I'm being fake protective?"

"You can't fake anything," his wife said. "You're too honest."

Bowman shrugged, acknowledging this. Then he gave Whit a look. "Just watch it."

Piper hit Bowman's leg again, trying to communicate that just because Liam had sent her into a tailspin, that didn't mean she needed protection or sympathy. Bowman squeezed her shoulder, letting her know she was getting it all the same.

"Welcome, rodeo fans!" the MC boomed over the speakers. "Outcrop Rodeo, the loudest little show in the West!"

Piper had to admit, there were less fun people to watch a rodeo with than Whit Benton. He wasn't a hardcore fan, but he knew enough to appreciate the athleticism. The night started out with calf roping, which Whit and Jet both understood on a practical level. They launched into a spirited discussion of calves that had gotten away while Piper and Clara cheered on the competition.

"Come on," Clara murmured, leaning forward and keeping her eyes on the calf. "Let's go!"

The calf cut right, avoiding the cowboy. The man spun his lasso again, managing to get it around the clever little bovine but not pulling it tight quick enough.

"Yes!" Clara shot up, raising both arms and whooping as the calf slipped away trotted to the other end of the arena and off the field.

Whit stared at her, then whispered in Piper's ear, "Is your sister cheering for the calves?"

Piper nodded, keeping her eye on the next pair of wranglers. "She always roots for the stock."

"Why?"

Piper looked up, shocked at the question. "That's the whole point of the rodeo, a test of wit and brawn between animals and humans. There's nothing wrong with rooting for the animals."

Whit glanced around. "If there's nothing wrong with it, then why isn't anyone else doing it?"

Piper shrugged. Whit raised one eyebrow. Piper's eyes

shone as she tried to keep from smiling. "I have no idea. Ask them."

As the last of the calf ropers left the arena, Nate the rodeo clown took the field, filling time before the bronco riders came out. He threw a football into the stands, joking with the crowd over his headset as he played catch with various spectators in the arena. When he threw the ball into their section, Ash's fiancée, Violet, lunged for it because it was a football and she was incapable of doing anything else. Her return throw was so hard Nate stumbled backward when he caught it. But he took it all in good humor, gesturing to her and saying, "Ladies and gentlemen, let me present Violet Fareas, head coach of the Outcrop Eagles!"

A cheer went up through the stands, with no one cheering louder than Clara and Piper. They'd been so thrilled when their terse, bossy, wounded oldest brother had fallen head over boots for his son's football coach.

"And if it's not our own candidate for county commissioner, Whit Benton, in the stands—" Nate theatrically covered his mouth with the back of his hand, saying to the rest of the crowd "—with *another* pretty girl."

"I heard that, Nate!" Piper called back.

The clown looked up, eyes wide. He didn't have to mug his shocked expression. "Is that Piper Wallace?"

She pulled off her Stetson and saluted with it.

"As I live and breathe." The clown shook his head, then got a sly smile on his face. "Unless she tries to knock the wind out of me."

"Thinkin' about it!" she called back.

"Piper, stand up." Nate gestured for her to rise. Piper stood and waved. "Folks, this little lady—"

"This reasonably sized woman!"

"This…person was one of the most popular barrel racers back in the day."

"You were a barrel racer?" Whit asked.

"How do you not know that about me?"

He widened his eyes, suggesting they'd spent less than five hours together in the last seven years.

Good point.

"Folks, let's see if we can get Piper to join us on the field." The clown started clapping, and the crowds joined in. "Come on down here."

Piper waited for the insistence to build, then climbed over the rail and down over the chute. Nate took her hand and helped her into the arena.

"What are you doing back in town? Last I heard you moved to—" he paused dramatically, then said in a Darth Vader voice "—Portland."

The crowd laughed as he made fun of the big city. Piper pointed up at Whit. "I still live in Portland, but I've been making more and more trips back to see my boyfriend."

"You and everybody else," Nate joked.

Piper pulled the microphone toward her. "Now, Nate, I know you've seen that hysterical ad Marc Holt put out, and I have two things to say about it."

"Just two things?" He looked out at the crowd. "I've never known Piper to be so shy."

She pulled the football from his hands and bopped him on the head, buying herself time. She needed to play this right. Whit was a good guy. And yeah, he had been out with a lot of women. What did the audience need to know about him? How could she spin this to his advantage?

She glanced at Marc and Bunny, then up at her fake boyfriend. He looked good tonight in the vintage T-shirt and Stetson. He looked completely nervous about what she might say, but good.

And that's our key to spinning this.

Piper smiled. Nobody wanted a playboy for a politician,

but if *Bridgerton* taught her anything, it's that everyone loves a reformed rake.

"First off, it's not a crime to look good tubing on the Deschutes River. Am I right?"

A largely female-led cheer went up through the crowd. Whit covered his face with his hand, looking at her through his fingers.

"Secondly—" She held Whit's gaze. She was trying to find the right words and hoped she came off looking dazzled by him. "He's amazing. He's smart, he listens and he cares so much about this beautiful place we all love. So yeah, Marc's ad makes one good point, I had a lot of competition for this guy. But you *do* remember my defining characteristic as a racer, don't you, Nate?"

"What was that, Piper?"

She grinned at the crowd, then looked back at Whit. "I always won. That man is off the market, ladies. Sorry!"

Nate laughed, then pulled her into a hug. Over his shoulder, Piper saw Marc Holt looking like he was about to spit barbed wire. Whit shook his head as though he'd found not one but eight holes in his life raft. She jogged toward the chute and climbed back up to the family seats.

Whit gave a terrible fake smile as he took her hand and helped her back into the seats. "What. Was. That?" he spat out.

"That was fun," she told him.

"That may have destroyed my campaign." Panic was clear in his eyes.

Piper put a hand on his cheek, gazing at him as though she were in love. "Look around you," she whispered.

Whit drew his eyes up to the arena. Rodeo patrons were gazing at them. Everyone was smiling, interested in the two of them, happy for them.

"Everyone loves a reformed rake."

Whit's gaze connected with hers. "But I'm not a rake."

"Not anymore. Would you please kiss me? It's what they're waiting for."

Whit drew in a breath, then brushed his lips across hers. Piper was surprised by the jolt of feeling that came at his touch.

She was not at all surprised when the crowd burst into applause.

Whit blinked, dazed. "I think you might be right."

"She is right." Ash leaned between the two of them. "That was brilliant, Piper. I knew you'd know how to handle this."

"Ash?" Piper placed a hand on her chest. "Was that a compliment? Did you literally just give me a compliment?" She turned to Clara. "Ash said a nice thing!"

"He's never given *me* a compliment," Clara said.

Ash snorted, turning away from their teasing.

"He hasn't given you a compliment...*yet*."

Ash looked at Whit and shook his head. "I know she's a lot, but when you have to accomplish something, Piper's your best bet."

There were those words again, *a lot*. But somehow, coming from her brother it didn't feel like an insult.

"I am a lot," she told Whit. "I'm an enormous amount, but you only have to put up with me for three more months."

Whit gazed at her, opening his mouth to say something that was probably going to be a thank-you or an apology or whatever. Piper didn't need to hear it. She might be too much for the average man, but she had a feeling she was just enough to help Whit win against Marc Holt.

The rest of the rodeo was somehow less eventful, even if it did include bull riding, barrel racing and steer wrestling. Piper felt energized by her first clash with Holt and ready for the next one. She glanced across the arena to where he was still watching them with those watery gray eyes.

Bring it on.

"That concludes the events for tonight," the master of ceremonies said. "Time to head on over to the Eighty Local events center for the dance. Just remember folks, drive responsibly. If you've been drinking, leave the keys with someone else and ride your horse."

Piper stood and stretched, then looked around at her siblings. "Dance?"

"Yes," Bowman said, pulling Maisy to her feet and spinning her right there in the stands.

"A country Western dance is going to be an entirely new experience for me. We're even taking the night off to enjoy it," Ani said, then she nudged Hunter in the ribs. "But don't be surprised if one or both of us winds up in the kitchen."

"Caleb's got it," he said, raising both hands in innocence. "I'm just heading to this dance to have fun. And possibly work behind the bar if they need me."

Hunter had come so, so far in allowing others to help with his restaurant and events center. A year ago, he would have been working a solid forty-eight hours to prepare for this dance on his own. Now he was here, having fun, trusting that his employees had it covered. Piper gave Ani a grateful smile for…what? Being an amazing woman and falling in love with Hunter? Ani shrugged one shoulder in acknowledgment, as though being happy and in love was the least she could do.

"We need to stop by Wallace Ranch. Bob's going to spend the evening with his grandparents," Jet said, cradling his sleeping son.

"Bobby," Clara corrected him.

Jet glanced at Hunter then Bowman, who both tried to

keep from smiling. Clara glared at her brothers then her husband. "We agreed to call him Bobby."

"You have to admit he looks like a Bob."

"He's a baby!" Clara said.

"Bob the baby." Jet held up his son and gazed at him.

Piper was completely on Clara's side here, but Jet had a point. The kid did look like a very small, bald Bob.

"His name is Robert, after our dad. But everyone calls Dad *Bob*," Piper told Whit. "We need to call this little guy Bobby, so people don't get confused."

"Right." Hunter faked a cough. "Because folks are going to mix up a sixty-five-year-old man and an infant."

Clara launched herself at Hunter, who roped an arm around her neck and messed up her hair. Clara responded by whacking Hunter on the arm, and Piper couldn't let her sister go it alone. She reached out and grabbed Hunter, but then Bowman joined in the fray, going for her tickle spot, and soon they were all laughing and arguing and trying to convince anyone listening of the correct nickname for baby Robert.

"Well, if it's not the Wallace clan."

They stilled as Marc Holt appeared in the bleachers next to them.

Something about his voice just made Piper's skin crawl. Who did this guy think he was, interrupting them as they argued about what to call the baby?

"It *is* the Wallace clan. A lot of us, anyway." Piper stalked down the steps and held out a hand. "I'm Piper, and I already know who you are."

Whit came trotting up behind her, his determination to be civil pulsing off him like the country music coming through the speakers.

"Nice to see you, Marc." He held out a hand and shook. "Bunny." He nodded politely. "Did you enjoy the rodeo?"

"We did," Marc said. "It's a wonderful heritage event. I think as more people build vacation homes in the area, it will continue to be a draw."

"Are more people building vacation homes here?" Piper asked.

Marc narrowed his eyes but kept his smile in place. "Over time."

"I'm surprised we haven't seen you before," Bunny said. "Seems Whit has a secret weapon in you."

"I'm not a secret. And I'm only considered a weapon when I'm destructive. I'm a matchmaker. Totally harmless."

"You're a matchmaker?" Bunny let out a saccharine, high-pitched giggle. "How cute of you."

Marc turned his watery gray eyes on Piper, a watery smile to go with them.

"Cute?" Piper asked.

"I'm sure it's a really sweet hobby," Bunny said. "Just like your brother's horse breeding operation."

Ash had taken over the family's breeding operation after eighteen years in the National Guard, and he was making bank. There was nothing "cute" or "hobby" about anything Ash did. Ever.

Piper took a step into Bunny's personal space. Whit put his hands on her shoulders, trying to draw her back, but Piper kept her stance firm and her smile bright. "In the last six years, my sister and I have matched up hundreds of people, all of them living fuller, happier lives because of their bold decision to take steps to find the love they deserve. It's not a hobby. And my brother supports his family quite well with the profits coming from Wallace Ranch."

"Is that so?" Marc glanced at Ash. "I'm glad to hear it. Property taxes will inevitably go up, so it's good to know you're doing okay."

"Inevitably?"

Whit had a tight hold of her shoulders now, and Piper realized her mistake. She'd gotten mad. She walked right into their trap.

She looked at Bunny, then Marc. They had a hundred traps lying in wait. These people knew how to dive low to get what they wanted.

Winning this election wasn't just a matter of making Whit look more responsible. They were going to have to use every weapon in their combined arsenals to fight Holt.

Piper lifted her chin, feeling the calming power of righteous anger sweep through her.

Because Marc and Bunny didn't recognize *their* mistake.

They'd just made this battle personal.

CHAPTER FOUR

MUSIC POURED OUT of the timber-framed structure, reaching down the side streets, pulling people from all directions into the Eighty Local events center. It couldn't look less like the place he'd met with his campaign manager and the ranching federation a few days before. As Whit pushed through the door, they were engulfed by the crowd. The only part of Piper he could see was her hand, and that was because it was in his. A live band, rather than the computer projector, was set up on the dais. Party lights sparkled from the rafters, the place was packed and these people weren't worried about a thing.

Everyone was here: rodeo patrons, bull riders, barrel racers, even the clown had changed his clothes and come to hang out.

Everyone, that is, except for Marc and Bunny Holt.

Piper had completely thrown them off-balance. Whit was alternately panicked and impressed as she worked the crowd at the rodeo. What was it she'd said? *Everyone loves a reformed rake.*

He glanced around at the crowd, everyone watching as he and Piper entered the dance. Apparently they liked what they saw, but whether that had more to do with the vintage T-shirt he wore or how reformed he might be, he didn't know.

None of this was going down as he expected. When Dan had first suggested a public relationship, Whit imagined himself showing up at events with a neatly dressed woman who would nod approvingly as he spoke to potential voters. He hadn't stopped to imagine the volunteer fake girlfriend would have any personality.

"Love this dance!" Piper tugged him toward the dance floor. "Let's go!"

Yeah, safe to say Piper Wallace was the last thing he'd expected.

"I don't know any line dances," he called back.

She turned her large brown eyes on him. "Well, no wonder you're behind in the polls. Time to learn."

He was about to make an excuse about needing to campaign. He and Ash and maybe Piper's other siblings could work through the crowd, drumming up votes. Unfortunately, all the Wallace siblings were heading to the dance floor. Bowman was the first one there, drawing his wife out with him, a smile lighting his face as they moved to the music. Hunter and Ani didn't know the dance, but jumped in on the edge of the floor, watching, learning and laughing at themselves as they tried to follow along. But it wasn't until Whit saw Ash and Violet on the floor that he realized he had no choice. If Ash was dancing, everyone was dancing.

Whit gave a frustrated sigh. "I thought we were here to campaign."

"This *is* campaigning."

"No, this is having fun, exactly what the Holt campaign is accusing me of having too much of."

"This is you, local rancher, at a community event, spending quality time with his girlfriend's family. Please start smiling, we look like we're arguing right now."

Whit faked a smile. She countered with a sincere expression, then flexed up on her tiptoes to whisper, "You really are horrible at smiling when you're not happy."

"My apologies for having principles."

Piper dropped back on her heels. Her face softened. "What is it?"

"Nothing." He probably looked as frustrated as he felt and knew how that would read to the crowd. He glanced down at her hand in his, then admitted the truth: "Everything."

She stilled for a moment, like she had the day before at his house, when her energy seemed to shift. "When was the last time you went dancing?"

The last time he'd danced was at his sister's wedding, five years ago. It was the family's last-ditch effort to hold it together publicly. They failed. The reception ended in a screaming match, and everything fell apart.

"It's been a while."

As though reading his mind, Piper placed a hand on his back. "This one's pretty easy. Want to try?"

Fifteen feet away, Bowman and Maisy were adding a moonwalk and running man, when the instructions were only a slide and step to the left. "It's *not* gonna be easy if we let Bowman take the lead," Whit said, gesturing. "Let's get out there."

Piper's mischievous grin spread across her face, her dimple flexing as she tugged him onto the floor, right up front, next to Bowman and Maisy.

Whit kept his eyes on Piper, trying to ignore the crowd as he followed her movements. She clapped her hands, then swung her hips as instructed by the song. Whit awkwardly followed along.

"Step left," she called to him.

Whit crashed into the woman on his other side.

"Left!" Piper said again, laughing.

He'd never been fantastic about knowing his left from his right, and trying to remember it with Piper, looking stunning in a white tank top, dancing next to him was almost impossible. Then they were spinning, sliding to the right, and Piper was clapping, swinging her hips again. But it was fun to move to the music, and every time he messed up, it was just an opportunity to laugh at himself and look like the regular guy that he was. Whit eventually learned the simple dance, the crowd cheering for him and his two left feet as they figured it out.

The next dance was a two-step. He quirked an eyebrow at Piper. "You willing to get your feet trampled if I attempt this?"

Piper lifted her foot to show off cowgirl boots. "I'm in."

Whit slipped a hand around her waist and did his best to remember how this all went down.

They'd only run into a few other couples by the time Whit remembered he used to enjoy dancing. Eventually he relaxed, and dancing got easier. Ash commandeered a table next to the dance floor, and Piper and Whit joined him. The family and all their friends flowed between the dance floor and the table. Jet and Clara arrived. Hunter and Ani brought drinks over, and what they called the "Family Special," Eighty Local leftovers and other people's messed-up orders.

The Wallace clan was a powerful social conduit. Their table attracted local ranchers, medical professionals from the hospital in Redmond, teachers from the high school, women from the Bend Equestrian Society, parents of kids who had been at some camp at Wallace Ranch, all the fans of the high school football team, firefighters and seemingly every person Clara or Piper had ever matched up.

And almost all of these people asked Whit about the campaign. He was able to talk about the issues casually, connecting with others in a way that felt natural and easy.

If he could just keep himself from staring at Piper, this might work out.

It wasn't only that she was pretty, although "textbook definition of beautiful" still stood. He liked the way she moved, quick and decisive. She was uninhibited and interested in those around her. She was just so... Piper.

When a pop song came on, Whit begged off dancing and watched as Piper and her friends took to the floor in a clump, bopping around to the music. The rodeo clown moved in on the group, dancing wildly, making Piper and her friends laugh. Whit felt a twinge of something like jealousy. Fake jealousy, to go with their fake relationship?

Hunter nudged Bowman's shoulder and pointed to the dance floor.

"How many times did Nate ask Piper to marry him?"

"You mean *begged* her to marry him."

"He did get pretty desperate toward the end there. Six? Or six that she told us about, anyway."

Okay, maybe it was real jealousy. But not because other men wanted to date Piper or marry her, in the case of the rodeo clown. Whit wasn't romantically interested in Piper. Sure, she was beautiful and funny, but she was complicated. Whit's life was complicated enough. He didn't have the time or space to fall in love with anyone and certainly not someone who lived three hours away in the city of Portland. Or someone who argued every single point he made, down to his favorite color.

Piper's laugh rang out as Nate grabbed both her hands and spun her dramatically.

Whit forced an image of the sausage dog in a frog hat to the forefront of his mind.

No, he *didn't* want a romantic relationship with Piper. But in college, he valued his position as her chief rival. Most guys were just trying to get her attention. He had that. As her nemesis in debate, in class or over the library cubicle, there was respect. He understood that other men would always want to date Piper, but could they hold their own in an argument with her?

"Phew," Piper sighed, dropping into the chair next to him. "My feet need a rest. What's this?" She looked at the food spread out on the table. "Oooh! Guacamole." She dipped a chip in it, then looked up at him. "Did you try the guacamole?"

"I have eaten everything of Mexican inspiration that Hunter serves," Whit assured her.

Clara slid in next to Piper. "Have you checked your social media since the rodeo?"

"No." Piper pulled out her phone. Whit's own phone had been steadily buzzing in his pocket all evening. He'd been hesitant to look.

Piper's eyes widened as she gazed at the screen. "Oh."

"Right?" Clara said.

"So many happy voters saying nice things!" Whit looked over Piper's shoulder to see a flood of reactions and comments to her pictures from the rodeo. Her real smile flashed. "I'm literally helping you!"

She was. Piper wasn't what he expected, or necessarily wanted, but she was helping. She scrolled through the comments, pointing things out to her family. Whit rested a hand on her shoulder, still warm with the exertion of dancing, to steady himself as he looked at her phone.

Then she stopped talking abruptly and stared at the screen.

"What is it?" Clara asked.

"Nothing." Piper's eyes were dark, and she bit her bottom lip. Whit had the sense that *everything* might be closer to the truth.

Clara reached for the phone. Piper tucked it away.

"Piper—" Clara started to express sympathy, but Piper held her hand up to stop her.

"Hunter, I *so* appreciate the beer, but do you have any pinot gris?"

Clara tried to reach into Piper's back pocket to grab her phone. Piper clamped a hand over the pocket.

"I have the bottle of pinot gris I keep on hand for when you're here and you ask for it. Can I pour you a glass?"

"I'll get it." Piper hopped up.

"Let me get it for you," Hunter insisted.

Piper spoke over him. "In the main restaurant?"

"Yeah—" Hunter stood, ready to go pour a glass of wine for his sister, but Piper shot off toward the restaurant on her own, leaving her family and Whit staring in her wake.

As she pushed through the door, everyone at the table seemed to exhale at the same time.

"What was that?" Whit asked.

"Liam?" Bowman guessed.

Clara nervously tucked her hair behind her ears. "It must have been."

Hunter shook his head, disgusted.

"I hate that guy," Ash said.

Whit looked around, waiting for someone to explain. They all looked at each other, as though wondering if they should explain.

He lowered his voice and leaned across the table so only Wallace family members could hear him. "Look, I know I'm just the fake boyfriend, but it would help to understand what's going on."

Clara placed a gentle hand on his arm. "It would help all of us to understand. She's not—" Clara blinked, like she'd been hit with a rush of emotion. "She's not telling us anything."

"You knew her pretty well in college, right?" Hunter asked.

"Yeah."

"And I bet in those four years you never saw her with a broken heart," Ash said.

"I saw her breaking hearts, but she never seemed to get too involved with anyone."

"We don't know what happened with this guy, or why it hit her so hard," Clara said. "But she won't talk to us about it, and she's been distracted every time she's been home in the last few months. We're worried."

"It's like she's going through the motions of being Piper." Bowman ran his hands over his face. Maisy rested her hand on his back. "I miss her."

Whit thought through the conversation he and Piper had in his living room, when she admitted to being the odd duck out in her family. Her siblings were all still here in Outcrop, connecting with each other daily. They were getting married, having children, moving into new phases of their lives. Whit might not understand Piper, but he could see that she didn't want to intrude on their joy with her unhappiness.

Whit cleared his throat. "I think maybe she feels a little like a duck sometimes."

The family turned on him in one motion, like a school of offended fish.

"What duck?" Clara asked.

"Did you just call my sister a duck?" Bowman glared at him.

"You know, like the odd duck out." They continued staring. "You all live here, and she lives in Portland."

"That doesn't make any difference," Hunter said. "We love her."

"If she is a duck, she's like the director duck, the one who tells the rest of the flock what to do."

He tried another tack. "You all live here, and anytime

she wants to see you, she has to come home. Maybe you should visit her in Portland."

"Because she likes coming home," Bowman said, then crossed his arms and dismissed Whit by glaring past him into the crowd.

"But it might be nice if you visited her on her own turf, let her take you to her coffee shops or art galleries."

"She likes my coffee," Hunter said. "To quote Piper, 'it's literally the best.'"

Whit refrained from pointing out that Piper had never been shy with hyperbole.

"It's got to be weird for her, though. Always coming home, having half her life here and half in Portland. Being the city girl in a family of ranchers."

"She's *Piper*. She's happy living there and coming home to visit. The problem right now is Liam." Bowman turned away, muttering, "Or you."

Whit drew in a breath. Piper had told him that she didn't feel like she fit with her family in confidence. She probably wouldn't like him sharing it with her family, and they certainly didn't seem to like it either.

Why can't you just let it go?

An inability to let things go was Whit's worst trait, but he wasn't going to reform right now. "I can see that from your perspective, she fits right in. But she might see it differently."

Ash, arguably his most important and helpful supporter in this campaign, leaned across the table and spoke quietly, his voice deep and threatening. "What would you know about fitting into our family?"

Whit kept eye contact with Ash as he sat back. This would be the time a smart man would apologize and say he must have it wrong. *"Sorry, folks, Piper doesn't con-*

sider herself the odd duck out, just one of the regular, odd-emus-in running around here."

Then Clara, the kind, empathetic person that she was, patted his arm. "We're a pretty tight-knit family, and I know it's a lot getting thrown in like this. But trust me, we couldn't love Piper more." She gave each of her brothers a stern look as she said to Whit, "It's really sweet that you care."

Ash nodded, then glanced at his brothers. "It *is* good that you care. That's more than I can say about Liam. And this campaign is giving her something other than him to think about."

The storm seemed to have mostly passed, although Bowman still hadn't uncrossed his arms.

"Is that why you asked her to do this?" Whit asked. "To distract her from Liam?"

Ash gave him a wry smile. "I asked Piper because she's the most capable woman I know. I think her performance at the rodeo this afternoon was proof of that." He glanced at his phone, then held a text out to show everyone at the table. "Dan is calling it the Piper Effect."

PIPER LEANED HER head against the wall and exhaled. She'd tucked herself into Hunter's favorite spot behind the bar. In the rare moments the restaurant wasn't busy, she could find her brother here, his lists and clipboards piled around him. During the day, this spot was made cozy by sunlight pouring in from the windows. Right now, streetlights from Main and the occasional set of headlights were the only illumination. The music and noise from the events center were muffled.

In the half dark, with muted music, Piper felt a familiar isolation wrap around her.

Tears pushed at her lower lids, and she blinked them

back. How much longer could she stay here, in the dark silence of the main restaurant, while the party clattered on in the events center next door?

Not long. Clara and Bowman were probably already arguing about who was going to come in and comfort her. She should just pour herself a glass of pinot gris, plaster on a smile and head back in.

The last thing she needed right now was alcohol, which would only intensify her sadness. And the last thing she *wanted* was anybody's sympathy. She just wanted to be done with this annoying depression.

Piper pulled out her phone and engaged the social media app. A picture of her and Whit came up; there were hearts and likes and *oh my* faces. Over a hundred comments expressed excitement and wished her and Whit all the best.

She scrolled down, skipping through the litany of love and joy, until she got to a terse phrase near the bottom.

Happy for you, Liam had written.

Three words. Happy for you. That was it.

Piper moved her thumb to stamp a like on the comment, then stopped herself. Then started again. It would look weird to have a solo comment hanging out there without a like on it. It would make her look like she cared. She started to type a response, Thanks! then erased it.

What she wanted to say would take hundreds of words, paragraphs of information. She didn't want him to be happy for her. She wanted an apology. Maybe, I'm sorry I made you feel small when I accused you of being too much. Possibly a note to Whit, admonishing him to be a better man than Liam had been.

The happy, golden start of their relationship had been so easy, back when he cared, back when he was sweet. They weren't a perfect match, but they had fun. He was all in, moving heaven and earth to get her attention, to secure her commitment. She thought it could work. It was like she'd confidently bought a ticket and boarded a flight to a gorgeous paradise island of happiness, then wound up deplaning alone in an abandoned freight yard.

It had been nearly a year since the breakup, and she still couldn't shake the blow to her confidence. That was the worst part; she felt trapped, like nothing was ever going to lead out of this sorrow.

The door from the events center opened. Piper ducked behind the counter where Hunter kept a bottle of pinot gris for her. "Be right there!" she called to whichever sibling had come in to check on her. "I forgot where he kept it, then remembered."

"It's just me."

Piper peeked over the counter. Whit stood on the other side of the empty restaurant, hands in his pockets.

"They sent you?"

"I sent me."

She stood, crossing her arms and eyeing him. He glanced behind him toward the events center, then said, "I slipped out when they were debating whether or not you wanted to be comforted. I figured you didn't." He took a few steps toward her. "I'm terrible at comforting people, so here I am."

Something about that honest admission from her fake boyfriend made her gray world a little brighter. It felt like coming across a lone wildflower in that abandoned freight yard.

Piper smiled. "That's the sweetest fake boyfriend thing you've ever done."

"It's the least I can do, after everything you're doing for me."

Piper gazed at him steadily. She might be depressed,

not heartbroken, just…broken. But she was mad at Marc Holt, and that gave her something real to fight.

"I'm one hundred percent in for this campaign, Whit. I know I wasn't your first choice, but it's personal now. I'll help where I can. I mean it."

He nodded, a real smile emerging. "It's hard to admit I need help, but I do. According to the social media reactions, your help is exactly the kind I need."

She held his gaze for a moment, then nodded. Her sadness didn't lift, but it was tempered with the anger Holt inspired in her.

He glanced down at his boots, then gestured to her phone on the counter, still open to Liam's comment, still no response from her. "You want to talk about it?"

"Nope."

"You want to argue about something else?"

"No, let's just get back in there." She pulled a wineglass down from the rack. "I love this song."

Whit, hands back in his pockets, made a face as he twisted around toward the events center. "This isn't real country music."

Piper looked up from the glass and frowned. "Yes, it is."

He raised one eyebrow. "No, it isn't."

"A man is singing about his truck. I hear a fiddle. How is this not country music?"

"His truck is running, and the woman he's dating is sitting in it with him. That's far too positive to be a country song."

"Oh, don't be ridiculous. There's plenty of classic country that's positive."

"Name one song."

"Johnny Cash, 'Walk the Line.'"

"'Walk the Line'? No, that's depressing when you

think about it. He has to subvert his true nature to be in a relationship."

"His true nature was being a jerk. And who even *thinks* about country music? The whole point is you're supposed to enjoy it, not think about it."

"Nothing that has been produced in the last thirty years can even be considered real country music."

"What makes something real?"

He rolled his eyes. "Don't try to turn this into a debate about the nature of existence."

"I'm just saying. Modern country music *is* country music. It's largely produced in Nashville and put out by country labels and played on country stations. That makes it country music."

"New country has just become an industry, an image."

"As opposed to what it used to be? Back in the good old days when musicians didn't want to make money?"

"Country music used to be performed by honest, hardworking, heartbroken musicians."

"Then I guess today most people find the tunes by dishonest, affluent, happy people a little more catchy."

Whit sputtered out a laugh, then winked at her. A warm feeling spread through her chest as the realization of what he'd done hit her. He'd argued her out of a funk.

"Feeling better?" he asked.

She laughed, shaking her head. "Somehow, yes. Thank you. That's exactly what I needed."

He took a few steps toward her. "Thank *you*, Piper. I don't know what's going on—" he gestured to her phone on the counter "—but I appreciate your help. Ash is right. You're the perfect woman for this job."

She scoffed. "I'm the only single woman between the ages of twenty-three and thirty that Ash knows."

"Well, then, he knows the right woman."

She felt a little heat rising up her neck at the unexpected compliment. But it was dark in here, and he'd never know. Still, she ducked back under the bar. "I guess I should find the wine and get back in there before we're missed." Piper knelt to open the small wine fridge and pulled out several bottles of white until she found the lone pinot gris. There was a note stuck to the label that read, "Piper's wine. Please don't serve to customers unless you want to feel her wrath."

Tears crushed at her eyes. She had the *best* family.

"You okay down there?" Whit called.

"Just fine," she answered, wiping her eyes. She composed herself, then stood and held up the bottle. "Want a glass of pinot gris?"

"What is that, exactly?"

"What is it?" Piper positioned the bottle under Hunter's fancy, wall-mounted corkscrew and opened it. "It's wine."

"I assumed. What's it taste like?"

Piper poured a glass and passed it to Whit. "What are you afraid it's going to taste like?"

He sniffed it. "Argumentative matchmaker."

She poured herself a small glass, out of love for a brother who kept this on hand for her. "What could possibly be more refreshing?"

The door from the events center opened, letting in noise and light. Ash's frame filled the doorway. "Piper? Whit?"

"Hmm?" Piper glanced over, doing her best impression of herself when she'd been interrupted.

"I have some news I think you'll both be interested in. I just talked to Dan."

Whit strode toward Ash. "What did he say? I know it's too early for real information about the Piper Effect—"

"The Piper Effect?" she echoed.

"What's the verdict?" Without pausing for Ash to answer, Whit continued, "Because I think she's doing great."

Ash dropped a hand on Whit's shoulder to settle him, just like he did with his son, his brothers and even the horses. "She is. Dan just got a call from Holt's campaign. They're pulling the advertisement. Seems it's only making people more excited about your relationship with Piper."

Piper's arms shot up in victory, and she let out a whoop. "I told you everyone loves a reformed rake!"

Whit shook his head. "I'm still not sure what you mean by *rake*, or if it even applies to me. But you nailed it, Piper."

"Right? He's pulling the ad. That's what we wanted. Mission accomplished."

"Is he offering an apology?" Whit asked.

"A private one. According to campaign officials, Marc and Bunny weren't aware of the content."

Piper snorted. "So, that bit at the end about, 'I'm Marc Holt, and I approve this ad,' was what? An oversight?"

She laughed, but Whit didn't seem to be feeling her happiness. He slipped his hands in his pockets and gazed down at his boots. His eyebrows furrowed like they used to in college when he got flummoxed in an argument. Ash didn't seem to understand the reaction either.

"This is good, right?"

Whit looked up and gave her a quick nod. "It's good. It's just coming awfully easily."

"Because he knows he lost and made himself look petty." Piper couldn't understand why Whit wasn't more excited about this. She'd been asked to help because of one campaign ad, and in less than three days, they'd pulled the ad. How satisfying was that?

"He did. And because he knows that, he's going to be on the offensive, looking for another way to strike." Whit let out a breath. "He's not retreating. He's reloading."

CHAPTER FIVE

HELPING SOMEONE CAMPAIGN for county commissioner included an inordinate amount of time spent on metal bleachers. This wasn't Piper's first 4-H livestock auction, but it sure felt like the longest. Piper shifted as she spoke on the phone to her client, while Whit chatted with the couple on their right about water rights and salmon restoration. The steady voice of the auctioneer droned in the background as kids brought their animals into the dusty arena.

When Holt's campaign pulled the slanderous advertisement, she and Whit had less than forty-eight hours to celebrate before the opposition came back swinging. Rather than one powerful blow, Holt let loose a swarm of smaller insults, like an army of well-trained mosquitos whining in the ears of voters.

Whit was still convinced something big was coming, but Piper couldn't even imagine what that would be. Whit's business dealings, his intellect, his commitment to the environment, even his choice of truck were all called into question. Seriously, what was next? His haircut?

Piper glanced up from her call. Whit's light brown hair was sliding onto his forehead again. She reached up to push it back under his Stetson. Her move distracted him from talking about spawning salmon for half a second, but he looked better this way. Okay, maybe not *better*. She'd always liked the way his hair fell against his forehead in an enthusiastic mess, but he seemed more serious this way.

At any rate, their mission was *not* accomplished once the slanderous advertisement was pulled, and Piper had to spend more and more time in central Oregon with her pretend boyfriend. This was her fourth trip in three weeks. She didn't mind helping him, and he needed her help. It was just a lot, what with the various life incidentals she had going on. Little things got in her way, like her home, the business she ran and a pregnant dachshund to care for.

All of which added up to taking calls from distressed clients while sitting on metal bleachers at a livestock auction in Redmond.

"Are you okay?" Whit asked her.

Piper nodded, then shuffled her bidding card to her other hand and cradled the phone to her ear so she could better communicate with Svetlana, a lovely, if overly nervous, client. "You have your first date on Tuesday."

"What?" Whit nearly jumped out of the bleachers.

Piper indicated her phone, and Whit let out a sigh of relief. She patted him on the shoulder with her bidding card, mildly aware of the auctioneer saying, "I have four fifteen from number eighty-three, do I hear four twenty? Four twenty."

Speaking to Svetlana, she said, "He's in his late fifties and works in finance. Remember, this is just a practice date. You don't have a lot riding on it."

"Practice date?" Whit gave a dramatic shudder. "Real dates are bad enough."

Piper scowled and bopped him with the bidding card.

"I hear four twenty-five," the auctioneer rambled.

Piper widened her eyes at Whit, imploring him to stop responding to her conversation. He could be such a pain sometimes. Whit wrapped an arm around her waist and kissed the top of her head as though there was nothing more adorable than a multitasking woman trying to run her business while being on a fake date at a 4-H auction.

"You're going to be fine, Svetlana. I want you to open up to the possibility that this might even be fun."

It wasn't unusual for clients to lose their nerve for dating just as they finished all the personal work they needed to get ready for that first date. It was like they'd spent so much time dreaming about finding the perfect partner, they were more comfortable imagining a relationship than actually being in one.

A text came in on her phone, just as Svetlana began a downward spiral of self-doubt. Piper shifted her bidding card to her other hand, and she held out her phone so she could read the text.

"I hear four forty," the auctioneer said. "Four fifty?"

"Piper?" Whit tried to get her attention again.

She held her bidding card to shield her phone from the stream of sunlight coming in so she could actually see the text. Over the speakers, Svetlana questioned her ability to find something to wear as Piper scanned a message from another client. *Ugh.* Brian didn't like Keith, either. That man was so picky, she wasn't sure she'd ever find someone for him.

"Four forty-five, going once."

"Piper!" Whit said, more sharply.

She held up her bidding card to silence him for a moment as she spoke into the phone. "Svetlana, you can do this. You can."

Svetlana admitted she was scared. Piper infused enthusiasm into her voice. "You are a sixty-two-year-old woman. You left a terrible relationship, moved halfway around the world, started your own company. You go after everything you want, and you succeed. You can have coffee with a nice man."

The auctioneer's gavel hit the podium as he said, "Sold, to number eighty-three!"

Whit waved a hand in front of her face as she wrapped up the conversation.

"What?" she mouthed.

Whit turned her bidding card around so she could see the number.

Eighty-three.

She looked up at the auctioneer who was pleased with the price, then around the metal bleachers, where 4-H supporters were applauding her generosity. Piper was now the proud owner of more beef than she could eat in five years.

She let out a very long breath, then spoke into the phone as calmly as possible. "Svetlana, I need to take off, but know I'm cheering for you. Text me as soon as the date finishes up and let me know how it goes, okay? Yep, you too. Goodbye."

Piper cradled her face in her hands.

"Did you just buy a cow?" Whit asked.

Piper glanced up to see a twelve-year-old nodding his thanks to her as he drove the animal out of the arena. "Looks like."

He patted her on the back. "Only you, Piper."

Piper still had to respond to the urgent text from Brian, would probably be getting another distressed call from Svetlana and now owned upwards of a thousand pounds of beef.

Was this rock bottom?

"Why did you even get a bidding card in the first place?" Whit asked.

"Because we're at a 4-H auction. That's what you do."

"That's what *you* do. I'm here to drum up votes."

"Yeah. I hear the middle-school farm enthusiast is a powerful voting block."

Whit gazed at her for a moment, then turned his attention to another kid leading her steer into the arena. He dropped his voice so he couldn't be heard by anyone sitting near them. "You doing okay with all this?"

She pressed her lips together. Okay or not, she *needed* this. Exhausting and near-constant multitasking kept her from slipping back into the bleak, murky lap pool of her own thoughts.

"I'm fine."

"You accidentally bought a cow."

Piper gazed at the phone in her hands. "True. But I also got a lovely sixty-two-year-old woman to go on her first date in over thirty years." She looked up at him. "That feels pretty amazing."

He grinned at her, that smile making her feel pretty amazing too. Whit had myriad ways of smiling at her. There was *smug smile,* after he'd made a good point during one of their arguments. *Fake smile* made him look more like a Halloween decoration than a boyfriend. His *sorry smile* came out when she was trapped in some painful campaign situation. *Reluctant respect smile* when she did something he wasn't sure was a good idea that then turned out to be.

But she couldn't pin a name on this smile. It was sweet, like he was both surprised and humbled. Like she'd exposed a side of herself he wasn't expecting.

He turned his eyes back to the arena. "That's cool. You like your job, don't you?"

She pushed her hair back behind her ears, inadvertently flashing her bidding number. Whit snatched it out of her hands, then placed it at his feet.

"I love my work," she said, ignoring his subtle suggestion that she was on the cusp of buying another kid's 4-H project. "I love it. There's nothing in the world more important than what I do." She nodded regally, lowering her voice to say, "When we're done with all this, and you and I have our fake breakup, I'm going to match you up with someone perfect."

The color drained out of his face. "Whoa. Wait. I never said—"

"Oh, but you did say. The first day, when I agreed to all this, you said that when the campaign was over, you'd figure out why you can't commit and that you'd let Clara set you up."

He glanced around to make sure no one was listening, then whispered, "I said I'd let Clara set me up, not you."

"And the difference is?"

He coughed out a laugh. "Where do I start?"

"So, wait, you trust me with your world-saving, all-encompassing political campaign, but not with your heart?"

He gazed at her for a moment. "Yeah. Exactly."

Piper propped her feet up on the bleachers and rested her elbows on her knees. "You get that I'm really good at my job, right?"

"I have no doubt."

"Then what's the problem?"

He watched as a girl guided a hog nearly three times her own size into the arena. "I don't know. I guess I feel like if you set me up with someone, you'd get super serious about it. And then I'd be—"

"In a relationship?"

He chuckled, eyes widening as he said, "Yeah. Scary."

"You're as bad as Svetlana."

He set his feet next to hers on the bleacher and imitated her posture. "How do you start with a client like Svetlana? It's gotta be hard to help someone who is afraid of what they want."

"The same way we start with everyone, having them memorize the love rules."

"You make your clients memorize rules?"

"Yep. And you're going to have to memorize them eventually. Want to get started?"

"I'm not a client yet."

"You will be. I'll give you this part of the service for free."

Whit held his hands out, grasping for any excuse. "But what if I fall in love with someone before you have the chance to set me up?"

Piper rolled her eyes. "If you can run your ranch, win this election and fall in love all before November seventh, I'll be impressed. We may have to hire you as a freelance matchmaker if that's the case."

He laughed. "Okay, fine. Hit me with the rules."

Piper gazed at him for a second. Would she get the mystery smile after she explained the rules? They were relationship gold; she had five years of evidence to prove it. But would he see it that way?

Well, whatever. The rules *were* gold, and he could take them and lead a happy life or leave them and be miserable. His choice.

"Number one, never waste time on someone who isn't into you."

Whit nodded, then glanced at his hands as a flush ran up his neck. Piper grinned at him. "I'm guessing there were a few women who broke this rule with you?"

"I tried to be clear, but sometimes it seemed like the more distant I was, the more convinced they became we were supposed to be together. I would try to be nice—"

"Oh, yeah. It's the 'nice' that gets them every time." Piper patted his back. "It's all about the intermittent reinforcement."

"What's intermittent reinforcement?"

"It's what gets people addicted to gambling or checking their social media feeds or playing video games. Intermittent reinforcement is when you're randomly rewarded for a specific action, and it is *the* most powerful way to shape behavior."

Whit wrinkled his brow like he was confused, but understood that he really needed to know this information.

Piper continued, "In relationships, things can start off strong, with intense emotions. But if one of the partners starts to drift away, the other can get caught up waiting for the hits of pleasure you get from a text or a kind word or a kiss. You stop seeing the whole picture. It doesn't matter that you logically know you're not very happy, intermittent reinforcement keeps your focus on those rare moments of sweetness. Like a gambler only thinks of the jolt of pleasure from winning, and a social media addict is living for the likes and comments and shares, rather than real human connection."

Whit gazed at his hands for a long time. Piper imagined he'd been guilty of intermittently reinforcing the attachment of any number of women. But then he looked up and said, "Yeah. I remember falling for someone like that back in college."

"You?" Whit had always seemed so sure of himself; she couldn't imagine him pining over anyone.

He gave her a long look, then gazed back out at the arena. "Me."

This was starting to feel way more serious than she'd intended. Piper cleared her throat and jumped back into the rules. "Love rule number two—to find love, love yourself first. Super important. Number three—know your core values and find someone who shares them."

He looked at her, the respect smile emerging. "Can

you imagine what would happen if everyone followed that advice?"

"Total world peace, am I right?"

He chuckled. "Maybe not total world peace—"

"*Total* world peace," she asserted, holding eye contact. "Think about it. Think about all the human misery that comes as a result of fear and greed. If people were happy and had strong connections with others, be it a partner or friends or family, they wouldn't seek to harm others in an attempt to feel better." Whit tried to interrupt her, but she spoke over him. "They'd already feel better because they'd cultivated strong human connections."

He held out a hand indicating a truce. "Let's save this argument for the next time you and I are speaking at the United Nations. What are the rest of the rules?"

Piper glowered. She wanted him to admit she was right, but she also wanted him to learn the rest of the love rules while he was still listening. "Okay, love rule number four—know your love chemicals. Choose when, and with whom, to release them."

"The chemicals are—?"

"All about canoodling. Canoodling releases chemicals like vasopressin and oxytocin, making you feel like you're in love."

He laughed, and Piper couldn't help but continue, "If you release love chemicals with someone you're not in love with, you're going to feel attached, and that can lead to bad decisions."

Whit nodded. "Got it."

"Number five—and a personal favorite—look good, feel good."

He glanced down at her outfit, then his eyes ran to her face and hair. "You've got that one hammered in, don't you?"

"As will you, by the time we're finished with all this."

He smiled at her, and there it was. The mystery smile she couldn't quite pin a meaning on. It felt good. A little too good, if she were being honest. And given that the smile was intermittent and reinforced her behavior of trying to impress Whit, it was time to look away.

"That's really all you need to know. Follow the rules, put yourself out there, you'll find someone in no time. Then you'll fall in love, and the world will be a better place." She nodded firmly. "You're welcome."

He bumped her shoulder with his, his smug smile flexing. "How come you're not in a relationship, then? If love saves the world?"

Piper's throat constricted. She blinked hard, willing herself to make a snappy comeback. She tilted her head, like she did when they sparred, opening her mouth to say something funny, something light and witty. The cold, watery sadness flooded her system again, blocking her throat, exhausting her. She froze, unable to snap back like she should. Unable to do anything she should, just stuck in this frustrating, panic-fueled sadness.

Whit started talking quickly, leaning down so his Stetson covered the expression on her face. "I'm sorry, Piper."

She shook her head, wanting to say it was no big deal, but her throat was too dry to speak. He was still talking, apologizing. His apology was now longer than Liam's had been when he walked out. She couldn't hear him over the rush in her ears.

Piper drew in a breath, then put her hand on his arm to stop him. Whit ran his hand over hers, then wound their fingers together. The gentle touch stilled her, helped the air reach her lungs. The sounds of the arena came back to her; the pounding of her heart subsided.

Whit was very close, speaking quietly. "For what it's worth, your brothers think he's a fool."

Piper nodded, but it wasn't Liam who was a fool for dumping her. She was a fool for allowing the breakup to knock her down like this.

Love rule number one: don't waste time on someone who isn't into you.

Or even worthy of you.

According to Liam, she was also a fail on number three—know your core values and find someone who shares them. "We don't want the same things," he'd said during that last, short conversation, "and it's too hard for you to give on key issues for me."

She was too selfish, too attached to her way of doing things. He'd told her that her core values were to put herself first, her family second and he wasn't even sure he came in third.

While it felt like a slap in the face at the time, there was some truth to it. She liked the things she liked: good espresso, short-legged dogs, her downtown loft. Avocado toast. It had been hard to pin down exactly what Liam's values were, so how was she supposed to know if they shared them or not?

And of course her family was important. She'd been under the impression that Liam might join her family one day. When he didn't get along with her brothers, it was impossible to see his point of view.

So yeah, she was a hard fail on love rules number one and three, and if she were honest, she'd pushed number four a little further than she should have. As far as love rule number two went, she thought she loved herself going into the relationship, but now that it was over, she wasn't so sure.

Thankfully, she was nailing rule number five: look good, feel good.

Except for the part about feeling good.

Whit placed a hand on her back, rubbing slow circles. Piper blinked. They were here to campaign for heaven's sake. She needed to get it together. The auction was over, and they still had another stop to make. She pulled in a deep breath.

"Do you want my cow?"

His gaze connected with hers, and he shook his head, questioning the abrupt change of subject. She pushed on. "Seriously, let me give you the cow. I don't have a freezer."

"Piper, I'm a rancher. I already have cattle. What am I going to do with an extra thousand pounds of beef?"

"What am *I* going to do with it?" Piper stood and dusted off her behind, then stretched.

Whit picked up her auction number and his jacket. "Feed it to your family?"

"Jet supplies the family with beef." Piper pulled her sunglasses over her eyes and headed down the bleachers. "He's aggressive about it."

Whit laughed, then reached out and grabbed her hand, keeping it in his as they walked to his truck. It felt so natural. And while holding hands was a long way off from canoodling, she felt the tiniest spark of oxytocin flow, helping her feel a little better. Not in love or ready to make a bad decision, but just…better.

He gave a light tug so she spun toward him in the parking lot. "Piper, helping me with this campaign is a huge commitment. You've got your business and a life."

She waved a hand in front of her face. "I don't really have a life right now."

His grip tightened. "If you need a break to get your work done, or to just have a break, let me know. Because

Dan's gonna have us both running nonstop until November unless you tell me otherwise."

She cleared her throat, looking from his face to their hands. "Helping you is helping me." With her sunglasses on, he couldn't see the tears that were gathering. He couldn't see how much she needed this right now.

"Okay. But you have to promise to tell me if it gets to be too much."

She rolled her eyes and resumed her march toward the truck. "There's no such thing as too much."

"Really? Because you accidentally bought a cow."

"You purposefully bought those pants." She eyed his slacks with an exaggerated frown. "That's a cry for help."

Whit started to defend the choice of fabric he had covering his legs when Piper asked, "Where are we headed?"

"The home builders' expo." He opened the passenger-side door for her, and she let him help her into the truck.

"Ooh! Fun."

"Are you being sarcastic?"

"Oh, no. I love home...stuff." She pulled off her sunglasses and checked her makeup in the drop-down mirror. "I'm really into looking at homes, despite the fact that I never plan on living in an actual house."

"You don't?"

She shook her head. "I'm happy in my loft." Whit closed her door and trotted around to the other side of the vehicle. As he hopped behind the wheel, Piper continued, "My home is perfect. I'm in the Pearl District, overlooking the river. I have what's technically a two-bedroom, but really it's more like one bedroom, one really large closet." Her phone buzzed again. "Seriously. My clients are so super needy today. Is it a full moon?"

"I don't think so."

As she checked the text, her phone rang. "I'm so sorry. Do you mind?"

"No, go ahead. Maybe you can get them to take some beef?"

Piper grinned at him as she answered her phone.

But Whit never caught her smile. He'd pulled out his own phone before starting the truck. His face fell, blood rushing from his cheeks, hair falling against his forehead, as he studied the screen.

Piper put a hand on his arm. He shook his head, dropped his phone in the console and started the truck. Was it possible that Marc Holt found a way to strike even lower?

"Thanks so much. I appreciate your vote," Whit said to the high school teacher he'd been talking to. The man nodded, then picked up a few pamphlets to distribute to his friends. The moment he walked away, the image of the email attachment Dan had sent earlier flooded back to him. His stomach clenched. It was no surprise that Holt would stoop to this, but Jana?

Yeah, Jana. His sister never had been able to resist the drama, or the limelight.

"Whit is actually super tidy, like his house is pristine," Piper was saying to another possible voter, bringing his focus back to the task at hand. "I wouldn't have expected it either, but he's pretty organized."

Whit tried to focus on the positive. They were getting a lot of attention at their booth at the home show. Dan gave all the volunteers shirts that said Ask Me Anything about Whit! Piper had pulled out a Sharpie and amended her shirt with Literally. Ask Me Anything. I'm in the Mood to Dish.

But just as she was about to convince this woman to vote for him based on the cleanliness of his kitchen, her phone rang, again. She rolled her eyes at him. "Ugh. Do you mind?"

"You've got a business to run. I support small businesses, remember?"

Whit forced a smile and gave Piper space to take her call. She'd been working so hard on this campaign, and her chatty, cheerful presence in the booth was a welcome distraction from Dan's email. It wasn't that Holt's latest ad was some type of political ace in the hole. It might convince a few people to vote for him, but it wasn't going to sway the election. It was just so mean and petty. How did Holt even know about this wound, much less know just how to strike at it?

The disintegration of his family, and Holt's willingness to exploit it, was enough to make him wonder if there was any good left in the world.

"So glad to hear it's going well," Piper said into the phone. "I knew you could do this, Seth."

The man on the other end of the line mumbled something back. Piper grinned as though he was a student and had just learned the complicated math formula she'd been trying to teach him for weeks.

"Okay. Go have fun. And text to let me know how it goes."

Piper disengaged the call, then leaned her head back, heaving out a sigh.

He laughed. "Everything okay?"

"It will be." Her phone buzzed with a text, and she glanced at it. "Svetlana just did a dry run at the coffee shop." Piper raised her arms in victory and whooped. "She's gonna do it!"

Whit let Piper's simple joy warm him. There was a *lot* of good in this world, and some of it was even in the booth with him right now.

"What?" she asked, noticing him staring.

"I don't think I've ever seen anyone so excited about someone else getting coffee."

"Getting coffee is always exciting. Speaking of which, do you think the Bend Expo Center has decent espresso?"

Whit did not think the Bend Expo Center had what Piper would consider good espresso. It was just a question of what would inspire more wrath, bad coffee or no coffee.

"Do you want to take a break and find out?"

"Nope, I'm gonna stand right here and answer questions about Whit Benton." She gave him a rogue grin, then nodded to a woman lingering at the edge of their booth. "How are you this afternoon?"

The woman smiled, then launched a string of questions at the two of them. Some of them even had to do with the upcoming election.

Piper's effect on the crowd was electric. Once she started chatting, people began laughing and having fun. This drew more people in, and soon their booth was thick with potential voters.

She was extraordinary. It was like the more she had to do, the happier she got. You'd never know the vivacious, cheerful woman gently teasing him had ever had a moment's disappointment her whole life.

"Hey!" She waved at a family slowing down on the outskirts of the crowd. "What can I tell you folks about Whit Benton? Besides his favorite color."

A man in the group stepped toward the booth, and Whit felt a wave of shock pass through him.

"Well, hello," his father said.

"Dad." Whit held out his hand, then realized how silly it was to shake his own father's hand. He offered his arms in a hug, but there was a table in between them, so hugging was even more awkward than it might have been. "Good to see you."

"Good to see you." Dad's words were forced, overly cheerful.

"Hi, Whit." His stepmom waved, dragging her son in next to her.

"Hi, Melanie. Hi, Rory."

Whit did his best to act normal in front of his father's second family. Dad had cut out on the Benton family roller coaster early on. He'd been a good parent when Whit was young, but dealing with Benton drama was more than he could handle. Or was willing to handle. When he fell in love with Melanie, she and her son became his new family.

It was fine. Good, even. Dad, Melanie and Rory were a happy family; it was what he wanted for all of them. Whit just wasn't a part of their happy family.

Piper's hand came to rest on his back, as if questioning him. *Are these people in on our charade?*

They weren't. Whit wasn't even sure he had his dad's vote.

Whit shifted, pulled an arm around her so she was slightly in front of him, like Piper could ward off the awkwardness. "Dad, Melanie, Rory, let me introduce you to Piper."

Piper's adorable smile flashed, and she skirted the table to talk to them. "So great to meet you."

"We saw you two were dating," Melanie said, a little nervous, the way she always was around him. "It was on the news."

Piper laughed. "That's probably my fault."

Dad, also nervous, seemed to shore up his resolve. "I don't know what else you could have done with the way Holt was coming after Whit here."

Relief, pure and primal, rushed through him with the realization that Dad was on his side.

Heck, it felt good to know his dad was even aware that he was running for county commissioner.

"And you're Rory?" Piper asked, focusing on his step-brother.

Rory nodded and gave a deep, one-syllable response. "Yeah."

"What year are you in school?"

Rory glanced at his mom. He had a speech impediment that made some letters extremely difficult for him to pronounce, and he was always shy about speaking to strangers. Melanie was about to respond for him when Piper threw up her arms dramatically.

"Oh my God, that's like the worst, most annoying adult question in the world, isn't it? Right up there with, 'What do you want to do when you grow up?'"

Rory blushed, then gave Piper a second, deep, "Yeah."

"Lemme try again. How do you feel about emu murals? I'm pro."

Rory was now completely spellbound. He risked a sentence with a couple of his tough letters and said, "Like the one in Outcrop?"

"Yes! Exactly. Yea or Nay?"

Rory thought for a moment, then said, "Yea."

Piper offered him a high five, and he slapped her hand back. Melanie turned to Rick, widening her eyes in awe, then she gave Whit an impressed nod. She was fiercely protective of Rory and deeply grateful to anyone who could see past his speech impediment. Piper, of course, could charm the socks off a centipede.

"How's Benton Ranch?" Dad asked.

"Good. I've had trouble hiring help this year, but I'm

still afloat. So long as Holt's plan for Hummingbird Ranch doesn't come through, I'll continue to make a profit."

Dad nodded. "That's good. You did the right thing, stepping up to run against him."

Whit had no idea how much his dad knew about the campaign. Had he been following it closely? If so, why hadn't he reached out earlier? They stood awkwardly, watching as Piper chatted and laughed with Rory and Melanie.

"You hear from your sister?" Dad finally asked.

"No. You?"

Dad shook his head, hands in his pockets. After a beat, he asked, "You see that advertisement she made?"

"Uh, yeah."

Dad caught his eye, then let out a breath. That pretty much summed up the situation.

Whit knew he should move the conversation forward, but what do you say? Dad had his new life now, and Whit didn't begrudge him that. His sister was sabotaging his campaign, and that was her MO. He'd refused to pick sides in his grandparents' divorce, so neither of them spoke to him anymore. Everyone had moved on except for him, hunkered down in the family home, waiting for everyone to show up and be a family again.

"Wouldn't that be a good idea?" Piper's chipper voice interrupted his thoughts.

"What?" Whit glanced up to see Piper beaming at him.

"If Rick, Melanie and Rory came out for a barbecue. Rory was just saying he hasn't been out to the ranch since he was little."

Whit remembered every detail of their last trip out to the Benton Ranch. His grandparents still owned the place, and Whit was a sophomore at OSU. Dad had met and married Melanie within a six-month period. The family didn't even know he was dating anyone until he called to suggest a get-together to meet Melanie and her son. Whit had come home from college, argumentative and full of himself, to find out he had a stepmom and brother. He wasn't upset, just confused and hurt that Dad had gotten remarried without so much as a text to him. The rest of the family, as expected, blew up at the announcement.

When the argument started, Whit offered to take Rory to see the cattle. He'd carried the six-year-old on a piggyback ride away from the bellowing humans to see the placid livestock. They'd had about an hour together, and he remembered it being surprisingly fun. A tiny oasis of good feeling in the midst of another huge family argument. Rory, for whatever reason, seemed to think his new stepbrother was pretty cool. As Dad and Melanie walked to the car, heads high, expressions tight, Whit had followed them, not sure of what to say or do. Dad was so angry he got straight into the driver's seat and started the car. Whit helped Rory into the back seat and gave him a fist bump. Rory's eyes watered as Whit's grandmother yelled at Dad from the front porch. But he gave Whit a little smile and whispered, "Bye, brother."

But then Whit was back at college, and Dad was moving on with his new life. As much as he wanted to be a brother to Rory, it all felt too hard. Now ten years had passed. They'd seen each other maybe twelve times since that day.

Whit shook out of the memory to find Rory's eyes fixed on him, his hopeful expression now tempered by age, but still there.

"Absolutely," Whit said. "Sounds great."

Dad and Melanie reacted with vigorous head nodding and loud agreement, masking the gamut of emotions that had to be moving through them.

"Perfect," Piper said. "You all eat beef?"

Their willingness to consume Piper's cow confirmed, Whit watched as his stepfamily drifted off. It was such a strange relationship. They weren't bad people; they just weren't *his* people. Not like Piper's family, who seemed to exist in a huge, noisy, flexible, loving mass.

"Are you mad?"

Whit looked down to see Piper vaguely gesturing. Her manicured fingers were splayed as she rotated her hands in a way that seemed to say, "Because I invited your estranged father and his second family to your home in a poorly masked attempt to get rid of some beef."

"No."

She held eye contact, calling his bluff.

"I'm not mad." It was true; he wasn't angry at Piper. Annoyed, but not angry. His anger was currently reserved for his sister, and there was a lot of it.

"Okay. I just don't want you to be mad. Rory said, like, three things about how cool the ranch was, and I offered without thinking. So I'm sorry, even though you're not mad."

"Piper, it's fine. They won't even come."

She looked shocked. Then shook her head, muttering, "Well, yeah, if you don't follow up, it's pretty likely they won't come."

Okay, now he was a little mad.

But more and more people stopped by the booth, and Whit could stuff down his feelings as they focused on the campaign.

After an hour, there was a brief lull. Piper seized the opportunity to make a break for it.

"It's past time for espresso. I'm going to give it a try, and I promise to campaign all the way over to the coffee stand and back. Can I bring you some?"

"No, thanks."

"No, thanks? I just offered you coffee."

"This would be a different conversation if you offered me a taco."

Piper rolled her eyes.

"You want me to go get the coffee for you?" he offered.

"We can't have the Whit Benton booth with no Whit in it."

He put his hands in his back pockets, fingers inadvertently brushing his phone. Sometimes he wondered.

Piper grabbed her bag. "I'll be right back."

Whit watched as she wound her way up the aisle, chatting with people, smiling brightly. He waited until she disappeared to pull out his phone.

His email was still open to the message from Dan, Heads up written in the subject line. The attachment was a simple social media advertising post of Marc Holt talking with a woman in her early thirties. She wore a denim jacket over a T-shirt with a sparkly flower on it. In the background, two kids played together on a swing set, and Whit had to assume they were his niece and nephew. The text was simple, "I'm in favor of a strong economy for central Oregon. That's why I support Marc Holt." The woman was identified as Jana Benton Brice.

The advertisement didn't come out and say it was his sister, but it had to be pretty obvious.

Did she really support Marc? Or did she just love the drama that much?

Whit slipped the phone back into his pocket and attempted to look interested and interesting. He kept the flow going, but he had to admit it was a lot easier with Piper in the booth.

"How amazing am I?"

Whit looked up to see Piper balancing a paper plate on top of two coffee cups.

"On a scale of one to ten?" he asked.

Piper nodded to the plate with her chin, and Whit lifted it off the cups.

Tamales.

It was a simple, innocent gesture that overwhelmed him. He hadn't realized how hungry he was, how much he needed to feel like someone cared, even just a little bit. And now Piper was handing him a whole plate of spicy cornmeal-wrapped goodness, smiling like it was just what you did for your fake boyfriend on the campaign trail.

He gazed at Piper, ready to thank her for this, for everything. She spoke first. "And the lady who made them is definitely voting for you. Drink this." She handed him the coffee.

"Thank you."

Coffee he didn't want and tamales he didn't ask for turned out to be the most thoughtful gesture he could imagine. That was the whirlwind known as Piper Wallace. One minute she was matching up a client, the next she was meddling with his family, then supplying the snacks. He had no idea what would happen with her from one minute to the next.

"It's an Americano. I figure that's the hardest thing to mess up." She pulled the lid off her coffee and took a whiff. "Although they may have managed to do just that."

Whit picked up the plate of tamales and took a bite, just as a group came up to the booth. Piper chirped in with information as he swallowed. The folks were smart; they had some good questions and listened thoughtfully to his answers. By the end of the conversation, they'd decided to vote for Whit, *and* go visit the tamale booth.

The crowd picked up again and remained steady throughout the afternoon while Piper's phone continued to buzz with clients. They were exhausted but sustained by the less-than-stellar espresso and thoroughly delicious tamales.

By six o'clock, the expo center began to clear out. Piper typed out a message on her phone, then sent it, letting out a huge sigh.

"Welp. This has been a day."

"You'll have a whole five days off from me, starting tomorrow," Whit reminded her.

Piper looked a little uncomfortable, as if she didn't want the time off. "That's true, but then we have, like, four campaign events in one weekend, and one of them is the Utner-Kim party."

Whit wanted to let out a groan at the idea of the Utner-Kim party, a fancy event at the vineyard of a wealthy tech entrepreneur. But you couldn't groan out loud at your own information booth.

"And then, maybe we could have your dad and his family over on Sunday?"

Whit stared at her. His fake girlfriend, solely around for the duration of the campaign, was already interfering with his family. Only Piper Wallace.

Whit shook his head. "Not until the campaign is over."

"You know they came here to support you today."

"They came here to get some ideas for kitchen tile and happened to see me."

"It's possible your family's not as completely messed up as you think it is."

"You think?" Whit pulled up Holt's newest campaign ad on his phone and handed it to her. "Check this out."

CHAPTER SIX

PIPER SAT ON the back steps of the family home at Wallace Ranch contemplating Bowman's shirt. The short sleeves were one type of plaid, the body was another, with a button placket and collar that were yet a third plaid. It was the embodiment of warring Scottish clans.

It should have been impossible for a designer to think this was a good idea, or for a factory to go through with production. How could a buyer in a clothing store look at that shirt and choose to stock it? Yet they had, and somehow at the end of all those bad decisions, her brother had chosen to pull it out of his closet and put it on.

Bowman was a very good-looking man, objectively the most handsome of her brothers. If he spent half a second thinking about what he wore, it would be amazing. Instead, he looked like he'd escaped from the rubbish bin outside a discount-clothing basement.

On a normal day, she'd take him to task for the shirt. But today, she couldn't even muster up the energy to complain about it.

All in all, she was not feeling like herself.

But she *had* to be herself. They'd had an intense round of campaigning over the last few days and were headed to a massively important party. Hunter planned this afternoon's family barbecue so she could have a relaxing break in a wild week.

What her family didn't understand was that the minute she stopped running, her thoughts came crowding in, setting her adrift into the cold, dreary sadness. She was different and floating steadily away from this tight-knit family.

"Whit, go long!" She heard her nephew Jackson yell. Whit jogged farther out into the yard to catch the throw. Her fake boyfriend launched the ball back. He was fitting in better than she did these days.

Piper gazed out at her siblings. Ordinarily when she felt out of place with her own family, she'd spend time with her sister. But Clara was rocking a fussy baby Bob in hopes of a nap, and given the set of her sleep-deprived sister's eyes, Piper imagined Clara would be getting in on that nap if she had the chance.

Piper leaned back on her elbows, looking around for something to get her out of this funk. She could pick a fight, but that seemed like too much effort. Offering to catch the ball for Jackson would result in a ball being thrown at her, and that had never been her thing. She studied Whit. He'd been a champion debater in his youth, but not an athlete. You wouldn't know it from the way he hopped up to catch the ball and launched it back at Jackson. He was relaxed and easy.

Tears pushed at the back of her eyes as she thought about Whit's sister and his whole complicated, estranged family. She was sitting around feeling sorry for herself because she was a little different from her siblings, while Whit's own sister was out actively campaigning against him.

"I'm in favor of a strong economy for central Oregon. That's why I support Marc Holt."

What was worse? Whit's sister corroborating with Marc Holt, or Marc Holt asking in the first place?

Or anyone suggesting that Holt would be good for the economy?

Piper gazed out at her family's ranch: snug stables, riding arena, the big red barn. Grassy fields, kept green with the swift running irrigation ditches, unfolded down to the two ponds. Beyond them, a hillside blanketed with Aspen and Oregon white oak rose to the north. All of this was at risk if Holt remained county commissioner.

Piper felt eyes on her and turned abruptly. Bowman had his arms crossed and was staring at her, speaking in a low voice to Maisy. *Great.* Her intuitive brother had picked up on her depression and was calling in his doctor wife to fix the situation. She was not going to disrupt this family gathering by talking about her problems.

Piper gathered Bernice into her lap and sat up straight. "Who all is going to the Utner-Kim party tonight?" she asked.

"We'll be there," Ash said, nodding seriously.

"I cannot wait to see that house," Violet said. "I heard they had it built stone for stone to resemble an actual French château they stayed at on their honeymoon."

Whit caught another pass from Jackson, but Piper could tell he was listening in on the conversation.

Jet glanced over from where he was trying to help Clara soothe the baby. "It's massive. I don't know how Lance and Bettina find each other in that house, especially considering they were living in their Airstream trailer for two years during the build."

"How do you know these people again?" Piper asked Jet. "Fancy French château-builders don't seem like your type."

Jet grinned. "I had an internship with Lance when I was at the University of Washington. Then Bettina and I worked together for a while before she and Lance started RanTech."

"Are they weird?" Piper ran her hand over Bernice's head. Her puppy eyes drooped, also exhausted. "Because they seem a little too smart and rich not to be."

Jet laughed. "They're a little weird. No more so than anyone else around here."

Whit tucked the football under his arm and moved closer. "You do know Lance and Bettina Utner-Kim are probably the most important social influencers in central Oregon."

Jet shrugged. "You'll like them."

Piper gave Whit a wry smile and widened her eyes at Jet's casual appraisal of the situation. The Utner-Kims had made an obscene amount of money in the tech industry, then left Seattle to start a vineyard in central Oregon. They had the nerdy-chic glamor of two smart, hardworking people who'd made it big and were now gleefully enjoying their money. Piper had no doubt that they'd vote for Whit. Most people who put half a thought into the process would. The problem was that most people didn't have the first idea of what the county commissioner did. Holt was a popular, likable incumbent who hadn't made any major changes…yet.

Whit's campaign needed the Utner-Kims' outward support. They would inspire others to put up lawn signs, to share posts and, most important, to vote. Whit's campaign needed their endorsement.

A little money would be nice too.

Clara looked over the head of her squalling baby. "You're going to love them. Bettina has great style, and their house is *amazing*."

Piper's heart dropped in an unexpected free fall. She fought to keep her flippant tone.

"You've been there too?" she asked, but Clara didn't hear her over the squalls of little Bob.

Of course, Clara had been to their house. The Utner-Kims were friends of Jet's and new friends for Clara. They had kids; Clara and Jet had a kid. They all preferred middle-of-nowhere Oregon to the big city.

Piper swallowed hard. There was nothing wrong with Clara making new friends.

It's fine.

Her sister should totally make friends who lived nearby, had great style and kids and a château. It wouldn't override *their* friendship, their sisterhood.

It couldn't.

"Cool. I'm glad everyone's going." She flipped her hair back behind her ears. "It's super important."

A dry ache formed in the back of her throat. It was so frustrating to have these moments sneak up on her. But she couldn't shake the feeling that Liam had dumped her because she was fundamentally flawed, selfish, too much. Unlovable.

And maybe it was only a matter of time before her family caught on to her flaws too. They would all just become closer as the years went on, and she would be drifting solo, a hundred and fifty miles away in a completely different world.

"Piper?"

She looked up to see Maisy striding toward her, concerned-doctor smile firmly in place. Piper tried to give her the conspiratorial grin that generally worked on Bowman's wife, but it must have fallen flat because Maisy asked, "How are you feeling?"

"I'm fine." Piper picked up the sleeping dachshund and placed her on the grass next to her. Bernice shifted, then snored. "I'm hungry." She cupped her lips and called over to Hunter, "Because my brother's taking forever!"

Piper glanced at Jet and Clara's overtired baby. That was how she felt, so bone-tired that she couldn't rest.

Maisy made eye contact with Bowman in obvious husband-wife communication before saying quietly to Piper, "You don't seem like yourself."

Piper eyed her coolly. Maisy lifted her chin and stared right back.

There was nothing worse than a trained medical professional recognizing your signs of distress.

"Yeah, no, I'm good. I'm um…" Piper faked a cough, then pointed to the house. "I'm gonna grab some water."

Before Maisy could stop her or Bowman could get involved, Piper trotted up the stairs, into the kitchen. She wasn't going to ruin this perfectly nice family afternoon talking about her problems.

Piper grabbed a glass and headed to the sink, as if she had to go along with her own charade even when she was alone. The kitchen was crowded with family memories, even when empty of actual family members. Big discussions, lazy afternoons, epic piles of dishes when Hunter experimented in here, learning to cook. The first time they had Jet over to dinner and Clara ran smack into him. The time Ash paced around, growling at the family like a big, nervous, love-struck tiger as he waited for Violet to arrive for dinner.

Piper and her unwanted glass of water moved into the living room. In her childhood, this was the epicenter of pillow fights and forts. Once Ash took over the family home, the room straightened up like a soldier waiting for inspection. But while it was regularly cleaned with military precision, the occasional pillow fight still broke out, particularly when her parents were home from their travels.

She glanced out the window to where Ash stood in the yard, his arm around Violet. They'd be married soon, and

Ash might have more children. If anyone could help her oldest brother relax and enjoy a living-room fort, it was Violet. There would be a hundred new memories made here, and she wouldn't be privy to any of them. She'd just be the aunt who came in from Portland from time to time. She used her pinky finger to pressure her tear ducts into getting it together, then gulped in a breath.

Okay, she might just be the aunt from Portland, but she *would* bring the best presents.

The back door creaked open. Jet's careful steps trod into the kitchen, followed by Clara's. Their silence suggested they had a sleeping baby, and if Clara saw Piper moping around in the living room, she'd feel compelled to skip her nap and comfort her.

Piper slipped to the front door. From the porch, she could hear the voices of her family. The scent of Hunter's grilling reminded her that she was legitimately hungry. The ranch waited for her, as it always did. The ponds shimmered in the afternoon sunlight, with Clara's running path looping around them. The simple bunkhouse her brothers had shared through their twenties looked exaggeratedly rundown when contrasted with the snug red barn they'd cleaned up for Clara's wedding. The gardener's cottage was ringed with flowers Hunter had planted for Ani. But the part of the property Piper was drawn to today was the stables. Growing up, she'd spent hours there, the horses helping her develop confidence and independence. She'd started teaching riding lessons when she was still in high school and tried barrel racing on a lark. In the stables, you could be alone, while not alone at all.

Keeping her eyes forward, she launched down the front steps and walked quickly across the yard. She slipped into the barn, letting the familiar smell of sweet hay and horses wash over her as her eyes adjusted to the light.

She scanned the aisles until she found the friend she was looking for. Midnight walked to the front of his stall and let out a breath. Piper draped her arms around the gentle, sweet animal and finally let herself cry.

"Lunch is ready!" Hunter called from the big red barn.

Whit breathed in the scent of barbecue mingled with the "family special" from Eighty Local. He'd never met a family where a simple gathering was as big a deal as this. When these people wanted to get something done, they went all in: political campaign, holiday sales event, lunch.

It was impressive and more than a little depressing when contrasted with his own family.

"I'm in favor of a strong economy for central Oregon. That's why I support Marc Holt."

It was unlikely Jana knew the full definition of *economy*, much less the intricacies of what made this one tick. It was even less likely that she understood Holt's plans for the area. All she needed to know was that her little brother was receiving a lot of public attention right now, and she wanted her share.

Whit's stomach turned and his throat tightened as he thought of the look in his sister's eye in the photograph and of the two children in the background whom he'd never met and who would be raised to hate him. It all felt so hopeless, so pointless.

"Grab a plate!" Ash said, slapping him on the shoulder as he walked to the barn.

Ordinarily, the instruction to "grab a plate" was one of his favorites, and he appreciated being included in the family gathering. But he needed a few minutes off from the family. Their happiness rubbed at the wound Marc Holt and Jana had opened.

"Uh, yeah." Whit put his hands in his pockets and

turned, scanning the well-kept property. "Just a sec. I need to send Dan a quick text."

The family jostled into the barn, laughing and teasing each other. Bernice woke from her nap and waddled in behind them. Piper was probably inside already, directing traffic.

A late summer breeze wafted across the fields, bringing the scent of the creek that ran along the property. Whit would give himself five minutes to let the anger at Jana flow, then he'd stop up the dam of emotions and try to enjoy his time with the Wallace family.

He strode across the back lawn, not headed in any particular direction. The sleek brown Canadian horses were in their turnout pens alongside the stables, watching him as he walked past. Whit climbed over the split rail fence and hopped into the riding arena. The space was open to the stables on one end, with a half wall overlooking the tack room. The tidy structure and orderly ranch were the product of this well-functioning family. Piper's parents had bought the land and built this place all while teaching full-time. As the kids grew up, they helped with the operation. Whit could imagine Piper in the arena, fierce and focused as she practiced her barrel racing.

It took a minute for Whit's eyes to adjust to the dim light as he slipped from the arena into the stables. He was impressed by how Ash ran the place. He had the help of his siblings and sometimes the parents, when they weren't traveling.

Yeah, the Wallaces were an incredible family. It was enough to make a man wish he were in a real relationship with Piper Wallace. Almost.

But she would be back in Portland the minute the last ballot was cast in this race. And with any luck, and a lot of help, he'd be the Deschutes County commissioner.

A soft nicker echoed down the aisle, almost as though a horse were calling him. Whit glanced up to see Piper leaning her forehead against the shoulder of a large, dark animal. It looked like she was...

Yes. She was crying.

The horse pushed his nose into her shoulder, and Piper wrapped her arms more solidly around the animal.

Whit was at a loss. Consoling crying women had never been a strong suit of his. It was part of why Piper appealed to him: she was so completely capable. His sister was the one who cried, and his mother made those tears everyone's business. Whit was suspicious of anyone over the age of sixteen crying, and while that was something that could clearly land him in a therapist's office, it was what it was.

That said, he had his part in these tears. Piper had been burning the candle at both ends and melting the wax in the middle as she tried to help him. She had to be exhausted, which would exacerbate whatever it was in her personal life she was refusing to share. He'd suspected this was all getting to be too much for her, and the 4-H auction really hammered it home. She was capable of running her business, her life and this campaign, but it was taking its toll. He needed to offer her the last thing he wanted to give her: an out.

Whit gazed at Piper, slumped against the horse, tears slipping down her cheeks. He knew her well enough to understand that she would not take kindly to being comforted. But if he returned to the barbecue without her, a member of her family would come in to comfort her.

Was pathetically bad comfort from him better or worse in this situation?

It didn't really matter. Whit knew what he had to do: offer her a chance to gracefully back out of all this. He needed to help her into a situation where she didn't need comforting.

He approached her slowly, then reached out and patted the horse with her. She let out an exasperated sigh but didn't move away. He shifted closer, patting the horse, the soft noises of the stables filtering in around them, the occasional bursts of laughter or conversation from her family wafting through from the open arena.

"You've got a lot going on right now," Whit forced himself to say.

"I'm good at a lot."

He cleared his throat. "Maybe you should take a break."

She shook her head the way she did when she was frustrated with him. "I don't want to take a break. I want to pet this horse and cry. How is that a problem?"

Whit put his free hand in his pocket and studied his boots, finally saying the last thing he wanted to, "I feel like I should let you out of this. If it's all too much, I can campaign on my own."

"No," she snapped, finally looking at him. Even in this dark barn, with her tear-stained face, she was gorgeous. It was as though one day she'd just decided she was going to be the most beautiful woman in Oregon, then followed through with a step-by-step plan. "We can't stop now. That would look suspicious. Anyway, this is my fight too. I'm in."

Whit let out a breath. "What do you need?"

"I need to stand in this dark barn, pet a horse and cry. Why are you making a fuss about it?"

"I'm not making a fuss."

"Yes, you are. That's your fussy face."

Whit shifted. "Every time I try to talk to you about something serious, like the fact that you are clearly overwhelmed, you turn the tables and deflect."

"I'm not turning anything. I'm just asking why you're making a big deal out of nothing."

"Because I don't think crying in the stables when your entire family is enjoying a great meal is nothing."

She glared at him, but a loud hiccup completely ruined the effect. He tried to hold back his smile. She turned away, but he could tell she was stifling a laugh as well. She splayed her fingers, gesturing toward the party. "Sometimes my family can be overwhelming."

"Always. Your family is always overwhelming."

That got him a grudging smile. "They just all have so much happening right now, and it's good. And I'm, like, in Portland."

Her words made no sense at all, but Whit could sense her meaning. He took a guess. "Is it hard for you? Your siblings are all getting married, and Clara and Jet are starting a family?"

She raised her chin. "I couldn't be happier for my sister. Bob is a perfect miracle."

"I didn't ask if you were happy for your siblings. I asked if it was hard for you."

She held eye contact for just a moment, and then her body seemed to sag with the relief of admitting the truth. "It's silly."

"Tell me."

She leaned her forehead against the horse. After a long moment, she said, "I'm jealous."

That actually *was* silly. What could anyone else have that Piper would possibly be jealous about?

"Of…?"

"I don't even know. That's the problem, it's like a complex jealousy, full of conflicting hopes and needs. I'm not jealous of what my sister has. Clara deserves more happiness than any human on earth. She is literally the best person. It's just—"

"It's just that she's moving in one direction, and you're still headed in another?"

Piper nodded, tears filling her eyes. "We always thought we'd do this stage of life together. As kids, we planned these ridiculous, elaborate double weddings. We named our future children, strategically planning the number and timing of girls and boys for maximum cousin fun." She wiped her palm against her cheek. "But we grew up. I fell in love with the city. Clara fell in love with Jet."

"But you're still best friends."

She blinked, her brown eyes shining as tears wavered on her lower lids. He'd struck a chord, and it seemed like a deep, painful, confusing one.

"I don't even know sometimes. Clara has Maisy and Joanna, Ani and Violet to hang out with. And probably Bettina Utner-Kim. She has everything in common with these women. Sometimes it seems like the only thing we still share is DNA."

Whit's heart lobbed out a ridiculous suggestion, involving him, Piper and a future on a similar track as Clara's. His frontal lobe grabbed a racket and tried to send it back but missed. The idea of him and Piper and a life together dribbled out of control through his mind.

"I'm not jealous of the life these women lead, but of the fact that they all seem so satisfied with it." She held her arms up, like nothing was more ridiculous than someone being happy living in a small town. "I could move back to Outcrop in a heartbeat, but I don't want to. I want my city, my local espresso bar, the art museum, trendy workout studios, specialty cheese shops and overpriced glasses of pinot gris. I love the energy and opportunity of the city. I'm not going to wind up on a ranch."

All right then. There was zero possibility of a future with Piper. Good to have that cleared up. Completely.

Whit shook his head, destabilizing the tennis match between his good sense and his emotions. He and Piper were friends. She was helping him with his campaign. And maybe he could be part of helping her out of this funk.

Whit summoned his strength and said, "Of course you won't. Portland's great. It suits you."

She nodded, more tears gathering in her eyes. She pressed a palm over her heart, her voice raw with emotion. "But sometimes, the overwhelming sadness of watching my sister's life move forward without me feels like a... like a boulder balanced on my heart. Like I can't breathe. It's so heavy."

Whit gazed down at Piper, his arms involuntarily rising to wrap her in a hug. He'd never seen her so vulnerable. Having her open up to him felt intimate, but it didn't scare him. He felt called into action, as if supporting and caring for Piper were the tasks he'd been waiting for. There wasn't a romantic future for the two of them, but there was a future where Piper could move past this emotional tough spot. It would be an honor to be the one to help her through it.

"Piper, I'm new to all this—" he gestured toward the barn "—family fun." She gave a dry laugh. He continued, "But I know how much they love you and depend on you, and if there's anything I can do—"

"Hey! What's going on in here?"

They both jumped as Bowman came striding into the barn. Piper stepped away, avoiding the almost hug and severing the connection between them.

Bowman took one quick glance at Piper, then turned on Whit. "Is there a problem?"

She groaned, burying her face in the side of the gentle horse. Whit fought the urge to hold up his hands and start babbling excuses. Fortunately, Piper took the reins, turning the tables and deflecting like only she could.

"Yes, there's a problem. Your shirt."

Bowman glanced down in confusion. "What's wrong with my shirt?"

"What's wrong with your shirt?" She shook her head. "Seriously, Bowman. What's wrong with *you*? It's like you do it on purpose."

"Look, I didn't come in here to discuss fashion. You need to tell me what's up. Why are you crying?"

"Because that shirt is enough to bring anyone to tears."

"Piper, knock it off." Bowman reached a hand out to the horse, as though letting him know he had the situation under control. "Maisy bought me this shirt."

"Why? To keep other women from hitting on you?"

"Piper—" Bowman started, but she cut him off.

"I'm fine. I just came in here to spend some quiet time with Midnight. You come in here all the time when you need a break." She turned away, running her fingers through the horse's mane. "Just because I'm not singing doesn't make my barn time any less valid than yours."

Bowman crossed his arms. She steadfastly ignored him, petting the horse as if it took all her focus to run her palm along his clipped fur. Finally, she sighed and said, "If Maisy bought you the shirt, you should wear it."

"I wasn't waiting for your permission."

She eyed him coolly, face still tear-stained, clearly grappling with extreme exhaustion and lingering sadness, then said, "Why won't you let me help you?"

Bowman turned to Whit, shocked and baffled. Whit shook his head, saying, "The irony is so strong, you'd think she was doing it just to mess with us."

"Speaking of clothes, we need to eat up, then go get you dressed for the party tonight. I have high hopes for Grandpa's magical closet." Piper strode toward the exit, leaving Bowman and Whit staring after her. She turned back, gesturing for them to follow. "Come on. Lunch is ready. You know Hunter's going to freak out if we're not there."

She slipped out the bypass door.

"I don't know…" Whit started, but he wasn't sure how to finish the sentence.

Bowman laid a hand on his shoulder. "Me neither."

CHAPTER SEVEN

WHIT DROVE IN silence down Lower Bridge Road. Not because he didn't want to talk, but because his thoughts were looping on repeat in his head. Piper, true to form, had left him and Bowman staring after her in the barn. She'd clipped back into the house, washed her face, fixed her makeup and come out onto the back lawn holding a glass of water like she'd spent forty minutes AWOL just filling a glass from the tap.

She'd been laughing and confident and completely Piper ever since.

Maybe she did just need to pet a horse and cry?

He had to admit it sounded a lot better than going to this fancy party. Small talk, high stakes: it really wasn't his thing.

"Are you nervous?"

Whit jumped at Piper's question, wishing he could shoot back a cool "No," but aware that nothing he could say could make up for his reaction.

"I'm not nervous. I'm…apprehensive. I want this to work."

"Me too. These people have a lot of money. I'd love to see some of that money flowing into your campaign."

"It's not just the money. They're also…"

"Right."

This party had to go well. If the Utner-Kims took an interest in him, a lot more people would too.

"I get it," she said, glancing out the window. Young grapevines of the new vineyard rolled by. "They are über-wealthy, and they command a lot of influence in the area, but Jet says they're great. And he's not the world's most social person by a long shot."

"But he's also brilliant like they are, right?"

"Oh, for sure," Piper said, not expounding on it, as though his intelligence was something the family took in stride, along with his emus.

"How did he meet your sister?"

After a faint stutter in her expression, Piper relaxed. "Jet was a year ahead of us in high school. He fell in love with Clara pretty much the moment he saw her. That's not super unusual, a lot of people fall in love with Clara. But Jet and Clara…" She trailed off, a smile crossing her face. "Jet and Clara are a really strong match. And his high-school self must have understood that because he basically spent his whole adult life trying to get back to her. I'm so happy for them." She looked up into his eyes. "Really."

He took a hand off the wheel and squeezed hers briefly. "I know you are."

"They're the exact opposite of us," she said.

His smile faltered. She went on, "You didn't like me from the minute you met me."

"That's not true."

She rolled her eyes. "You hated me."

"I did not."

"Okay, maybe *hate* is the wrong word."

He gazed at her. He'd always been drawn to Piper, but in a way that felt dangerous. Like he was a small child holding a fork, heading to an interesting-looking electrical outlet. "It was more like adversaries at first sight."

She grinned up at him. "I did love arguing with you in college."

"Remember when the coach made us work together?"

"The Gonzaga debate?"

Whit laughed, remembering the massive fights that exploded as they prepared for the debate.

"I really thought I might lose it." Then she stilled and smiled up at him. "But we always won when we worked together."

He let himself bask in her smile. "Every single time."

She held eye contact for a moment, then pulled out her phone.

"So, we're going to win this election." She opened a notes application. "You're nervous about tonight, and honestly I am too. I don't know what to expect from these people, and there's a lot riding on this evening. Let's make a plan."

He let out a dry laugh. "We can do that? Just make a plan, and I won't be nervous anymore?"

She raised her brow. "Whit, how many nervous people do you suppose I work with in an average day of matchmaking?"

"All of them?"

"Just about." She checked her list, then looked at him. "I have a list of suggestions for engaging in social situations. Want to hear them?"

"Like the love rules?"

"Yep."

"Hit me."

Piper read from her phone. "Number one, wear comfortable clothes appropriate to the situation." She gave him a once-over. "You look fantastic. How do you feel?"

He shifted his shoulders. The dress code for the night was "vineyard elegant," whatever that meant. Piper had dressed him in dark slacks, a vintage button-down, no tie and a blazer. He'd felt a little awkward until she showed him a picture of a Hollywood film star in a similar outfit.

Both he and Dwayne Johnson looked good.

"I feel great, thank you. And you look beautiful, if I didn't already say so."

Piper shifted, turning from him to look out the window. The sunflower-yellow silk was out of place in his truck, but he liked it there. Her dress was long, like something a Greek goddess would wear. Piper paired it with simple jewelry, her hair pulled back in a messy bun.

"Thank you." She consulted her list again. "Do you know about the three conversational topics that never fail?"

He looked at her skeptically. "There are topics that won't fail?"

"For the most part. I mean, you can't talk to some people no matter what. That's a them problem, not a you problem. But the vast majority of people will talk freely about topics in one of three categories—care, choice and creed."

"Oh." He mugged a thoughtful expression. "So, it's *not* politics, money and religion?"

Piper laughed. It felt good to make her laugh, to relieve a little of the pressure weighing on her.

"No, although you will be talking politics tonight."

"Understood."

They were both quiet for a moment, remembering just how much was riding on this party, this election.

Piper consulted her list again. "Care topics are the safest. Find something a person obviously cares about and discuss. Bonus points if you have the same thing in common. For example, if we get there and they have a dog, that's where I'll start."

"You like dogs, they like dogs—"

"—hours of conversational possibility."

"For you," he grumbled, nervous again as they drew closer to the château.

"They own several thousand acres of land, as do you. You can probably talk about anything having to do with property—rainfall, invasive species, mule deer."

He chuckled. He had a lot of feelings about the mule deer who nibbled the feed he intended for his cattle.

Piper continued, "Children are the ultimate care topic. People can talk forever about their kids."

"We don't have any kids," he joked.

"Do we want kids?" Piper tilted her head to one side. "Fake kids, I mean. Because folks will ask."

Whit thought for a minute. "You know, I don't know. Do *you* want fake kids?"

Piper looked up from her phone and gazed at him, understanding his real question. Did she want kids? Did he? Not with each other, obviously. Hypothetically.

"I've always thought I did. But now I'm not sure. I'm a really good aunt."

"The best, if we're asking Jackson."

"But kids?" Piper frowned as she considered the question. Then she shook her head. "If anyone asks, let's just smile slyly."

"Like this?" Whit tried the expression.

"Your fake sly smile is worse than your normal fake smile, which is saying something."

"Again, I apologize for my authenticity."

"Anyway, *back* to conversation topics. At this party, every time you meet someone, figure out what you both care about and go from there. All these people care about Deschutes County, so that's an easy one."

Whit nodded, feeling a little better. "What about choice and creed?"

She grinned. "Creed is a topic you can take a stance

on, but the trick is to keep it light. Pick some hill you'd die on, but that maybe doesn't matter too much in the grand scheme of things, like the oxford comma or pineapple on pizza."

"Abomination," he said.

"Or maybe, the use of mayo as a frying agent on a grilled cheese sandwich. Or whether or not men should cuff their pants. You introduce the topic as a question and let the other person express their feelings—"

"I'm still back on pineapple," he said. "I'm not sure we can be in a fake relationship if you put pineapple on your pizza."

She laughed. "I think I've made my point."

"Pineapple, yes or no?" He was almost ready to pull the car over because weird hits of warm fruit on a savory tomato, basil, cheese combination were not acceptable.

"No. And thank you for supplying evidence that people can talk for hours on the most trivial points."

"Oh, wait." Whit took his eyes off the road and stared at Piper. "Emu mural."

She flushed, her eyes lighting up at the insight. "Exactly. I'm crossing the parking lot of my brother's restaurant and see you for the first time in seven years. I was nervous. I didn't even know if you'd remember me. So, emu mural."

Whit gazed at her. How could she think there was a man on earth who could forget her? She was Piper Wallace: star of every class discussion, leader of every campus activity, funniest girl at every party, most fashionably dressed woman at any debate tournament by a long, long shot.

"I remembered you."

Piper's brown eyes connected with his, as though weighing his words. She must know that he, and probably every other man she'd ever so much as passed in the street, couldn't forget her. Even the fool who'd broken up with her probably had trouble sleeping at night. The tiniest smile bent her lips, like she could hear his thoughts, then she turned away abruptly.

"You know what I feel strongly about? Keeping your eyes on the road." She gestured to the blacktop. Whit kept his eyes on Piper a second longer, just to annoy her. "This is a *two-lane road*, a literal hill we could die on if you don't focus on driving."

Whit forced his eyes back onto the road. Which was fortunate, because he would have missed their turn. He pulled off the two-lane onto the long, narrow drive. Vineyards rippled out on either side, the leaves appearing almost purple in the setting sun. He focused on the beauty of the landscape, tried to steady his breathing and *not* think about the beauty beside him, Piper in her summer-yellow goddess dress.

Where were they heading again?

"We need to finish planning for conversations."

Right. High-stakes fancy party. At least he was heading out of the fire and into the frying pan this time.

"The final topic is choice," Piper said. "People want to feel like they've made the right decisions in life. So ask about a choice they've made and affirm it." She gestured out the window. "How did you choose this grape varietal, this part of Oregon, this type of fencing? Anything where they had to make a clear choice, but that's not too personal."

Whit nodded, sneaking another glance at Piper. *How did you choose your dress? What made you leave those wisps of hair falling around your neck? Who was this man who broke up with you, and what could he possibly have been thinking?*

"The final conversational tip, for you, tonight, is just

talk about the issues. Everyone at this party supports you—that's why they're coming. You don't have to win them over, just inspire them to spread the word."

Whit nodded. He could do this.

They crested the hill and pulled up in front of a huge mansion. He glanced at Piper, whose jaw had dropped in an uncharacteristic display of shock.

"Care, creed, choice," she muttered, almost to herself.

A young woman appeared at his window and asked to park the car for them. Whit's heart pounded as he handed over the keys, then helped Piper out. He did not release her hand as they walked to the door.

"This is going to be fine," she said quietly as they passed an ornate fountain.

Whit drew in a deep breath. They walked up the steps to a covered entry. Climbing vines surrounded the front door and gargoyles glared at them from the top of the portico.

"Do those critters look a little judgmental?" Piper asked.

"You're one to talk," he muttered back.

"Are you calling me a gargoyle?"

Whit laughed and reached a hand out to ring the bell, just as the massive door flew open.

"Welcome! *The* Whitman Benton is here!"

Lance Utner-Kim himself, trademark mussy hair and bright smile, beamed at them. He was wearing a tuxedo, shirt untucked, no tie, no shoes. A baby with wide, startled eyes stared at them from a front pack.

The Whitman Benton?

Whit muttered out a hello, then cleared his throat, scrambling back through Piper's advice. Something about care and kids. He glanced at her, and her golden dress shimmered almost pink in the setting sun. Everything he'd ever learned swirled together in his brain.

Whit reached out to shake Lance's hand, then said in

the most confident manner he could, "I see you're wearing a baby."

Piper's fingers dug into his palm, like she was glaring at him with her soul.

The tech mogul just grinned. "I am! Jet was wearing his tonight, so I thought, why not?"

Whit paused another moment, glanced at Piper, then asked, "How did you choose that type of baby carrier?"

THE UTNER-KIMS HAD six different baby carriers. They'd done prolific research, and Whit would be hearing about that choice for the next hour unless Piper helped him out. But if she got anywhere near him, she was going to start gushing about her feelings again. She'd overshared this afternoon, and that didn't need to happen ever again.

What was it about him that made her want to delve into her complicated family dynamics? From the first afternoon they'd spent alone, she was admitting her real fears about being an outsider in her own family to her fake boyfriend. Was that weird? She felt like a therapist would call that weird.

But then again, *weird* was probably on a list of words therapists weren't allowed to use.

Piper glanced across the massive living room to where Whit was now being shown a wrap-style front pack, as the various pros and cons were explained. He gave her a pleading look. She raised her glass in a toast, then turned to gaze out the windows.

This house…no, this *château* was amazing.

Built on modified plans from a seventeenth-century country home in the Loire Valley, the gorgeous residence was made of local stone and timber. The bones were all Louis XIV France, while the furnishings were sleek and modern. It was taking all her self-control not to shoot off like a squirrel through the place and check out all the rooms. She crept toward what looked like hand-carved window molding and reached out to run her fingers along it.

"You must be Piper."

Piper spun to see a petite, nervous-looking woman in a gorgeous floral dress holding a bottle of wine. She gestured to herself with the bottle. "I'm Bettina. I'm so g-glad you and Whit could come tonight."

Piper gave herself half a second to be jealous of the woman who could potentially become her twin sister's new best friend. Then she glanced at the bottle.

Pinot gris.

Okay, there are worse people for Clara to be friends with.

"Thank you for having us. Your home is amazing."

Bettina followed her gaze. "Right? I-I don't want to brag—"

She sounded like she was about to apologize for her incredible abode, and Piper wasn't going to let that fly. "It's not bragging. It's acknowledging that this is fabulous."

Bettina laughed, then filled Piper's glass as she said, "Would you like a tour?"

Piper glanced back at Whit. Jet, with Bob in his front pack, had joined the group discussing baby-carrying apparatuses along with a few other new dads. He was fine.

"One hundred percent," Piper said. "Let's grab Clara."

Twenty minutes later, Clara and Piper were both pretty sure this house fulfilled any and all childhood fantasies about being princesses. Or empresses, in the case of Piper's young imagination.

"Did you see this sink?" Clara asked as they stood in a gorgeous bath on the lower floor of the château. "It's the most beautiful sink in existence. I want to marry this sink."

Piper ran a finger over the pale green freestanding fixture. "If I lived here, I would never stop washing my hands."

Bettina laughed. "I was really happy with it. Lance and I were so busy with RanTech when we had the house built, I left most of the decisions in the hands of the designers. I'm still discovering cool things about my own home."

"How will you babyproof it?" Clara asked.

"The left wing is already babyproof, so we'll hunker down in there, and as the kids get older, we'll expand into the space."

They left the bath and ambled along a great hall. To the right was a wall of windows with sweeping views to the north, and on the left were large dramatic pieces of abstract art. The floor was a geometric pattern of poured concrete. "I thought this would be fun for roller-skating," Bettina was saying.

"I love roller-skating!" Clara clapped her hands.

Piper could just imagine Bettina, Clara and however many combined children they wound up with tearing up the room wearing knee and elbow pads, trying not to bump into the art. It was fine, fantastic even. Clara was at a new stage in her life, and Piper was *not* going to begrudge her sister's roller-skating friends with babies.

She took a sip of her wine and gazed out the window. The vineyard spanned acres across the rolling hills, until the property abutted a wildlife sanctuary. A Cooper's hawk circled over the vineyards, playing on the thermal drafts. In the distance, a herd of mule deer grazed near a pond.

"Piper?" Clara called, and from her tone it sounded like the second time she'd called.

"Oh. Sorry. Roller-skating?"

Clara walked over and slipped her hand through Piper's arm, drawing her close. "What are you looking at?"

She gestured with her glass. "That's where the first phase of Hummingbird Ranch would be built."

Bettina followed her gaze. "That's a wildlife sanctuary. No one can build on it."

"No one can build on it so long as it's designated as a wildlife sanctuary."

Comprehension shifted across Bettina's face. "The county commissioner can do that?"

"A county commissioner like Marc Holt can pave the way. He did the same thing back in Colorado. The backers of Hummingbird Ranch have already put a lot of money into this. They come in, do a quick, cheap build. Then the houses are bought as third homes by non-residents, so they won't contribute to the tax base. To offset the cost for infrastructure, taxes are raised on current residents. We lose protected wildlife areas, pay more taxes and the only jobs the development creates are minimum-wage service positions, at the loss of family-owned farming operations and small businesses."

"I-I knew Holt was bad, but I didn't—" Bettina trailed off, looking out at the land. "You and Whit *have* to win, don't you?"

Piper drew in a breath. *You and Whit have to win.* This wasn't just Whit's campaign anymore. She mattered. And she'd left her partner in this high-stakes tango upstairs, trapped in a web of baby carriers, a single man surrounded by married dads discussing dad gear.

"We do." Piper smiled at her hostess. "Speaking of which, I should go check on him. Despite what Holt's campaign wants you to believe, he's not exactly Mr. Party."

"Me neither." Bettina raised her glass to clink with both Clara and Piper. "Lance is social with no fear. It never occurs to him that someone might not like him, or that he might care if they didn't. But I've had a really hard time making friends since we moved here."

Piper had a brief but successful wrestling match with her jealousy. "I don't completely live here—"

"Or even mostly live here," Clara added.

"But you have great taste in wine and sinks and art, plus you want to roller-skate in your own home. I feel like we should be friends."

"Absolutely," Clara agreed.

Bettina shrugged her shoulders repeatedly and grinned, like the bashful, gorgeous tech-industry billionaire genius she was. "Yay!"

Piper drew back, biting the inside of her cheek as Clara threw out the idea of a meet up at Second Chance Cowgirl. Bettina led the way back up using a second staircase, as the two planned a shopping trip for the coming week.

It's fine.

"How did you meet Whit?" Bettina asked.

Piper paused as they climbed the spiral staircase. It was steep and honestly a bit of a workout.

Clara laughed. "They were college debate rivals."

"Oh, that's fun!" Bettina said.

Piper nodded. "I don't actually remember meeting him. He was just there. I showed up at OSU, and there he was, ready to argue."

"That's adorable! I love your story. And now you're in love and fighting Marc Holt together."

Piper shifted uncomfortably. She hated lying. If Bettina and Clara became good friends, would they eventually have to tell her this relationship was fake? Or would it be some weird secret her family just didn't talk about for the rest of their lives? Piper glanced out one of the windows, eyes landing on the wildlife sanctuary. Whit *had* to win.

They were an impossible couple, but together they could turn this election.

Just like the Gonzaga debate. Neither of them could have beaten that team with any other partner, but together they were unstoppable.

Even if they nearly killed each other in the process.

Piper quickened her step. She should not have left Whit alone with all the dads. She was going to be better at this, more supportive, less self-indulgent.

They emerged from the stairs at the edge of the massive living room, which had filled up in their absence. There had to be seventy people there. Whit's campaign manager and Piper's brothers had arrived with their partners. She was happy to see Bowman in a less-than-horrible shirt. The mayors of Bend *and* Redmond were here. People were milling around, having fun, but not too much fun. There was an energizing urgency to the gathering. It was a support-a-strong-political-candidate level of enjoyment.

And at the center of it all was Whit. He was talking seriously to a large group of people, pointing to the window, just as she had to explain where the first phase of Hummingbird Ranch would be built.

He reminded her of college Whit: smart, in control, unstoppable.

There was a funny feeling in her chest. Anticipation mixed with...something.

"He looks good," Clara said.

Piper grinned. "Right?"

He'd always been handsome. To be honest, that had been part of the problem in college. But at twenty-two, he was scruffy and cute. At twenty-nine?

Well, she could understand how he'd gotten all those dates Holt was anxious to point out.

"I found all of those clothes at his house. The jacket is

vintage, but he bought those slacks and shirt on his own. It's like he has good instincts, he just needs my help pulling it together."

Clara leaned in. "Like the campaign."

At that moment, Whit looked up and saw her. She must have been smiling, and who wouldn't? He looked good, and she was partially responsible. Maybe not for the deep blue eyes or bright smile. Definitely not responsible for the hours this guy was putting in at the gym.

But she could claim the outfit. And maybe a little of the confidence that went with it.

He smiled back, that mystery smile she couldn't quite figure out. He was getting good at this charade.

As he answered another question, Whit held out a hand to her. She moved to his side, winding her fingers through his. The group reacted to her presence. Everyone loves a young couple in love.

"Well, I'm impressed," an older gentleman said to Whit, then looked back at Lance. "A few weeks ago, I thought your campaign was doomed."

Whit squeezed Piper's hand and glanced gratefully at her.

"I'm glad Holt ran that ad," she quipped. "We were keeping quiet about our relationship until after the election."

"I never liked that idea to begin with. And now we get to campaign together." Whit reached his hand around her waist and purely by accident tapped her tickle spot.

Piper shouted out a laugh and twisted away.

"You're ticklish?" he asked. She shook her head but couldn't stop herself from laughing. "You are!"

Piper drew in a breath and looked him straight in the eye. "No."

Whit reached out with both hands, and she started

laughing when his fingers got within a foot of her rib cage. She batted his hands away, but Whit caught her and tickled her again. Piper laughed, tears pricking her eyes as she tried to tickle him back.

"That's not fair! That's my tickle spot."

Whit held up his fingers, a smile splitting his face. "I've discovered the one weakness in Piper Wallace."

She tried to grab his fingers to keep him from tickling her, but at the same time really wanted to be tickled. This just made her laugh even harder.

"How did you not know she was ticklish?" Lance asked.

Whit dropped his hands. Piper sobered immediately.

Lance Utner-Kim had a super good point.

"You've been dating for months," Lance reminded them.

Piper's gaze met Whit's. Had they been caught? Would their charade be called out here in the home of their most important supporter?

Whit took a few steps away from Piper and stood next to Lance, gazing back at her. "I didn't know." He spoke to Lance, easy and honest sounding. "Piper's always been two steps ahead of me and slightly out of reach. Since the first time I saw her, in line at freshman orientation, she was just a little bit smarter, a little bit funnier. I try to keep up, but she's a lot to keep up with."

Ash chuckled, but what was funny about her oldest brother's laugh was that it sounded real. Like he wasn't pretending they were dating, but honestly found this amusing.

Whit smiled at her, a sincere smile with something else layered in there, like he was making a confession. "Sometimes I forget that we're finally dating. I forget that I'm not pursuing her anymore. She's here. She's committed to me, even through this wild campaign. And in those moments, I still get overwhelmed with the miraculous understanding that I am dating Piper Wallace, after all these years. I'm the one who gets to sit next to her, argue with her, comfort her."

He held eye contact, and warmth rushed through her at his fake confession of how much he cared.

"My discoveries about Piper keep unfolding: how much she loves her family, how committed she is to defending even the silliest-looking dogs, how strongly she feels about public art involving emus." He put his hands in his pockets, studying his shoes for a moment before glancing up at her, speaking to her. "She's still smart, still two steps ahead, but what I didn't understand about her before is that she's always willing to reach back and help others join her. When she slips her hand into mine, a little of Piper's magic rubs off on me, making me a better man."

Piper flushed, looking past Whit to avoid his eyes. Unfortunately, that landed her gaze on her sister, who had covered her heart with a hand and was looking like she was about to cry. Bowman had caught Hunter's eye and raised his brow, suggesting that Whit might be more for Piper than a fake boyfriend.

She needed to shut that right down.

But not in front of Lance and Bettina.

She gave Whit what she hoped was a shy, grateful little smile, then she reached out a hand to him. He slid his palm against hers, and again she was surprised by the jolt of chemicals moving between them. She felt good, excited, energized. Like his magic was rubbing off on her, making *her* a better woman.

Then Whit tugged her to him and caught her other hand in his grip.

"Oh, no—" Piper cried, as Whit teased his fingers against her ribs again, sending her into screams of laughter.

"I also never knew how ticklish she was," he said, laughing as she tried to jump away.

"You are asking for it, Whit Benton!" she warned, but she couldn't stop laughing as she did.

Then he wrapped both arms around her and kissed the top of her head. Over his shoulder, she saw Bettina give Lance a look that said something along the lines of *Awww!*

And truth be told, she was feeling a little *Awww!* herself.

But this relationship wasn't going to happen. Whit was among the best men she'd ever met, and he'd given a beautiful performance to save their charade. She would always want her city life. The Deschutes County commissioner had to live in Deschutes County. Period.

THE UTNER-KIM PARTY was a success.

Somehow, Whit had relaxed and managed to connect with his supporters. Once they were in the clear with the tickling incident, the party became rowdier, more fun. At some point, Lance suggested they all head outside to watch the moon rise. Now seventy-some people walked to the ridge overlooking the Utner-Kim vineyard, bathed in silver and blue from the rising moon.

"Over there?" Lance asked, pointing to the wildlife refuge.

"That's phase one," Whit confirmed.

Lance and Bettina looked at one another. He placed a protective hand over his baby's head, then nodded at Bettina, some communication passing between them.

"We'd like to get involved," she said.

Whit nodded. He didn't feel a rush of gratitude or relief. He felt like he had two new team members on his side, lined up in the fight against Holt.

"Thank you. Your support will mean a lot. My campaign manager will be in touch about ways you can help."

Lance turned back to Bettina, eyes bright. She took his hand, and he spun her around, then wrapped both arms around her as they gazed out at their vineyard.

"Whit?" He turned from the couple to see Clara approaching.

"Hey." He took a few steps, closing the gap between them. "What's up?"

Clara looked over her shoulder to where Piper was walking with Hunter and Ani. Her dress billowed out behind her. If the makers of pinot gris had any idea how beautiful she looked consuming their product right now, she'd have a modeling campaign in minutes. Not that Piper would ever have the patience to stand still long enough to have her picture taken more than once.

Clara drew in a deep breath. "I was thinking." She tucked her hair behind her ears. "I've been thinking a lot about what you said about Piper not always feeling like she fits in."

Whit put his hands in his pockets. Piper definitely hadn't authorized him to discuss this information.

"You mentioned that she always comes to see us." Clara glanced back at her sister again. "We're just so used to Piper being the one who supports everyone else, we honestly don't know how to help her."

"She's not great about accepting help."

A spark lit Clara's eye. "You get her."

Whit warmed at the compliment. He did get Piper. He would never be the man she fell in love with, but he took great pride in being the man she was at least willing to spar with.

"So, I was thinking, I'd like to plan a girls' trip to Portland."

"She'd love that," Whit said.

Clara held out a hand. "You haven't heard the whole request."

"You don't need to ask me if you can visit your sister in Portland."

She shot him a look.

Whit began to understand the situation. "But that would take away time from the campaign?"

"We'd have to do it on a weekend. Maisy works at the clinic, and Violet has daily doubles for football."

Piper's laugh drew his attention. She was talking with Lance and Dan now, and by the way she was gesturing, it looked like she was doing her imitation of Marc Holt.

He could campaign for one weekend on his own, couldn't he?

Technically, yes. He did fine on his own, but with Piper this whole thing kicked up a level. Dan wasn't going to like it one bit. They both knew the Piper Effect was powerful. She brought the soul to his well-crafted arguments; she was inspiration for action in the face of immobilizing bad news.

She was exactly what he needed.

The weekends campaigning with Piper were frustrating, fun, exhausting and exhilarating. The weekdays between her visits felt dull and listless without her.

Clara's eyes were trained on him. He knew what he needed to say here.

"Of course. Put it on the books. I'll make sure we don't schedule anything she needs to be at. If she balks, go anyway."

Clara grinned, her smile and resulting dimples an exact replica of Piper's, but somehow worlds different.

"It's a great idea," he forced himself to say. "She'll love it, and it's just the break she needs."

And it was clearly the break he needed too. Because if the feelings building in him tonight were any indicator, he was in as much danger of falling for Piper as he'd ever been.

CHAPTER EIGHT

"EVERYTHING IS SET for maximum fun!" Piper cried as she swung open the door to her loft. Bernice squeezed her narrow nose between Piper's ankles, welcoming the women.

Well, the women and baby Bob.

"This is fabulous!" Violet said, walking into the open apartment.

Ani scampered over to the nearest wall and leaned her head against it. "Exposed brick." She ran her hand along the rough, cool texture. "I love it."

"It really is fabulous and loveable, isn't it?" Piper had purchased the loft as an investment. It was in a renovated warehouse in Portland's Pearl District. The lobby of the building was sleek and modern, but the open lofts retained an eclectic feel. Her large front room had windows spanning across its length. A living room was set up at one end, furnished in the sunflower yellow Piper loved. At the other end was a modern kitchen, and in between the spaces was a reclaimed-wood dining table that she was more likely to use as an office than a place to eat. Today, a bouquet of golden carnations graced the table, along with a note from Whit that said, "Enjoy the weekend!"

Maisy scanned the view of the river and city beyond. "I think you can see my old apartment from here."

Clara, who'd spent a lot of nights in this loft until she fell in love with Jet, slipped her hand into Piper's. "It's great to be back."

Piper wrapped both arms around her sister. "It's so good to have you here." She looked down at her sweet nephew in the front pack. "And Bobby. How'd you wrestle him away from Jet for the weekend?"

"It was *not* easy."

She'd been surprised when Clara told her—not asked but *told her*—that they were coming for a girls' weekend. She suspected Whit had something to do with it, inasmuch as he was always on her to take a break. And while she didn't love other people interfering and telling her what she did or didn't need, this was the type of break she loved. She was surrounded by her favorite people with a list of fun activities to shepherd them in.

Plus—and Whit would never need to know this part—each of the activities had a dual purpose. Piper was taking her friends to places that held difficult memories from her last relationship. As she spent more time with Whit, she realized she wasn't so much upset that Liam had dumped her, but that she'd wasted so much time with a man who clearly wasn't right for her in the first place.

This weekend, she would expunge that regret. Streets and shops she'd been avoiding would be overlaid with new memories. A landmark would go from being *that place Liam got frustrated when I tried to stage an intervention about his misuse of the words* affect *and* effect, to *the place where I held my baby nephew and laughed with friends.*

This was going to work. She'd suggested the same tactic to multiple clients, and it had worked brilliantly. Ergo, her mixed-up feelings over Liam and their breakup would be cured by the end of the weekend, right?

"Where should we dump our stuff?" Ani asked.

"Okay, that's kind of funny," Piper said. "How much stuff did you actually bring? You have the least amount of gear of anyone I know."

Ani held up a tiny canvas tote bag, the sort of thing one would get at a specialty olive oil shop.

"How do you travel so light?" Clara asked.

Ani laughed. "Practice?"

Piper pointed to the tote. "I bet she's got one of her magical outfits in there, the ones she can dress up, down and sideways with a simple change of earrings." She kissed her almost sister-in-law on the cheek. "Follow me to the guest room aka closet. The guest closet, if you will. Clara, you're in my room."

The back half of the loft held her room and a guest room. She initially planned to use the guest room as an office, but over time she'd set up sturdy metal racks around the edge to hang overflow from her closet. It was like decorating with clothes, and she was surprised more people didn't do it.

Piper got everyone settled, showed them how to work the Murphy beds in the spare room and hoped that no one had a problem sleeping surrounded by her wardrobe. Once her friends dropped their bags and finished exploring her loft, she gathered everyone in the living room and clapped her hands.

"Okay! Ready for the schedule?"

Maisy grinned. "I'm always ready for a good schedule."

Piper read from the list on her phone. "First up, espresso at North End." *Subject of the breakup avocado toast argument.* "Then shopping. There are a few new boutiques I want to take you to." *Where I bought clothes for dates I thought meant more than they did.*

"Perfect. I love shopping with you." Violet turned to Ani and grinned. "When Piper and Clara are around, I don't have to make any decisions."

"Lunch at Papa Haydn—" *not actually a sore spot, but incredible desserts* "—and there's a new gallery that just opened in Northwest near the restaurant. Ani, I think you'd love it." *Liam didn't love it, but Ani would.* "At that point, I'll need to bring the pup back here because her little legs will be tired, and she'll want a napper. If anyone else wants a napper too, that works."

"I love this plan so much," Clara said.

"I'm not done! Après naps, I thought we could head downtown." *Where Liam never wanted to go because he didn't like parking there and felt the ten blocks from her apartment was too far to walk.* "Violet, there's a football situation happening at Portland State that we could check out, and Maisy, if you want, we could go to the rock gym. I thought you guys could climb, and I'll hold Bobby."

"You've thought of everything!" Maisy said.

Piper just grinned. "For dinner, I bought a ton of snacks and wine." *Snacks were a favorite meal of mine that drove Liam up the wall; he didn't like having too many choices.* "And we can eat here and stay up late, and Clara and I will give you all the dirt on our brothers." She set her phone on the coffee table and looked around. "Sound good?"

"It sounds perfect," Violet said. "I have spent most of my waking hours with teenagers and men this summer. This—" she indicated the clean, open loft "—is heaven."

Piper tilted her head, challenging her. "I thought heaven was the front porch with Ash."

Violet grinned. "That's nice too."

"Oh, and tonight, after brother gossip, I thought we'd plan your wedding."

"Shouldn't Ash and Jackson be here for that?" Maisy asked.

"The only thing Ash cares about is being married to Violet. He literally won't notice anything else. And so long as there's a pickup football game sometime during the festivities, Jackson will be happy."

Violet laughed and pointed at Piper. "Truth."

"Is Hunter still planning on catering your wedding?" Clara asked Ani.

Ani covered her face with her palm and groaned.

"So that's a yes?"

"So far, Hunter is planning on having the wedding at the house we're remodeling, the reception at the events center of Eighty Local and providing all the food, which is an extensive menu. This is after I suggested a simple ceremony at the courthouse and a trail ride back at your family's place."

The women burst out laughing.

"What's next? Becoming a minister and performing the ceremony himself?"

"Don't give him any ideas."

"Speaking of which." Piper clapped her hands and looked at Clara, who nodded vigorously. "Wedding dress shopping tomorrow?"

"Please and thank you," Violet said.

"Okay then, let's go! Everyone has shoes they can walk in?" Piper scanned feet as she grabbed Bernice's leash. Violet wore a pair of trendy sneakers, Ani had on vintage boots, Maisy wore high tops and Clara had on walking sandals. They'd all gotten, and followed, her memo.

"So excited!" Clara said, waving little Bobby's arms. He chuckled, a deep, gurgly sound that struck Piper in the solar plexus.

"Did he just laugh?" Piper leaned over to look in Bobby's eyes. His brown eyes met Piper's, and he chuckled again. A complete miracle.

"He's the most amazing baby ever, in the whole history of babies."

"Right?" Clara agreed.

Bernice whined, so Piper picked her up so she could

see the baby. Bobby flailed his arm out toward the puppy, a big smile lighting his face, just like Jet's did.

This moment was worth the whole trip. If nothing else happened for the next forty-eight hours, this chuckling, gurgling baby trying to pet the world's most adorable dachshund was all anyone really needed.

An abrupt buzzing interrupted it.

All the women turned from where they were watching Bobby and Bernice to see Piper's phone on the coffee table.

Her phone buzzed again, jumping slightly, as though this call felt it was more important than your average call.

Everyone stared at it. How was it that the ringing felt ominous?

"You gonna get that?" Violet asked.

Maisy bent over to look at the name, then glanced at Piper.

"What?" Piper continued to attach the leash to Bernice, unwilling to ruin this day with a call from anyone, much less the automated scam call most likely coming in.

Maisy picked up the phone and held it out to her.

The phone continued to ring accusingly in her hand. Piper finally glanced at the caller.

Dan, Whit's campaign manager.

"What could *he* want?" Piper asked, clicking to accept the call.

"You did *what?*" Whit demanded, then lowered his voice. The ballroom of the Bend Country Club was still full of supporters. They'd responded well to his speech; this stop had been more than worth his time. Whit was finally finding his stride, able to relate to constituents but still keep everyone focused on the issues.

He had Piper's influence to thank for that, and thank-

ing her didn't include ruining her weekend by asking her
to present at the Oregon Cattlemen's Association.

"We double-booked you," Dan defended himself. "That
speech was in your calendar as much as mine. We both
overlooked it."

"And asking Piper to do it was the only solution?"

"Piper was the best solution."

Anger flashed in Whit's chest, masking something
deeper. He was mad at Dan, but *panicked* about Piper. She
was going to be furious, and rightfully so. He knew how
Dan could get when persuading someone to do something
they didn't want to. It was part of what made him a great
campaign manager. But he must have coerced Piper into
doing this speech, and once it was over, she'd be fuming.

"You should have asked me first," he said in a low, controlled voice.

"You were busy." Dan, who didn't seem to think there
was anything wrong with ruining Piper's weekend, headed
toward the door, expression grim.

A constituent stopped to shake Whit's hand. He flipped
his expression into a smile and thanked the elderly woman
for her support. As she joked and patted his arm, Whit
thought of his own grandma.

Would Grandma Benton be voting for him?

Probably not.

Whit jogged a few steps and caught up with Dan.
"Look, I know how hard you're working, and I appreciate
it. But Piper needs a break."

"For what? So she can take her dog to the salon?"

"So she can run her business," Whit said, more sharply
than he wanted to.

Dan flexed his eyebrows. "Matchmaking?"

Whit glowered, then brushed past him to grab his blazer

from the rack. He clearly wasn't getting an apology out of his campaign manager.

"Look, I did what I had to," Dan said. "You were double-booked. I needed someone to fill one of the spots."

"What about Ash? What about you?"

Dan gave him a bland look.

Good point. Piper was significantly more engaging than either of them.

But she deserved a weekend off in all this insanity.

And he needed a weekend off from a gorgeous, argumentative matchmaker.

"I knew what I was asking of her," Dan continued. "This campaign is life and death for our community, and I made the decision to call her. I provided her with a speech. All she needs to do is read it, then answer a few questions."

"That, and drive three hours from Portland to give a twenty-minute presentation."

"Piper's 'me time' isn't my first priority right now."

"I get the sense that Piper hasn't had more than twenty minutes of 'me time' in the last five years," Whit snapped.

Dan's lips set in a thin line across his face, a clear sign this conversation wasn't going to get any better. Whit needed to walk away before he fired his campaign manager.

He stalked to the door, trying to shake his frustration. "Next time, just ask me first."

"I'm supposed to ask you what Piper wants to do for this campaign? Seems like that's her business."

Whit hit the crash bar on the exit door and headed into the bright sunlight.

"Where are you going?" Dan asked.

Whit pressed his fingers into his twitching eyebrow. "I'm going to try to get there before she does."

"The speech starts in ten minutes. You're twenty-five miles away."

Whit shoved his arms into his blazer, trying to steady his breathing.

"I can get there in time to help her out and apologize for ruining her weekend."

Dan let out something between a grunt and a laugh. His campaign manager wasn't happy with him, and that wasn't going to change. If Whit could keep Piper from being mad at him too, that would be at least a partial win.

Who was he kidding? Piper was going to be furious.

Whit shook his head and headed across the sun-washed parking lot. It was foolish of him to try to get to the Cattlemen's Association on time. Piper had already driven three hours from Portland. The girls' weekend on her home turf was ruined. The best he could do was show up, take over the speech that she would have gotten started by then and offer to rent her and her friends a place at Sunriver for the weekend.

Highway 97 seemed to grow longer and more congested as Whit rushed to the meeting. Whit's heart pounded, closing up the back of his throat as he pulled into the Cattlemen's Association building at 2:17 p.m. He ran across the parking lot, pausing only briefly to consider what he was wearing. It was one of the old snapfronts Piper liked, nicer jeans, a blazer and clean boots. It was a look she called "rancher grabbing lunch in town." It was going to have to do. He pulled open the door.

The sound of laughter hit his ears.

Piper's voice was indistinct but cheerful. He ran across the lobby and into the presentation room. It was wall-to-wall with grizzled ranching men and women, every seat taken, with as many more on their feet along the walls. Jet and Ash were behind Piper on the podium. Clara and the rest of the girls' road trip stood near the back. Dan hadn't just ruined Piper's weekend, he ruined *everyone's* weekend.

But Clara and the other women didn't look upset.

"So, he's like, 'Piper!' and I look down and *I'm* holding number eighty-three!"

The room exploded into laughter, and Piper laughed with them. "I'd bought a thousand pounds of beef without even knowing it." She shook her head, inspiring even more laughter.

Clara waved him over, grinning. Not exactly the facial expression he expected from someone just cheated out of a fun weekend in Portland. Whit scooched past people to join her, ready to start apologizing, but Clara just pointed back at Piper. Maisy waved at him, holding the sausage dog. Bernice was wearing a white crocheted bonnet with black spots today, making her look like a mini cow. The dog eyed him coolly, as though daring him to comment.

Once the laughter died down, Piper looked up, eyes thoughtful as she scanned the crowd.

"I tell you this story, not so that you'll invite me to your child's 4-H auction—" people chuckled again "—but because it's another wonderful example of the gem we have in Whit Benton."

Warmth spread through his chest. It was silly to feel like it meant anything; she was just talking him up. Of course she was speaking well of him. This was supposed to be *his* campaign speech. But something about the way she said it...

"Whit is observant, and he's got the kind of mind that can quickly connect relevant facts to see a bigger picture. He's able to walk into a room and respond to everyone. Most of us tend to find people like ourselves and gravitate to them. Whit can find the good in everyone." Her lips quirked up in a self-deprecating smile. "Even me."

The crowd gave a collective sigh at young love. Piper continued, "Whit is able to hold an enormous amount of information in his head. He's one of those people who can meet you once, have a five-minute conversation about your grandpa and he'll remember both your name and your grandpa's name when he sees you five years later."

Clara glanced at him, eyes widened as though asking if this were true. He shrugged and nodded. He did have a pretty sharp memory.

"He's brave. If something matters, he won't back down. And on that note, sometimes he won't back down on lesser issues either, like pineapple on pizza." The crowd chuckled again. Piper gave a wistful smile. "But beyond all that, he cares. Let me be honest, Whit is not stoked about a political career. He's a rancher, like you, and this campaign is taking a lot of time away from his work. He's doing this because someone had to step up, and he was the best option. Whit doesn't just *want* to beat Marc Holt, he is *compelled* to. Saving our farms and ranches from outside interests is his mission, and he will sacrifice his own time and well-being to get the job done." She contemplated the podium for a long moment, then looked up into the faces of the ranchers. "Whit is the best man I have ever known. I didn't realize men like him existed—smart, principled, kind, honest." She paused then added, "Super good-looking." Whit reddened as a few whoops of appreciation peppered the audience. "I'm just so grateful for the time I get to spend with him."

A roar of applause sounded throughout the room. Whit noticed for the first time that Ani was filming the speech on her phone.

Piper gave the crowd a wry smile. "And, he'd better be

good at grilling because the two of us have 365 days of beef for dinner coming up."

The crowd cracked up again, launching into another round of applause. Piper joked with a man in the front row about getting his marinade recipes. People were already clamoring to ask her questions, to connect with her more deeply.

Everyone was swept away by Piper. Whit was transfixed.

"We can't outspend Marc Holt." Piper glanced briefly at her speech, then flipped it over and continued to disregard it. "His pockets are deep, bottomless. But we can do absolutely everything else. We can talk to our friends and family about Whit. We can get the word out. We can support him on social media. We can put up lawn signs, field signs, whatever kind of signs work on your property. And most importantly, on November 8, we can flood the polls with votes for Whit Benton. I'm all in. Are you with me?"

The crowd of cattlemen spanning generations leapt to their feet, applauding. Piper stood, hands resting easy on either side of the podium. She was relaxed and in control, like she was having the time of her life up there.

Whit had never seen anyone so beautiful.

How had he ever thought he could win this campaign before Piper? And what was he going to do when the campaign was over? She would return to her life in Portland, and he'd be rambling around in a five-bedroom house unable to fill the oceanic hole Piper would leave.

"Thank you all for coming today," Piper said. "I'm going to stick around in case you have any questions. My family members are here too—you all know my brother-in-law, Jet." Jet waved from behind Piper on the podium. She looked around the room, pointing out her brothers and even the group of women who were supposed to be enjoying themselves in Portland right now. "We're all here and—" She broke off abruptly as her eyes landed on him. She stood, staring. Whit braced himself for her scowl.

Instead, she blushed.

She was shocked to see him; that was obvious. And she was *blushing*.

The audience turned their heads to follow her gaze and saw him, gazing back at Piper. Then she covered her face with her hands and let out an embarrassed squeak, possibly the least Piper-like noise in the universe.

"How long has he been there?" she asked the crowd.

"Just after you started talking about how hot he is," Bowman muttered.

Piper peeked through her fingers. He knew this was all for show, but somehow it seemed like she really was embarrassed that he'd heard all of that. Was he the best man she knew? No, that was probably her dad or one of her brothers. Or one of the nephews she was so fond of.

But that last line, "I'm just so grateful for the time I get to spend with him."

That sounded real.

And now they were staring at each other in front of a room full of cattle ranchers.

Piper kept her gaze trained on him and raised her right eyebrow as high as she was able. He responded with what she called the full-on Bond villain brow flex, just to make her laugh.

She gripped the podium, dropping her head in acknowledged embarrassment and said to the audience, "Welp! So much for playing it cool." She shook her head, laughing at herself. "The man himself is here, so I'd suggest if you have any further questions, you talk to Whit. I clearly need to stop talking at this point. Thank you for coming, everyone!"

She gave one final, bright smile and stepped away from the podium.

Whit had questions, and feelings. He glanced briefly at Clara, but she was obscured by a woman in a canvas jacket with ideas about limiting the spread of Scotch thistle. Whit did his best to focus as people stepped forward and spoke with him, but he was hyperaware of Piper's voice lilting across the room, of her laugh as it rang out.

He needed to keep focused on the goal. They were getting closer; he could feel it. Something about today felt like a major shift, like they'd been slowly gathering momentum, but Piper's speech kicked the campaign into another gear.

And right now, he wasn't getting questions about how he was going to help these people; he was getting questions about how *they* could help his campaign. But it felt like the only thing he could focus on were the snippets of Piper's voice floating across the room.

"Okay, I'm literally about to faint from hunger. And by hunger, I mean a lack of espresso. But also hunger."

Whit glanced over to the door where Piper stood with Clara, Maisy, Ani and Violet. He then looked back at the man he was speaking with, ready to apologize for excusing himself. The man surprised him by slapping him on the back, grinning.

"I've known Piper her whole life. I was her high-school history teacher. You want something done, give it to Piper."

The man's wife, a tall, stunning woman, leaned toward him saying, "My husband may have known her since she was born, but I bet I know her better. You're a lucky young man."

"I am."

"Piper!" The man called out, getting her attention. "That was a rousing speech. Even better than the one you gave as student body president, when you tried to convince the school to adopt a cat."

"Coach!" she called, sweeping over. Piper hadn't met Whit's eye since stepping away from the podium, and she kept her gaze averted now. "Hi, Christy!" She hugged the couple. "You met Whit?"

"We did. I approve," Coach said.

"He has nice style." Christy gave his outfit a once-over.

"That's all Piper," Whit admitted.

"It is," Piper confirmed.

Whit found his fingers weaving through hers, tethering her to him; he was ready to offer her lunch, a place at Sunriver for the weekend, his heart, soul, even his favorite comic books from childhood.

She kept her eyes on Christy. "Hey, is the shop open? We had a whole shopping extravaganza planned for Portland, but honestly nothing's better than Second Chance Cowgirl. It's time to get Ani and Violet wedding-ready."

Christy's face lit up. "Oh, I already have three possible dresses for Ani to try."

"You do? You're the best!"

"I'm keeping an eye out for you girls. I have some ideas for Violet as well."

"Are we going with a cream, jersey knit?"

"It seemed to work so well the last time." Christy and Piper laughed. Coach looked at Whit and shrugged. His wife continued, "Are you staying at Wallace Ranch? I could bring a few things out."

"Oh, actually…" She turned to Whit, as though she were about to make a request.

He opened his mouth to offer a place at Sunriver, but she spoke first. "Can I ask you for a favor?"

"Yes." He turned to Piper and took both of her hands in his, hoping she understood he was not pretending right now. He was deeply, legitimately grateful and a little bit in love. "Whatever you want. Coffee, lunch, whatever Christy has in her shop."

Piper grinned. "Can I have your house?"

Whit stammered because for a second his subconscious was saying, *"Yes! The custom home of my best childhood memories is no less than you deserve for ruining your weekend and giving a speech for me."*

But his logical mind suggested that wasn't entirely the case.

His subconscious rallied with ideas of sharing the house with her.

"Just for the night. For the girls' weekend."

Whit laughed. "Sure. That sounds great. Can I order in—"

"We're going to Whit's house?" Clara interrupted. "Perfect!"

"Christy's coming too. Hey, I know Joanna couldn't come for the whole weekend, but do you think she could stop by tonight?"

"Already texting her," Clara said.

Whit was caught in the tornado that was Piper and her family, but this time he was less inclined to run for the basement. Plans ricocheted between the women, and in less than five minutes, the takeover of his abode was planned.

He was offered a spot in the bunkhouse at the Wallace ranch.

Coach clapped him on the shoulder as he and Christy prepared to leave. The older man gave him an astute look, like he was reading Whit's thoughts in a series of bullet points. "You do the right thing," he said.

Whit swallowed, then nodded. Waiting in case the man wanted to offer some clarity as to what the right thing was.

He did not.

Slowly the room cleared. Whit had a few lingering conversations with constituents. Piper also met with constituents, while planning for her party and taking a quick call from a client. Until, finally, it was just the two of them left.

Piper let out a sigh, a satisfied smile on her face.

Whit took steps toward her across the empty room. "Thank you."

She met his gaze for a moment, smoothing the hair off her forehead. "Yeah. You're welcome. It was fun."

"It can be fun, can't it?"

She nodded. "There's a little part of me that likes—" She gestured, not quite able to find the words. "This? The complicated rush of it all. Does that make sense?"

"I get it. I'm sorry Dan roped you into this but—"

"Dang! That guy?" Piper shuddered. "He does *not* mess around."

"He does not. He's a good campaign manager. I'm furious with him for asking you to come today, but he was right that you were the best option."

She smiled, her dimples appearing. "I like being the best option."

Whit gazed into her eyes, then delivered a sharp mental slap to his heart. He cleared his throat.

"Was that the speech Dan gave you? Because, somehow, I feel like he didn't write that part about the 4-H auction."

Maybe it was the light, but it really did seem like Piper was blushing again. "I might have gone off book."

Whit raised an eyebrow.

"Okay, fine, I was never really on book. The speeches sound good when *you* give them, but when I do, it sounds like I'm describing a cardboard box."

Whit laughed, then slipped his hands in his pockets and studied the floor. He and Piper were not in a real relationship. She was marvelous and wild, but this wasn't real.

He glanced up to find her studying him.

It's not real. She's pretending so you can win this important election.

"What?" she asked.

"Nothing. Let's get out of here. Get you some coffee."

"That's a good idea. And lunch. Possibly cookies."

"Cookies for all. Hunter's expecting us at Eighty Local."

Whit gestured to the door, and Piper headed out. Instinctively, he placed a hand on the small of her back. She paused for just a moment, so brief he couldn't be sure it had happened. Then she stepped into the sunshine.

CHAPTER NINE

"OKAY, ONE HUNDRED percent honest?" Clara leaned forward in one of Whit's Adirondack chairs on the back veranda. "I'm a little bit in love with the idea of you and Whit Benton."

"I thought you had designs on Bettina Utner-Kim's sink."

"The sink is just a passing crush. I'm ready to commit to you and Whit."

Piper tried to glare at her sister, but it wasn't working. She glanced through the big windows where Ani, Violet and Maisy were looking at dresses with Christy Kessler. She and Clara needed to get back inside and help them make decisions. Ani was fine, but left to her own devices, Violet would get married in a tracksuit.

Piper just desperately wanted a few more minutes alone with her sister.

"Let's not talk about Whit."

"Okay." Clara took a sip of her wine and gazed out at the valley below. The sun was just beginning to set, a cooling breeze blowing across the veranda. "Let's talk about Whit's view. It's amazing."

"Stop it!"

"Or how Whit couldn't take his eyes off you at lunch today."

"We were in a public place. He's supposed to look like he's in love with me in public."

"I'm just saying, I think he *was* in love with you in public."

Piper buried her face in her hands. She didn't know what had gotten into her with that speech today. Dan's script was dull as dirt, and when she looked out into the faces of the ranchers who'd come to listen, it felt like a waste of their time to drone on about something they could just as easily read off a website. They wanted to know if Whit was someone they could trust, someone capable of seeing Deschutes County through this difficult time. So, she talked about the man she knew. And once she got rolling on how great he was, it was impossible to stop.

She could still see him gazing at her from the back of the crowd after she'd spoken, unfiltered, about her respect and admiration for him.

And yes, she'd noticed Whit watching her at lunch, picked up on the attention he gave to her comfort, watched him wrangle with Ash and Hunter about who would pay the bill for lunch and cookies for ten.

She leaned back in her chair and took a sip of wine.

"I'm in the process of setting Whit up."

"Seriously?" Clara asked, kicking out her legs, clearly frustrated. "You're the worst. You're worse than I was when I was falling in love with Jet. Who are you possibly going to set him up with?"

"His family."

"Oh." Clara paused, leaning down to scratch Bernice's ears. "I guess that's okay."

"He's estranged from most of them, but his dad and stepmom want a relationship. And his stepbrother, Rory, idolizes him."

"Families are complicated," Clara said.

Like she needed the reminder.

"So are romantic relationships. Anyway, I feel like I

could really help here. I want to leave Whit with something when this campaign is over."

"You could leave him with a promise to love and argue
with him forever."

Piper tossed a cracker at her sister, who adeptly caught
it and nibbled on the edge, still grinning.

"I invited his family to the Deschutes Brewery debate
next Sunday, then over to dinner after."

"Whit is debating a brewery?"

Piper laughed. "No, the Holt campaign suggested a
friendly, town hall-style debate in Bend. The brewery offered to host."

"No offense, but I'm not sure it's a good idea to mix
beer and politics."

Piper nodded in acknowledgment. "Good point. But it's
on the books, and as evidenced today, if something is on
the books, Dan won't drop it."

Clara's phone buzzed, and she took a look at it. "Ooh!
Speaking of people we set up, Joanna can make it tonight."

Piper's heart took a tiny surge of jealousy, and she
forced herself to say, "Yay!"

Clara looked up from the phone, pinning her with a look
only Clara could throw.

Piper sighed and finally admitted an ugly truth. "Sometimes I'm a little jealous of Joanna."

Clara blinked. "You're jealous of Joanna? I mean, no
shade, but she wears vintage statement sweaters with little
animals on them."

"She's a grade-school teacher. Animal sweaters are stylish when your audience is eight." Piper took a sip of her
wine, then forced herself to voice her fears. "I'm jealous
because of you. You're my best friend, and sometimes,
with everything... I don't know. Sometimes it seems like
there might be a time when I'm no longer your best friend."

Clara stared at her, clearly not comprehending.

"Because, you know, Jet and Michael are best friends, and you all live here, and Joanna's really funny, and you all go out to brunch together."

Clara thumped her wineglass on the table between them and stared at Piper.

Piper twisted uncomfortably in her seat. "Sorry. I know it's super petty, but it's how I feel."

Clara stood and walked over like she was going to get in her face. Then she dropped and scooched into the chair with Piper, accidentally brushing the ticklish spot and making her laugh. The chair really couldn't fit both of them, but Clara was determined, hugging Piper as she tried to sit beside her. "You shush. Don't you ever say that."

"But I feel it sometimes."

"You are my *Piper*." She looked at her sternly, but the effect was somewhat lost in the silliness of her trying to fit into the chair. "You will *always* be my best friend."

Piper hugged her back. Clara was literally in her lap at this point, and it was kind of hard not to.

"I adore my husband. He's amazing and balances me in a way I didn't know was possible. I love my son. Being a mom is even better than I imagined it would be. But you are my *sister*. You're the other half of me, the half that's brave and outspoken and funny. I get to live vicariously through your glamorous life, while I have all the comforts of staying behind."

Piper squeezed Clara more tightly.

"Don't be jealous. Just be Piper."

Piper blinked at her tears. The last year had been such a whirlwind. Clara falling in love, and Piper helping her keep steady through the scary part. Then Liam, pulling over a block from home, declaring out of the blue that she was too much, asking her to leave his car. And then...everything else. Bowman and Ash meeting incredible women. On a whim, she and Clara hired Ani to paint a mural for Hunter, and now Christy was bringing wedding dresses over for her to try on. Then the baby. Now this.

Maybe she'd been holding on to the frustration of Liam so tightly because she was really trying to hold on to the past. She was used to being the one in motion, with the expectation that she could come home to the same family she drove away from all those years ago. But they were moving on too. Her parents were growing older. Jackson was practically out the door.

She'd never loved Liam. She'd planned an incredibly stylish wedding for the two of them, and there was a three-bedroom in her building that was coming up for sale. They'd had good times. When he was pursuing her, he went hard, sending bouquet after grand bouquet of roses and lilies that made her sneeze. She thought that meant love. What it really meant was he loved the idea of her more than the reality.

Clara looked down at her and grinned. "Also...what about Whit?"

"No!" Piper pushed at her sister, laughing at her persistence.

"Just a little bit of Whit?"

"There's no such thing as a 'little bit' where he's concerned."

"Fine." Clara sighed and kissed Piper on the forehead. Then she stood, holding a hand out to Piper. "We should go help with the wedding dresses."

Piper lingered in the chair a moment longer. If she was going to not be jealous of her sister's friends, she may as well go all in. "Should we text Bettina Utner-Kim? Invite her over? She said she was having trouble meeting people."

"That would be super sweet."

"Well, that's just me."

Clara pulled Piper out of the chair, then wrapped both arms around her, and they headed back into the house. "It is. No one is sweeter than you."

THE HOUSE WAS silent as Whit approached the front door the following morning. He debated knocking. It was only eight thirty. They were probably still asleep.

Whit glanced up at the sky, clear and blue. The women were going rafting today, in lieu of whatever they had planned for Portland, but they had hours to laze about before their trip. He, on the other hand, was meeting with a group of Quakers before their Sunday morning meeting for a simple Q and A. He needed to be in Bend by nine fifteen, hence the early arrival. He'd just sneak into the kitchen, leave his gift and go.

Then he'd be back in the afternoon to actually work on his ranch. He was running for county commissioner as a rancher, but he'd had precious little time to devote to the work he loved in the last month. Once Piper and her friends were gone, he'd ride out to check the grass level and see about finding some men to help drive the cattle to a new pasture next week.

Whit stepped up on his front porch, steadied the two cardboard carriers and tried to use his elbow to open the front door. It flew open before he even made contact.

"Hey! Good morning!" Piper stood before him wearing running shorts and a tank top, her hair pulled back in a simple ponytail. "Whit's here!" she called over her shoulder.

"Hi, Whit!" someone called back, and she opened *his* front door to allow him into his house.

He really needed to stop being surprised when Piper surprised him.

"I brought coffee," he said, holding up the trays.

"That's really—" Her sentence cut off as she lifted a cup. Her right eye narrowed. "Pony Espresso?"

"Tumalo's finest."

Piper heaved a sigh. "I guess it's the thought that counts. And the caffeine."

"I was just going to sneak in and leave them in the kitchen. I didn't expect anyone to be up."

"Oh, Maisy, Clara and I just got back from a run. I don't know about everyone else."

Whit glanced into the living room on their way to the kitchen. It looked like a slovenly eagle had tried to build a massive nest out of clothing and snacks. Violet was curled up on one sofa fast asleep, while Christy sat gazing out at the view, baby Bob content and sleeping in her arms.

The kitchen didn't look much better. Every dish he owned seemed to have been taken from its cabinet and filled with something that someone only nibbled at before moving on to something else. Every single cabinet door was open. His grandmother would be rolling in her grave. Or rather, rolling in the RV she and her new husband now lived in.

"Fun times?" he asked, setting the coffee on the counter.

Piper nodded, her lips pressed in a smile, keeping some secret to herself. "Fun times. Thank you." She picked up a cup and examined the writing on it.

"I didn't know what everyone would want, so I just got one of everything."

"That's super sweet. Thank you."

Her gaze connected with his, and he got a little lost in her brown eyes. Then movement distracted him, and he looked up to see Bettina Utner-Kim shuffle by in an adult-sized onesie that made her look like a dinosaur.

"Mornin'," she said, waving sleepily.

"Good morning," he said to one of his two most wealthy and influential supporters. He gave Piper a questioning look.

She shrugged. "Bettina's fun. And she *loves* dinosaurs."

Whit took another glance toward the living room, not because a tech mogul in a dinosaur onesie was particularly interesting, although it was, but because staring at Piper was becoming problematic. She was stunning on a normal day, in her carefully chosen clothing, perfect makeup and hair. But in simple running shorts and a tank top, she was breathtaking. Wisps of hair fell into her face. Whit could imagine this being just a normal morning with Piper, grabbing coffee as his wife went out for a run, then planning for the day ahead as they sat on the deck and sipped espresso.

A small burst of laughter erupted from the living room.

Okay, a normal day married to Piper might not include seven other women and half the contents of a clothing store in his living room. Or maybe it would? And on that note, there was probably no such thing as a normal day with Piper Wallace.

She lifted a paper cup, examining the large, looping handwriting of the teenage barista. "Is there a cortado?"

"I don't think the Pony Espresso serves a cortado."

"Flat white?"

"Unlikely."

"Pour over?"

"Not this morning." Whit reached past Piper and grabbed the cup he thought she'd be most interested in. "This is an Americano. You said that was the hardest to mess up, so I had them make it a double."

She took the cup and turned it, reading where the barista had written "Probably Piper" on the side. She looked up at him, her brown eyes connecting with his.

"Thank you."

"Thank *you*," he said. "You ruined your whole week-end by coming out here. You gave a brilliant speech. The least I could do was coffee."

Piper lifted the cup to her lips, holding his gaze as she took a sip. The kitchen was still, the only sounds muffled conversation coming from the living room. Whit's heart raced as Piper kept eye contact. He placed one hand on the counter, his body inexplicably leaning toward her. She swallowed. If she noticed or minded that the space between them had diminished significantly, she wasn't saying anything. Her secretive, tight-lipped smile broadened.

"This coffee is not horrible."

"That's what I was aiming for."

Piper's eyebrow twitched, as though acknowledging he was much closer to her than he'd been a minute ago, and yes, he remembered how she liked her coffee. Then she glanced down at the cup and nodded.

Whit felt *something* flow between them. He couldn't put a name on it, but he was sure Piper could. Some heady force making every cell in his body want nothing more than to be a little closer to her. Piper cradled the coffee with both hands and flexed up on her toes. She hesitated a moment, then her lips brushed his cheek so lightly, like a beat of air coming from a hummingbird's wings.

That tiny kiss seemed to knock him off his feet, send him spinning, floating. Did she mean to do that?

No, she had no idea how far reaching the Piper Effect was. He'd arranged this weekend to give her a break and allow himself to take a step back from her. One tiny kiss and all his best intentions flew right out the window. His conscious mind had now ganged up with his subconscious, and both were trying to browbeat him into dropping on one knee, immediately, and begging her to marry him.

So next weekend she absolutely had to stay in Portland. Give him a break from all these... *feelings*. He had an important job to do, and losing sight of that could be catastrophic for central Oregon.

Whit forced himself to take one step back. Piper's gaze met his, as though she knew exactly what he was wrestling with. He took another step back.

"Hey, Piper?" Clara padded into the kitchen, holding her phone. "How many times does something have to be shared before it's considered viral?"

Bettina's voice answered the question, "Five million hits within a week is the standard." She walked into the room, dinosaur hood pulled back, and looked at Clara's phone. "Oh. Dang!"

"What is it?" Whit asked.

Clara turned the phone around, and it took Whit a moment to realize the beautiful image of Piper laughing was from the Cattlemen's Association the day before.

"Is that my speech?" she asked.

"The last three minutes of it," Ani said. "Ooh! Coffee." She rummaged through the carriers and selected a chocolate caramel latte.

Everyone turned to stare at her.

"You uploaded the last three minutes of my speech on YouTube?" Piper asked.

Ani shrugged her left shoulder. "It's cute." She took a long drink of coffee. Everyone continued to stare. "What? I'm just trying to be helpful to the campaign. Now that I've become a local, I need Outcrop to keep existing." She took another sip of coffee, but Whit could see her smile behind it.

His phone buzzed. He pulled it out to see a text from Dan.

You and Piper just received an invitation to the Bridge Coalition fundraiser. They want to support your bid for county commissioner and, I quote, "any future political ambitions." Call me.

Piper leaned over his shoulder to read it. She looked up, her brown eyes wide. "Whoa."

He nodded, unable to fully respond. The Bridge Coalition was the most important political fundraising group in Oregon. They sought out and supported candidates willing to work across the aisle and support all Oregonians. It was a huge honor to be invited, much less supported, by the coalition.

"That's held at the Portland Art Museum," Piper said, grinning. "You'll be on my turf this time."

Whit knew all about the formal fundraising event. Enough to make his stomach constrict in nervousness. And the thought of spending the evening there, continuing what for him was no longer a charade with Piper?

A typing indicator appeared on his phone, then another text from Dan.

She should plan on attending next week's debate and all other weekend campaign events with you throughout the month. We're closing in on this election, and Piper is key.

Whit glanced up to see Piper reading the text over his shoulder, a smug smile crossing her face. "I'm key," she said, pointing to the screen. "You hear that, everyone?"

Clara grinned at Piper, and something about Piper's reaction suggested she was uncomfortable with that smile. "To the campaign," Piper clarified.

"Sure," Clara said, with an exaggerated shrug. "To the campaign."

Piper took a sip of coffee, then grabbed Whit's hand and pulled him toward the hall. "The Bridge Coalition gala! Let's figure out what you're going to wear."

"I have a meeting—"

"Two minutes in Grandpa's closet. Let's go!"

Whit sighed and gave into the literal pull of Piper Wallace. Resisting the emotional pull was going to be even harder.

CHAPTER TEN

"*THIS* WAS THE most-watched video in Oregon last week?" Piper asked as they headed down Bond Street on their way to the Deschutes Brewery in Bend.

Whit nodded, skirting a display of hiking boots outside a shop as they strolled past. "Dan was as close to giddy as I've ever seen him."

Piper glanced sideways at Whit. He'd apologized profusely for Dan's behavior, despite the fact that it all turned out well. She patted his shoulder. "Dan just wants to win."

"Me too. But he's acting like your speech going viral was a result of his planning."

"To be clear, it's not the speech that's gone viral—"

"It's the last three minutes of the speech, I know."

Whit shifted his shoulders. Piper looked decisively into the window of an art gallery and took a long drink of her espresso. The last three minutes of her speech: the part where she'd gone off about how much she adored Whit, the part where she got so embarrassed she actually squeaked and covered her face like a crushed-out baby marmot.

So, basically, just the mushy parts.

The *fake* mushy parts.

Their social media erupted in the wake of her speech. Pictures of her and Whit, and speculations about their future, ran rampant. Marc Holt's campaign countered with a series of pictures of Marc and Bunny and their kids and grandkids, but they looked so staged in light of the snapshots that kept floating around of Piper and Whit. Pictures of the two of them laughing, her checking his outfit to make sure he looked fine, him checking out her outfit because she *did* look fine.

Piper tried for a joke to clear the air. "I've had six direct messages asking when we're getting married. Two of them offered a discount on a wedding dress if I'd post a link on Instagram."

Whit laughed. "I got a DM asking if you were pregnant."

Piper stopped abruptly, nearly spewing her espresso across the sidewalk.

He rubbed a hand on her back as she coughed. Piper did her best to recover. "Sorry. I'm just not sure if I'm ready for fake kids."

He chuckled, keeping his hand on her shoulder as they walked. "I thought it was funny too. My favorite ones have been people asking when you're going to launch your political career. The invitation to the Bridge Coalition fundraiser was issued to both of us."

Piper wrinkled her nose. "Political career? No, thank you."

"No?"

"No." She gave one strong shake of her head. But a little part of her heart whispered that her name on the invitation wasn't an accident. She was getting good at this. And she didn't hate making that speech.

But she already had a job and a life in Portland.

As they approached the brewery, Piper could make out the Whit Benton volunteers in their Ask Me Anything about Whit! T-shirts. Among them was a young man, earnestly handing out fliers.

Whit's steps slowed as he noticed Rory. She gave his hand a little tug.

"He wanted to help," she told him.

"How do you *know* he wanted to help?"

"He told me so," Piper obscured her face with the cup, "when I called and asked him if he wanted to help."

"Piper."

"Don't *Piper* me. Rory idolizes you. When I talked to your dad, he said—"

Whit stopped completely. "You talked to my dad?"

Piper kept her eyes on her coffee, knowing she was pushing the limits with Whit, but also knowing they needed to be pushed. "I called to set up a time for them to come over. For hamburgers."

Whit pressed his fingers against his twitching eyebrow. "I appreciate you did this out of a sincere desire to help, but you don't understand the whole dynamic."

"You're right. The only thing I understand is that your dad thanked me five separate times for calling, and your teenage stepbrother jumped at the chance to come downtown and hand out fliers today."

Whit gazed down the street to where Rory stood outside the knot of other supporters. A group of stylish women in their early fifties approached, and Rory bravely stepped forward and offered them fliers. Whit's expression softened.

He needed this. As much as he pretended to not care about his family falling apart, it was everywhere. She couldn't change his sister, couldn't put his grandparents back together. But Piper knew a thing or two about interpersonal relationships. She could help Whit reconnect with a father who didn't know where to start in all this mess.

"Oh, actually, I know one more thing. Rick and Melanie are coming to the debate this afternoon, then they'll all join us at the ranch for dinner." Piper turned to take a sip of coffee, but Whit snatched the cup out of her hand.

"Are you for real?"

"Give it back."

"You invited them over tonight?!"

Whit's face mottled red, and Piper suspected she'd gone a little too far. Still, it wouldn't have mattered when she told him, he was going to react this way. May as well just rip the bandage off and get it over with.

"It was the only night available. Melanie's got Rory scheduled six ways to Sunday."

Whit closed his eyes and shook his head. "You're impossible."

Piper reached for her coffee. "*You're* impossible."

Whit raised the cup higher. "You're unreasonable. In fact, you're so far from reasonable, you couldn't find a flight to get you there in less than seventy-two hours."

Piper jumped for her coffee; Whit took a step back.

"*You* couldn't find reasonable with a map and compass," she snapped.

"If you *could* find it, with literal step-by-step instructions from Google Maps, you wouldn't recognize it when you arrived."

Piper grabbed his arm and tried to wrestle her coffee back without spilling it. "I'd recognize it because *you* wouldn't be there!"

Someone chuckled, and it wasn't Whit. Piper lowered her arms and realized they were now the center of *a lot* of attention, right outside the venue for Whit's first debate since he'd launched his campaign. The golden couple arguing over who was the worst, in front of everyone. Rory was staring wide-eyed, flier still extending to a woman, who was also staring wide-eyed.

Piper met Whit's gaze. After a shared moment of panic, he slowly lowered her coffee, smiling like it had all been a joke. "You can have it back, after I get a good-luck kiss."

Piper sighed dramatically and said loudly, "You don't need luck. You're gonna crush this debate."

He raised his right eyebrow. "But I do need a kiss."

The crowd was now completely transfixed, as though this was a scene in a cute rom-com. Whit had smoothly turned the tide.

Except now she had to kiss him.

She glanced at his lips, nervous. When she'd kissed him the other day, she'd been shocked by the wave of tenderness that accompanied the brush of her lips against his cheek. She hadn't one hundred percent thought it through. It was more of a reflex. He'd brought her coffee, after all. It wasn't unusual to want to kiss a man who brought you coffee, was it? But what started as a quick thank-you peck on the cheek wound up feeling like so much more.

A real kiss seemed like a way to get the two of them into a whole lot of trouble.

But it was, at present, the only way to get out of a whole lot *more* trouble.

Piper rose up on her toes, turned her face to Whit's. He wrapped his free hand around her waist, brushing her tickle spot so she squirmed and moved closer. She steadied herself by resting her hand along his jaw. His gaze met hers, unreadable. Then his eyes slid shut as her lips brushed his.

It was the softest kiss, like a sweet breeze across her lips, almost apologetic in its lightness. In response, her heartbeat grew steadily stronger, faster, flooding her system. His arm tightened around her waist. Piper kept her hand on his jaw, not wanting the kiss to end. She heard a sigh that felt like it might have been hers. A wild sense of freedom expanded inside her, pressed at her heart, the walls aching in their effort to contain it. Whit pulled her closer, deepening the kiss. His scent wound around her, seemed to lift her off the sidewalk. Piper had been running since she was born, and this kiss felt like the destination.

Whit pulled in a deep breath, keeping his forehead against hers. Piper unflexed her toes, letting the distance between their lips grow but keeping her hand on his jaw.

They'd done the thing. Now they could step apart and get on with the campaign.

"Piper," he whispered.

She nodded, understanding all the meaning behind that one word. They shared attraction and a common goal, and that was it. *They* were impossible. A relationship between them wasn't reasonable by even the most generous standards.

She leaned up to whisper in his ear. "Do you remember love rule number four?"

His gaze met hers, his pupils were large and dark, his face flushed. "About the chemicals?"

"Yeah. We just broke it." She leaned her lips toward his ear to whisper again, "We need to be really careful."

He grinned but kept his face next to hers, the faintest stubble brushing her cheek. "You know what's not helping?"

"Hmm."

"Whispering in my ear."

It took extreme willpower to pull back, but she did it. The crowd around them clapped; someone called out something about Piper getting her coffee back. She snatched her drink from Whit's unsuspecting hands and took a sip. It was a little disappointing.

Was it possible she'd found something she liked more than espresso?

No, that was just the chemicals talking, or rather singing. She glanced up at Whit, who'd been knocked out just as hard by that kiss. It was okay. They'd get through this.

Their bodies were responding just as human bodies were supposed to—with a loud and vibrant suggestion that they should commit to one another and raise a family.

But that wasn't their story. She lived in the city; he lived here. He didn't like complicated; she was as complicated as they came. They just needed to be careful and not have perfect romantic kisses on street corners, or anywhere, ever.

Dan, always guaranteed to knock the fun out of any situation, came trotting over. That was all they needed, Dan standing in between them at all times.

"Perfect, you two." He gave Piper a grudging smile. "You really know how to make this look real."

She nodded, avoiding Whit's eyes.

"Now, this should be a pretty straightforward debate," Dan continued. "You're solid on the issues, but what the audience needs to see is a responsible, relatable hometown rancher, stepping up for his community."

Whit nodded, still looking a little dazed. Piper could almost see Dan's words bouncing off his skull and clattering on the sidewalk below.

"What you want to focus on is how *they* feel. People are here to have a good time. Our volunteers and Holt's will take care of any hecklers. You need to get up there and make these voters trust you, like you."

Whit nodded, turning slightly. Then he straightened, the stars falling from his eyes as he refocused elsewhere. Piper followed his gaze to where Rory offered him a wave.

Oh, right. She'd added to the stress of this day by inviting his estranged family along for the ride.

"Hey, Dan—" She was about to tell him Whit needed some time to speak to his brother, but he beat her to it.

"Excuse me for a minute," he said, then stepped around Dan, toward his brother.

Piper let out a breath as she watched him approach

Rory. This was what she'd leave him with, a renewed relationship with good people who wanted to be his family. She might never get to be his family, but an incredibly lucky woman would. When this campaign was over, Piper was going to set Whit up with the most amazing woman. Someone grounded and calm, who would live in that fabulous house with him, adopt a big messy dog they'd both love. And on every other Sunday when she gathered for a family dinner at Wallace Ranch, Whit might be doing the same at his place.

She would give him everything he needed for his happily-ever-after, even if that ending never included her.

WHIT HEADED OVER to his stepbrother, his head still swimming from Piper's kiss.

What happened there? It was like stepping through Alice's looking glass into a world of color and music, like everything came together when her lips met his.

"We need to be really careful," she'd said.

You think?

Life with Piper was unpredictable. It felt like she was a small, reckless child and he was the stuffed animal she dragged around and got into trouble with. He couldn't do anything about the kiss now, except try to forget it. Or at least not replay it continuously for the rest of his life.

Rory, on the other hand, needed his immediate attention. He had no idea what he was walking into here. How had Piper convinced them all into showing up today then coming out for dinner? Did they really want to spend time with him? Or did they just feel guilty, and today would assuage their guilt for another year or so?

Rory glanced over, then offered a flier to a man walking down the street. Whit drew in a breath and walked up to him.

"Hey, good to see you." He started to offer a hand to shake, but that was weird. A hug? A piggyback ride to go visit the cows? He gestured awkwardly to the leaflets. "You having fun with this?"

"Yeah," Rory said, but with a smile. He didn't *look* miserable.

"Well, thank you. I appreciate it."

Rory took on two of his challenging consonants as he said, "No problem."

"Thanks," Whit said, again. They looked at one another, unsure of what to say. Whit stuffed his hands in his pockets. "How's, uh, soccer?"

Rory nodded. "Good."

"Cool."

Rory handed out another flier. Whit waved at the person awkwardly, as though he, the candidate, were getting in the way of Rory campaigning for him.

Whit fished around for something else to say, finally coming up with, "You guys are coming over tonight?"

Rory nodded again. "Yeah." His tone was different this time, like he was excited. Then he smiled. "It'll be cool to see the house again and the cattle."

Whit got it. There was something about that house. He'd loved going there as a kid, as a teen, even now he looked forward to returning home in the evenings. Something about the way the house unfolded, rambling in all directions, connected at the heart with the living room. It was special.

"Okay," Whit said. "See you after the debate then." He didn't know what possessed him, but for some reason, he held up a hand for a high five. Rory slapped it back.

This might just be okay.

And if nothing else, Piper's reckless driving through what was supposed to be the steady path of his life was bringing part of his family back. She might give him a heart attack before he was ever able to enjoy the relationship, but it was nice to know there'd be some family there to call the medics.

"Whit? You ready to go? Debate starts in five," Dan said.

"Let's do it."

Whit felt light as he walked into the Deschutes Brewery. The crowd was cheerful, as though this were a comedy throwdown, rather than the life and death battle he and Holt were locked in. He let that energy rub off on him. Or he told himself that, anyway. It was the crowd's energy that had him feeling so good, and not the lingering effects of sliding an arm around Piper's waist, feeling her breath warm against his cheek, her lips on his.

"Welcome!" The mediator was a local radio personality. Whit listened to his show every morning, and his familiar voice was calming. "We're here for a friendly debate this afternoon, two gentlemen expressing their views in a pub, the way God intended. There is to be no heckling, no low shots, no fighting, understood?"

"Not even a little bit of heckling?" Piper quipped from the back.

"Not even a little bit," the announcer said.

"What if we're heckling the guy we're rooting for?" she asked. The audience chuckled, and one man good-naturedly suggested she save the heckling for marriage. Piper raised her glass in a toast to him.

Whit rested his hands on the podium. Whomever Piper married was going to get a lot of heckling.

Lucky dog.

He shook the thought of Piper's future husband out of his head and turned to greet Marc. As usual, his opponent's gray eyes were cold and watery, while his face was pressed into a fake smile.

And for once, Whit's heart didn't freeze up in Holt's presence. The sight of Marc, his pandering, greedy, soulless opposition, just made him sad.

Sad because Holt was about to get destroyed in this debate.

Whit had his faults—that was undeniable. But he was a nationally ranked debater in high school and college. Showmanship in intellectual argument was his happy place.

The mediator started off with a softball question, "Where do you see Deschutes County in four years?" Marc gave a brief description of nothing changing at all, except every man, woman and mule deer would be holding wads of cash because he was going to "crank the economy right up!"

When it was his turn to answer, Whit took a thoughtful pause, gazing out at the audience. "That depends on what happens over the next few months. I hope to see the people of Deschutes County continuing to work together, balancing our love of this land with sustainable economic growth for our community. Local businesses, family farms and living-wage jobs can be sustained if we continue to care for the land like people in these parts always have." He scanned the audience and saw his dad and Melanie at a table, smiling at him. Encouraged, he let out a sigh. "That is my *hope* for the future. My fears, on the other hand, are all outlined on Marc Holt's re-election website. I don't pretend to understand Marc's motivations, but the proposed Hummingbird Ranch will cut off wilderness access in key areas and redesignate the Rodgers, Muha and West Lake wildlife sanctuaries as commercial real estate. I don't need to explain how that would affect the environment, and the outdoor tourism profits that are dependent on our beautiful wilderness areas."

Marc chuckled and shook his head. "I think you're over-simplifying things, Whit—"

"It's on your website." Whit turned back to the audience. "Grab your phones, head to re-elect Marc Holt and download the PDF for the Hummingbird Ranch proposal. It's all right there. Increased taxes on local businesses and any designated farming property under 10,000 acres fund the infrastructure for Hummingbird. You will be paying for pavement that gets laid across the Muha bird sanctuary, among other protected areas. Rather than taking your annual hunting trips to the Upper Deschutes, you'll have access to a strip mall."

The audience grumbled to one another, hands shot up with questions. Marc was sputtering out an excuse, but half the audience had already downloaded the wordy PDF, snorting in disgust as they discovered for themselves the extent of the plan.

"Okay! Let's save the rest of these questions for after the debate. I know both candidates plan on hanging around." The mediator was overly cheerful as he attempted to move on to the next question. "Gentlemen, we'd like to hear some good news. What's your favorite thing about Deschutes County?"

Marc attempted to redeem himself by talking about the wildlife he was about to force out of a home. He rambled on so long it became clear he was trying to make up lost ground, and no one was buying it. The crowd gave him an almost polite smattering of applause.

When it was Whit's turn to answer, he did so in six words. "Piper Wallace in a yellow sundress."

The crowd applauded and whooped in response. He grinned at her, and she closed her eyes, shaking her head.

Then Whit continued, "And although you didn't ask, my second favorite thing about Deschutes County is the rest of the people living here. Resilient, caring, hardworking. There's something about the people who chose to live here, on this plateau in the middle of Oregon. We love this place. Some of us have families who have lived in this area for thousands of years, some of us immigrated here from other countries, some just came up from California." That earned him a chuckle. "But our common denominator is that we know that for us, there's no place we'd rather settle than right here."

Again, with the loud and raucous applause.

The debate continued, and while Marc had shown himself to be a cold and calculating opponent over the last few months, he just wasn't very good at thinking on his feet. Whit had been doing that for years, and time spent with Piper had been a think-fast boot camp.

"I got a question." A man stood in the front row and shot a glance at Piper. It was Nate, the rodeo clown. The guy who'd asked her to marry him at least six times.

"How'd you do it? How'd you get Piper to commit? Because I know at least half of us here must've tried at one point or another."

Whit grinned conspiratorially at the man and said, "Very carefully."

The brewery erupted into laughter. Sensing the audience, the rodeo clown continued, "You hanging in there?" Whit mugged an expression and waved his hand like he was doing so-so. "How are you feeling?"

Whit gripped the sides of the podium with mock seriousness. "Out of my league, but confident."

The audience cracked up. Marc was clearly annoyed, and that just made the debate all the more fun.

"This has been charming, but if we could bring the debate back to the issues, that's why we're here," Marc said.

Whit turned to Marc. He'd been polite, professional, beyond patient as Marc had tried to sabotage his campaign. That was all busting out the window for the afternoon.

"I agree." Whit nodded to Marc, then gave into the flush rising up his neck as he remembered Piper's kiss. "But you were the one who brought my love life into this campaign to begin with."

Whoops and catcalls exploded from the audience.

Whit glanced out to see Piper, eyes shining as she watched him. His gaze skipped to where his dad and Melanie sat with Rory. They were enjoying themselves too, laughing as he tripped up Marc. It felt good to have them here.

The mediator had a hard time getting the debate back on track, but seemed to enjoy watching Whit run circles around Holt as much as anyone else. For every question about infrastructure and land use, there were three questions about him and Piper.

And every time, Whit managed to answer a question about his love life with more information about the campaign.

What was their favorite place to have dinner? At any of the locally owned spots in Deschutes County, but particularly her brother's place, Eighty Local, which bought at least eighty percent of all ingredients served from local suppliers.

When did he know Piper was the one? When she went all in on this campaign, as determined as he was to do anything to preserve the best in their community.

"What are your plans for after the election?" a woman asked, looking meaningfully at Piper.

Piper answered the question for him. "His plan is to be the Deschutes County commissioner."

Applause came from all corners of the room, and this time the mediator could not stop it. The debate was over, and Whit had destroyed Marc's credibility while appearing down-to-earth and likable.

Professor Arturo would be proud.

Marc glared at him, his watery gray eyes angry and determined. Then his fake smile spread, and Marc crossed the space between them, holding out a hand in defeat. Whit did not want to shake his hand, but it would be petty not to.

Marc gripped his hand tight, attempting to crush his fingers, but Whit had been running a ranch for the last few years, so that wasn't happening. The older man gritted his teeth, saying under his breath, "You are nowhere close to winning this, Benton. Nowhere close."

Whit grinned back, continuing to shake his hand as he spoke quietly. "I see you're threatened enough to finally be rude to my face. That must mean I'm somewhere close."

Marc ran his watery eyes to Piper. "I think it's interesting you found such a perfect partner on such short notice. My people are looking into it."

"Look as hard as you like," Whit said, dropping his hand and returning to the podium.

"If you're so serious about her, where's the ring?" Marc said, loud enough so people could hear. "In my day, men didn't mess around if they were serious."

"Yeah!" A slightly tipsy woman called from the audience. "Where's the ring?"

"Where's the ring?" Melanie called out cheerfully, jumping in on the joke.

A number of other audience members joined in, and Whit involuntarily looked to Piper for help. She held her hands out and lobbed the question right back at him. "Great question, Whit Benton. Where's the ring?"

"Okay, I feel a little bit bad. But I wish you could have seen the look on your face. It was priceless."

"Glad to know you can't put an exact dollar amount on my discomfort." Whit reached over Piper's head to open a cabinet and pull down a pitcher for lemonade. All the dishes were his grandparents', and he stuck to serving the same things in each. Not that he'd done a lot of serving in the years he'd owned the house.

Still, it would be weird to make lemonade in anything other than Grandma's lemonade pitcher.

"Look, we just need to ride it out through the campaign," Piper said, as though the kiss they'd shared and the public demand for an engagement were nothing. She set the can of lemonade concentrate on the counter and peeled back the plastic ring. "If people want to think we're getting married, fine. We're not going to wind up married just because a bunch of people we've never met before want us to."

Whit stalked away, grabbing glasses to set on the tray as he muttered, "At this point, they might issue a recall if we break up after the election."

"Don't be ridiculous," Piper snapped. But Whit could tell by the way she refused to meet his eye and her seriousness as she made the lemonade that the day had caught her off guard too.

"Don't be flippant about the whole thing." Whit set the glasses on the tray. "You said yourself that we need to be more careful in this…" Whit paused, gesturing between the two of them, unable to come up with the word for what *this* had become.

Piper abandoned the lemonade. She crossed her arms

as she turned on him, reminiscent of college Piper when she'd had enough.

"Don't be such a worry wart."

"Don't be so calm."

"Don't be such a Whitman Benton."

"Stop Piper-ing!"

Her lips pressed together as she tried to hold back a laugh. Whit gave in first, inspiring Piper to giggle even harder.

She finally pulled in a deep breath. "This really was a day."

He glanced into the living room where Dad, Melanie and Rory sat, waiting for them. "It still is."

"Just to be clear, I will never apologize for inviting them here." Piper finished stirring the lemonade with a flourish. "Even if this whole election goes sideways, which it won't, you need to do this."

"I know." He sighed. It would be nice if he didn't have to save Deschutes County, keep himself from falling in love with Piper and reconnect with his estranged family all at the same time.

But it all felt strangely doable as Piper abandoned the lemonade and wound her arms around him in a hug. He nestled in, losing himself in her warm, summery scent. He ran a hand along her silky hair and found himself leaning down to press his lips on the crown of her head.

All of it felt doable, except the not falling in love with Piper part of the plan.

She jumped back abruptly. "Why am I hugging you?" Whit lifted his hands from her and held them up, as though he'd somehow been complicit in making Piper hug him. "Seriously. Love chemicals. So problematic."

He nodded, but in his case, he couldn't blame the chemicals. It was Piper who was problematic.

"I promise to stop hugging you."

He nodded again, not at all interested in holding her to that promise.

"You've got the tray?" she asked.

He picked it up: lemonade and glasses, a dish of Hunter's house salsa and another of guacamole. Piper held a bowl of Eighty Local house-made tortilla chips.

Okay, there were definitely some perks to fake dating a Wallace.

Dad stood as he and Piper entered the room. It was both touching and sad how uncomfortable Dad was in these situations. Whit noticed Piper and Melanie making eye contact. They were clearly in cahoots on this project, and that was probably for the best.

He set the tray on the coffee table, then poured lemonade, hoping Melanie and Piper would also be in cahoots about keeping the conversation rolling.

"The debate was fun," Rory said, surprising Whit with his willingness to speak. "You smoked that guy."

Whit gave his brother a smile. "Debate's the only thing I've ever really been good at."

"Oh, that's not true, you're good at lots of things," Piper said. "Arguing, bickering, squabbling."

Dad and Melanie laughed as Piper gently poked fun at him. Then Melanie gave Dad a meaningful look, and he cleared his throat. "You did a great job today. Both of you."

Piper waved away the comment, but Melanie wouldn't let her off the hook either. "No, really. You two make a great team." She picked up her phone. "I've been following all the hashtags."

Piper narrowed her right eye. "Hashtags?"

"On social media, hashtag PiperPlusWhit, hashtag ElectWhitBenton, hashtag WheresTheRing?"

A flush ran up his neck at the memory of Piper gazing

at him across the pub, that mischievous grin on her face as she said, *"Great question, Whit Benton. Where's the ring?"*

Piper laughed, but Whit could tell she was nervous too. Melanie continued, holding out her phone, open to the search of a new hashtag. "But I think this is my favorite."

Piper took the phone and stared at the screen, a little bit thrilled, a bit petrified. It wasn't an expression she often wore. He moved next to her, gazing over her shoulder at the screen.

It was a gorgeous shot of Piper from the Cattlemen's speech, followed by #PipersTurn. Piper scrolled down, Melanie's phone lighting up with a series of posts suggesting that after Whit won the seat for county commissioner, Piper needed to run for office.

"I love it," Melanie said. "Piper's turn. You should think about it."

Piper shook her head but kept her eyes on the screen. Whit ran his hand down her back. Of course people wanted Piper to run. She was smart, personable, creative and the only person he knew with a five-step plan for total world peace.

"We were both invited to the Bridge Coalition gala in Portland next week," Whit said. "They want to talk about this campaign, but Piper received her own invitation."

"Wow." Melanie was impressed. "Are you nervous?"

"I am," Whit admitted. "It's a Portland crowd. There's gonna be a lot of confusing silverware. But now that the public is calling for Piper's political career, I'll just yell out 'Piper's turn' every time I make a mistake."

She slapped his arm, but he could tell her heart wasn't in it. She was still mulling the idea around.

"You ever think about public service?" Dad asked her.

Piper shrugged. "I don't know. I mean, no, I'm not thinking of running for anything." She gazed up at Whit, the same look she'd had at the Cattlemen's speech crossing her face. "But I never would have considered *this* either. Somehow, I spend a few months in the company of Whit, and suddenly I'm feeling all public service-y and selfless."

The company laughed. Whit gave into the wash of confusion in his chest. She sounded so sincere. And when he was with Piper, he felt like they could do anything together. There was no fear, no sense of lack or anger. Like he was the vast expanse of the sky and had just been waiting for the roiling bright energy of Piper to illuminate him.

She set the phone down decisively and turned to Rory. "What about you? Is there a debate team at your school?"

Rory startled, eyes darting to his mom. Then he shook his head, tough consonants slowing his words as he said, "I'm not good at public speaking."

"Yet," Piper amended.

Dad wasn't having it either. "You've been coming along with the new speech therapist. She said you're one of the hardest working kids she knows."

Rory reached for a handful of chips, but Whit could see the effect the compliment had on him. Dad was getting it right this time around.

"And you're really good at soccer, right?" Piper asked.

"He's on the travel team," Melanie boasted.

Piper looked impressed, but Whit was willing to bet good money she had no idea what a travel team was.

"Ooh! Like the Harlem Globetrotters?"

Yeah, not a clue.

Rory laughed like she was making a joke. Which she wasn't.

Piper sighed. "I literally don't even know the rules to soccer."

Rory frowned. "But it's *soccer.*"

"That's about all I know. Hey, Whit's about to head out to the grill. Let's go out back, and you can show me."

"Do you have a soccer ball?" Rory asked.

Piper turned to Whit. "Do we have a soccer ball?"

Whit started to say something about checking in the game room, but nothing came out as he looked down into her big brown eyes. This would be so much easier if she would stop being wonderful and smart and helping him connect with his family.

"There are probably five in the car," Melanie said, standing up. "Let's go. You and Piper can scrimmage before dinner."

Piper stood as well. "I'm warning you now, I make up rules."

Rory tentatively attempted to banter back, "I'm warning you, I can still win."

"It's on." She headed for the door, calling over her shoulder, "We'll meet you guys out back."

Piper, Melanie and Rory spilled from the room, taking the easy conversation with them. Whit was alone with his father for the first time in over a decade.

Dad stood but didn't follow the others out. Whit waited with him.

Finally, Dad cleared his throat. "Let's, uh…let's talk for a second?"

"What's up?" Whit asked, trying not to come off as nervous as he felt. He masked his discomfort with a smile.

Dad put his hands in his pockets and studied the floor. Piper and Melanie's voices faded down the hall, and the door closed behind them. The women would understand if it took the two of them longer to make it out there. They'd be happy he and his dad were talking.

If either one of them could find anything to say, that was.

Dad let out a dry laugh and shook his head. "I'm sorry,

Whit. I'm not sure how to do any of this." Dad met his gaze. "It was just so hard, with your mother, and my parents."

Silence fell over them again. Whit wanted Piper back in the room. She could smooth things, resolve this strained relationship. But it was his issue to solve.

"I know." Whit wrestled with the words. "It's okay. You're happy. I'm glad."

"It's not okay. I should have done more to include you."

Whit nodded, his throat tight. "I could have tried harder too. I'm an adult. This is as much my responsibility as it is yours."

"No, *I* should have done more. I'm going to do more."

Whit was catapulted back in time to his sophomore year in college, the confusion and frustration he'd felt at not knowing how to connect with his dad, not even having the words to express what he wanted. He'd pretended to be self-sufficient, an adult who didn't need the family that was falling apart all around him. He'd built walls he wasn't even aware of, until Piper showed up with a sledgehammer and pickaxe to break through.

He swallowed hard and managed to say, "I'd like that."

Dad met his eye and smiled. "Me too. And Rory. He's always thought you were as cool as they come. He was sure impressed by that debate today. I was too. I'm proud of you for standing up to Holt."

Whit grinned. It had been a whirlwind of a day, but he *had* smoked Holt in that debate. "I'm always at my best in the middle of a high-stakes argument."

"That must be why you're doing so well with Piper."

Whit faltered. He didn't want to lie to his dad. They'd missed years with each other, and now they were taking the first steps to repairing that relationship. He didn't want to start off by lying.

But what was he going to do? Estrange his father further by admitting the truth?

"She's something else."

Dad grinned. "She is. She caught you off guard today, taking Holt's side and asking about a ring."

Whit did his best to try to make his laugh sound natural. "We'll get there when we get there."

Dad's face turned serious. "Don't make her wait. A woman like Piper doesn't come along too often."

Women like Piper never came along. There was only one.

Dad reached into his pocket and pulled out a box. "Melanie suggested we swing by the house and pick this up on the way here. You don't have to give it to her, but I wanted you to know it's yours if you'd like it."

Whit stared at his dad, unable to flip the lid on the small red box.

Dad cleared his throat. "It was your great-grandmother's." He laughed nervously. "It was passed on to me, but I didn't give it to your mom. It never felt right. When I met Piper, I thought, 'Now, that's why I held on to it.' It's for you to give to whomever you choose, but I think you'll agree it would look right on Piper's hand."

Whit forced his thumb to flip the latch on the box. A large sunflower-yellow diamond was flanked by two good-size white diamonds on either side, set in an elegant gold band.

"That's what you call a—"

"Coffee diamond," Whit finished for him. He held the ring up to the light. The diamond glittered between a golden yellow and warm brown. The ring was elegant, audacious, beautiful, one of a kind.

It was Piper's ring. No question. No debate.

Whit's throat closed up. Dad could have given this ring

to Melanie or kept it for Rory to give to someone. Or sold it and bought a bass boat.

But he gave it to Whit, to give to his fake girlfriend.

Whit let out a breath, then hugged his dad. Dad chuckled at the display of emotion, but hugged him back, hard.

CHAPTER ELEVEN

WHIT GAZED UP at the massive brick-and-glass structure, then back at his truck parked out front. His dusty vehicle couldn't be more out of place in front of Piper's building. He felt the same.

She lived in a renovated nineteenth-century warehouse, to which modern glass and steel accents had been added, including the ultra-lux lobby that he was currently trying to find his way into. The building was a mishmash of style and function that was pure Piper. People were moving in all directions, and he'd never seen so many designer dogs in one place. Every other person came with a canine: Chihuahuas; basset hounds; Dalmatians; greyhounds; big, square-headed bulldogs; tiny, smush-faced pugs. And all of these animals just went about their business, no scuffles or barking, just dogs passing other dogs, as aloof as their owners.

Whit steadied his shoulders and headed to what he hoped were glass doors and not another window like the last one he'd tried. A tall cement planter box, full of succulents, ran along a pathway. Piper had told him to text when he arrived, then use the code to open the door and she'd meet him in the lobby. Whit stared at the electronic pad, which was entirely blank, not sure of what he needed to press to get started.

A man behind him trotted up and reached in front of him to flash a card at the box, and the door swung open.

His fabulously well-groomed, off-leash Australian cattle dog walked into the lobby ahead of him.

"Great boots," the man said as he passed.

Whit glanced up, intending to nod his thanks. The man was about his age, fit, with a neatly trimmed mustache and what had to be the type of expensive vintage clothes that Piper went on about. He looked like a well-dressed yuppie from the early 1980s, with the exception of a string of pearls he wore around his neck.

Whit stared at the pearls, not able to make sense of them.

"Did you find them in town?" The man was still talking about Whit's boots. Whit was still staring at his pearls.

Finally, he forced his gaze down at his own outfit. Piper had decreed a tuxedo worn with boots for the occasion, which felt as eclectic as the building he was entering, but that was Piper for you.

"Uh, no. I got these at the Boot Barn in Madras. But they're old."

"Cool." The man and his dog took off across the lobby, where they met up with a woman, also wearing pearls, who gave each of them a kiss.

Was the dog wearing pearls too?

He didn't have time to investigate because the elevator doors opened, and suddenly Piper was in the lobby. Somehow she managed to knock the rest of the world out of focus, the sight of her the only thing he could really see clearly. She wore a long, blue silk dress that floated around her like she'd just stepped down from the clouds. The fabric shimmered faintly, the color shifting around her from pale to deep blue. Her hair was up in a messy bun, the wisps framing her face, again reminiscent of a goddess.

She stopped to speak to the couple in pearls, kissing

the air near their cheeks, then leaning down to pat the dog and comment on who might be a good boy.

Only Piper could look right snuggling a dog while wearing a silk gown.

She must have felt his eyes on her because she looked up, her full, dimpled smile flashing.

"Whit!"

The couple turned to look at him as well. Whit awkwardly pulled a hand from his pocket and waved. How do you greet a goddess? If he'd ever learned, he really couldn't remember.

"Is that Whitman Benton?" The man in the pearls asked.

Piper gestured for them to follow as she streamed toward him. Whit steeled himself. He was going to kiss her cheek, hold her hand and that was it. Piper walked up and set both hands at his waist, rising up on her toes. Whit cupped her cheek with his palm and kissed her other cheek lightly.

Lightly, that was what he was calling it. Not reverently.

"Hey! Meet my friends Emily and Geoff."

Geoff held out a hand, which meant that Whit had to remove one of the arms that had somehow gotten itself wrapped around Piper and shake. "Great to meet you," Geoff said. "We are huge Piper fans."

"The biggest," Emily said, holding out a hand as well.

"Maybe top ten?" Whit challenged. "I think I get to claim biggest fan."

Piper wrapped her arm a little tighter around his waist and leaned into him, which wasn't helping anything.

The couple laughed, then launched into a story of how Piper was their matchmaker. He wasn't entirely listening. He watched Piper as she soaked in their gratitude. She really was changing the world, one relationship at a time.

"—then we bought these pearls as an engagement promise," the man was saying, "and were married a month later."

Whit snapped out of his meditative trance on Piper. He placed a hand over the breast pocket of his blazer.

Engagement pearls? Is that a thing now?

"Welp, we've got a gala to crush," Piper said. "See you in the dog park tomorrow morning?"

"We'll be there."

Piper slipped her hand into Whit's, tugging gently. Her dress fanned out behind her as she led him to the exit. "Twenty-minute walk?" she asked. "Pro or con?"

"You want to go for a walk?"

"I want to get to the gala, and it's at the art museum, about a mile away. Walk? Or do we negotiate that massive truck in traffic?"

Whit chuckled. "A walk sounds great."

They emerged onto the street, which was alive with people and their pets on this warm summer evening. Folks were cheerful as they headed into posh delis, grabbed slices of pizza and sat at tiny tables sipping glasses of wine.

"You're in the Pearl District right now," she told him.

"It's nice."

"That's where I get my coffee." She pointed to a shop alongside a dog park. "And that's where I get my olives and hard cheeses."

"You have a store specifically for hard cheeses?"

"Obviously. Italian deli for hard cheese, French for soft." She shook her head, like everyone knew this and had access to such things. Then she pointed out a little corner store. "That's the best bodega for Cuban coffee."

Whit nodded, watching Piper's face as she pointed out all her favorite spots.

They passed what looked like a fitness center, but with

orange lights everywhere. A young woman came rushing out. "Piper!"

Piper waved back, and another extremely fit young woman ran out, waving. They looked like a sorority that had gotten hit by a tattoo parlor.

"When are you coming back?" one of the women asked.

"As soon as the business of this election dies down."

Whit's heart sank a fraction of an inch. She was planning on working out here, a few blocks from her home, in Portland. Not going for long runs on his property.

Unless something happened to change her mind.

She tugged his hand, and they kept walking up a hill, the sunset flashing through tall buildings on their right as they walked. "I'm going to take you on a little detour."

"Do we have time?"

"It's literally the world's smallest detour."

"How can you prove that?"

"Who wants someone to prove the length of their detour?"

"I'm just saying, don't go making claims you can't prove."

"You're going to love this detour."

"And the evidence for that might be—"

"—on the detour. Come on!"

Whit sighed, but he followed. Piper ducked down a side street, and they emerged into a parking lot full of food trucks. "Are you prepared to love this? Because you're going to."

"Aren't we heading to a big meal?"

"This is a tiny snack on the way. Plus, we're walking. You have to channel my nephew and not let anything spoil your appetite."

He didn't tell Piper it was unlikely he'd be able to eat

at the Bridge Coalition gala because he wouldn't be able to figure out which fork to use.

The spaces between the trucks were narrow, filled with a variety of people. No one seemed to think the most gorgeous woman in a blue silk gown leading a tuxedoed man in boots through the warren of international food options was anything to gawk at.

"Here we are."

Whit looked up at the sign, simple and welcome: Tacos al Pastor.

He gazed down at Piper, who was grinning at him.

There couldn't be anything sweeter in the world. And this was just one of a hundred thoughtful gestures she did for everyone. Looking out for her siblings, figuring out how to engage with his family, crocheting ridiculous hats for her nephews and dogs alike.

Whit took her other hand and pulled her to him. He was nervous about tonight, nervous being with Piper, nervous being in the city. She'd brought him to the one place she knew he'd love. He wanted to say thank you, but the words felt so grossly inadequate, they wouldn't form in his mouth.

She gazed up at him, looking a little nervous too. Like they'd turned some kind of corner and neither of them was very interested in returning.

"Piper Wallace," a somewhat surprised, also nervous male voice said.

Whit turned to see a man holding a noodle bowl moving toward Piper.

There was something about the guy Whit didn't like at all.

"Liam, hi." Piper brushed her hair back around her ear. "How's the pad thai?"

Whit dropped a hand around her waist and anchored her to him.

Liam looked absently at his bowl, like he'd expected just about anything other than a question about his meal choice. "It's good." He looked into her eyes, something apologetic in his expression. "How *are* you?"

How are *you?* What kind of question was that? She was fine—better than fine, she was on her way to a gala with the Bridge Coalition.

Whit pulled her closer, then danced his fingers across her tickle spot so her answer was interrupted by a gale of laughter. Piper slapped her hand on top of his and held it so he couldn't tickle her again. He pulled her even closer.

"Hi, I'm Liam," the guy admitted. Whit didn't like his tone, like he knew how he'd hurt Piper and needed to man up to it. While that happened to be true, he didn't like Liam's sense of his own importance. "You must be Whit. It's good to meet you."

To shake his hand, Whit would have to unwind his arms from Piper, and that wasn't happening.

He nodded, about to spew some nicety about it being good to meet him too, but Piper interrupted. "Must he be Whit? Is that a requirement?"

Whit laughed. "I think I have to be."

"True, *you* don't have a choice, but *I* could be running around buying tacos with any number of people."

"But would you?" Whit countered.

"Well, no, of course not. That's not the point. I'm just not sure you *have* to be Whit Benton." Piper grinned as she warmed up to the debate.

"No. I *have* to be Whit Benton. It's impossible to change that fact." Whit kept his fingers on her tickle spot, in case he had to resort to underhanded methods to win the argument.

"You could change your name."

"But I'd still be me."

Liam cleared his throat, reminding them that he was still there. He gazed at Piper, a little bit of longing, a little bit of challenge in his voice as he said, "You haven't changed at all, have you?"

Which was almost word-for-word what Whit had said to her after not seeing her for seven years. It was what he'd said when she threw him off balance.

"You haven't changed" really meant "I still can't keep up with you." Piper was always going to be a little too smart, too pretty, too funny. A man just had to learn to hold on and get comfortable with the fact that she was a force.

Whit tightened both arms around her, pulling her back against his chest as he said to Liam, "Why would she ever change?" He gazed down at her, and if she was surprised he was holding her so tightly, she wasn't complaining. "Could there be anything more tragic than Piper changing? I don't want to imagine this world without Piper running around being exactly who she is." He met Liam's gaze. "No, she hasn't changed a bit. Nobody could knock the Piper out of this one." Then he smiled and reached out and slapped Liam's shoulder, just slightly harder than he needed to, for Bowman's sake. "Good to meet you, man. Enjoy your noodles."

Liam said something that neither Whit nor Piper were listening to, then receded into the crowd. Whit felt strangely light, better.

"What are you smiling about?" Piper asked.

"That guy." Whit looked over his shoulder to where Liam was skulking away. "He's not what I expected."

"What did you expect?"

"I don't know. I just thought he'd be more—" Whit couldn't come up with the word. He figured Liam would be more intimidating, more worthy of Piper. In the end, he was just some guy, and not a terribly interesting one at that. "I just thought he'd be *more*."

Piper's fingers wound through his.

"His problem with me was that I was too much."

"Well yeah, you're way too much for that guy. I'm not even sure he's up to that bowl of noodles."

Piper laughed, and Whit felt heat and bravery wash through him. In college, he'd been the only man who could keep up with her. Could he still be that guy?

"You want a taco?" a grumpy woman barked through the window of the food truck.

"Yes, please," Piper said. "Two."

Whit's stomach became acutely aware of the promise of taco goodness. "Just two?"

"You'll spoil your appetite."

"I thought I was supposed to be channeling Jackson."

Piper glared at him as she snapped open her purse and laid cash on the counter. Two small, perfect tacos were deposited on a plate and slid across the counter: pork, cilantro, salsa.

Whit picked up a taco and took a bite.

Piper gazed at him, her wide brown eyes tracking as he tasted the taco. Whit was cognizant of the fact that he was wearing a tuxedo, standing in a crowded parking lot with the most amazing woman, eating a taco. He closed his eyes, savoring the moment.

"You like it?"

The setting sun washed through an opening in the buildings, bathing Piper in pink and golden light. A breeze pushed a tendril of hair across her face, and she brushed it back as she grinned at him.

"Yeah." He nodded, letting every feeling and hope he had regarding Piper flow through him. "Absolutely perfect."

"Just keep still another second," Piper said, adjusting his tie. She really needed to step back, because he smelled amazing.

No, he *was* amazing.

The depression she'd suffered after Liam had very little to do with Liam. It had to do with getting comfortable with the choice she made to embark on a different path than her siblings. She'd thought that if she were married, she'd be keeping up with them, have more in common. She'd have a husband her brothers could befriend; she and Clara could plan her wedding. And, if she were honest, she wouldn't be as lonely in her beautiful loft.

Liam had served as the focus of her confusion, not as the real heartbreak.

But he was still kind of a jerk, and it was awesome to watch Whit defend her. In Whit's arms, the truth sounded more like a declaration of love than an accusation. She *was* Piper Wallace, and she didn't have much of a choice in the matter. He made it sound like being Piper was the best anyone could hope for.

And then there was the not-very-subtle slap on the shoulder he gave Liam before sending him off to his noodles. She could feel her brothers high-fiving him from across the state.

Piper looked over Whit's shoulder at the park blocks unfolding behind them. On this warm night, the pathway through the city was lively, green and leafy in the middle of the concrete city. While it would be fun to stroll through the city on Whit's arm, they had work to do.

And she was not going to take one more step along the slippery banks of falling for Whit Benton.

Tonight was about launching what could be a real political career for him. He'd given her her confidence back. She would repay him with support, help, tacos, whatever he needed. And when he was ready, she'd set him up with a wonderful match. There would always be a piece of her heart in his hand, and that was okay. She was getting comfortable knowing she might not always be next to the ones she loved, but she was going to love them all the same.

"Is my tie straight enough?" he asked. "Or are you making it artfully askew?"

"That's not a thing."

"I just had a conversation with a man in pearls walking an Australian cattle dog. Anything can be a thing now."

Piper gave him a grudging smile. His eye caught hers, and her body involuntarily shifted closer.

"You look really pretty," he said.

Piper flushed. She'd spent a lot of time making sure that was the case.

"What color blue is your dress?" he asked, stepping back to admire it. "It seems to change as you move."

"That's what it's supposed to do." She glanced at him from under her lashes. "Sky blue."

The admission seemed to hit him, and he swayed slightly, a smile spreading across his face. A warm breeze floated over from the park, shifting her dress around her legs. Piper met his gaze, attempting to raise an eyebrow in challenge. Whit, show-off that he was, raised his right brow even higher.

He'd caught her out. She wanted to look pretty for him, and he knew it.

She reached back up to adjust his bolo tie. "Your tie is ridiculous."

He was still looking at her, resting a hand across the breast pocket of his jacket. It was beyond time for her to disengage.

Keeping her eyes on his tie, she said, "I'm just going to walk in there and pretend I'm your girlfriend. If anyone asks about a ring, I'm going to imagine it's in your jacket pocket tonight, just waiting for me."

He dropped his hand abruptly, then gave a nervous chuckle. "Isn't that what we've been doing all summer?"

"Yes. Obviously. I'm just getting ready." She slipped her hand in his and headed for the entrance. "Let's go get it."

The Kridel Grand Ballroom was stunning. Golden walls shone in the warm light of the chandeliers, as did the crystal and china on the beautifully laid tables. Everywhere she turned there were massive standing arrangements of yellow roses, Portland's signature flower. Piper was delighted to see so many people she knew, and extra smug when she introduced Whit to the lovely woman who ran the shop where she procured her soft cheeses.

"I've been following your campaign," Michael Lane, the über-wealthy owner of a running shoe company, said. "I'm impressed. You've been patient—you've risen to every challenge Holt's thrown at you. Throughout everything, you kept the focus on your message, while responding to the desires of your constituents."

"Thank you." Whit shook his hand. "I never expected a career in politics. I'm only running because someone has to step up."

"That's the basis of all good leadership. A call to do the right thing."

Piper squeezed his hand. "We're so lucky to have him."

"He's lucky to have you," Lane said, turning to Piper. "There are several people who want to talk to you this evening as well."

The familiar temptation ran through her. Should she think about getting involved in local politics? No, her work kept her busy enough. She smiled at the shoe mogul. "I already have my calling."

Forty minutes into the event and Piper was glad they'd

stopped for tacos. Everyone wanted to talk to Whit, and her. There were trays of delicious-looking hors d'oeuvres floating around, but there was no time to grab so much as a crostini, much less eat it.

Also, watching Whit's face as he enjoyed that taco was a memory she'd replay for the rest of her days.

Or maybe they could spend more time eating tacos together? Like on a food tour of Mexico…

No. There would be no future taco eating with Whit. Every time her heart started to trot down that path, she needed to wrestle it firmly back onto the straight and narrow. It was just the love chemicals getting her into trouble.

Or was it?

Yes, it's the chemicals, she barked at her subconscious in an imitation of Ash's old drill sergeant. She and Whit were impossible. And this time, she was going to prove to herself, and the world, that she wasn't as selfish as Liam thought. She would step away from the gorgeous, funny, principled man and set him up with the woman of his dreams.

"Here?" Whit asked as they approached their table. They were in the center of the room, seated with some of the biggest players of the evening.

"Right where you belong," she said.

Whit pulled out her chair, giving his head a slight shake as though to remind himself this was really happening. When he dropped into the chair next to her, he stared down at the place setting in horror.

"What is it?"

"So many forks," he whispered.

Piper repressed a smile. "It's fine."

"It's not fine. Why so many forks?"

She smiled at the distinguished woman to her left, then

dropped her voice. "What would you prefer? A steak knife and a spork?"

"Yeah," Whit said. "That sounds about right."

She kicked him under the table. He nudged her knee with his.

"It's great to meet you both," a man from across the table said. Whit and Piper looked up at the same time. "I'm curious to hear what you have in store next."

What Whit had planned for his future and what these people had planned for it were clearly two different scenarios. They saw Deschutes County commissioner as a start, not the end goal. But Whit, being Whit, listened with an open mind. The country was facing a political crisis that could only be cured by good, reasonable people stepping up to do their civic duty. What Piper had thought of as *unappealingly Greek* was apparently the answer for these folks.

And Whit wasn't the only budding politician they hoped to support. People were asking about her plans too.

A server set a wedge of melon on a salted kale leaf in front of Whit. He didn't pause in his conversation as he reached for his dessert fork to cut into it. Piper gently took his hand and guided him to the correct fork. He tapped her knee with his in thanks.

Then he looked down at what he was supposed to be eating.

"What's this?"

"Delicious," she responded, not breaking her smile.

"It looks like cheat day for a mouse." He glanced behind him to see if a waiter was coming with more food. "I'm starving. I should have had eight tacos."

"Have some bread."

"I already ate mine."

She took her roll and set it on his plate. He started to

put it back, but she blocked his hand and engaged a man across the table in conversation. Whit dropped the roll and caught her hand, his index finger and thumb lingering for a moment on her ring finger, brushing softly across the spot where a wedding ring might someday rest.

Piper caught his eye, something powerful and intimate passing between them. He let go of her hand, but smiled at her like she was the only woman in the room, or even on earth.

Her heart beat rapid-fire, sending out clear and detailed plans for a future with Whit at every pulse.

"Have you met the chief of police?" a man asked, gesturing to a woman in her midforties who'd stopped at the table.

"Not yet!" Piper shook her head and focused.

She lived in Portland, she loved small dogs, she was a matchmaker. She was a matchmaker, and the chief of police was *not* wearing a ring. Piper forced her thoughts from Whit by mentally running through her client list.

Oh, and actually there was Luis, who had a thing for powerful women with Venus of Willendorf figures.

She held out a hand. "I'm Piper Wallace. So great to meet you."

Six courses and six correctly used forks later, music filled the room, and couples were making their way to the dance floor. She could officially call the evening a success. The Bridge Coalition had committed funds to Whit's campaign, and he'd made connections that would serve him for a lifetime. Meanwhile, Piper had a new client.

She leaned back in her chair and sighed with satisfaction, only to watch as Whit stood and held out a hand to her.

"Dance?"

Could she enjoy one celebratory dance with Whit? The

evening had gone off better than anyone could have fore-seen. She was officially over her funk. Whit's campaign would be well-funded, and the plight of Deschutes County brought to the attention of some very powerful people.

Yeah. With all that in the books, she could allow her-self a dance with Whit Benton.

Piper slipped her hand into his. "One hundred percent."

Her dress floated around her legs as he led her to the dance floor. He took her right hand in his, cradling it near his chest as he wrapped his other hand around her waist. The music was a murmur of brass instruments under the thudding of her heart.

He smelled warm and Whit-y. If it had been anywhere near appropriate, she would have buried her nose in his neck, inhaling him.

"You just know everything, don't you?"

She looked up, surprised.

"You can line dance, slow dance. You know which fork to use, which taco truck to visit. Everything you do is Piper Perfect."

She gazed at him. "Almost everything."

He readjusted his fingers around hers, the slight-est brush lingering on her ring finger again. She could feel herself slipping further, falling. She couldn't do this, couldn't let them get any more tangled up together.

Whit had to win this election. And when he did, he had to live in Deschutes County.

And while it was clear he was attracted to her, what kind of chance did they really have with one another? His problem with relationships was that they were too compli-cated. She was as complicated as they came.

And, to quote Whit, she wasn't going to change.

He leaned down and spoke in her ear. "How am I going to repay you?"

Piper swayed on her feet as the warmth of his breath brushed her shoulder. She closed her eyes for strength, then gazed up at him. "You have to promise me that when this is all over, you'll open up to a real relationship."

His breath caught. His feet stopped moving, and they were staring at one another in the middle of a crowded dance floor. Then he cleared his throat and gave her that mystery smile.

"I promise."

WHIT PACED TO the window of the Airbnb apartment and gazed out across the dog park to Piper's building. He strode back across the bamboo floor and picked up his phone. Two twenty-five.

There was no way he was getting to sleep any time soon.

Whit paced back to the window. She was less than 200 yards away, but still light years ahead of him.

But watching her shine tonight, Whit knew one thing with absolute clarity.

He was in love with Piper Wallace.

And if he allowed himself to really think it through, he'd been a little bit in love with her since first hearing her argue with an upperclassman at check-in for orientation their freshman year at OSU.

The gala tonight made it clear that he had a career in politics if he wanted one. It made sense. Public service was the perfect use of his education, upbringing and personality. He was uniquely qualified to help his state, and possibly his country during these difficult times. The Bridge Coalition was ready to help him step up.

But he didn't want to move forward with anything without Piper by his side.

It was on him to make a relationship with her work. The

complications of geography, her business and his political career were no small obstacles. But with Piper by his side, anything was possible.

"I'm just going to walk in there and pretend I'm your girlfriend," she'd said. *"If anyone asks about a ring, I'm going to imagine it's in your jacket pocket tonight, just waiting for me."*

Whit reached into his pocket and pulled out the red leather box with his great-grandmother's ring. She had no idea how right she was.

CHAPTER TWELVE

BERNICE TOOK OFF running for the dog park the moment Piper had the coffees in hand, if you could call what happens when a pregnant dachshund is in a hurry "running."

Piper took a sip of her coffee and watched Bernice greet her friends. Anticipation fluttered in her stomach as she glanced up at the building across the park where Whit had an Airbnb rental for the night. Today, she got to show him *her* Portland.

She pressed her lips together, refocusing on the puppy. Bernice was sporting a pink pig bonnet this morning. Piper was pretty sure all the other dogs were a little jealous.

Without her explicit permission, Piper's eyes returned to Whit's building.

Stop it.

Her eyes suggested they weren't doing any harm, just admiring the front door of a building, out of which Whit Benton would be striding at any minute.

Piper puffed out her cheeks in a big breath and turned away. Her behavior last night had been unacceptable. As much as she'd love to blame him or the organizers of the gala or the magic of the Park Blocks, she knew she had no one to blame but herself. Heat rose to her face as she thought about the dress, the detour to the taco truck, the dance. She wasn't pretending to be Whit's girlfriend last night. She was a girlfriend, and a love-struck one at that.

It needed to stop right now.

"Good morning."

She looked up to see Whit striding toward her. He wore jeans, a vintage denim jacket and the old feed-supply T-shirt. His hair was still damp, standing up around the forehead. His smile was bright and inviting.

Maybe being his girlfriend could stop in four hours? After they explored the city together?

No.

She closed her eyes against the urge to throw herself into his arms, then acted as close to normal as she was going to get.

"Hey." She held out one of the coffees to him. "I wasn't sure what you drank in the morning, so I got you a cortado because it's what I drink in the morning." He chuckled, gazing at her with his warm blue eyes. Something about his smile was different. It was brighter, like he was hiding a surprise. "But I'm happy to grab you something else if you like." She looked over her shoulder at the coffee shop with the intention of keeping her eyes there, but her head swung right back around toward Whit as though her neck were in cahoots with her eyes.

He was still smiling.

"This is great. Thank you."

"We're just out for the morning waddle." Bernice perked her head up but didn't growl when she saw Whit. "I'm super excited for today."

"What's on the docket?" Whit asked.

"I'm going to show you everything you never knew you loved about Portland."

His gaze connected with hers. "I feel like I already know what I love about Portland."

She let herself get a little lost in his eyes, then snapped herself out of it.

"One taco truck does not complete a love story."

He dropped his gaze and laughed. "I beg to differ."

"Beg all you want—I will broker no differing." She gave a little tug to the leash. "Miss Bernice, let's show Whit our city."

He startled briefly as she said *our city*, his gorgeous smile faltering. Then he nodded. "Let's do it."

"Do you want to know where we're going?"

"Nope." His smile was back, and she nearly reached out for his hand. "But promise you'll tell me when we reach your favorite place in the city."

"Why?"

"Because."

She raised an eyebrow. He responded in kind, raising his so high she laughed out loud.

"Well, we're like twenty feet away." She gestured to the promenade overlooking the river. "You want to check it out?"

Whit blanched, looking suddenly nervous. "It's—it's right here?"

Piper glanced up at the cloudless blue sky overhead, thinking it through. She nodded slowly. "Yeah. I love being outside in this city. I mean, I really love exploring the permanent collection at the art museum. And there are a lot of cool places in Southeast Portland and North Portland. But if we're talking absolute *favorite*, favorite spots?" She pointed to a place where the path curved with the river. "That's it."

Whit followed her gaze, then nodded. "Okay." He ran a hand over the breast pocket of his jacket. "Show me."

They'd made it about five steps in the right direction when they were stopped.

"Good morning, Piper," Mrs. Coleman said. Her French bulldog approached Bernice with a similar greeting. Mrs. Coleman was very old, very small and as sharp as they came.

"Hello, Mrs. Coleman—"

"Who's this?" she asked before Piper was able to move onto the second half of her sentence, which would have answered the question.

"This is—"

"Whit Benton," Mrs. Coleman surmised.

Whit practically had to bend in half to shake her hand, but he could hear her loud and clear as she made several demands of him relating to his treatment of Piper.

Whit nodded, acquiescing to each politely. Yet another person who would be disappointed when she and Whit ended this fake relationship.

But do you have to end it?

Piper sat with the question as Whit charmed her elderly neighbor. What would happen if they let this play out, gave in to the connection building between them?

No, she knew what would happen. Whit would win his bid for county commissioner because he *had* to win. And she would be the one who had to make the sacrifice by moving. And all of the life and vitality of the city would be left behind, and she would always be a little bit mad and a little bit sad about it.

Unless there is another compromise?

No. Anything other than her moving would be complicated beyond words. Whit didn't do complicated. That was the whole problem with her to begin with, according to Liam. She was always going to be on the edge of anyone's limits for too complicated and throwing a 165 mile drive into the mix wasn't going to help anything. She just needed to enjoy the day for what it was: a time to show her friend Whit the home she loved.

"Wow. She loves you," Whit said as Mrs. Coleman shuffled away.

"She looks out for me. We've been neighbors for four years now."

Whit's head swung around from where he was watching Mrs. Coleman walk away. Something about the sentence seemed to unsettle him. Then he dropped his hands into his jacket pockets.

"She's a sculptor," Piper told him. He didn't respond right away. "We'll see several of her pieces when we duck into a few galleries this afternoon." She felt somehow uncertain but forced herself to continue, asking, "If you want to see galleries, I mean."

"Yeah, sure."

Piper came to an abrupt stop. Something about the conversation with Mrs. Coleman had upset him.

"You're acting weird."

"No."

"Yes, you are. Did Mrs. Coleman say something?"

"No, of course not." He shook his head, then gazed at her. "She's been your neighbor for four years?"

"You say that like it's an accusation."

"No, I'm sorry." He waved his hands, trying to erase this awkward conversation. "I just didn't get much sleep last night."

"Are you too tired to tour the city?"

"Not at all. I've been looking forward to it. I want to see the city with you."

"You sure?"

He held up a hand in a Boy Scout's pledge. "I swear."

"Okay." She nodded, satisfied and capable of dealing with the situation. "Finish your coffee. Then I'm getting you another."

Whit chuckled. "I'm fine. Let's go see your favorite spot."

"I'm serious. And this coffee shop is my second favorite spot, so worth stopping by for comparison."

Whit held her gaze as he took the last sip of his coffee, the humor returning to his eyes. "Happy now?"

"Almost."

Piper gave in and grabbed his hand. He wound his fingers into hers as they walked and seemed to settle at her touch.

"This is the best morning coffee place," she told him when they approached the door.

"Should one of us stay outside with Bernice?"

Piper scrunched her forehead in confusion. "If Bernice stays outside, how will she get her treat?"

"You're buying coffee for the dog?"

"Don't be absurd."

"You're the one taking a dog into a coffee shop."

Piper rolled her eyes and pushed open the door.

"She's back!" Dhruv, one of her two favorite baristas on the planet, called as they entered.

"You all have to meet Whit. And Whit has to meet you."

Everyone who worked at North Point and half the customers called back some iteration of, "Hello, Whit!"

He waved, a little stunned. "Are they always this friendly?"

Piper glanced around, then said under her breath, "I drop a lot of money in this place. Pretty sure Dhruv had to declare my tips when he applied for financial aid at the Fashion Design Institute."

"What will you have this time?" Jude asked from behind the register.

"I'd love to stick with the cortado." She glanced at Whit. "I feel like a double Americano wouldn't be amiss for this guy."

Whit nodded, but he seemed more nervous than exhausted. Maybe coffee wasn't the best idea?

Who was she kidding? Coffee was always the best idea.

Dhruv made their drinks and pocketed his tip as Whit loaded his with cream and sugar. Bernice sat patiently waiting for Hollis to give her a doggy treat.

"When is she due?" Hollis asked.

"Less than a month!" Piper clapped her hands. "I can't wait."

"Will Micha be home by then?"

"Yes." Piper sighed, then bent down to snuggle Bernice. "I have to give her back."

Bernice looked up at Piper, reminding her that her work as a good dog here was finished. Piper was out of her funk and moving on with life. Piper tried to communicate that she still loved puppy-sitting, even without lingering depression. Bernice, not one to get all mushy, looked away.

Whit took a drink of his coffee and held the door. "Is it going to be hard for you, giving up Bernice?"

"Horribly hard," Piper said as they emerged into the sunshine. "But I'm on the waiting list for two of her puppies."

Whit's face fell, like she'd just told him she had three months left to live.

"You're adopting a dachshund?"

"I'm adopting two dachshunds, yes. If I can get off the waiting list. Is that a problem?"

He let out a breath and rubbed his chest with his free hand, like she'd just kicked him there.

"What's *wrong*?" she demanded. Because something was wrong.

Whit turned away quickly, as though he were holding back tears. Piper grabbed his arm and caught a glimpse of his face. He was upset, distraught.

They'd been together for fifteen minutes at the most: one dog park, one elderly sculptor, two coffees.

"What *is* it?"

His gaze met hers, and somehow the whole situation felt painfully familiar. *One minute you're laughing and having fun, the next he's pulling the car over and asking you to leave.*

WHIT TOOK ONE step back, then another. He was about to lose it over what should have been a mundane revelation. She was adopting a couple of short-legged puppies. This was not a surprise. It wasn't even a problem. The problem was his own inflated self-confidence in thinking he had anything she wanted more than this life she'd created for herself.

But the evidence had been stacking up from the moment he met her in the park.

She had no intention of leaving Portland, ever. Not for her family, and certainly not for him.

Now he was trapped in a dog park, surrounded by hipsters, holding a seven-dollar cup of coffee, about to fall apart over a woman he'd always known he had no chance with. Piper had been out of reach from day one. Why would he think their connection meant anything to her? Or if it did, it didn't mean half as much as having a hard-cheese shop on one corner, a soft-cheese shop on the next and the perfect Cuban coffee somewhere in between.

And that just made him want to fight.

"Why do you…" He gestured to Bernice. "How could you *want* a dog like that?"

"How could I *not* want a dog like that?"

"I'm just saying, it wouldn't last two minutes on the ranch."

Confusion clouded Piper's face, like she couldn't tell if they were having fun or seriously arguing. "Two things. One, you're wrong. Dachshunds are some of the best guard dogs."

"They are not—"

"Google it. Second, Bernice doesn't have to last two minutes anywhere other than the city."

Whit glanced around him at the tall modern buildings, the stylish people, the dogs that came with paperwork rather than a free round of shots from the animal shelter.

And that settled the argument right then and there.

"You love it here, don't you?"

"Yep." The playful light was fading from her eye. Whit hated himself for wanting that light to fade, for wanting her to feel how desperate this situation was.

"You prefer a hundred food carts to your brother's restaurant."

"Prefer isn't the right word."

"But you're here with the food carts."

"I'm here, and I like food carts. And small, niche restaurants. And big fancy restaurants. This is not new information."

Whit put his hands in his pockets and paced a few steps away.

Piper approached, placed a light hand on his arm. "I get that you're upset. What I can't understand is what I did, and why you won't tell me."

He had to get it together. He depended on her help for this campaign. He couldn't let her see he was mad at her because she liked where she lived.

"Do you want to…" She gestured with both hands, trying for humor. "Do you want to see my favorite spot?"

Whit glanced over at the promenade. He'd seen this day unfolding very differently. He'd imagined the magic from last night overflowing into the morning. He'd imagined her smile shining up at him as they explored the city together. He'd imagined arriving at her favorite spot in Portland at the end of their day, and just assumed it was the top-floor restaurant of some fancy building. There they'd finally stop fighting their feelings, and he would offer her the ring that was so clearly meant to be hers.

And in this fantasy proposal spot, they'd order pinot gris to celebrate, and they'd return to it on anniversaries for the rest of their lives.

But for Piper, there would be no coming back to Portland, because she wasn't going to leave in the first place.

"Because I know you love rivers, and this urban river is super cool, with big ships and warehouses. It's fascinating."

It was like she had a whole box of Morton's salt to slowly pour on his wounds.

"The point of rivers isn't commerce."

"Try saying that to any civilization ever in the history of rivers and boats."

"Why are you—"

"Why are *you* trying to back me into a corner?"

Whit gazed down at her, somewhere between giving in and getting mad. "I just want you to admit it."

"Admit what?"

That you love the city more than me. That you choose this.

That I've never been anything more than a project to you.

Piper's brown eyes connected with his, concerned but frustrated. She let out a short breath and looked away. She'd planned a whole day for them, and he was ruining it.

"You are *cranky* this morning."

"I'm not cranky."

She gave him a wry glance. Whit held her gaze, willing her to see what he was feeling, to take on some of his pain.

"Drink your coffee." She bent down to pick up Bernice and snuggle her, like she did when she was feeling stressed. "Then let's get some breakfast in you."

"I don't need breakfast. I need—" Whit broke off and turned away because looking at her wasn't helping. He'd been foolish to imagine this would work. Foolish to even think he had a chance. He was just another Nate the Rodeo Clown to her.

He ran his hand over his jacket pocket, feeling the small, square box. What had he told himself last night? That it was on him to make this relationship work. His job was to find a solution.

Sounds of the dog park drifted around them: morning greetings, happy barks as dogs frolicked, the faint sounds of traffic. He was aware of Piper setting Bernice down, of her hand coming to rest on his back.

"What is it?" she asked, in the same kind, caring tone he'd heard her use with countless clients, with her sister, with him as she urged him to make amends with his family.

He wanted to melt into her touch, turn and pull her into his arms.

She continued, "I was really looking forward to today, and if I did something to upset you, it was unintentional."

Whit closed his eyes. Now he'd disappointed her, on top of everything else.

He shook his head. "You didn't do anything. I'm sorry, Piper." He turned, gazed down at her big, disappointed, slightly annoyed eyes. "This is just you, isn't it?" He gestured to the city around them.

Her eyes narrowed. "It is."

"That's cool." His attempted shift to casual didn't fool her. She further narrowed her right eye, and Whit found himself saying, "I don't think I fully understood."

"You don't understand that I love Portland?" She was clearly getting frustrated, heaving out a sigh and stalking to a bench. Bernice, in an absurd pig hat, wagged her lower half, and Piper scooped her onto her lap.

He shoved his hands deep in his pockets. His eyes were fixed on the grass between them, but he could still see every detail of Piper; he would always be able to bring her image into sharp focus.

"Why does it matter?" she asked, voice low but clearly hurt. "I get that no one from home understands why I'm so happy here, but I'm not asking you to."

"It's just—" He flailed his hands in the air, frustrated and unable to say what he needed to. "Why do you have to have two cheese shops?"

She glared back at him, legitimately angry now. "Why does it matter?"

He'd pushed the argument too far, like he always did. Why couldn't he just drop it and let Piper be Piper?

She wasn't going to change. And that meant they were never going to be together.

WHIT STARED AT HER, hurt and betrayed, like patronizing more than one cheese shop was some kind of personal affront. Like getting along with her neighbors and planning on adopting two puppies was breaking the Whit Benton moral code.

It all felt a lot like her final argument with Liam. Her gaze inadvertently flickered to the spot, not two blocks away, where Liam had pulled the car over in the middle of a similarly ridiculous argument about avocado toast.

But the look in Whit's eyes was wholly different. He seemed desperate, hurt on some level she didn't understand. Whit kept eye contact with her, then dropped on one knee before her. Her breath caught in her throat as he took her left hand and stared at it.

"Because it's always been you." The words came out more like an accusation than a declaration. He focused on her face, as though trying to get her to see how desperate the situation was. "You are the only woman I've ever felt anything for and—" He broke off, gesturing at the city around them.

Piper pressed her lips together, trying to hold on to her emotions as they raged and scattered.

Half of her heart was elated, the other bruised and exhausted. Because once again, caring for her was *such* a burden.

He continued, "All those women I've dated over the last few years? It's not that I can't commit, it's that I didn't *want* to. I want you."

She held his gaze, feeling hopeful and annoyed and mad at him for making her hold the conflicting emotions in her heart. He wanted her, but he wished he didn't.

"You don't think I've considered—" She waved a hand between them, not even sure what to call their situation. "But I'm not blaming you for wanting to remain in central Oregon. I don't take it as a personal affront."

Whit reached out for her other hand, hesitated, then drew her fingers into his. Sweet warmth rushed through her at his touch. He pulled her hands to his lips, pressing light kisses to her fingertips. His exhalation brushed across her hands as he said, "I've only ever wanted you, but you're always two steps ahead and slightly out of reach."

Piper closed her eyes as his confession hit her.

She got it now.

Whit wasn't any more in love with her than Liam had been.

It was the *idea* of her he was chasing.

Piper removed her hands from his. The tightness at the back of her throat was painful to speak against, but she got the words out. "Maybe that's why."

Whit gazed up at her, confused. She clarified for him, "Maybe that's my appeal. Two steps ahead, slightly out of reach? You don't have to open up to a relationship if you can just dream about being in one."

Whit shook his head. "No, Piper. I've always felt this way for you. You are—" He blinked, studied his hands as he got control of his emotions, then gazed into her eyes. "You are the most amazing woman."

Piper swayed, dizzy with grief. God, she wanted this so badly, wanted Whit's love and friendship. But she didn't have his love. She was a brass ring to reach for, to fight for. It was her impossibility that made him interested.

"Sure." She nodded, glancing over her shoulder at the corner where Liam had asked her to get out of his car. "I'm amazing. My point is, you're not feeling love, you're feeling longing, an emotion you are much more comfortable with."

Whit's gaze connected with hers, and she could see just how hard her observation landed. Whit stood and paced to the end of the bench. Piper crossed her arms.

"You can't tell me how I'm feeling," his voice was low, warning as she poked at his most sensitive spot.

"You want a family, but you can't make the most basic call to a stepbrother who adores you. You want a girlfriend but say you can't handle the complication of a relationship."

He let out an incredulous laugh, his eyes dark with hurt. "That's low."

"It's the truth. You're interested in me because you think I am out of reach. I'm safe."

"Piper, nothing about you has ever been safe."

She faltered, then raised her chin. "Well, maybe the reality of me is not nearly as appealing as the idea."

"I didn't say that."

"You don't have to. I get it. I'm like a Monet painting— I'm better from a distance."

"I think of you more as a Jackson Pollock."

His gaze met hers, and the tiniest smile appeared on his lips.

Okay, that was fair.

Whit dropped onto the bench next to her. She involuntarily leaned into him. His arm wound around her, like it was created for no other purpose.

And that just made everything worse. All she wanted was here on this bench: Whit, a dachshund, espresso.

But he didn't want her. He wanted the idea of her.

Piper straightened, moving away from him. He gave an exasperated sigh, like she was being unreasonable by not wanting to have this painful conversation while snuggling.

"You don't want me, you want the feeling of wanting me. A woman you don't think you can ever have is perfect for a man who doesn't want the complications of a relationship."

He ran a hand over his face, then gazed at her. "Could I, Piper? Could I have you? Think it through. Could we ever make this work?"

"You don't think anything can work. Not us, not a relationship with your family—"

"That's not fair." Whit stood abruptly, moving away from the bench. "I'm trying with my father."

She pressed her lips together. He was right; he *was* trying. She was just mad now and wanted to fight, reaching for anything she thought she could hurl at him. Her gaze met his, and she tried to tell him everything—she wanted this relationship, wanted the dizzy feeling he inspired in her, wanted to spend as much time tucked up under his arm as physically possible. Moisture gathered in his eyes, and it felt like he heard her. Then he looked away, shaking his head.

"I'm in love with you," he spat out, like it was her fault, like he was angry at her for making him feel this way.

"You say that like it's a bad thing," Piper cried, her emotion raw and open and ugly. "I mean, wow. You're hurling your feelings at me like accusations."

"You don't know what it's like, loving you. Your siblings will back me up here—it's not easy."

His words landed like a heavy swing of a club to her heart, knocking all the wind out of her. That was it, wasn't it? She was too much.

Piper stood, needing to get away from him before she started bawling in the park.

"I guess I'm just too complicated then, right? Heaven forbid a woman should be anything for a man other than a soothing balm."

"Piper, I don't want you to be anything other than who you are."

She held her arms out, her voice rasping against the back of her throat as she said, "This is me, Whit."

Complicated, different and hard to love.

Bernice whined, pushing against her ankles. Piper bent down and picked up the dog. A tear escaped, and she gritted her teeth, determined not to cry.

He glanced at the city surrounding them, then placed his hands in his pockets. "And you can only live here?"

If she thought for a second that Whit truly loved her, she'd be ready to talk. But he loved the feeling of longing for her, not her. He'd never throw down an ultimatum like this if he did.

"I *want* to live here."

He let out an incredulous laugh, examining the tall buildings surrounding them. Then he gazed at her, sad, hurt and with something that did look a lot like love. Those eyes were almost enough to make her reconsider. But after a few seconds, he turned away and started to walk back across the park.

The argument was over. Everything was over.
"So, that's it?" she asked, barely above a whisper.
He stopped, but didn't turn around. "I think it has to be."

CHAPTER THIRTEEN

"WHEN IS SHE coming back?" Dan demanded, pacing in front of the wall of windows in Whit's sunken living room.

Great question. Whit had turned away from her, irrationally, unforgivably crossed that dog park, got in his truck and left two weeks ago.

"She has a life in Portland," Whit said, again.

"She made a commitment to this campaign," Dan reminded him, glancing at Ash to confirm this.

Whit leaned forward on the sofa and cradled his head in his hands. When he'd walked away from Piper, he hadn't thought things could get worse. But voters, it seemed, weren't interested in him alone. Teasing comments about Piper and real concern at her absence greeted him at every stop. Holt's campaign picked up on her absence as well and kept up a steady stream of speculation.

Every single time her name was mentioned, it felt like a bull's hoof straight to the chest, leaving Whit winded and unable to respond.

He needed to come clean, admit to Dan that he'd lost it over dachshund puppies, causing his fake girlfriend to dump him.

He'd lost the support of the one person who managed to air all his flaws and make him better. No, he hadn't lost her support. He'd hurled it into the murky, industrial river flowing past her city loft. There were a million ways he could have handled it, but he'd struck right for the core of who she was.

He'd known he couldn't handle the complications of a relationship, and he was right. He couldn't even manage a fake one.

Dan sat down in a chair facing him, as though he needed to remind Whit how serious this was. "Look, the Bridge Coalition gala was a huge coup. The pictures of you and Piper alone could turn this election, not to mention the support and money. We are so close."

Whit dropped his hands and met Dan's eye. "I know."

"Please get her back here."

"I'll try."

"Most voters intellectually support you, but Piper gets people to the polls. She makes this interesting."

You can say that again.

Ash interrupted the discussion, clapping a hand on Dan's back. "They're both exhausted, Dan. Let's lie low for the weekend and pick back up in a few days."

Dan looked from Ash to Whit, sensing something was off but probably not wanting to step into a mess he didn't strictly have to. Not that he wouldn't wade in if he thought he needed to drag Whit and Piper by the scruffs of their necks and hurl them into a campaign stop together. "Can you promise me she'll be back for Outcrop, Outside, that small-business festival you guys hold? Whit is speaking, and it's on her home turf. There will be questions if she doesn't show. There are already questions."

Whit wasn't going to make one promise regarding Piper's commitments, but Ash said, "She'll be there."

Dan accepted this with a nod. "Whit, I understand you're trying to protect her. But I got word that Holt is planning something big."

"What could he have left?"

Dan stood, grabbing his messenger bag as he got ready to leave. "With Holt, nothing is off the table. We know that."

Whit leaned back on the sofa, taking the second hoof to the chest. This campaign was real, and so much bigger than him or Piper. Everything he loved about Deschutes County would be lost if Holt won. He nodded to Dan. "You're right. Thank you, Dan, for all of this."

Dan paused on his way to the door. "Thank *you*, Whit."

The words sent a wave of shock through him, rattling around in his empty chest. Dan's eyes were serious as he continued, "You're the right man for this position, and the only reasonable candidate willing to take on Holt. This is hard, and I'm being hard on all of us, especially you. But don't think I don't understand the sacrifice you're making."

Whit accepted the rare, almost kind words. If Dan had any idea how badly he'd bungled this, he wouldn't be so generous.

Ash followed Dan to the front door, low conversation rumbling between them as they prepared to leave. Whit stayed where he was, staring out the window.

What had gotten into him? He just dug into the argument with Piper and refused to drop it. It was no surprise she'd turned on him, accusing him of only caring about her because their relationship was impossible. It couldn't be further from the truth. He'd fallen in love with her *despite* the fact that their relationship was impossible.

He'd destroyed everything. Any chance he had with Piper, any chance he had at winning this campaign. He wasn't even confident he could continue forward with this new relationship with his dad and his family.

When the campaign started, he stepped up full of confidence, ready to take the bull by the horns. Now he was lying in the dirt, assessing how many bones were broken and questioning his ability to get back in the saddle.

The front door opened, and he heard Ash and Dan exchange goodbyes. But when the front door shut, a heavy tread of footsteps returned to the living room.

Great. Now he was about to experience the wrath of Piper's stern oldest brother. The scrappy twins would be after him next, and there was no telling what Clara would make of his remains.

Whit leaned back in his seat, ready to face his fate. There was nothing the Wallace clan could do to make him feel worse than he already did.

He opened his eyes to find Ash standing before him, arms crossed, feet planted wide, his face locked in...

Concern?

"You okay?" Ash asked.

Whit was so surprised a dry laugh escaped him. "No."

"You wanna talk about it?"

Did he want to relive the worst mistake of his life? *Not really.*

Ash took a seat next to him, leaning forward and resting his elbows on his knees. "You mind if I take a guess?" Ash didn't wait for him to respond, so whether or not he minded didn't seem to matter that much. "You went to the gala and saw Piper in her element."

Images of Piper in her sky blue dress, grinning up at him, slipping her hand in his as they wound through the crowded parking lot to her favorite taco truck came flooding back. Whit nodded.

"And if I'm to judge based on what I've seen between the two of you, you've been hoping she's not as attached to the city as she professes to be."

Whit rubbed a hand over his stubble. "That's correct."

He expected a myriad of reactions from Ash, but not the

smile that spread across his face. He set a hand on Whit's back, grinning. "That's half the reason I asked her to do this. I figured you two might like each other."

Whit turned on Ash, horrified. "You did this on purpose?"

"I did it because you have to win this election, and Piper is the perfect woman to help you do it. She's argumentative, smarter than most people she meets and has a huge heart. There aren't that many men out there who can keep up with her."

Whit closed his eyes briefly, letting himself soak in this new information. Ash had set them up? You really could not judge a man based on his Stetson.

Whit shook his head. "I blew it. I backed her into a corner and just couldn't let it go."

Ash looked up sharply. "You're talking about a verbal sparring corner?"

"Yeah."

"Not an actual corner."

"No."

Ash relaxed against the back of the sofa. "I can imagine what happened pretty well because we've all had the same argument. We want Piper to come home. We've never understood why she loves that city so much. To tell the truth, I'm glad she's willing to settle for Portland. She'd probably love LA or New York or Paris given the chance."

Whit's heart scrambled with panic in his chest, like it could hop out and keep Piper from moving halfway around the world.

"She's different from the rest of the family. Being true to herself and continuing her relationship with us takes constant sacrifice on her part. But she does it. She comes home every other weekend and for every birthday, special occasion or crisis any of us works up."

It was true. Piper's complicated schedule was created around maintaining a connection with her family.

Ash continued, "She *can* come off as selfish—I know that. But only because she knows what she wants."

"Espresso?"

Ash laughed. "Espresso, pinot gris, different-sized forks for different foods."

"Oh, man. You should have seen her with the forks at the gala."

"I can imagine she was pretty happy."

That word, *happy*, hit him hard. She'd been so happy that night. And they *did* have a connection; she cared about him. Or at least, she had.

"A lot of people in this world never figure out what they want, and they spend their lives expecting others to make them happy. Piper knows what she wants. And I believe she wants you."

"We're impossible."

Ash shook his head. "Hard, maybe. But not impossible."

"But she loves the city. I'll have to live here if I win."

Ash nodded. "And after that?"

"After what?"

"After four years as county commissioner. You have a large group of well-funded people who want to support your political career. I think it's likely you may be spending a lot of time in the state capital in a few years."

Whit let that idea roll through him. Would he continue his political career? If he knew Piper was going to be with him, for sure. She was the wind in his sails, and the howling gale in every opponent's face.

"Who knows? You might find yourself living in another city out of necessity. Like Washington, DC."

Whit's head jerked up as he considered the implications

of Ash's words. There were probably a lot of fancy cheese shops in DC, and a couple of dachshunds would fit right in.

But he was getting way ahead of himself. Right now, Piper wasn't speaking to him, and he was about to lose his bid for county commissioner.

"I don't even know how to get her to come back to the campaign."

"Have you tried asking?"

Whit gazed out the window and admitted the truth. "I'm so afraid to hear her say no, I don't want to ask."

Ash stood. "You expect she's just gonna swoop back in and fix this without anyone asking?" Whit met his eye, and Ash chuckled. "Yeah, that is her MO. But you should take the lead in this."

Whit nodded. An inkling of a plan was beginning to form. It was a desperate plan, but no more desperate than his original bid against Holt.

He stood and walked Ash to the door. "I'm going to call her tomorrow. If you could send her a text after that, reminding her about Outcrop, Outside, I'd appreciate it."

"Why wait until tomorrow?"

"There's something I need to clear up, a misconception Piper has about me."

Ash gave him a nod, then set his hat on his head. "Let me know how it goes." He waved and headed toward his truck.

Whit closed the door behind him and looked out at his home. He bought this place trying to save a family that didn't exist anymore. He hadn't changed a thing, waiting for the day his grandparents came back and Christmas was what it used to be.

That wasn't happening. It was time to make this place his own. He didn't mind Grandma's taste, but threadbare towels from 1985 weren't holding up anymore. It was time to go through the house. As Piper had noted, there were plenty of great vintage finds here. He'd keep the things he wanted but get rid of anything he was just holding on to because it had been there when he was twelve.

Piper was right: he *had* been longing for the past and unwilling to do what was uncomfortable to ensure a future with what little family he had left. His sister was a lost cause, and his mom was so wound up in a codependent relationship with Jana that he wasn't ready to reach out to her.

But his dad wanted to move forward.

Whit had been hurt when Dad got married with barely a word to him. It was wrong; Dad regretted it and clearly wanted to move on. Melanie did too. And while there was no reason at all whatsoever for Rory to look up to him, he did. Spending time with the three of them had been fun, and he needed to make that happen again.

Whit grabbed his phone. He stared at the lock screen for a minute. A selfie from the rodeo, Piper smug with her victory, Whit staring at Piper.

Then he opened the phone and clicked on his contacts, nervous but ready as the phone rang.

"Hello?"

"Hey, Dad. How's it going?"

"Great! Great to hear from you! How are you doing? Any word on the new polls?"

Okay, Dad was a little nervous too. It was harder to do this without Piper's easy charm making everything run smoothly. He managed to get through the greeting phase of the conversation, then made his request.

"I need to clear out this house. I never packed up Grandma and Grandpa's stuff, and I'm still sleeping in the bunk beds in one of the guest rooms."

Dad laughed. "You've probably outgrown them."

"I have. Look, I don't know what you all have going on tomorrow, but I was wondering if Rory might want to come over and help me go through stuff? Then maybe you and Melanie could come have lunch with us."

Dad was silent on the other end of the line, and Whit wondered if he'd pushed it too far. Then his father cleared his throat and said gruffly, "He'd love that. We'd love that, son."

Whit then had to clear his own throat before the emotion overwhelmed him. "Great! Why don't you put Rory on, and we can make a plan?"

CHAPTER FOURTEEN

PIPER'S PHONE VIBRATED with an incoming call at the same
time it twitched with a text.

She lunged at it, then stopped herself.

It wasn't Whit. It was never going to be Whit again.

How had she let things go so wrong, so fast? There *was*
a spark between her and Whit; there always had been.
Rather than acknowledging it and allowing herself to believe that spark and their friendship might equal something
more, she dove for her deepest insecurities. A brilliantly
executed, headlong dive right into her feelings of fear and
unworthiness. In doing so, she lashed out at Whit in the
harshest way possible, accusing him of searching for longing, rather than love.

An image of his face when he realized she'd taken him
to a taco truck washed through her. His gaze hadn't held
an ounce of longing for the future, but rather the sense that
his future had arrived.

The phone buzzed again, insistent, like Bernice when
it was time for breakfast.

Piper snatched up the phone. Both the call and the text
were from Clara.

Clara.

Piper slammed her thumb against the screen to answer
the call. "Is everything okay?"

Noise from the other side clouded the line: the sounds

of the road, Bobby crying, strains of *Legally Blonde: The Musical.*

"Hey!" Clara called cheerfully.

"Where are you? And is Bobby okay?"

"Bobby is upset because I have him strapped into a car seat. He'd prefer to be wiggling around on a blanket, or possibly driving at this point. I'm just pulling onto Twelfth Street off I-405."

"You're in Portland?" Piper walked to the window as though she could see her sister through the buildings between them. "You shouldn't talk on speakerphone in traffic."

"I'm perfectly safe, eyes on the road. Just giving you a heads up that I'll be there in five."

"What's *wrong*?"

Clara was silent on the other end, Bobby plaintively wailing from the back seat, not happy with the situation. Piper wished she could wail like that. Cry and complain until she fell asleep and her problems solved themselves.

Clara cleared her throat. "I texted you a video that I want you to watch. I was going to just send it, then I realized you'd probably need someone with you after you watched. It's…it's pretty bad."

Piper pulled the phone from her ear so she could see the text. The video was from Marc Holt's campaign. Piper's stomach sank.

"What's he done this time?"

"Watch the video. I'll buzz myself in."

Clara signed off, leaving Piper staring at the image on the video link. It was another sketchy-looking picture of Whit, this one captured by a high-powered camera. He was talking to her, and by his stance, she could see they were bantering.

It was the argument they'd had outside of the Deschutes

Brewery, where he'd stolen her coffee and only gave it back after a kiss.

That conversation had ended in her head spinning with the aftereffects of Whit's kiss. But the camera had caught the one moment it looked like they were actually mad.

Piper hovered her finger over the link, then clicked play.

"Whit Benton has a problem," the suspicious announcer began.

"A problem named Marc Holt…" Piper mumbled.

"He's a habitual liar."

Piper's heart twisted as she spoke to the screen, "More like painfully honest."

"Whit Benton lied to voters when he accused Marc Holt of being anti-environment." On the screen was a picture of the Deschutes Brewery debate, with Marc looking defeated and Whit looking smug. All Whit had done was point out information available on Holt's own website.

"Whit Benton lied to voters about his own conservation record."

"He literally doesn't have a record to lie about!" Piper yelled at the screen. "It's his first election."

"Whit Benton has lied about everything, including his relationship with Piper Wallace."

Several less than flattering photos of the two of them flipped across the screen. A camera managed to catch them as they turned away from each other or fought over something as trivial as using anything other than whole milk for a cappuccino.

Not that milk choice was super trivial.

"He's even lied to Piper."

An image filled the screen of Whit talking with Bettina Utner-Kim as she left his house after the girls' night; at the bottom right-hand corner of the image was the date and time.

Another image flashed, this one of Whit laughing with Violet after football practice.

Then one of him and Maisy, his hand in hers, Whit gazing down at her. Zero mention of the fact that she was looking at a bad splinter on his palm.

"Or was he lying *about* Piper?" the suspicious announcer went on. "Whit Benton will stop at nothing to get your vote. Marc Holt only wants you to ask yourself why. What's in it for Whit if he wins this election?"

Um...four years of grueling, thankless hard work?

A woman Piper recognized as Whit's sister, Jana, appeared on screen. "My brother has always been able to convince people of whatever he wants. But this election isn't about him, it's about *you*, the voter." She gave the camera a sincere look, tilting her head to the side, just the slightest threat in her voice as she asked, "What do *you* want for Deschutes County? Post your ideas on social media with the hashtag ElectMarcHolt."

Piper dropped into a chair, fear and regret shuddering through her. She looked back down at her phone. The video already had six hundred views, and who knew how often it was being aired on television or run with YouTube videos.

This was her fault. She could have stuck in there, continuing with her commitment to the campaign. Instead, she was right where she'd been at the beginning of the summer, moping around her apartment, depressed.

Piper paced to the window, angry at Jana, furious with everyone from Marc Holt's campaign and deeply disappointed with herself. She had to *do* something. Getting in other people's business, fixing their lives, was legitimately her favorite thing. But in this situation, she didn't know where to start.

There was a tap at the door, and Piper raced to open it.

No matter how badly the world spun off its axis, hugging her sister was priority number one.

"I'm so glad you're here!"

"Of course. I came immediately."

"Even if it meant torturing my nephew with his car seat." Piper bent down and unclicked the straps Bobby was straining against.

"You'd think he hates being safe."

Piper looked up. "Careful what you say. We don't want him taking after Bowman."

Clara batted at her arm lightly, then came back with a second, harder hit. "Not funny."

"He's gonna take after his responsible dad," Piper amended. Bobby straightened his legs and let out a wail suggesting he'd take after whomever he pleased, thank you very much.

Piper wrapped her arms around the baby, quieting him as she pulled his warm little body against hers. This was what mattered, her family. Piper closed her eyes against Bobby's head.

And finally, with her best friend by her side and her beautiful nephew in her arms, Piper acknowledged the truth to herself. She wanted Whit to be a part of her family. And she wanted to be a part of his.

Her heart expanded, blocking her throat until she could only get out a whisper. "How's Whit?"

Clara was silent, and Piper knew her well enough to imagine the emotions moving across her face.

"What is it?"

Clara pulled in a breath. "Whit's not doing very well."

Piper looked up from her nephew. She and her sister didn't need to speak. Whit had so much going on, and she'd just left him in the lurch. "What did he say about the video?"

"I'm not sure he's even seen it yet. He's not been himself for the past two weeks."

That makes two of them.

"What happened?" Clara asked. "What happened, and why didn't you tell me?"

Piper pressed her lips together. She didn't want to bother anyone with her issues. Nor did she want to admit to anyone that she even had issues.

She risked a glance at her sister. Clara inexpertly narrowed her right eye, making Piper laugh out loud.

"That's my move! You can't make me talk by using the eye trick."

"I can't make you talk...yet."

Piper laughed even harder, and Clara wrapped her arms around her and Bobby. The three of them stood there, in the perfect apartment, in the gorgeous city, laughing until Piper finally let herself cry.

"I don't know." Piper drew in a breath. "He just...he was like, 'You love it here. You have to have two cheese shops.' Then I was like, 'What's wrong with liking my life?' And he got mad, and I said some awful things about him not even wanting to like his life. And then he—" Piper choked up, unable to speak as she imagined him walking away again. Clara wrapped her arms more tightly around her, squeezing.

"He's right," Piper whispered. "I'm just selfish."

Piper expected an even tighter squeeze, but Clara dropped her arms and stepped back, delivering a cold hard glare.

"That is unsubstantiated nonsense."

Piper choked out a laugh. "You totally sound like Mom right now."

"Thanks." Clara crossed her arms. "You are one of the least selfish people I've ever met."

Piper scoffed. "Not true."

"True."

"Um. Not true. I'm literally the most selfish person in the family."

Clara rolled her eyes. "You wouldn't even make the top five."

"Stop cajoling me."

"I'm not cajoling! Look at you. You put your entire life on hold to help Whit win this election. You put your life on hold to help me when Bobby was born. You put your life on hold every time one of us needs anything."

Piper had to physically absorb each statement. Nothing Clara was saying was untrue, but...

"Seriously, sis. You've come home just because Bowman was wearing something horrible and clearly needed your help."

Piper shrugged. Okay, she was pretty good in a situation.

Clara placed a soft hand on her arm. "There's nothing selfish about wanting a career, espresso and a dog with short legs. And knowing what you want only makes you less selfish because you're not bumbling around waiting for someone else to make you happy. Ash says so all the time."

Piper shifted as the uncomfortable feelings meandered through her. Did her siblings really view her this way?

"You're the best."

Piper opened her mouth to contradict Clara because that was just nonsense. Clara was the best human on earth, and there was no contradicting that statement.

But Clara spoke first. "Whit loves you."

Piper shook her head.

"He does."

Piper cleared her throat, needed to get ahold of this situation, of her feelings. "I don't know what he feels, but it's not going to work. It's too much of a stretch."

"Is it? Because from what I've seen, you two work pretty well together."

"No. He can't stand complications. I don't want to move. We're not in for a happily-ever-after like you and Jet."

Clara smiled at her, her dimples flashing, eyes warm. "You're right. You'll never have what Jet and I do." She rested her hands on Piper's arms. "You'll have whatever you and Whit create. Not every relationship looks the same. You'd be bored out of your mind with my life, even *with* the emus. Jet spent his life trying to create a stable family environment, which is exactly what I need to thrive. You need someone willing to jump into the fray and do battle by your side."

Tears unexpectedly flooded Piper's eyes at Clara's insight. She pressed her lips together and nodded, admitting her deeper fears, "But what if we don't work out? What if I messed it all up already?"

Clara didn't take on these unanswerable questions, just as neither of them would take them on with a client. Instead, she said, "No matter what happens with Whit in the future, right now he needs you."

Piper glanced at her sister. There were so many unknowns ranging around her, but Whit needed her, whether he wanted her or not at this point. It was time to Piper up, get in Holt's business, fix the lives of the residents of Deschutes County.

"How much is your son going to hate us if we drive straight back to Outcrop?"

"Nothing five or six years of therapy won't cure." Clara grinned. "Let's go."

CHAPTER FIFTEEN

"THESE TAKEOUT MENUS are from the last century," Rory said, both fascinated and horrified.

Whit looked over his brother's shoulder at a pizza advertisement. The place hadn't existed for the last twenty years. He chuckled. "Yeah, I think we can recycle that."

Rory dropped the menu in the very full recycle bin and continued cleaning out the kitchen junk drawer.

Whit opened a cabinet and examined the contents. "What do you think about these?"

Rory glanced at the North Star "George Jetson" plates.

"Stay," he said without hesitation.

"Absolutely," Whit agreed.

The two of them were nearly finished with the kitchen, with some boxes to go to charity, others to be recycled and a bunch of plain old garbage. Rory had amassed a small pile of mementos for himself, and Melanie offered to shop with Whit for new towels, sheets and other household items that needed replacing.

It had been a big twenty-four hours.

After Whit called his father, then made plans with Rory, he'd started on the primary bedroom. He cleaned out all of his grandparents' old things, with the exception of the clothing Piper liked, and moved in. It would be a while before he could get around to removing the hydrangea wallpaper from the bathroom, but then again, it was probably the only thing that went with the blue fixtures. He could live with it.

Moving bedrooms kept him busy until one in the morning, and by two he was actually able to get some sleep. Rory arrived at ten the next morning, and after an awkward start, they found their groove.

It was almost enough to keep him from overthinking the call he needed to make to Piper.

He didn't know where he stood with Piper. He was ready to go all in, but if he could salvage a friendship out of this, or even just a grudging acceptance that he wasn't all bad, he'd take it. He needed her help. That was clear a week ago. And this morning, Dan texted him Holt's latest smear ad with one sentence: We need to talk.

Whit didn't respond to the text, hadn't watched the ad yet. He'd return one of the five calls from Dan after spending time with Rory, his dad and Melanie.

Piper had asked one thing in return for helping out with his campaign, that he open himself up to a real relationship. A relationship with his family was going to have to do because he wasn't interested in dating anyone other than Piper.

"It's you," Rory said, holding up an old newspaper.

Whit glanced at the picture. It was of him at the national debate tournament, senior year in high school. Whit blinked, nearly moved to tears.

"Yeah. Wow. I can't believe they kept this."

"Dad said you were really good at debate."

Whit nodded, warmth moving through him that his grandparents and father had remembered, or even noticed, in those last few years as the family fell apart. Rory probably needed to know that people noticed him too.

"Dad says you're really good at soccer."

Rory shrugged, continuing to dig through the junk drawer. Then he said, "My club team has a game on Thursday."

"Cool. Can I come?"

Rory nodded, hiding a smile as he pulled long-spent pens from the drawer. Keeping his eyes on the pens, he asked, "When we're finished here, do you need any help with the ranch or something, like with the cattle?"

"I do, actually. I've got some guys coming next week to help me drive the cattle to a fresh pasture. Want to help? We'll be on horseback."

"On a horse? Yeah!"

Whit chuckled at Rory's enthusiasm. "Great. I hope you like it because I've had a heck of a time hiring help. If you're any good, I'm gonna expect you to cowboy up and help out around here more often."

"Can I miss school?"

"No."

"How about a half day?"

Whit laughed. "Forget it. All cattle drives happen on weekends, no-school days and summer break."

Rory started a new line of negotiation, but a knock startled both of them. The door opened, and Ash's voice called from the entryway. "Whit?"

"In here," he called back.

Two sets of footsteps tramped toward the kitchen.

"What's going on?" Dan demanded as he barged into the kitchen with Ash behind him. "Are you moving?"

"Just cleaning a few things out." He held Dan's gaze. "I'm sorry I haven't returned your calls. I'm spending some time with my brother today."

Ash and Dan looked at each other, the communication fast and unspoken. Ash cleared his throat. "You haven't watched the video yet?"

A chill ran down Whit's spine. "No." He shook his head. "No, sorry. Rory and I have been pretty busy."

Dan was clearly struggling to understand why Whit was taking two seconds to do anything except run against Holt. Ash dropped a hand on the campaign manager's shoulder to settle him. "We're sorry to interrupt. Looks like you're getting a lot done." Ash tried to smile, but it didn't come out right.

Whit steadied himself against the worry flooding his system. "Is the ad that bad?"

Dan closed his eyes. Ash nodded. "We should respond as quickly as possible."

Every possibility ran through Whit, then it hit him. Had Holt gone after Piper? Had he brought her family or business into this? He pulled out his phone to find the video.

Ash put a hand on his arm, then gestured to the living room. "I think you might want to sit down."

Three minutes later, it felt as though every solid thing had been unhinged, that gravity stopped working and the pieces of his life now spiraled apart. They'd accused him of the one thing that would never, never be true. He was all in with Piper, as serious about a woman as any man had ever been.

He dropped his head into his hands. Ash and Dan were trying to create a strategy to deal with this, but Whit couldn't hear them. Piper would know what to do, and she'd make him laugh while getting it done.

Why hadn't he just called her yesterday? Why hadn't he called her two weeks ago?

"Whit," Dan's voice roped him back. "We have to respond. This is resonating with people because you two haven't been campaigning together."

Rory looked from Dan to Whit. He still thought Piper

was his girlfriend. His dad was so convinced he gave Whit his grandmother's ring.

It was one thing to lose this election, to lose the trust of the voters. He couldn't lose his tiny grasp on his family.

Think. There had to be something he could do or say. Anything.

From the entryway, Whit heard the front door bang open. He let out a groan at the thought of dealing with anyone else. What next?

"How many boxes are you planning on putting on your front porch? Because you only have a thousand square feet of veranda, so you might think about adding on."

A wry smile spread across Ash's face as Piper's voice rang through the house. Dan dropped into a chair in relief.

"Seriously." Piper, preceded by Bernice in a mouse hat and followed by Clara and Bobby, who wore a matching mouse hat, stalked into the living room. "What *are* those boxes? Or is that your plan for protection against Holt's invasive cameraman?"

Whit's heart had launched itself into his throat, scrambling up his windpipe to get to Piper. He stood, unable to speak or do anything other than stare at her in wonder and gratitude.

She crossed her arms and gazed at him, then uncrossed her arms. Emotion welled up in her eyes, and she held her arms out to him, looking just a shade hesitant. Which was as hesitant as Piper was ever going to be. Whit took three long steps, crossing the room and folding her in his arms, pulling her closer, refolding his arms around her as though he had to repeat the action to understand that she was really here. He tried to speak, to give voice to every feeling inside of him, but he couldn't get a word out.

Piper's arms wrapped tight around him. Her lips were close to his ear as she said, "And they didn't even get your faults right in that commercial. Marc Holt accuses you of six million things, and he doesn't include your actual issues. How is he even our county commissioner?"

Whit laughed, a few tears escaping as he pulled back to look at her. Textbook definition of beautiful, but with a little redness around the eyes that suggested that she, too, hadn't slept well for the past two weeks.

"I'm so sorry, Piper."

She waved the apology away. "We all have our faults—yours are just more frustrating than most."

He caught her hands in his, bending slightly to look into her eyes. She was trying to obfuscate, using her uniquely Piper mix of humor and bossiness to flip the channel. He wasn't going to let her get away with it. "I'm sorry. I missed you."

Her eyelids fluttered down, then back up as she read his face for honesty. He nodded. "I always miss you, every second I'm not with you."

She pressed her lips together as she wound her fingers more tightly into his.

And that was all the vulnerability he was going to get for that day. Piper dropped his hands and scanned the room. "It looks great in here," she accused. "What'd you do?"

"Rory and I have been cleaning the place out, making it my own. We've had a fun day."

Piper became aware of Rory and everyone else in the room. She nodded, understanding what he was saying. Then she wrapped her arms around him again, whispering, "It's about time."

He nodded. It was time for a number of things. First and foremost, though, was letting Piper off the hook for this campaign, so she could live the life she chose in Portland.

He took a deep breath. "I think we need to come clean. Let's just admit that we're not in a relationship."

The room reacted. Rory was confused and disappointed. Ash was skeptical. Dan was livid.

"That would be a disaster," Dan said.

"I won't have Piper dragged through the mud—"

Dan started to argue, but Piper held up a hand to stop him.

"I don't know that it would be a disaster to say we're not in a relationship," Piper said. "But more than that, it would be a lie."

Whit looked at her sharply.

"This *is* a relationship." She gestured between them. "We have a friendship as real as any, and probably a lot better than Marc and Bunny's marriage."

Whit gazed into her big brown eyes. It *was* a relationship: a messy, beautiful, confusing relationship with a woman who'd captivated him from day one.

"People will construe our connection to be whatever they imagine. But when we changed our social media status to 'in a relationship' that wasn't a lie. We went into this charade to prove that you are steady and trustworthy, and you *are*." A little smile appeared on her lips. "Also, that hug was likely longer than any shared by Marc and Bunny in the last twenty years, just sayin'."

"You're willing to come back and help?" he asked.

"I wouldn't dream of letting you all try to clean this up without me." She slipped her hand into his and said quietly, "It's the least I can do for my friend."

Whit opened his mouth to say thank you, to let her know how much he cared, how much he felt for her. But with her sixth sense and ability to ward off his mushy rush of emotion, she said, "Let's get out of here, go do something public."

"Rory and I were going to meet Dad and Melanie for a late lunch."

"I'll tag along. Then what? Bowling? Wallace family vs the Bentons?"

"There are four of us and fifty of you."

"Okay, exaggerate much?"

"I'm in," Ash said. "I'll call Violet."

"Jet and I will be there," Clara said.

"Are you sure about this?" Whit asked.

Piper turned on him, exasperated. "Yes. I said I'd help, and I'll help. This campaign matters. You matter. I know that I'm complicated and this is hard, but I'm not leaving you to fight Holt on your own." She gazed up at him. "I'm not leaving you."

Whit allowed himself a long moment to soak in her words. She was going to stay and help. She believed in him, in their friendship. Piper Wallace was possible.

But he still needed to clarify his original point.

"I meant, are you sure about bowling? Have you ever been?"

"No. How hard can it be?"

"Do you know about bowling shoes?"

Her face screwed up in confusion. "Bowling *shoes*?"

Yeah, there was no way Piper was putting on bowling shoes.

"How about mini golf?" Rory suggested. "There's a place with mini golf and laser tag, and they have pizza. We could meet my...we could meet our parents there."

Whit nodded to his brother. "Sounds good to me."

"I love it," Clara said, grinning at Rory. "I'm sending a family text now."

Whit gazed at Piper. She avoided his eye, bending down to pick up Bernice, fussing with the mouse hat. She was distracting from her selfless, thoughtful nature again, and he wasn't going to stand for it.

He placed his lips near her ear. "You are amazing."

She kept her focus on the dog. "Thanks. I put 'amazing' on my vision board two years ago and have been making steady progress."

Whit shook his head and spoke again, "You are *the* most incredible woman."

She let her eyes connect with his. A lot moved in that gaze, but Whit wasn't entirely sure what it was. Then Piper turned away. "*You're* amazing. And wonderful." Then she gestured to his torso. "And you need to change your shirt. I'm gone for a couple of days, and you fall apart aesthetically. I'd be impressed if I weren't so horrified. Please tell me you didn't recycle the magical hipster closet."

"I wouldn't dare."

CHAPTER SIXTEEN

PIPER AND WHIT emerged from the back room at Eighty Local hand in hand as they headed for Outcrop, Outside. She could feel eyes on them and knew what people were seeing: Central Oregon's golden couple, heading to battle. Whit wore jeans, boots and a blazer, looking more handsome than any politician had a right to. She was in a golden yellow sundress, a nod to the comment Whit had made at the Deschutes Brewery debate.

He gave her hand a squeeze. "We can do this."

She nodded, repeating their game plan, "Remain calm, answer the questions truthfully."

A spark lit his eye. "Kinda hard to remain calm when you look so pretty in that dress."

She kept her eyes ahead but wound her fingers more tightly through his. She was here to support her friend in an important election, not speculate as to whether or not he meant it when he told her he loved her.

Main Street, Outcrop, had outdone itself for adorable vibrancy. Sparkle lights were strung across the street. Local businesses had their doors open and half their wares displayed on the sidewalk. Enterprising locals brought their own folding tables and sold honey, homegrown produce, dried flowers, pottery and other home-produced crafts. Hunter had the Eighty Local booth set up. He and Ani, with the help of Bowman and Maisy, were serving barbecue and his town-famous kale-slaw. Music drifted from the park, where a group of her old high-school teachers had an Eagles cover band. They only played at Outcrop, Outside, and they always played at Outcrop, Outside. It just wouldn't be the business fair without them.

"Nice to see you home, Piper." She looked up to see Mr. Fareas nod from the front porch of Outcrop Hardware, Tack and Feed.

"Hey!" She waved. "How's business?"

"Tolerable." This was a massive understatement. Mr. Fareas had the business sense of a modern-day Medici. He looked at Whit. "Can I bother you with a few questions?"

"That's what I'm here for."

Piper watched Whit jog up the steps and lean forward to shake Mr. Fareas's hand. He listened as the local business legend gave his take on a proposed tourism tax, then asked clarifying questions, explained his position and finally handed Mr. Fareas a card with his email on it, urging him to keep in touch and email with his thoughts on other issues as well.

It was the exact right thing to do. And Whit would do the right thing, over and over, his entire life. That was just who he was.

Piper turned and scanned Main Street. The last few months had been intense and hectic, but fun. As much fun as Piper could remember having. The high stakes of the campaign were stressful and invigorating. Her business continued to flourish. *She* was flourishing.

"Aunt Piper!"

Jackson's voice startled her out of her thoughts. She looked up to see a football hurtling toward her and reflexively ducked, as one does. Fortunately, a young woman in an Outcrop Football sweatshirt jumped in front of her to catch it.

"Nice catch, Carley!" Violet called from where she was chatting with Coach Kessler and Christy.

"Yes, thank you," Piper said.

The girl was quickly swamped by Manuel Garcia, who seemed to be spending every last second before he left for Cornell University trying to get Carley's attention. If he were a few years older, she'd give him some advice. But young people really did need to make their own dating mistakes; he'd be ready to listen to reason by his midtwenties.

Piper gazed down the street. On the side of Second Chance Cowgirl, a new mural brightened the building. Coach Kessler, nearly a year in remission now, stood before it, wrangling people into his wife's store. Jet and Clara strolled past, then he held the door to Three Sisters Chocolatier for her, his eyes on his wife, rather than the chocolate displays. Ash had Violet's hand and was leading her to where people were dancing on the lawn. Maisy and Bowman were dancing in the Eighty Local booth because wherever there was music, Bowman was incapable of keeping still or quiet. Ani was trying to convince Hunter they could switch up his usual sandwich-serving routine; Hunter was stubbornly resisting, and the two of them were laughing so hard they could barely take orders. Maia, a shy fifteen-year-old, snapped a picture of them. Then she gazed down at the new camera she'd bought with money she earned painting murals with Ani, grinning. She raised the camera and caught Piper's eye, gesturing to her and Whit.

Piper tugged Whit's hand. "Look like you're in love with me."

Rather than give an exaggerated sigh and mumble something about trying, Whit stepped in close to her. He took both her hands in his and gazed at her for a long moment.

His voice dropped low as he said, "How's this?"

Piper's heart seemed to expand with each beat, growing impossibly large as she gazed back at Whit. It was un-fathomably sweet, and a little frightening. There was so much happening, this campaign, her business, her changing family. Whit seemed to engulf all of that.

She glanced down at the sidewalk, then back up at Whit as the certainty spread through her. "I was thinking—" Her sentence dropped off. What was she planning on saying here? *I was thinking I'm in love with you? I was thinking we should spend the rest of our lives together, no matter how much juggling and compromise that would take?*

I was thinking we could ditch this campaign stop and head back to Eighty Local because I know for a fact it's gonna be empty for the next hour at least?

He grinned down at her. "What were you thinking, Piper Wallace?"

"I was thinking… I was wondering. Would you be willing to revisit your feelings on *complicated*?"

He laughed.

"I mean it. Everyone is always saying we should simplify, say no, do less. But, I like this. I like feeling like I have a lot to love and a lot to do in this world. I don't mind being busy. I thrive on busy. I am ready for things to get complicated." She pulled in a breath. "Are you?"

He gazed into her eyes, as though he couldn't quite figure out where she was going with all this but really wanted to. If a person liked complicated, her attempted declaration of love was certainly that.

"What I'm trying to say is that I was thinking—"

"Piper," he cut her off. He dropped one of her hands and placed his in his jacket pocket. Her hand was pretty upset about it, and definitely jealous of the other hand. "I've been thinking too."

Her heart seemed to teeter, like it was standing on the edge of the high dive, unsure if it was safe to launch off the edge, but with no intention of turning around to climb back down the ladder.

"Ladies and gentlemen…" Ash's commanding voice over the PA system startled her. She looked around. Why were there so many people here?

Oh. Right. Outcrop, Outside campaign stop, what have you.

"Six months ago, Whit Benton stepped up to run against Marc Holt for county commissioner. It's been an uphill battle, but one Whit was made for. He's here today, and I think we can convince him to say a few words."

The crowd applauded their encouragement. Whit kept his gaze on Piper.

She didn't know where he was going with all this, but it didn't matter. He had to know how she felt. If there was a future for them, fantastic. If there wasn't, well, he needed to walk into his future knowing just how much she cared for him, valued him and was grateful for their time together.

"Whit?" Ash scanned the crowd for the man who was supposed to be walking on stage right about now.

Whit spoke quickly, "Piper, there's something I need to say to you."

"Okay?"

"Piper, you—I mean, I…" He flushed, gazing at their hands and pulling in a deep breath. "You and I—"

He wasn't making much more progress than she had. Ash's eyes landed on the two of them, and he glowered with a "get yourself on stage right now and deal with whatever situation you two have stirred up later" sort of vibe.

As annoying as it was, he was right. They had a county commissioner's seat to lock down. Piper squeezed his hands.

"Go make your speech. I'm not going anywhere."

Whit nodded. "Okay." He brushed her cheek with his lips, then jogged toward the stage.

"Except maybe to grab one of Mrs. Garcia's tamales!" she called after him. He turned back, longing in his eyes at the mention of tamales. "For you," she finished.

A smile spread across his face, then he glanced down and it almost seemed like he was blushing.

WHIT USED EVERY last pocket of strength to walk away from Piper and head up on the stage. Honestly, it felt a little unfair. These people had been waiting for two minutes. He'd been waiting for Piper since he was eighteen.

Whit let out a breath, then glanced back over his shoulder. She shot him a grin and looked meaningfully at the tamale stand. He wasn't sure what she meant by embracing complicated, but he had a pretty good idea of what that meant to him.

The irony wasn't lost on him. He'd spent years trying to avoid complications, only to find the complication was within him. He'd limited relationships because he was afraid of being hurt the way he'd been when his family fell apart. Piper and her small army of a family were simple compared to the complex system of battlements and barbed wire he'd set up around his heart.

Letting it all go and allowing himself to love Piper was simple in comparison.

Whit stepped onto the small stage. The musicians remained in place, a reminder that he wasn't the main attraction here. A high-school band director with a wicked riff and the promise of "Hotel California" was what the crowd came to see. But folks were cheerful and receptive. This was Piper's home turf, and the audience was filled with her friends, former teachers, people she did business with, not to mention the whole huge Wallace clan.

But she wasn't the only one with friends in the crowd. Dad and Melanie were off to one side. Rory had been absorbed by Jackson and his crew, who all seemed to be getting free food at the back of the Eighty Local stand and were debating the relative merits of soccer and football.

Whit stepped up to the microphone, allowing himself to feel Piper's support. "Thank you, Outcrop, for having me here today."

"You're welcome!" Coach Kessler called from the crowd.

Whit chuckled, then stilled as a chill crept through him. In the back were several people who were *not* smiling. They looked like any other resident of the area but had buttons signifying them as Holt supporters. Whit pulled in a breath.

This speech mattered. What happened after this speech mattered more, but he could keep it together for five minutes before sprinting back to Piper. He glanced over in her direction.

That was all the inspiration he needed.

"I love Outcrop. I've loved watching this community thrive over the last ten years. The citizens of your town have responded to changing times with innovation and enthusiasm. I remember driving through here as a kid, and half the buildings on Main were empty." He gestured back to the crowded, thriving streets. "You haven't just built businesses, you've had fun doing it, creating a town where people can raise their families and thrive professionally. A town where visitors and new residents alike are accepted and integrated into community life." He cleared his throat. "And if anyone needs proof, they don't have to look any further than the twenty-foot mural of Larry the emu welcoming everyone to town."

Cheers went up through the crowd. He noticed Piper

offer a high five to a young woman with a camera, who smiled shyly as people applauded.

"But no matter how long you're staying in Deschutes County, we're here because we share similar values. We love being outside." That got another cheer, as they were technically at Outcrop, Outside. "Our youth matter to us, and we will do what we can to secure a future where they can grow and innovate like we've been able to. There will always be tourists in Deschutes County because why wouldn't people come here?" Another cheer, this one led by Hunter. The Holt supporters in the back were stubbornly still, arms folded across their chests. "But as county commissioner my job would be to support residents. That means keeping our small businesses open, our ranches and farms running and our wildlife thriving in their natural habitat. I want the best for my neighbors. I may not be the best person all the time, but I try." Most of the audience responded to this admission of humility, but he heard one of the men in the back grumble. "I want the best for the county I grew up in and live in."

The crowd applauded, but at the back someone yelled out, "Liar!"

A smattering of concern rippled around him. The familiar voice, feeling an advantage, called out again, "He's a liar."

Whit didn't turn to his heckler, but instead glanced over at Piper. She gazed back at him and nodded. He was transported back to their Gonzaga debate, when they'd been backed into a corner by a prep school team. Piper had given him the same nod, and the two of them let loose, intellectually destroying their opponents.

It was time to shut down these Holt supporters.

He straightened his shoulders and scanned the back of the crowd. "What was that?"

No one responded. "I thought I heard someone call me a liar."

People shifted uncomfortably, craning their heads to the back of the crowd. Every moment of debate training came back to him. Over the last few months, he'd come to learn that there were times he just needed to let an argument drop, but this didn't feel like one of them.

Finally, the voice from the back responded, "You've been lying about everything, from the beginning." The crowd in the back shifted to reveal a woman in a denim jacket with a bright T-shirt underneath.

His sister.

Whit stared at her, all the hurt and frustration rushing through him. He glanced down briefly to gather himself, then out of the corner of his eye, he saw a flash of movement. Dad was heading back to her, ready to take care of this situation for him.

As grateful as Whit was, it was time to take her on himself.

"What have I been lying about? I'm curious."

"Well, her for starters." Jana pointed at Piper.

Whit gazed at Piper, remembering that the sooner he wrapped this up, the sooner he could get back to that conversation they'd been having.

"I am in a relationship with Piper," he stated, using her words from two days ago. "And yeah, it's complicated. Because she's Piper Wallace." The crowd chuckled at this, but Whit held a hand up to silence them. "I'm complicated too. This is complicated." He gestured to everything around them. "I chose to run for office against a well-funded incumbent because I don't like his plan for Deschutes County. I don't want a huge chunk of land taken over for a third-home community. I like the wildlife sanctuaries, the wilderness access. Small businesses are good for our economy and good for the consumer. I think most other people agree with me, so I'm gonna fight for it."

"It's just awfully convenient for you to suddenly have a girlfriend," Jana said.

Whit glanced at Piper, then at her siblings. He shook his head. "There is nothing convenient about Piper."

The crowd laughed. Piper rolled her eyes, but she was still smiling.

Whit met his sister's eye, trying to communicate how annoyed he was, and also that they didn't need to do this anymore. But if she chose to antagonize the family, that was her affair. He was going to move forward. Forward, and in a direction that didn't include her negativity.

"Jana, you of all people should know I've always been interested in Piper." His sister stepped back, shocked at the use of her name, shocked that he was acknowledging her. By now, Dad had reached her side, but Whit kept going. "I talked about her all the time in college. I thought about her all the time after graduation. I even…" Whit hung his head in embarrassment about what he was about to admit in front of the entire town of Outcrop. "I even used to find her on social media, so I could see what she was up to and if she was still as beautiful as ever."

A chorus of "aww!" and a smattering of laughter rose from the crowd. He snuck a glance at Piper, who was attempting to raise an eyebrow.

"Don't tell me you never Googled me," he said. She shrugged, theatrically casual, sending the crowd into more laughter.

"I love every minute I get to spend in Piper's company. I can't wait to see her again when we part. She is the smartest, most beautiful woman I have ever met." Whit turned from the crowd and looked at Piper. "I am in love with her."

Piper's eyes widened and color rushed to her face.

Whit said it again. "I'm in love with Piper Wallace."

Clara was now at her side, wrapping an arm around her. Whit kept his gaze connected with Piper's, willing her to hear the truth.

"I'll do anything to make this work, and that's going to be hard because she lives in Portland, and I'm going to win this race, so I'll live here. She likes sausage dogs in frog hats. I run cattle. But we are two determined, hardworking people. There's nothing we can't do."

By this point, the crowd was half in tears as he declared his love for the woman the whole town adored. Even Jana was having trouble not tearing up. But then the man next to her called out, "If you're so in love, where's the ring?"

Whit gave himself two seconds to glare at the man. Like Piper had said, they didn't even have his faults right. There were so many things Holt's campaign could hammer him for—his arrogance, his stubbornness, his inability to drop a fight. But how could they possibly accuse him of not loving Piper?

Whit turned to Piper, who had stepped into the protective arms of her sister at his declaration. Then he glanced back at the man. His inability to drop a fight was about to get the better of him again. He took a deep breath and reached into the pocket of his blazer.

PIPER PULLED CLARA'S arm tighter around her shoulder, which was hard because Clara was bouncing on her toes like she did when she was happy.

This whole flirty speech had started out like a lot of others but took a dramatic turn that had her unable to stand on her own feet. Whit's brow was furrowed. He was about to verbally launch into that man in the crowd, she could see it in the set of his shoulders. He'd slipped his hand into his pocket and was formulating some kind of response while the crowd waited, rapt with attention.

And she was a little nervous.

Had Whit just told her he loved her?

He'd told his nasty troll of a sister, a woman whose outfit was a clear and desperate plea for help, that he loved her. The whole town of Outcrop heard it.

And then he'd turned to her and said it again.

"I'm in love with Piper Wallace."

Blood rushed to her head. This was what "weak in the knees" meant. She really wasn't sure she'd still be standing if Clara wasn't propping her up like a crutch. A really nice crutch that smelled like orange and ginger and had a huge smile on its face.

But despite the whole weak-knee situation, Piper felt strong, flexible, powerful. She felt like anything was possible.

"Is he in love with me?" she whispered.

"Wrong question," Clara whispered back.

"You can't question my question."

"I'm not questioning anything. I'm telling you." Clara turned her attention from Whit and focused on her. "Piper, look what he's holding."

Piper needed an answer from her sister first. They were both experts in love and relationships, but where Piper could line up the pros and cons and intellectually predict the outcome of a match, Clara had a stronger sense of intuition. Piper just needed a quick confirmation from her sister before any more time passed.

"Is he in love with me?"

"Piper." Bowman nudged her shoulder. "Pay attention."

Piper glared at Bowman, who looked like he'd done battle with the laundry facilities at a frat and barely escaped with his life. Bowman never bossed her around.

That wasn't how their brother-sister relationship worked. She bossed him and he ignored her; it was a well-established pattern.

Piper glanced at the stage, feeling like she was going to self-combust if she didn't get an answer. Also feeling like it would serve her siblings right if she did self-combust since they were being so frustrating.

Whit contemplated a small box in his hands. A very small, red leather box. The crowd was silent.

Piper's heart began pounding like it was replacing all her blood with good espresso.

Whit flipped open the box and turned to the audience. "Here," he said simply. Then he smiled, that mystery smile she'd never been able to pin down. "This was my great-grandmother's ring. I've been carrying it around for weeks. I take it everywhere, and I keep bungling my chances. I took it to Portland, and there was a perfect moment at a taco truck, and I just let it slip." He glanced down at the ring. "It's Piper's ring. I mean, look at it." He held the ring out to the crowd, but Piper couldn't see it. That felt wildly unfair. But then he said, "I just want this so much, spending my life with Piper. Being her partner. I think about it all the time. But I'm not sure if she's ready, and I can't stand the thought of her saying no. I can't stand the thought of asking her and hearing no."

Like that *was going to happen.*

Clara unwound her arms from Piper, and Bowman's hands pushed her forward. She felt like she was floating to the stage. She didn't one hundred percent have a plan for when she got there. At this point, the crowd was completely bananas, applauding and whistling, but the noise was somehow muted.

She approached the steps. Mr. Katz, the band director from the high school, held a hand out to her to help her up.

Whit looked up from the ring and gazed at her, his eyes questioning, cautious and so full of love. Piper wasn't sure her knees would hold out. She reached out a hand to him, and while she had no idea what her face looked like, Whit must have liked what he saw because his eyes lit up, his gorgeous smile broke out and he pulled her close to him.

He opened his mouth to speak, and Piper bit her lip, nodding before he even got the question out. He pulled her closer, his forehead touching hers as he ran a hand along her cheek. "Will you?"

She wrapped her arms around his neck, flexing up on her tiptoes to smile up at him. "I'm far too selfish to let you slip away."

Whit's smile got brighter, then in one movement he stepped back and dropped onto one knee. Piper had a vague awareness of the crowd bellowing like a herd of really happy cattle.

Piper kept her gaze locked on Whit's until he gestured with the open box.

Oh. Right. There was some ring he'd told the crowd was meant to be hers.

Piper glanced down. *Whoa.*

She looked back into Whit's eyes, even more bright and beautiful than any diamond.

"Yes," she whispered. Her words somehow felt louder than the noisy world around them.

Whit slipped the ring on her hand, grinning as he anchored it on her ring finger with his thumb and forefinger. And that was just too adorable.

Piper placed her hands at the side of his face, trying to communicate how much she loved him, was grateful for his friendship, was willing to do what it took to make the two of them possible. Whit didn't have any trouble understanding. He stood, wrapping his arms around her waist, pulling her closer. Logically, Piper was aware of being on stage at the center of Outcrop, Outside, surrounded by her community, but the only thing she could see was Whit.

His lips brushed hers, and she wound her arms around his neck, letting his kiss sweep her away.

Yeah. That kiss.

They weren't going to have any trouble making this work at all.

Whit pulled in a breath, keeping his arms around her, his forehead touching hers. "The love chemicals are on our side now, right?"

"Absolutely."

Whit leaned in to kiss her again, and if there was any reaction from the crowd, they didn't hear a thing.

EPILOGUE

PIPER PEEKED AROUND a column into the courtyard of the Utner-Kim château.

"Hold still," Clara said, rearranging one of the tiny yellow carnations around Piper's artfully messy updo.

Guests were seated in gilt chairs facing a wedding canopy decorated with golden yellow roses and white peonies against a background of ivy. The crowd was a lively mix of ranchers, hipsters and everyone in between.

Piper flexed up on her toes, but she still couldn't see much from her vantage. The replicas of Baroque marble statues Bettina had commissioned were gorgeous but put a serious dent in Piper's ability to spy on her own wedding guests. Still, she knew that two horses, Bella and Midnight, were in attendance, along with Larry the emu, who she really hoped wasn't trying to eat the canopy right now. And somewhere in the crowd, Bernice was cheering her on, wearing a chic wedding cap with two golden yellow carnations next to her ears.

Yeah, Piper was a little smug about pulling off a massive wedding in a French château without ever having to leave Oregon.

"Perfect." Clara kissed her cheek and stepped back. "You are a complete goddess."

"That's what Whit seems to think," Mom said with a wink.

Her parents had returned home from a trip to Belize

to find Piper happier than she'd ever been, engaged to the Deschutes County commissioner and seriously considering a request from the Central Oregon Cattlemen's Association to run for state senator. Her siblings were thriving, Jackson had been accepted to Oregon State University, baby Bob was learning to walk and Bowman had finally broken ground on a house for Maisy by Fort Rock on Wallace Ranch.

Dad noted wryly that the best thing he and Mom ever did as parents was to get out of their kids' way. While Piper didn't completely agree with that statement, she had to admit her parents' willingness to let them make their own messes and find their way out of them worked out pretty well.

"I hope Whit thinks his wife is a goddess." Piper grinned at her parents. "All husbands should."

Mom laughed. "I taught you well."

"You did." Piper wrapped her arms around her, then pulled Clara in as well.

Over her shoulder, she saw Bowman point something out to Hunter. Something that was happening out in the courtyard.

"What?" she demanded.

Bowman held his hands up. "Nothing."

Piper's siblings, friends and her almost brother-in-law, Rory, jostled around her as Bettina and Joanna lined everyone up and directed traffic. Jackson, holding a wiggly baby Bob in a tuxedo and boots, gave her a big grin. "You ready for this, Aunt Piper?"

"I'm ready."

Jackson looked at Rory, and some communication passed between them. Everyone was acting a little funny.

It was like they all knew something she didn't.

Music floated up from the courtyard. Piper climbed onto the base of a column and could just make out the top quarter of Whit. He looked fabulous in a tailored linen suit, worn with his favorite Stetson. He was grinning, blue eyes bright as he scanned the edges of the courtyard. It looked like he was holding…something.

And why would the groom be holding anything?

Piper turned on her siblings. "What's going on?"

"Nothing," all four of them said, way too quickly. Piper narrowed her right eye and turned on Clara. Her sweet, kind sister just grinned at her.

"Let's go get you married," Clara said. "Ash, you have your guitar?"

Piper tried to glare at her sister, but she was in way too good of a mood. Plus, her wedding dress was amazing, long layers of floating silk in a look that was a cutting-edge reflection of ancient Greece. It was hard to glare at anyone when she looked and felt this good.

"Let's get this show on the road?" Dad asked, offering his arm.

"Dad, it's a wedding, not a rodeo."

He glanced meaningfully at the chaos all around them. "My mistake."

Ash scanned the courtyard over her head, and from his vantage, he could probably see Whit, which felt unfair.

"We need to get going." He picked up his guitar, muttering to Bowman, "Whit's surprise isn't going to last much longer."

He stalked off toward the aisle, but Piper managed to catch his arm.

"Wait, what surprise?"

"If we told you, it wouldn't be a surprise," Hunter said.

"That is the worst response. The most—"

"Annoying?"

"—thing you could say. Exactly."

Piper folded her arms over her chest. Bowman dropped a peck on top of her head. "It's all good, Piper."

She gave him a grudging smile because it really was all so very good.

Her brothers laughed, good-naturedly jostling past her, followed by Jackson and Rory, who walked Mom and Melanie up to their seats in the front.

Clara turned from the line of bridesmaids and grinned at Piper. Then she left the group completely and enfolded Piper in a hug, whispering, "You are the best."

"No, *you're* the best. It's been confirmed."

"By what agency?"

"By me." Piper winked at her sister. "The final authority on such things."

The music from the courtyard shifted. Piper could hear Ash strumming "You Are the Sunshine of My Life," which was one hundred percent appropriate as Violet, Ani, Maisy and finally Clara drifted up the aisle in their gorgeous, sunshine-yellow dresses. Some people thought it was a difficult color to wear, but it wasn't. One just needed to embrace the power of the golden yellow.

Finally, the tune changed. She couldn't see Bowman step up to the mic, but love for her brother surged as he sang Jack Johnson's "Better Together." Not only had Bowman volunteered to sing for the wedding, he'd picked out the song *and* managed to get here with his suit intact, clean and unrumpled.

She would bet good money he was looking at Maisy as he sang, but whatever.

Piper took her dad's arm and rounded the corner to the end of the aisle. Her pulse was fluttering warm and sweet through her body as she looked up at Whit. He grinned, his smile knocking the wind out of her, sending her spinning. She felt like the luckiest woman alive, but knew that hard work, compromise and confidence had also brought the two of them to this beautiful moment.

His mystery smile was shining at her, his blue eyes alive with joy.

Then she remembered there was some kind of surprise. She tried to tear her eyes away from his gorgeous smile to see what he was holding.

He knelt down and set something on the ground. No, two somethings. Two small, wiggly, brown—

"Puppies!"

Piper dropped her dad's arm and raced toward the twin dachshunds, scooping them up along with her bouquet. Their small bodies twisted in her arms, little tongues licking her face, tickling her and making her laugh. Whit jogged after them, then wrapped his arms around her and the two wiggling miracles of four-legged perfection.

He leaned his forehead against hers, but she could still see his grin.

"I figured we may as well start a family, since we don't have much going on right now."

Piper laughed. "You are all I want. But I'll take the dogs, our complicated work schedules and general geographic scramblings too."

Whit kissed her forehead softly, then whispered, "I love all of it, Piper. I love all of you."

Piper gazed up at him. She really did not want to mess up her mascara by crying, but...*wow*. She was holding dachshund puppies and on the verge of marrying the man of her dreams.

"Git on up here," Ash commanded. "You two need to get married and get on with your happy ending."

Whit laughed, wrapping an arm around her waist as they headed to the canopy. "I'm in!"

But Piper shook her head. "This isn't an ending." She gazed up at Whit, grinning as she said, "This is a happy beginning."

* * * * *

WESTERN

Rugged men looking for love...

Available Next Month

The Maverick's Marriage Deal Kaylie Newell
The Rancher's Secret Crush Cari Lynn Webb

Expecting A Fortune Nina Crespo
The Doc's Instant Family Lisa Childs

 LOVE INSPIRED

Recapturing Her Heart Jennifer Slattery
The Cowboy's Return Danica Favorite